# THE OTHERLIFE

# THE OTHERLIFE

## JULIA GRAY

ANDERSEN PRESS • LONDON

First published in 2016 by
Andersen Press Limited
20 Vauxhall Bridge Road
London SW1V 2SA
www.andersenpress.co.uk

2 4 6 8 10 9 7 5 3 1

British Library Cataloguing in Publication Data available.

ISBN 978 1 78344 422 9

Typeset in Adobe Caslon by Palimpsest Book Production Limited,
Falkirk, Stirlingshire
Printed and bound in Great Britain by
Clays Ltd, St Ives plc

For C.K.G.

Now, in the city of Asgard dwelt one called Loki, who, though amongst the Æsir, was not of the Æsir, but utterly unlike to them; for to do the wrong, and leave the right undone, was, night and day, this wicked Loki's one unwearied aim.

Annie Keary, *The Heroes of Asgard*

It is an ordinary day,
a sort of grey with boredom stirring in the streets.

Carol Ann Duffy, *Education for Leisure*

# A GUIDE TO THE NORSE GODS

*Here are some of the main Gods and monsters
that appear in this book.*

**Asgard**    The home of the Gods

**Baldr**    A handsome and noble God, the son of
Odin and Frigg

**Fenrir**    A fearsome wolf. Son of Loki and father of
Hati and Skǫll

**Freyr and
Freyja**    God and Goddess, brother and sister

**Frigg**    Odin's wife, mother of Baldr

**Hati**    The wolf who chases the moon across the
sky at night

**Heimdallr**    The God who keeps watch from Bifrost, the
rainbow bridge

**Hermódr**    The messenger God. (Also written as *Hermóðr*)

**Hǫdr**    Blind God and brother of Baldr. (Also written as *Hǫðr*).

**Jǫrmungandr**    The ocean-dwelling World Serpent

**Loki**    A mischief-making, shape-shifting God

**Odin**    Father of the Gods. He only has one eye, having sacrificed the other in exchange for wisdom. (Also written as *Óðinn*)

**Skǫll**    The wolf who chases the sun across the sky each day

**Sleipnir**    An eight-legged horse who is ridden to Hel, the underworld

**Thor**    Son of Odin and a ferocious warrior, whose prized possession is the hammer Mjǫllnir. (Also written as *Þórr*)

**Tyr**    A brave God whose hand was bitten off by the wolf Fenrir

# BEN
## MAY 2012

There's a God in the Stonehills' garden.

I've been out here for a while now, waiting for my T-shirt to dry. About a quarter of an hour ago I made the mistake of going into the library, where some girls were making Flaming Sambucas, cackling with drunken hysteria. Clear liquid splashed on the carpet; shot glasses cracked underfoot. Someone pushed past me. I staggered, and somehow, as one of the girls was waving a long-handled lighter like a malevolent wand, the hem of my T-shirt caught fire. Not just any T-shirt: my vintage, '94, Pushead-designed Metallica T-shirt, and the most precious item of clothing I own.

Pushing my way through the crowd, I drenched it in the downstairs bathroom, where a genuine Matisse stands watch over a shell-shaped sink. I lamented the scorch mark, a dark scar on white cotton. Then I retreated to the terrace, where the wicker furniture is set out in a mathematical arrangement and every potted plant is so beautifully maintained that it could have come straight from a gardening catalogue. Normally when the Stonehills have parties, there's a handful of people out on the terrace, drinking and smoking and shouting, and maybe a few

1

people here and there on the lawn. But for the moment, I'm the only one.

The low drone of guitars and drums surges in waves from the basement, where a jam session is going on. In a bit, the Stonehills will let off fireworks. More and more people will come, alerted by social media. Sooner or later the police will turn up. They always do. It's definitely time to go home, but I'm slightly too drunk to make the decision to leave. I've had three Coronas: too many, considering that it's a Wednesday night, and I have an exam in the morning. Nobody here cares about exams. Money will get them wherever they want to go. I don't have much in common with any of these people, apart from a love of metal.

I shouldn't have come to this party.

All day I've been feeling different. On edge, my head full of unwanted electricity. I've been feeling like something unusual is about to happen.

Now I think maybe it is.

Eyes unfocused, I look down the stretch of polished lawn. The garden is lit by solar lights, glowing like half-buried stars from the flowerbeds. Counting them, I let my gaze travel further and further back. And that's when I see it. Another light. A different light. Right at the end of the garden, past the fishpond and the organised ranks of roses and miniature lemon trees. Up where the yew trees grow tall and close together and the ground rises higher as it reaches the wall. There's an old treehouse that the Stonehills used to play in when they were younger, custom-made by some bewilderingly expensive company. That's where it is, this other light. Just under the treehouse. But it can't be a solar light. For one thing, it's the wrong colour. Also: it's moving. Fading in and out, circling, dipping . . . as though it's looking for someone. I have seen this kind of light before. I know what it means.

There is definitely a God in the Stonehills' garden.

And that means the Otherlife is back.

Down the terrace steps and along the path, past shadowy flowers and silent sprinklers. Tennis court to my right. I walk like a ghost, my feet light. The sides of my vision are soft. The nerves in my palms are glittering. I look for the light as I draw closer to the bottom of the garden. The early May night air is cold on my skin; my T-shirt clings to me wetly. There's a slight wind; the leaves rustle, as though the trees are breathing. I hesitate for a moment. Then continue.

Now I hear another sound. No more than a whisper: so slithery, so silvery, that it could almost be just a sharp breeze dragging a crisp packet over a scratchy surface. It's an old sound, an oceanic sound. A familiar sound.

'*Skoll . . .*'

I slow down, still looking for the light. The treehouse looms just ahead, with its peaked roof and shuttered windows. The trees are dark statues against the ivied wall.

'*Skoll . . .*'

Now I see the light. No: *lights*. There's more than one. Trickles, like the residue of fireworks, leaving gilded traces in the pre-dawn sky. One, two . . . there are seven, eight of them, flickering, assembling in front of me, pixelated against the trees. The eight lights are lengthening, gradually, into tensile, supple legs, and above them a body blooms: pale grey, pearlescent, itself made up of hundreds of filaments of light, rippling and pulsing. An elongated head. The suggestion of teeth. Now I am aware of enormous strength and vigorous movement; I know this is Sleipnir, the horse, and I am aware of his rider, too – not pale grey, but greenish bronze, and also formed of filaments of light.

Hermódr, the messenger God.

He presses his knees into Sleipnir's sides and the great grey horse takes a couple of steps towards me. A wall of movement pushes through the air: particles are displaced, hot and cold at the same time. Hermódr reaches one hand down, as though to beckon me closer. I cannot see his face, but somehow I know that he is sad.

He calls me again, by the name I used to call myself, and finally I hear myself, throat dry and corrugated, replying, in English: 'Yes. I am here.'

Hermódr speaks to me. I can't make out what he's saying. It's been so long since I read anything in Old Norse. He says it again – the same words, three times, four. But I can't understand him. In the presence of the Otherlife, this grand London garden and this mock-Tudor house with its palatial halls and staircases no longer exist. My burnt Metallica T-shirt no longer matters. Nothing matters but the messenger God and his eight-legged horse, and whatever he's trying to tell me. A little pulse begins near the old scar on the side of my head.

I wish I could understand him.

Hermódr turns away, and I feel the air move again, like an ethereal tide.

'Wait!' I call out. 'Please, wait!'

But the lights grow smaller, fainter, melting into the ivy at the back of the garden. Then, just as they are disappearing altogether, Hermódr turns his head to speak to me one last time. And finally there's something I think I recognise: a couple of words I think I know, something I must have learnt a long, long time ago.

'*Dead. He is dead.*'

Mum opens the door in her running gear. 'Oh *no*, Ben,' she says.

I avoid her eyes.

'Forgot my key,' I say.

'Not today. Not when you've got exams. I should put you on a lead.'

'It clears my head. Walking.'

'Plenty of daylight hours for that. I must say, though, your head doesn't look especially clear at this moment. *Don't* tell me you've been out all night.'

I follow her into the kitchen.

'No, not all night,' I tell her. 'Couldn't sleep. Went out about an hour ago, that's all.'

The kitchen is aggressively bright. There are too many shiny surfaces, reflecting too much light. On Radio 4 the presenter is snapping at the heels of a defensive politician, demanding answers to some unanswerable question. They always sound so angry on Radio 4. Mum manages to fill the kettle, throw bread into the toaster and clink the milk bottle so hard against the table top that I worry the glass will break, all at the same time.

Bright lights, loud sounds, sharp corners. It's impossible to sit comfortably in the plastic kitchen chair. I blink at the table top, my brain in soft focus. Mum puts a plate of toast in front of me. A cup of tea. The bag floats sadly, a shipwreck, at the top. Then, because I don't move, she digs a knife into the Lurpak and plasters butter over my toast. If she could eat my breakfast for me, she would. She's that kind of mother.

'And today, when we've got the French Listening paper.'

'*We* don't have a French Listening paper,' I say through buttered toast.

She ignores this editorial adjustment.

'It's a Big Day. Go and have a quick bath and I'll drive you to school.'

'Mum . . .'

'Not now, Ben.'

\*　　\*　　\*

Another Big Day: one of so many. My life is a series of small days leading up to magnificent, do-or-die, all-singing, all-dancing Big Days. And my mother is probably right: it wasn't especially smart of me to go out the night before a Big Day such as this one: the first of my GCSEs. But I find, sometimes, that I can't help myself. I need to go out at night. Not generally to parties, unless, like last night, they're going to be playing metal. Most of the time it's enough to be out and about, looking with different eyes at the buildings I see by day. Usually I'll find a park, or – even better – a cemetery, and stay there, like a soft-footed zombie, until I'm tired enough to go home. I don't really know why I do it; perhaps I feel like it calms me, in some indescribable way. I even have a name for it.

Nightwalking.

I make the bath as hot as I can stand. While it's running, I open the bathroom cabinet, and rummage around in the rubble of old bandages and nail-varnish bottles. I check in the woven baskets perched on the edge of the bath, where rolled-up flannels compete for space with those miniature shower gels and see-through caps that you get in hotels. I look in the medicine box, remembering that things are often in the likeliest place, and, sure enough, find what I'm looking for. A small brown bottle, with a single triangular apricot-coloured pill inside it. Filling a tooth mug with water from the tap, I tip out the pill and swallow it neatly. Then I climb into the bath.

*He is dead.* That's what Hermódr said, or what I think he said. I wonder about my grandfather, who hasn't been that well. But no: Mum would have said something, if anything was wrong with Granddad. Sometimes I think she hides things from me, but not about anyone as special as him. In the shallow water I watch my skin turn from blue and white to white and red, like a changing political landscape. I slide down, feeling the crack in the ceramic glaze scrape my shoulder blade, until only my nose remains out of the water. Now I listen for hidden sounds: the buzz of the fluorescent strip over the mirror, the gurgle of the radiator.

Why has the Otherlife come back now? That's what I can't understand. It's been gone for so long. I wish I knew what Hermódr was trying to tell me.

I hope nothing bad has happened to any of the members of Metallica.

'Be-en! *Ben!*'

I climb out of the bath. For a moment I'm surprised by a black smudge on my ribs, shimmering in the corner of my vision. I close my eyes, and it's gone.

My room is a small gallery. The Late Greats of metal adorn the walls, the ceiling, the cupboard doors. Most of them are vintage posters, found online or in Portobello Market. There's something almost holy about them. Flailing limbs and leather and halogen hair. Microphones and guitars and drumsticks, wielded like weapons. Under the stage lights, the faces and limbs of the Late Greats are ghostly, glowing green and blue.

My mother hates my posters. 'These people glorify death,' she'll say, wincing. As though she's imagining being there in the mosh pit, enduring the feedback and distortion and screaming. She finds metal distasteful, like the smell of drains. I don't agree with her. True: the Late Greats are, by definition, dead. There's Dimebag Darrell of Pantera, who was shot onstage by a gunman. Layne Staley of Alice in Chains, whose tale of addiction and self-neglect never fails to make me sad when I listen to his music. There's Randy Rhoads, Ozzy Osbourne's guitarist, who was killed in a plane crash. Gar Samuelson, drummer for Megadeth, whose reported cause of death was liver failure, at forty-one. And my favourite: Cliff Burton, who died in a road accident aged only twenty-four. Bassist in the best metal band of all time: Metallica.

But it's not death that makes them special. They died doing what they loved, and that's what matters.

I put on a white shirt. My hands shake. I unbutton it, do it up again correctly. Black trousers, a black and grey tie. Grey socks, black shoes. If my uniform was all black I'd like it more.

'Benjamin! We're going to be *ridiculously* late!'

I shut the door and run downstairs, avoiding the broken floorboard. Mum is holding my blazer out, an arm aloft, like a signpost. I take it from her. She hustles me out of the house.

'Do you have your revision folder? Do you have your keys? Do you have your—'

I tell her yes, yes, yes. I climb into the car and can't fit my legs in the space between the seat and the glove compartment. The early morning traffic rumbles and roars: a procession of lumbering beasts. Mum slams her door.

The drive to school is sluggish, fraught with roadworks and ill-timed traffic lights. Mum bangs the steering wheel and shouts at a lorry that pulls out in front of us. She fiddles with the radio until she finds a French station, and we listen to a discussion about the Olympics and the prospects of the French athletes. I have to get A*, or A at the very least, in all my subjects: I'm a Scholarship kid, ninety per cent of my fees paid by the school. The conditions: good behaviour and academic achievement.

'What do you think your grades will be?' Mum asks as we speed along the Westway. It's a question she's asked before. Many times. I watch the blur of houses, bus depots and railway lines, deliberately allowing my vision to distort so that they become a mishmash of line and colour.

'I dunno,' I say. She doesn't know this, but I'm predicted Bs in all the sciences and a C in geography. My standards seem to have slipped.

'Should we . . . perhaps we can find a tutor?'

I had lots of tutoring when I was little, and lots more in Year 8 to get me through Scholarship. It was great. I learned things I'd never have known about; I was taught to really use my brain. I wouldn't object to it. But I doubt we can afford it. Tutoring is a way of life for most of the people I know.

'I'll be fine,' I say.

'Well, it's good for you to be independent,' says Mum, pausing mid-flow while she negotiates a roundabout. 'Best not to turn out like your father. He can't do anything for himself.'

I only see Dad on alternate weekends. He and Mum split up a while ago, when I was twelve. She's probably right. He isn't much good at getting things done. I wonder if he goes on nightwalks too. I've never asked him.

'But, Ben, honestly – if they kick you out . . . I don't know *what* we're going to do with you.'

My school has a habit of rounding up the potentially lower-grade GCSE students and 'asking them to leave'; there are league tables and reputations to be considered, and it's a competitive world. Last year a boy was framed, in most people's opinion, for stealing a digital camera. He'd been predicted a handful of imperfect grades. Sometimes I think being kicked out would be a relief. But I doubt my mother would ever get over it. Even Dad, who is typically more laid-back, might be a bit disappointed.

It's not until we get to school that I find a moment to ask her, just as she's double-parking the car and wishing me luck with my French exam.

'Mum,' I say.

'What is it?'

'Is somebody . . . is Granddad OK?'

Her face at once is a screensaver of perplexed annoyance; then something softer takes over, but only for a minute, before annoyance returns.

'Of course he is,' she says as she switches on the ignition. 'You must learn to manage your anxiety better, Benjamin.'

School rises up out of the early morning mist: a ghostly monument in ochre stone. The giant clock in the courtyard never tells the wrong time. Shoals of boys in grey suits and black coats stream beneath it, dwarfed by the architecture. It's a lot like the courtyard in *The Shawshank Redemption*. Schools and prisons: not so different. The first couple of years I was here, I barely spoke to anyone. No one bothered me, and I bothered no one.

Solomon is in the locker room, doing Rosetta Stone on his laptop, waiting for me. He's one of those people whose face really lights up when they see you. He is one of the nicest people I know.

'Bennikin. What's up?'

I open my bag and tip it upside down. Books and papers clatter to the floor. My English file breaks apart, revealing a Seamus Heaney essay that is both unfinished and late. Chadwick has already issued several warnings to our set for shoddy work and unmet deadlines. It'll mean a definite detention. And a letter home.

Solly scrutinises me as I gather up armloads of index cards.

'Let me guess: another nocturnal perambulation?' he enquires. 'Such extraordinary things you choose to do with your time.'

'Not exactly. I went to the Stonehills'.'

'*Partying* on a school night! That's even worse,' says Solomon, in the exact tone of voice he used to play Lady Bracknell in *The Importance of Being Earnest* last year. But he doesn't go on.

I sit down on the bench, resting my head against the locker behind me.

'I haven't revised for French. And I've not done my essay,' I say.

'Relax,' says Solomon. 'I've done a spare. Just in case. Just for you. Different font, different line spacing, and some of those unmistakable Ben Holloway malapropisms. You always get *infer* and *imply* the wrong way round.'

'Thank you,' I say, taking it.

'As for the French, just take a few calming breaths now and again, centre yourself and it'll all come back to you.'

Solomon will make an excellent counsellor one day, though I think he has his heart set on running the country. He always knows when people are upset. He helps me sift through the debris from my bag, picking out unfiled A4 pages and stacking them together.

'Ben. What's the matter?'

'I have this feeling . . . I think someone's *died*,' I say.

Solomon replies, 'I've said it once, and I'll say it again: you listen to *too much heavy metal*. Songs about death, by people who are mostly dead, or who probably will be soon. Small wonder you're unduly preoccupied.'

For the first time today, I almost raise a smile.

The French listening exam comes and goes. I mark the boxes, indicate the true statements, doodle with inky magnificence on the back of the sheet. I watch the neat nodding heads of the columns of boys before and to the left and right of me. The exam hall rustles with the sound of sleeves and watchstraps catching on paper. In my earphones, solid, deliberate-syllabled French voices declare that they cannot attend the meeting, or explain that their working day begins at seven twenty-five in the morning. Sometimes the voices swim, fragment. Gaps appear. And another sound – a hollow, whipping-wind sound, a low rumble underneath – can be heard. Old Norse. On a piece of rough paper I begin to trace the words I think Hermódr said, the verb I think they came from.

*Deyja.*

To die.

To stop living.

But I can't be sure.

\*   \*   \*

14

After school there's Cold War revision to do, and a whole set of chemistry notes to hammer into my medium-term memory. On Friday it's my first maths exam, so I also need to revise for that. I make a pot of coffee and take it upstairs. I've always liked coffee. Not for the taste, but because it makes my nerves jangle and roar, my veins surge with caffeinated blood. It's like a cheap metal gig at the Camden Underworld.

My brain doesn't function the way it once did. I find it difficult to remember things now. Not, perhaps, surprising, given what I habitually do to my brain. I revise some equations, knowing that I am never again in all my waking days going to need to know what happens when calcium carbonate is heated, or added to water.

The knocking adds a polyrhythm that I don't notice until my door opens and Mum comes in, putting a plate of oatcakes and hummus near my elbow.

'Ben,' she says, 'your *ears*.'

I hit the iTunes tab and slide the volume down.

'Chemistry?'

'Yep.'

'Good . . . good. Don't let me interrupt you. I'm just off to my ballroom-dancing class,' she says.

'Oh yeah. That's cool. Have fun.'

Mum used to go to kickboxing on Wednesdays. Recently, though, she's switched to dancing. It's a good sign, I reckon: she's got less rage in her now. She explains what I need to do for dinner, right down to the number of minutes the salmon needs to cook in the oven for, the exact amount of tinfoil I need to wrap it in. We both know that I'll pop down the road and get some chips, if I'm hungry, which I probably won't be. But she'll leave the salmon anyway, like a ritual sacrifice.

Mum looks down at the rug. 'I may not be back till tomorrow,' she says, almost shyly. 'Reg is taking me out for dinner afterwards, and we'll be in Putney, so . . .'

Although I can't believe there are still people in the world called Reg, it doesn't bother me at all that Mum is seeing someone. She hid this from me for months. If I started seeing someone too, ours would be the most clandestine household in W9.

I haven't met Reg. Mum thinks I'd be rude to him.

'Mum. It's *fine*. I'll see you tomorrow after school, then.'

She hovers. 'I don't want to have to worry about you, Ben. No leaving the house at night. Please. I just . . . I'd just like to enjoy myself.'

She doesn't add *for once*. But we both know it's there.

As soon as she's gone, I put Metallica back on at top volume.

I revise for two hours, by which I mean that I listen to music while looking at things. I remember the revision cards I used to make at my old school, the colour-coded charts that logged my progress. I was better at achieving things when I was twelve. I go downstairs, take pity on the salmon and return it to the morgue of the fridge. I'm not good at

16

being hungry: my stomach doesn't know how to signal when I am, or else my brain can't read the signals. I have a couple of oatcakes and drink some juice from the carton.

Then I catch sight of the box on the kitchen table.

It's a mailbox, made of white cardboard. It must have been there all day, and yet I didn't notice it when I came home. Picking it up – it's quite heavy – I see that it's addressed to me. Mum must have forgotten to tell me. Now I am looking at it more closely, I can see that the box has taken a fair beating. Once a perfect cube, it's now scuffed and bruised and discoloured; the masking tape that secures the top, once white as well, is the yellow of stained teeth. I peer at the date on the postmark; it's hard to make out. At some point the box has been left out in the rain. I can't read the place it was posted from either. All I can say for sure is that it's been in transit for a very long time. The reason why becomes clear once I look at the address: it's been written in a looping, rather feminine hand, the letters squashed together and difficult to read. Although we live at 9B, it looks more like 98. Our street name's spelt wrong, and there's an error in the postcode as well. It's obvious from the various messages written by Royal Mail workers in irate biro – *Not known in Bevington Road. Try Bevington Crescent* – that someone's done a good deal of detective work in order to finally deliver this parcel. If the sender had written their own address somewhere, I suppose it would have been returned to them.

I take a pair of scissors and score the tape. The box breaks open and thousands of polystyrene packing chips, the ones that look like little butterflies, spill out onto the table. I plunge my hands in and pull out a folded sheet of paper with my name on it. It says:

> *Duvalle Hall*
> *17-12-11*
>
> *Dear Ben,*
> *Hope all is going well with your studies. I was clearing out some cupboards and came across these books, which I believe are yours. Sorry we held on to them.*
> *Friendly wishes from everyone here,*
> *Clothilde.*

With the eerie sense of unpacking an unexpected Christmas stocking, I take the books out, one by one.

My *Elementary Old Norse Grammar*.

My dictionary of Old Norse.

My book about the Gods, the one I used to take everywhere. It's warped and bloated, as though someone's dropped it in the bath.

My green notebook, where I once made language notes, adding bits of vocabulary as I came across them. *Bátr*: boat. *Dvergr*: dwarf. Just looking at the notebook, I start to remember them.

My red notebook, where I copied out parts of the poems that particularly appealed to me.

There's the children's book with the beautiful watercolour illustrations.

And finally, there's my Free Creative Writing book, where I once wrote stories of my own.

Once upon a time, these books were my most valued possessions.

Something has risen up out of the box along with the books and butterflies. I wish I knew how to describe it. Something like a pull. An undertow. A slow tide. Something that wants to draw me in, very deeply, and take me very far away. Far back.

To the beginning.

It cannot be a coincidence, that first Hermódr appeared in the small hours of the morning, and now my Norse books – long lost, long forgotten – have suddenly been delivered to my door.

I pick up the Old Norse grammar. It's a mildewed, disintegrating volume with ancient yellowed pages, full of footnotes and endnotes and tables. I wonder where I got it from originally. Wait: I know this too. Portobello Market. Autumn half term, Year 5. I remember now: fumbling through the massed heaps of old books, tracing my fingers down their spines. Opening the grammar slowly, almost reverently, like a church bible.

And a voice, soft and slightly lilting:

'It's your birthday tomorrow, isn't it, my friend? Here. I'll get this for you.'

I spend a few minutes flipping to and fro, taking care with its old pages, remembering how gentle I tried to be with this particular book. I look for the paradigm of *deyja*, but I can't seem to find it. Eventually, after comparing some different verb forms, and hoping that I still remember what it was that Hermódr said, I take the green notebook – and it's so weird to suddenly be using it, as though I am twelve again – and write:

*Hann er dauðr.*

He is dead.

I wonder if that's right.

There is something stuck between two pages of the Norse grammar. Slowly, carefully, I take it out. It's brittle and nearly square.

It's a photograph.

In the photograph I am twelve. In the photograph I am smiling. I did not often smile in photographs. I am smiling through a complicated red-and-gold mask, with a pointed snout and whiskers, and wicked tufted ears. I have a mouthful of fangs that glow with a sickly iridescence. I have something – bubblegum, I think – tangled in my fang-teeth. I am wearing a fur coat. I am a wolf. Next to me, in a similar outfit, is another wolf. Underneath his fur coat his clothes look pricier than mine, and where his mask ends you can see how curly and bright his hair is. Like me, he is smiling. He has his arm around my shoulders.

For a few seconds I sit totally still, holding the photograph flat in my palm. Then, unconsciously mimicking the image in front of me, I smile, unable to help myself. In a strange way I realise I've been thinking about it all day: being twelve, being at Cottesmore House, revising for exams. It makes an odd kind of sense that this photograph should have found its way back to me, along with everything else. Although I barely remember the moment the photograph was taken, it was certainly taken when I was in Year 8. And I do, for sure, remember the other person in the picture, though I haven't seen him for a long, long time.

It's my old friend Hobie.

# HOBIE'S DIARY

Monday 8th September 2008

Mr White has told us that even though we're back at Cottesmore House we're supposed to carry on with our journals. I seriously do not see the point. But now it's Year 8 and we're all doing Scholarship I suppose everything we do is meant to sharpen our brains and make us even smarter than we already are. Anyway, I have no intention of writing in this diary after this week, but I might just do some quick notes about the kids in 8 Upper – by which I mean the supergeeks, the Greekists, the teeth-grinding, book-toting weirdos, the Gifted and Talented lot who can't even speak properly, some of them, because their brains work too fast for their mouths.

I thought being put in the Scholarship form was quite cool until I realised how much work we're expected to do. I don't understand what's going on in Maths any more. In English we dissect poetry that makes no sense. Then there's a General Paper that's more like undergraduate-level Philosophy, so they say. Means nothing to me. And now I am basically stuck here.

Everyone in 8 Upper is obsessed, totally and utterly obsessed, with how Special we all are. There are nine of us altogether. We're doing Scholarship for a bunch of different schools but you can prepare for the exams in quite similar ways. Apart from me, there's:

Frodo, aka Fat Frodo, aka Hobbitboy. He is very good at Physics and can sing lots of show tunes from pointless old musicals.

Matteo, who has blond hair like mine but completely straight, that covers his head like an egg cosy.

Norville, who doesn't eat all day because he thinks nervous energy makes him a more efficient worker. He is very scrawny and his voice is breaking and he likes to share all his opinions very loudly, all the time. He can recite pi to the seventy-eighth figure.

The Nicholson Twins. I suspect that there is only one of them actually, because they are not interesting enough to be two people. They're called Peter and Ferdie. They like Greek.

Jean-Jacques, who does jiu-jitsu and aikido out of school and collects war memorabilia like bullets and things and lives in South Kensington, which is where French people live. Every Saturday afternoon his nanny takes him to do Warhammer off Kensington High Street.

Archie, who has lots and lots of freckles and plays the violin and is Chess Champion and would be, like, the perfect pupil if he wasn't hideously ugly with sticky-outy teeth that overlap.

Simon, who is allergic to lots of things.

Oh, and there's a new boy called Ben, who's been moved up from 7 Middle. I've never really noticed him because he isn't any good at Games and doesn't speak much to anyone.

He has dark brown hair that falls over his eyes in a heavy fringe and he looks like he's never taken any exercise at all, because he's really skinny and weak-looking.

Matteo says Ben needs to get a Scholarship because otherwise his parents won't be able to pay for him to go to a private school. If he gets a Scholarship it can be means-tested and then his next school will pay up to 100% of his fees, like something in Dickens. Norville and the Nicholson Twins are working extra hard now, just to be on the safe side. They don't want to be beaten by a newbie.

Apparently Ben's parents have just got divorced. If my parents got divorced I don't think I'd mind that much, because I'd just get two of everything then. Mum and Dad could have houses on the same street and Zara and I could swap round every few days so I wouldn't have to put up with her whining and moaning. I don't see what the problem would be.

## Wednesday 10th September

Miss Atkins stood over me during break while I sat my retest. Her legs are very thin but her ankles are quite swollen. She ought to wear boots. She told me my attitude was all wrong.

'Hobie, you really need to think about whether you're taking Scholarship work seriously. I don't expect to retest anyone from 8 Upper.'

I would have passed the test the first time, but I lost the sheet and we went out for dinner last night, and there wasn't time to call someone when I got back. It wasn't my fault.

Latin deponent verbs: they look passive, but are active. Like *morior*, I die, and *hortor*, I encourage. How ridiculous. What's the point of looking like one thing and being another? I asked Miss Atkins and you could tell she didn't know, because she looked in her silly teacher's bag which is covered with embroidered owls and told me to be quiet and finish the retest. I'm actually pretty good at Latin. When my grandfather, Hobart Duvalle II, was alive, he'd give me £100 every time I came top. That was a perfectly reasonable incentive, and even now he's dead I find that I don't have to make too much of an effort to do well. I was hoping for a lump sum when he died last year, but all he left me was his antique model-ship collection. To be fair, the ships are pretty awesome.

For lunch Clothilde my nanny, who is supposed to

improve my conversational French, brought me a tray from Feng Sushi, but it was left too long at Reception and the fish wasn't as cold as I like it, so I tried some of Simon's spelt fusilli but it was repulsive. He doesn't eat wheat, sugar or dairy.

This evening I had three homeworks (sometimes there's as many as four): a *Frankenstein* comprehension, simultaneous equations using the substitution method, and more Latin which was sentences using deponent participles. Clothilde brought me a hot chocolate. Mum emailed school to complain that they didn't refrigerate my sushi tray. She also told Clothilde to remember to drop off my lunch as close to lunchtime as possible. She was annoyed because Clothilde is supposed to make my lunch for me in the morning, but the Ocado delivery was late today, so she couldn't.

I have a tutor three days a week now. He's just there for support, which means if I don't understand my homework he explains it to me and he times everything I do and tells Mum if there are any problems, and he's very quiet most of the time and just looks through my books and things. His name is Jason and he's 24 or 34, I can't remember which. He is doing a PhD. He always asks for a Nespresso, which is coffee made with our special machine. Sometimes he doesn't shave properly and his clothes look old.

Mum and Dad both want me to get a Scholarship, because Dad got one. He got to wear a special badge for scholars and live in a special boarding house and I forget what else, but there must have been some other considerably cooler perks or else I can't think why he bothered. They've said it doesn't matter if I don't succeed and it has nothing to do with how much they love me. But that's only half true. It does matter. That's why Jason's always here. They want his genius molecules to float out of his brain and into mine.

Tonight we finished everything in an hour and forty-five minutes and Jason initialled my homework diary, and Clothilde cooked mine and Zara's supper which was pizzas made on our pizza stone, and I ate half of Zara's for her because I told her she didn't really need a whole pizza.

When I checked my Facebook after supper there was an invitation to join the group for 8 Upper and I thought for quite a long time about whether to accept, because there would be something quite cool about ignoring it. But I did join after all, because they probably use the group to share study skills, and I don't want to be left behind.

Thursday 11th September

Today Ben sat next to me in History. At Scholarship you're likely to get source questions about a time period you've never studied. It's about the skills you use to analyse the sources. We were doing an old paper that had been photo-copied several times – you had to really squint to read some of the questions. After discussing the sources in small groups, we had forty minutes to do the essay that went with them. The title was: 'Do great wars always have great causes?'

I spent the discussion part squirting the back of Frodo's head with hand sanitiser. When it came to the writing bit, I had no idea what to say. I mean, all wars are great, obviously, but I totally couldn't be bothered to sit there like a loser and come up with an argument and a counter-argument and a whole bunch of examples off the top of my head. I cast around the room to see whose ideas I could steal, and my eye landed on Ben. He was sitting in the next row of seats, up and to the right. He was using a laptop. He really knows how to type. His fingers worked the keyboard like one of those master jazz musicians you see on old TV programmes. He was making notes. I could see things like: 'Intro – analyse title – how do you define *great*? How do you define *cause*?'

I got out my Pelikan fountain pen and wrote: 'Before answer-ing the question it is important to attempt to analyse the title. "Great", for example, can have several interpretations.'

Then I waited for Ben to put down some more thoughts.

Pretty soon he started composing the essay. I simply copied everything down in my own words. I couldn't really follow his train of thought half the time. He opened with a quote from something called *For Whom the Bell Tolls*, all about soldiers and things. Then he started writing about something called Ragnarok, which apparently was a giant battle fought between some Gods and monsters where everyone died. According to Ben, the cause of Ragnarok was the death of some dude called Baldr. 'It was not a great cause so much as a catalyst,' wrote Ben. 'Baldr's death foretold the end of the Gods.' I wasn't convinced this was properly historical. Ben must have realised this, because he deleted his opening paragraph and began again, writing about something different this time. I think I made a noise, like a grunt of frustration or something, because he suddenly jumped and looked around at me. His eyes were completely black. He raised his hand, and Miss Flower, who had been reading an Excel spreadsheet from a wedding catering company while pretending to mark some books, came hurrying over.

'Please can I move to that desk over there?' Ben asked her. 'I need to plug in the power supply.'

He has a gruff, almost lispy voice. He can't quite do his Rs, but not the same way as Simon, who sounds like a four-year-old girl. Ben sounds more like a rescue dog that isn't sure whether to whine or howl.

I had to write my own essay for the rest of the lesson.

\* \* \*

Ben doesn't say much in class. I think he's quite weirded out by the lunatics in 8 Upper. Norville likes to rap whatever we've been doing, like the periodic table, or that thing that starts: 'Ah, Faustus, now hast thou but one bare hour to live, and then thou must be damn'd perpetually . . .' And then Archie and Frodo join in, because Frodo, stupid fat Hobbit, thinks he knows how to beatbox. Most of the teachers, apart from Mrs Ottoboni who does Art, let us make lots of noise as long as it's to do with the lesson. Ben just sits there looking out of the window or scribbling illegibly in his books.

There's only one time that I remember when Ben did contribute, sort of. Earlier this week we were looking at the Creation in Genesis and Mr White (who teaches RS as well as English) was reading us the bit where God creates the world in seven days or possibly six, and the Nicholson Twins were going on about how they'd read bits of the Bible in Greek (because they don't have any friends or anything more interesting to do with their time), and suddenly the room went a bit quiet and there Ben was, at the back, with his hand up.

And Mr White said, 'Yes, Ben? Do you have a question?' and Ben went red and put his hand down and shook his head.

Mr White said, 'No, go on. What were you going to say?'

And Ben took a deep and ragged breath and said something completely incomprehensible, about how in the beginning there was fire in the south and ice in the north

30

and a giant who gave birth to a man and a woman from his arms (Is that what he said? Sounds absurd) and a cow that turned up from somewhere, and then everyone pissed themselves with laughter and he shut up again.

'What's he going on about?' I whispered to Jean-Jacques, who shrugged.

'Comparative Mythology,' said Mr White. 'I wish we could discuss this further, Ben, but there isn't time today.' Ben meanwhile had retreated down into his blazer and definitely wasn't going to share any more thoughts with the group.

He's actually just as weird as the rest of them.

## Friday 12th September

We were changing for Games when I saw the scar. Or I thought it was a scar. Just below his ribs, sort of where you imagine Christ was pierced by the spear, although I have no idea why that came into my mind. Maybe because Ben's so silent and creepy and seems to know so much. You can kind of picture him healing the lame.

'Hey, what's that?' I asked him.

'What's what?'

'That weird mark.' I tried to grab at him, but he twisted away and pulled down his rugby shirt.

'It's nothing, just a transfer. Came free with a packet of chewing gum.'

Then Mr Voss came in and started barking war commands at us and we had to run out onto the pitch and I forgot about it, because I wanted to beat the hell out of everyone who got in my way. In the first lesson after the holidays I bloodied Simon's nose. And I totally got away with it, because it was Rugby.

If aptitude for Scholarship and a total lack of sporting ability go hand in hand, then I probably don't belong in 8 Upper. Apart from Archie, they're all malco lame-arsed old men who go in for tackles like they're on ice skates and cry in scrums. They want to go back inside and translate *Petit Nicolas* into fluent English. I, on the other hand, live for Sport.

I felt really strong today, stronger than usual. It must have been all the swimming over the summer, all the diving off the top of the yacht, cannonballing into the water inches away from where Zara was paddling around, washing her dolls' hair in the sea. I felt like the whole length of the pitch wasn't enough to wear me out.

I watched Ben lingering near the sidelines, and I found myself thinking about that weird mark on his ribcage. The skin underneath was pink like sunburn. And the mark was almost black. If it was a transfer, it was a pretty crap one.

Sometimes he looked over in my direction. I think he looked kind of *afraid*.

We had ICT last lesson. Ben was called halfway through by his harp teacher. Yes, he actually plays the harp. He left his books behind, which is the sort of thing he does because he apparently has mild dyspraxia and his organisation isn't that good. I picked them up and said I'd bring them back to our form room.

On the way I leaned against the wall and flipped through his homework diary. Nothing. Just his strange scribbly writing straggling all over the page. I would've investigated his laptop, but I didn't know how to log in. I unzipped his pencil case. Clothilde would be waiting to pick me up from the gate with my snack, usually a cherry and chocolate drop scone from Gail's and a Vitamin Water. But I wanted to find something. I don't even know what I was looking for.

In Ben's pencil case were about 100 Caran d'Ache water-soluble drawing pencils, two biros, a Pritt Stick, scissors, a calculator, the usual. I slid open the calculator.

And found something.

Taped to the back of the cover, a square of paper. Ben's writing.

He'd written:

*Skǫll . . . ~~son (?) Fenrir (genitive?)~~*
*<u>Skǫll sonr Fenris</u>*

Underneath was a drawing of a wolf, or a large dog like an Alsatian, done quickly with thick black lines.

And it looked a bit like the mark that I'd seen on his side.

## Monday 15th September

I watched the back of Ben's head in Assembly as we sang 'Dear Lord and Father of Mankind' and the organ blared away like a fire alarm and all the portraits of former and/ or deceased Headmasters stared down at us from above. My school is very old so there's a lot of them. Most of them are from the Cottesmore family. The school was started by Vincent Cottesmore in, like, 1850. (There's a mouldy falling-down museum behind the Science Block with some tragic-looking newspaper cuttings and commemorative plates and assorted crap which you have to show visitors when they come round.) So there's old Vincent, who looked practically dead by the time they painted his portrait, and then Alfred and George and Leonard and Richmond, then it skips to some other dude and then there's a whole bunch more Cottesmores and finally there's Roland, who's our current Headmaster and has hair growing out of his ears. I find this fascinating and repellent in equal measure.

I had a magazine with me, from my huge collection of Real Life Drama magazines that are so weird and gross that I find I just can't stop reading them. Celebrities are boring in comparison. What I like are stories about women who are so fat they squash their husbands to death or people setting each other on fire. Anyway, it was rolled up in my sleeve, ready to be whipped out and shoved under Simon's nose (he's especially squeamish and you can sometimes induce him to actually throw up), but for some reason I was too busy watching Ben. When he thinks no one's looking Ben tips his head back slightly and shakes it, like Zara's pony used to do, so that his fringe jumps. Now Zara doesn't ride any more because she's got to sit the 11+ and Mum and Dad think that all her spare time should be spent doing extra Maths and English. They didn't ask Zara what she thought about it, but I know she was scared of her pony, which used to bite her. So maybe she doesn't mind. Zara is scared of most things.

Ben was standing in between the Nicholson Twins, and even though they're grotesquely underdeveloped and have only ever used their muscles for carrying the Liddell and Scott *Greek–English Lexicon* up and down the library stairs, they made him look puny and weak by comparison. At the end of the hymn you're supposed to sing the line about 'O still, small voice of calm' really quietly. I made sure I didn't, just to annoy Miss Atkins, who was looking over and scowling.

Ben brushed past me on his way out of the hall.

'Hey,' I said.

'Hi, Hobie,' he said, not really looking at me. I kept pace with him as we went back to our form room to pick up our stuff.

'We probably need to bring our Science folders with us, and our French grammar notebooks and our RS homework,' I said as if to myself, but actually it was for his benefit.

I noticed, when we got upstairs, that he was collecting everything together. If you don't turn up with the right stuff you get a Demerit and if you get three Demerits you get a Detention and then you have to stay after school and it messes up all your clubs and activities and things.

'Don't forget the test on the water cycle after break,' said Simon, who carries everything around in a vintage satchel the colour of dog diarrhoea. I haven't mentioned that to him (recently) because he is very easily upset by things like that and it's not worth the hassle if someone catches you doing it.

Damn. The water cycle. I knew there was something I was meant to revise for.

Ben was looking at me sideways.

'I'll sit next to you in Geog, if you like,' he said.

What he meant was: I could copy his answers. I think that was what he was saying. But the other day he moved away from me when I copied his History essay. So what was different?

'Cool.' I shrugged. 'Whatever.'

And when it came to the test he made sure that his paper was turned towards me a bit and actually most of the key words came back to me because they're all derived from Latin and it was just a question of drawing the earth and sea and sky and getting all the arrows the right way round, and what possible use it could be to anyone is completely beyond me, but the point was passing the test. Scholarship

Geography is really, really complicated, all about quaternary industries and deforestation and Human Disasters.

I started thinking that this was going to work out well. For me. I could copy Ben's work, which looked pretty high-standard, and that would definitely keep me going for a few weeks while I got my head around some of the harder Scholarship stuff. I mean, I don't find it difficult, of course, but it's all such a massive effort.

We ended up sitting together at lunch too.

'Sushi?' he asked me, indicating my tray, extra bowl of edamame on the side. He looked as if he'd never seen sushi before, which is unlikely because most kids have at least one sushi-rolling party for their birthday at some point. Simon says that Ben's parents split up over the summer and it was really bad timing because then his mother lost her job and the Financial Crisis is happening so she can't get another good one. Now they live in some really small house, just him and his mum, somewhere off the Harrow Road. They probably can't afford sushi any more.

'You shouldn't eat sushi on a Monday,' said Frodo, who had one of those compartmentalised lunchboxes with all these different Italian deli items like breadsticks and mozzarella balls in it.

'Why the hell not, Hobbitboy?'

'Because,' he said, sneering, 'fishermen take Sundays off. So you're eating fish that can't be 100% fresh. That's why so many sushi restaurants offer deals on Mondays. To tempt customers that don't know better.' There was a puddle of oil from his artichoke hearts pooling underneath his elbow.

After that I didn't really want any sushi.

Ben unwrapped his sandwich.

'It's ham and mustard,' he said, holding one half out to me.

It looked totally boring, not on any particular artisan bread, no rocket or Gruyère or fancy ham like Serrano. Just: ham and mustard. But actually it tasted quite good. I'd forgotten some kids bring normal lunches to school.

'Cheers,' I said. I hate being hungry in the afternoons. Some kids, like Norville, don't eat at all until they get home. I can't imagine how they survive.

'No problem,' he said.

And then: 'Hobie?'

I knew there was something.

'I'd be really, really grateful if you didn't mention my . . . my transfer to anyone.'

'What, you mean that black mark on your ribcage? Why would I want to do that? Do you think I'm, like, obsessed with you or something?'

He looked down. 'I just don't want anyone knowing about it.'

'Sure,' I said. 'For all I care, it's just necrotising fasciitis.'

'OK, great. Thanks.'

'Whatever.'

As he was getting up to leave, I said, as if to nobody, '*Skǫll*. It's an interesting name, isn't it?'

Ben got that frozen look again, where his eyes look like marbles, and his skin actually went white.

'Can't think why that came into my mind just now,' I said. 'Thanks again for the sandwich, dude.'

'What's necrotising fasciitis?' Simon asked nervously, coming to sit down opposite me.

'It's a disease caused by *flesh-eating bacteria*,' I said, brandishing a piece of ham in his face.

I reckon I could've made him cry, but the bell was about to ring for the end of lunch.

In the afternoon we had English, and Mr White made us read out our Free Creative Writing homework. Mine was about a man that was addicted to drinking blood and eating car parts, which I'd basically culled from a couple of magazines and then added some INTERESTING IMAGERY to, such as 'his hunger was as lethal as a computer virus' etc. Mr White said I needed to tone down my imagination and be more subtle. I don't get that. Frodo had written a poem composed entirely from haikus about the decline of autumn and the slow, inevitable onset of winter, which the Nicholson Twins instantly recognised as having been ripped off from some famous poet. The lesson dragged on and on and I couldn't hear myself think for polysyllabic alliterative

40

phrases about multicoloured flowers and so forth. If that's being *subtle*, I can't see why anyone would want to be.

Finally it was Ben's turn. He shuffled to the front of the room, looking positively green in the face, and proceeded to read so quietly that Mr White made him start again. As he read his voice got louder and stronger until he sounded totally confident. It was like he was a different person.

This is what he said:

*The Gods lived peacefully at Asgard. Among them was Baldr the beautiful. He was a handsome and gentle God, but he was no longer as happy as he once had been, because of his nightmares. He went to the other Gods.*

*'I see a fiery red that prickles my dreams, and an overwhelming blackness,' he told them. 'Misty and dark, it covers my mind. Roots pierce my body.'*

*Now the Gods were very upset by this, but most anxious of all was Frigg, because Baldr was her son and she loved him dearly. So she went on a journey across all the lands and seas, and she extracted an oath from anything that could harm Baldr – the rocks, the trees, the plants, even the men from Midgard – that they would not hurt him. She went home to Asgard, happy that Baldr was safe.*

*The God Loki was unlike Baldr in every way. His smile was as crooked as Baldr's was open, and he was as mischievous as Baldr was kind. He was determined to harm Baldr if he could. He disguised himself as an old*

41

woman and went to Asgard to talk to Frigg. All the Gods were throwing stones and arrows at Baldr, which fell against the invincible God and dropped to the ground like feathers.

'What are they doing?' asked Loki.

Frigg told Loki what she had done to protect her son.

'Every growing thing has sworn an oath not to harm Baldr,' she told him. 'And every metal too, and every stone.'

'Every single one?' Loki asked, his eyes wide.

'All,' replied Frigg, 'except the mistletoe. It's such a young, tender plant. I don't see how it could trouble him.'

Loki went away gleefully, knowing what he had to do. At once, he returned to Asgard, to find Tyr and Thor and all the other Gods engaged in their usual pastime of hurling heavy rocks at their beloved Baldr.

Loki caught sight of Hǫdr, who was blind, leaning against a tree and listening to the cries of merry laughter.

Loki went to Hǫdr, and said, 'Why don't you join in?'

He handed blind Hǫdr a dart of mistletoe, smiling wickedly all the while. Taking the dart, Hǫdr threw it, trustingly, and Loki guided his hand.

Baldr looked up, and was stirred by the memory of the fiery red from his dreams – the exact same colour as Loki's hair. It was too late. The dart pierced his heart and he fell down, dead.

*The Gods stared, shocked. They turned on Loki.*
*'It was Hǫdr who threw the dart!' he protested.*
*But he knew he would not be forgiven.*


When he'd finished Mr White said, 'Ben, that's very moving. Boys, what do we think?' And everyone said things about adverbs and dialogue. Frodo, the pretentious gaylord, commented that 'the visual symbolism of red, the colour of danger, worked really well'. Ugh.

'Hobie?' said Mr White. 'Did you want to say something?'

I said Loki sounded pretty cool. I wondered if he got away with it. It seemed to be part of the same story as the war that Ben had been writing about in his history essay. For some reason it was obviously Ben's favourite thing, a bit like how Jean-Jacques feels about *Star Wars*.

I don't know why, but I kept my photocopy of the story. And then later, when I was having tutoring, Jason noticed it on my desk.

'I know that handwriting!' he exclaimed. 'That's young Ben Holloway.'

I asked him how he knew Ben, and he said that he'd worked with Ben like, three or four years ago. I couldn't quite work out the expression on Jason's face as he read the story. He looked sort of happy and sad at the same time.

'He's even put in the accents,' he said. 'Now, Hobie, that's the kind of accuracy that you should be trying to emulate in your work.'

43

I nearly asked Jason if he knew about Ben's tattoo. But I didn't.

I really need to know though. What's it *for*? If it's a wolf, why is it a wolf? Who or what is Skọll? What does it mean? Is it connected to the story?

Maybe I'll do some research.

Or maybe I'll just ask Ben.

# BEN

In my dream I'm swimming. It's unending tropical water, the sort I've never seen, let alone swum in – the kind of water you see in ads in the backs of magazines for all-inclusive island holidays. I'm floating, rotating this way and that, drifting further and further away from a palm-tree-lined, diamond-sand beach on the horizon. A yacht bobs on the surface, some way away. As I float backwards, the water darkens and hardens, becomes dense and heavy, like paint. I am swimming now, or trying to, struggling to pull myself back to the surface, but the paint is getting everywhere, and it tastes metallic and bloody. Powerless, I begin to sink. And through the darkening waves I'm dimly aware of a shadow coming towards me: a mass of scales and coils, a monstrous shape on the ocean floor, its jaws ecstatically wide. As it closes in, bent on the business of devouring me whole in the painted water, it hisses, almost conspiratorially, 'It's great to see you again, Ben.'

My eyes snap open.

My room is bright. It feels late, dead-of-night late, but I've only been asleep for an hour. The open window lets in waves of chill air. I stumble over and bang the window shut, draw the curtains. I realise that I am still holding the photograph of me and Hobie. It's a little crumpled at the edges. I smooth it out and lay it flat on my desk. Then, going back to the wall beside my bed, I slowly take down my poster of Cliff Burton. And then I take down the rest of the Late Greats. Dimebag Darrell, Randy Rhoads, Gar Samuelson, Layne Staley. As they come away from the wall, they expose, inch by inch, a vast, painted landscape. The mural I did when we moved into this house, shortly after Mum lost her job and Dad left. I trace my fingers over the ridges of acrylic, which stand out in relief because I laid it on thickly, with a palette knife. My hands are shaking, the way Dad's sometimes do in the morning. The paint is filmy with dust. I force myself to step back, so that I can see the whole of it. At the bottom, the sea. Grey-tipped waves, a deepening blue-black suggesting impenetrable depths. The World Serpent, Jǫrmungandr, just visible, a glimmering smear of green at the edge of the painting. Oceans of white cloud, with great cliffs behind, and then a stretch of rocky landscape studded with stones and lone trees. A longship appearing through the mist.

There were many windows into the Otherlife, but this is one I made myself. Gradually, as my collection of metal posters expanded, I covered up my mural, but – seeing it again, for the first time in a long time – I'm reminded of how deeply I cared.

And how truly I believed.

Now the air in my room swirls, shifts, changes, and –
seeing, unseeing – I become aware of a different light. Not
Hermódr, this time, but Frigg. Each of the Gods was a
different colour, and Frigg's colour was probably my favourite
of them all. She was a kind of lemony-green. The colour
you'd pick for daffodil stems, or a meadow in spring. She
was the gentlest presence, always, and the saddest, too, for
she loved Baldr very dearly.

Silently she weeps, a nugget of light against my mural. I
just can make out the curve of her jaw, the blur of a single
tear on her cheek, the folds of her shining hair.

Then she says, softly and urgently, '*Hjálpaðú . . .*'

And this verb I know: I don't need to check it.

*Help.*


Shaking a little, I reach for my laptop. I'm not a fan of
social media, but I've come to find that if I exclude myself
from sites like Facebook entirely I end up resenting not
being invited to certain events, even if I wouldn't have gone
to them anyway. Also, it's a good way to keep up with metal
gigs. I key in my usernames and passwords to Facebook
and Twitter, getting them wrong a couple of times before
finally getting them right. And I scroll up and down, flicking
from tab to tab, while my laptop – which is too old, really,
to handle even browsing the Internet – wheezes and
complains.

But there's nothing. No mention of anyone being dead.

Not anywhere I can see. And Facebook is always the first with this kind of information.

Probably because I can't stand to focus for too long on flickering screens, my head begins to ache. My hand travels automatically to my pocket. Nothing. I kneel, reach under the bed, remember that the bottle I had under there is empty. So is the bottle in the bathroom. I pull a shoebox from the bottom of my wardrobe and rummage through it. Finally I unearth a small brown bottle full of triangular pills.

I've had a problem with headaches for years. I was hit on the side of my head with a cricket bat when I was nine; the headaches started pretty much immediately afterwards. They weren't constant: they were worse when I was tired, or unhappy. I tried to live with them, since I couldn't seem to find anything – ice water, prescription medication, darkened rooms – that could make them go away. But then, one day, I discovered that Mum had these pills. Found a bottle in a drawer, maybe. There's nothing on the bottle – no prescription, no price, no dosage. I don't know what the pills are, or if they're legal; I don't know if they're meant to keep you ageless and unwrinkled or load your blood with iron. I don't remember when I took the first one.

Whatever they are, they are excellent at killing pain.

There's plenty of dealers in the sixth form at school; there's plenty of other things I could take, if I wanted to. But I wouldn't be able to afford them: the drugs people buy in the alleyway behind the tube, the powders they inhale at the weekend or the hothouse cannabis they smoke in the mornings before school. Anyway, I don't need to buy anything. The house is riddled with bottles of these triangular pills, buried like tiny Easter eggs in sock drawers and biscuit tins and laundry bags. I'm not sure what Mum takes the pills for. If she's noticed that I take them too, she's never said a word about it. Nowadays I need one a day.

Sometimes more.

I tip a pill into my palm and swallow it with the dregs from my cup. The softened corners hit my tongue with a glaze of sugar; then the bitter coffee washes the pill down my throat. I wait for the pain to subside. Sometimes, when it's bad, it's like a sign flashing in my head. Amber at first: *warning*. Then a sickly neon red. *Emergency*, it says. *Emergency.* These days I have a lot of emergencies, but today has been especially problematic.

Mistily, through my dissolving headache, I glower at my reflection in the wardrobe door. I am weird-looking; I know that. Girls don't notice me particularly – or, when they do, I imagine them getting round the corner and then turning to each other and saying, 'He's so weird, isn't he?' My skin is as dead white as the Late Greats, who, as Solly once commented, most certainly weren't getting their vitamin D. My nose is turning into my mother's: a wonky hypotenuse of bone. My eyes are all right, but generally puffy from sleeplessness, with an odd, pinched look just beneath them.

My hair is longish and dark brown. I do not have any kind of interesting haircut. I shake my head a lot; it's a habit I picked up when trying to stop my head from hurting. When I was younger I used to hide beneath my fringe. Mum would cut it with the kitchen scissors, and I'd beg her to let me keep it as long as possible. I was the kid who made dens behind the washing line, in the old fireplace, behind the garden shed. I loved to hide.

When I was at Cottesmore House and they suddenly moved me into 8 Upper, I was horrified by the free-for-all yelling, the chaos. The verb chants and war re-enactments and cut-throat debates. I was disorientated by the amount of work we had to do. Unyielding deadlines and unending past papers, each one denser and more challenging than the last. The kids in 8 Upper were like a different species: supremely confident in their opinions, forever training themselves to achieve fearsome academic feats, each with their own particular talent, like a set of cerebral superheroes. Norville . . . the Nicholson twins . . . Frodo.

But Hobie was the one who unsettled me most.

Finding the photograph hidden in my Old Norse grammar brings him to the forefront of my mind. It's so strange, to think of him now. Strange, and a bit confusing – that's why I don't often do it. As I sit back on my bed, still waiting for my headache to clear, I remember – I'm not sure why – going to the British Museum to an exhibition about a Roman emperor in the first week of September. It must be one of my earliest memories of Hobie. At first I don't want to let it unfold in my head. If it was one of those old-fashioned projectionist's reels, I'd try to halt it somehow. But, like the stories of the Gods, it seems to want to tell itself, and so I pull my knees close to my chest and let it.

Who was there that day? It was 8 Upper, 8 Middle and 8 Lower, and I think some of the Year 7 kids too. Miss Atkins was ordering us to walk in silence, not that anyone was listening to her. Miss Flower, who taught history, was also there, and one or two parent volunteers. Between them they just couldn't keep order. Hobie and Archie had managed to buy six cans of Coke from a vending machine and drunk the lot. They were running around the domed concourse, crashing into tourists and screaming hysterically. Eventually, under the threat of suspension, they allowed themselves, mutinously, to be led into the exhibition.

'Hadrian was a massive gaylord,' Hobie was saying loudly to anyone near him. 'Everyone knew that.'

'Don't be homophobic,' said Norville, who was copying all the writing on the walls into a Moleskine notebook. 'It's uncool to be prejudiced.'

I wandered away from the group. Over by the door, Miss Flower was surreptitiously checking her phone. Miss Atkins had the harassed, frantic look she always got when she was teaching our class. Trying to keep her voice down, she ordered us into a vague procession around the room. Each of us had a worksheet attached to a clipboard.

I watched Hobie mimic Miss Atkins's way of walking. She used to swish her hair from shoulder to shoulder in an eminently copiable style, her feet turning slightly outwards, like a duckling's. Behind her back, he was doing a very good job. Everyone was sniggering. I turned my worksheet over and drew a little sketch of Hobie on the back. Crouching behind a plinth, mouth wickedly wide in a blissful grin.

Planning mischief.

I stole a bit closer. Hobie was murmuring to Archie. With Miss Atkins and Mr Keynes occupied on the other side of the Reading Room, they crept over to where several small children, dressed in pink and grey uniforms, were dutifully looking up at an enormous marble head.

'Gosh, this is a really tremendous bust!' said Hobie, making his voice even posher than it already was.

'I simply *must* agree with you.' Archie was trying not to crack up.

Then, as if on some prearranged signal, they set off in opposite directions.

I peered at the small children. Some of them seemed disorientated, as though they'd been surprised by an ambush. One of them was beginning to cry, his face suffused with magenta.

Hobie bumped into me on his way back towards our group. He was choking with laughter.

'What were you doing?' I asked him. I was interested. Nothing, at the time, interested me about Cottesmore

House, about any of the people in it. But there was something about the freedom of the way Hobie moved. I liked the look of it.

For a moment his eyes burned into mine. They were extraordinarily blue. His canines, when he smiled, were slightly pointed. It made him look like a wild creature.

'Farting on little kids,' he said shortly. 'You should try it. Their faces are just the right height.'

That's what Hobie was like, when I first knew him. There was no one quite like him really.

I go back to the window. I've always wished I could see the cemetery from my bedroom, but it's on the other side of the house. From here I can see the garden – or what passes for a garden – and the backs of the houses in the next street along. For the moment, the Gods are gone. But I know they will be back. I hear their voices again: the delicate whisper of Frigg; Hermódr's velvety lament.

*Hjálpaðú.*

*Hann er dauðr.*

Someone is dead.

And the Gods are asking for help.

# HOBIE'S DIARY

Saturday 20th September 2008

Today it pissed with rain and I went to Football anyway because I don't care about getting wet. Mum drove me in our 4x4 and we picked up Archie and his mother too. Archie lives near us, the other side of Notting Hill Gate. He's almost as good at Sport as I am, which I don't mind because it gives me someone to try really hard to defeat. Archie's little sister Polly is the same age as Zara. His mum has the same red hair that kind of explodes off her head, but she isn't as ugly as Archie is. If she was I don't suppose anyone would've wanted to shag her.

Archie and I sat in the back taking turns on my Sony PSP while I listened with one ear to the conversation in the front.

Mum said, 'How are you doing with your 11+ preparation then? Is Polly finding it all a bit much?'

And Archie's mum said, 'D'you know, it's not as bad as I thought it would be. I mean we've been doing all the VRs and the NVRs since Year 4, so in a way it's taken some of the strain off this year.'

(VR and NVR stand for Verbal Reasoning and Non-Verbal Reasoning. A lot of it is saying which cube cannot be made from this net and which picture of a square with some squiggles coming out of it should be the next one in the sequence, etc. Presumably there are some vital life skills contained in there somewhere.)

You could hear Mum thinking for a while, and then she said, 'And are you getting any help?' By which she meant, tutoring.

'Actually, not at the moment. We think Poll is all right for now, though we might get someone in just before the exams.'

Then Archie's mum explained that she'd heard from the headmistress of a girls' school somewhere that statistically girls who were 'plump' tended not to do so well in the 11+.

'Really!' said Mum. 'What could she possibly have meant?'

Archie's mum said she wasn't sure, but it was something to do with being *hungry for success*. After that they talked about fish pedicures.

We won both our matches, 3–1 and 4–0. I did an epic slide tackle and mashed the other team's defender into the mud. He came off the pitch, and the kid they replaced him with was rubbish. When I came home I ate three pitta breads with Edam, blasted in the microwave for ten seconds. If you do it for longer the cheese goes hard and dimply like when women have cellulite. It must be so boring being a woman, always fretting about things like that. Mum said that Zara should wait until dinnertime because I'd been running around playing football and she hadn't. I reckon I know what Mum has started thinking.

I checked Facebook out of habit. 8 Upper was conducting a debate about the longest Latin word, with Hobbitboy holding out for the imperfect passive of *appropinquo* and someone (Jean-Jacques maybe) freaking out below that we aren't supposed to know the passive yet, or are we? I was about to start harassing them in simple but satisfying ways (picking on each of their most obvious physical defects until they all buckled under the cyber-strain) when I noticed that Ben was online.

He doesn't have a profile picture. Not of himself anyway. It's just a kind of blob of multi-coloured ink, spreading outwards in rings of blue and purple.

I clicked on the ink blob and composed a message.

*I want to know who Skoll is.*

Not a chance that he'd reply to that, I thought. Ben loathes direct questions of any kind. He won't even go up to the interactive whiteboard in class.

But he did. This is what he wrote back.

*I have no idea what you mean.*

*Yes, you do. Skoll. You wrote it in your calculator case,* I messaged, thinking I wouldn't bother explaining how it was that I happened to have seen that. I didn't want to come across like some kind of lame stalker.

There was a long pause.

*That is not the correct way to write it,* wrote Ben.

*Jesus H. Christ,* as my dad likes to say on occasion. What kind of loser puts accents in their Facebook messages? But I could see that I wouldn't get anywhere unless I made more of an effort. So I fiddled around on my MacBook Pro, typing and deleting a whole series of messed-up Skôlls and Skølls and so on and so forth until I was almost thinking of giving up completely when I finally managed it by doing a kind of copy-and-paste job.

*Skǫll!* I messaged in triumph. *Now tell me.*

*Why?*

*Because I want to know.*

There was another, impossibly long pause, and then:

*It's none of your business.*

Fine. So I went back on the Internet. There wasn't much on Wikipedia, but after some trawling through different pages (there's some kind of foundation called SKOLL and a satellite of Saturn which was mildly diverting) I found the right one. Skǫll was/is a creature from Norse mythology, a wolf, son of another wolf called Fenrir (and that's what Ben had written, wasn't it? *Skǫll, son of Fenrir*, only in some weird other language, not English.) It didn't mean much to me, but there were some pictures showing these fiendish-looking, spookily elongated wolves racing across the sky, chasing the sun and the moon in their horse-drawn chariots. I thought the pictures were quite impressive.

## Tuesday 23rd September

This afternoon, as we were running out onto the pitch for Rugby Training, I waited until Ben and I were the last pair (he runs pathetically slowly, so I had to lag a bit) and then I tackled him to the ground. He gave a cry, which I muffled with my sleeve, we rolled over onto the grass and I pulled up his rugby shirt. He was kicking my legs and trying to push me off, but of course I'm much stronger than he is.

I ran my fingers over the black mark. It really was a wolf. It was facing inwards, in profile, as though it was in mid-stride. The lines were quite jagged so it looked like its fur was sticking up.

'Get off me!' he hissed, his face blooming scarlet. Then he said something in another language which I couldn't understand, but it sounded like swearing.

I felt victorious.

'That's not a transfer. No *way* is that a transfer.' To prove it I slid my finger over the wolf's head as if to peel away the plastic and he squealed. I always think it's funny when other people have things that hurt.

'It's a tattoo,' I said.

He didn't reply. He looked the way Zara does when I knock over her Barbie house and watch it collapse like flat-pack furniture. Silent and furious.

Mr Voss yelled at us to get up and rejoin the group, so we climbed back onto our feet and set off at a jog.

'That must have really hurt. Where did you get it done?'

He was silent for a while, then muttered, 'Did it myself.'

'How could you even see what you were doing?'

'I used a mirror.'

'What did your parents think?'

'They don't know.'

'What about when we have swimming?'

'Yeah, well . . . that's not till the summer term. Maybe I'll stick a plaster over it.'

He threw an angry glance at me as if to say, *Why do you care anyway*?

What is it that grown-ups say? *He's a dark horse*. I can't quite believe he has a proper tattoo.

Wednesday 24th September

Today Dad returned from his business trip and we all had dinner together. Sometimes we have a chef who comes and cooks. Today he'd made roast chicken and a brown rice risotto and asparagus and watercress salad. Zara folded the napkins into ballerina slippers, or that's what she said they were meant to be. Mum mostly doesn't eat carbohydrates, and she prefers us to have wholegrains because they are better for you, but often she just lets us have what we want. It's like she hasn't really made up her mind what the rules are. I ate everything and I was still hungry and in the freezer there were six tubs of ice cream and Zara and I ate nearly the whole of a Spiced Cinnamon tub between us and I could see my mother looking at Zara and trying to decide whether she should say anything. She was probably thinking about what Archie's mum had said, about being *hungry for success*.

Then she made Zara do a timed Bond Assessment Paper in the playroom.

Mum and Dad asked me if I'd made any new friends in 8 Upper. I thought about Ben with his black eyes and spidery writing, his skinny shoulders and his home-made tattoo and wondered whether he counted as a friend.

'There's a new guy called Ben. Ben Holloway. He was moved up from the middle set.'

'Darling, not with your mouth full,' said Mum.

Dad said suddenly, 'Oh yes. His mother worked at Carrisford – you know, the legal firm that's just let go of half its employees. I once met her at the RAC.'

The RAC is the Royal Automobile Club. I always used to imagine a car showroom, but actually it's just a very expensive gym/hotel/restaurant place and they don't like it if you play cricket on the roof terrace, which is what I tried to do when Mum had her 40th birthday party there.

I said Ben was quite weird but then everyone else was too. I didn't say he had a tattoo that he'd done himself (surprisingly well) with a pot of ink and a sewing needle, though I really couldn't stop thinking about it. I told them Ben needed to get a Scholarship because he wouldn't be able to afford to go to a private school next year without one.

'He must be working awfully hard,' said Mum, pushing salad leaves around with her fork. 'You must have him over, Hobes, and then you can study together. That would be nice, wouldn't it?'

'Did you hear,' she said to Dad, 'they've given him an Assisted Place for the whole of Year 8? Thoughtful of the school, isn't it? Apparently it was a dreadful divorce. Did you know that—'

And then Dad said: 'Elsie, *pas devant l'enfant*,' which is what they always say and means *not in front of the child* in French, and they really should say it in Urdu or Swahili or something if they don't want me to understand. Plus Dad's French accent is really awful.

We heard Zara crying and she came trailing in saying she couldn't remember the difference between reported and direct speech and I groaned and said if she did Latin it would be incredibly easy, but Mum and Dad had already both rushed into the playroom to help her. They shouldn't stand over her so much. But they can't help it.

I pulled all the books off the bookshelf on the stairs trying to find the one about the Norse Gods that someone gave me a couple of years ago. Then I sat on the top step and read it and finished the ice cream. It was really more of a picture book. There was nothing about Skǫll, but there was a bit about his father, Fenrir, only the book called him Fenris-Wolf. The illustrations were quite good. I read the whole thing. Then I went on Google and found out that Skǫll had a brother called Hati. I loved how Fenrir died, with his jaw ripped apart by some guy at Ragnarok, which I realise now is the great battle that Ben was writing about before. The Day of Reckoning, when Skǫll and Hati chase the sun and the moon through the sky and devour them.

When I slept I saw wolves in my dreams. Giant wolves stalking the aisles of Hamleys, stacking their baskets really high with raw meat and Action Men. And when I woke, I'd decided something in my sleep.

I wanted one too.

Thursday 25th September

We had Art last lesson and we were looking at woodcuts by lots of different people. I was sitting with Ben. We had to draw portraits of each other on A4 paper, in pencil, to turn into woodcuts next lesson. Mrs Ottoboni lets us talk while we work, but sometimes she plays classical music, like stupid monk chants or the Planets thing by Holst, to keep us from getting too loud. Ben drew me first. He concentrates so hard when he works, like he's figuring out the hardest sum known to man. He's actually really good at Art for someone so malco and disorganised. He made me look like one of those Italian angels they put on greetings cards.

'You could have used one of these things, couldn't you?' I said, fingering one of the cutting tools that Mrs Ottoboni had laid out on the worktop.

'What for?' he frowned.

'You know what for. Your *t-a-t-t-o-o*.'

'Oh,' he said.

When it was my turn to draw him, I made his head too round and his eyes too small. I reached for a rubber and dragged it across the page, snagging it into a crease.

'Ben,' I said, 'I want a tattoo too. Can you do one for me?'

He made a gormless *what?* face at me.

'I want a wolf, like yours. Skǫll had a brother, right? Hati. Hati eats the Moon when Skǫll eats the sun.'

He looked surprised. 'How do you . . . ?'

Mrs Ottoboni came wobbling over with her too-large boobs bobbing under her art apron.

'That's not bad, Hobie,' she said. 'You must try not to rush your work though.'

Then she clapped her hands together and told us to pack away our things. I reached for Ben's elbow.

'I'll pay you,' I said. 'How much d'you want?'

His eyes went dark again.

I mean, it's not like I want to be his twin or anything, but it's cool. Those Norse wolves, I like them. I like how powerful they are. How they're the end of everything.

When I see something I want, I usually work out how to get it.

Zara has a tutor now on Wednesdays. She's called Rebecca. Mum and Dad think that Zara has some issues with working under timed conditions, so Rebecca is supposed to hold a stopwatch and get her to do all these 10-minute tests and also mark full-length papers which Zara does at other times. Zara really likes Rebecca, but she's starting to hate all the comprehensions and creative writing with rubbish titles like 'A Strange Journey' or 'A Winter's Day'. There's these particular questions which she just can't do where you have to find the missing three-letter word. The clue will be something like 'The prince fought a fire-breathing DON' and Zara will look at it blankly, and even though it's totally obvious, she just sees the word DON and she can't see any possible words other than that one and then Rebecca will make it easier, like this:

*The prince fought a fire-breathing D _ _ _ ON.*

And then Zara will start getting stressed out because she's worrying that she can't do it and by that stage she will never, never get that the missing word is RAG because the whole thing is DRAGON and if I'm in the room I will say, 'Za, for God's sake, what else d'you think would be fire-breathing?' And she'll look at me as if to say, *Shut up, Hobie, just shut up and go away.*

Mum and Dad blame themselves and think they should have started the tutoring in Year 5.

Sometimes Zara cries at breakfast.

## Friday 26th September

I asked Mum earlier this week if Ben could come round this afternoon so we could study together, and she looked really pleased and said I must be taking my work very seriously if I wanted to sacrifice my Friday playdate. But all we ever did on those playdates, me and whoever, was go on Facebook and eat Hummingbird cupcakes and maybe go to the cinema or to Byron Burger. And quite a few of the kids can't have refined sugar or hydrogenated fats and don't eat anything apart from chicken breast and salad, which is dull.

So Mum got Ben's mother's number from the class spreadsheet thing and she texted her and then didn't hear back for ages, but I explained that Ben's mother actually has a proper job – I don't know what it is but I think something involving the Citizens Advice Bureau or whatever she could get after losing her job at the law firm. Mum on the other hand is just a housewife or *femme de ménage* as I wrote in my French Oral Presentation last term. Thus (I said) Ben's mother might be too busy to check her BlackBerry every two minutes like Mum does.

And Mum hugged me and said, 'Hobes, I wouldn't swap being able to spend time with you for any job in the world,' and then she had to run upstairs in her high heels because her cab was waiting to take her to Pilates.

Ben's mother eventually replied and she said that was great and Ben could come home with me and then get a bus back to their house whenever we wanted to get rid of him.

And Mum, who has never allowed me or Zara out of the house without Clothilde or some other responsible adult practically carrying us over uneven paving stones, said she was surprised they let him wander around by himself, particularly when it was getting dark. You never know who's lying in wait, apparently.

And I thought, Lucky Ben. If anyone was lying in wait for me, I'd be quite interested to meet them.


So today, when Clothilde picked me up from school, Ben came home with us. I don't think he would've had anything else to do.

'*Ben, as-tu un snack?*' said Cloth-head, winding my scarf around my neck in a really irritating way that she has borrowed from Mum. I pushed her hands away.

'*Non, je n'en ai pas besoin,*' he replied.

I rolled my eyes at him. 'You don't have to answer her in *French*,' I said.

I ate a Pret pecan slice and a bag of dried pineapple rings. You aren't meant to bring nuts anywhere near the school because so many children have allergies. Once I put a peanut down the back of someone's shirt and was excluded for two days, which was convenient because my godmother was visiting and she wanted to take me shopping.

When we got home Clothilde made Ben a cup of tea and

me a hot chocolate with special flakes from Melt, which sells the most expensive chocolate in London, I've heard.

'Did you use to live in a house like this?' I asked him. (Our house has got five bedrooms and is just off Kensington Church Street.)

He shrugged. 'Not really,' he said. 'It was smaller. And we didn't have any of this sort of thing.'

He waved his arm, and I expected him to be pointing out the Bose speakers embedded in the skirting boards, or the triple fridge with the glass door, or the marble worktop in the kitchen and the sink with the tap that runs boiling water.

But no: he was pointing at the walls.

'You have so many photographs,' he said.

It's true. There's loads of me and Za, all in white frames. On beaches, in gardens, in uniform, in churches, in colour, in black and white. Hundreds and hundreds. Who gives a shit? They're not especially expensive or interesting. They're just pictures of me and Za.

'My parents don't take a lot of photographs,' said Ben, almost to himself.

'Let's go upstairs,' I said.

'Obie!' Clothilde called after me. She can't say the *H* in my name so it sounds like the guy in *Star Wars*.

'*What?*'

'I go now, quick, to pick up your sister. *Tu veux dîner à quelle heure?*'

'Whenever.'

I asked Ben if he had a nanny, and if so whether she spoke in a tedious foreign language, but he just shook his head and looked embarrassed.

We got up to the top landing, where mine and Zara's and Clothilde's rooms are. I pulled down the ladder that goes up to the loft, which is incredibly easy to do although Mum and Dad haven't realised I know how, and then climbed up it, telling Ben to follow me. The loft is quite an awesome space that hasn't been messed up yet with Farrow & Ball paint with a stupid name. Just unpainted floorboards, crooked ceilings and a bunch of boxes with 'The Gentleman's Moving Company' on the side. Mum wants to convert this into another bedroom, but what would be the point?

'Check this out,' I said. I moved one of the boxes, stood on it directly under the skylight and opened it by twisting the handle. 'Lucky you're skinny,' I told Ben. 'Frodes couldn't get through. Too many Hobbitburgers.'

I jumped up a bit and then used my hands to support my weight as I pushed myself through and out onto the roof. 'Hurry up!' I called back to Ben.

It took him a few goes.

The part of the roof we came out onto was flat. The sky was smeary with purple and gold, the sun just settling down towards the site of the Westfield shopping centre. London opened out on all sides.

'I like it when there are fireworks,' I said.

And Ben said nothing for a while.

It was like he could see something I couldn't. That's the best way I can describe it. His chest was moving out and in, as though he was drawing in big lungfuls of air, and he was turning his head from side to side. It made me feel like I'd never really absorbed the view. And maybe I hadn't. I only go up onto the roof to smoke, and to get away from Zara.

And then he said: 'From this kind of vantage point, you'd almost be able to hear the voices of the Gods.'

I extracted my Lucky Strikes from my back pocket and offered him the pack. He shook his head.

'*Je n'en ai pas besoin*,' he said again.

'It's not about whether you *need* a fag, it's whether you *want* one.'

'I don't,' he said.

The sun dropped and took the warmth with it. My skin started getting those little bumps, like the Thames when the wind starts rattling over it. I lit up and watched Ben sink down to a crouch on the tarmac.

I knew it. I knew I had something he wanted. I don't know how I knew. He might not have wanted a smoke, but he *definitely* wanted the view from the top of my house.

'You should come round every Friday, dude,' I said. 'We can get our homework done and come up here.'

He did his weird head-shake thing where his neck snaps back and his hair ruffles up.

'Don't your parents mind?' he asked.

Mind? Of course they'd mind.

'They don't know, do they? I only come up here when they're out. Which they almost always are. My dad is barely ever here anyway cos he travels so much.'

'Oh.'

'Now, about my tattoo—' I said. But he interrupted me.

'Look, Hobie, you don't know what you're talking about.' He closed his eyes for a moment. Then he put his hand on his right side, just under his ribs. 'I did this tattoo for a *reason*. Everything has to have a meaning; do you understand?'

No, I bloody well didn't. So I stayed quiet.

Ben opened his eyes again and he fixed them on some point far in the distance and he said, 'Skǫll is . . . he's a kind of symbol. He's like . . .'

'Your inner wolf?'

'No – yeah. Almost. But more than that.'

I waited.

'Skǫll represents the Otherlife. A place where beasts eat the sun and the Gods do battle with giants and it's cold, cold, cold . . . and people are savage and cruel and they live and die and all the colours are really big and bright. And there's no *X Factor* or reality TV or TV full stop and there's no texting and coffee shops and there's no bus stops and Oyster cards and . . . do you see? Everything is *real*.'

To me it sounded the exact opposite of real. But I also began to see what he was saying. A bit.

'What did you call it? The Afterlife?'

'The Otherlife,' he said.

And then it really was getting dark and cold so we climbed back down into the loft.

Even after he'd gone home, after we'd done our Maths and French and History homework and ordered Thai curries from Deliverance and watched four episodes of *South Park*, I kept thinking, Otherlife, Otherlife, Otherlife.

# BEN

When I wake up, I'm flat on my back, on a bench in Kensal Green Cemetery. I must have nightwalked again; I don't even remember doing it. Maybe it's the painkillers. I'm starting to worry about the painkillers. I peel myself off the bench, leaving an outline of my body in the condensation. My legs and arms ache, and so does my head.

I make my way home, past delivery trucks and mail vans, the world organising itself for another day. It moves with speed and assurance in perfectly straight lines. The edges seem a little more blurred than usual, and I wonder, suddenly, whether I need to go back to the ophthalmologist. I hope not, because I don't know how Mum will pay for it. I feel for my scar: a tiny dent, like a slanting staple-mark, on the side of my head, and remember again the day – long ago now – when I was hit by a cricket bat.

It was some kind of charity event: a team of writers versus a team of actors, or else maybe television presenters. I can't remember. My dad was never famous, but there was a time when his books sold reasonably well. For whatever reason, he was on the team. Mum and I had come with him, our car smaller and dirtier than the rest when we parked behind the pitch.

Lunch was served beforehand: a lavish, many-coursed affair, with cheesecake and four different kinds of bread roll, and salmon sweating in a pastry shell. Those sugar granules that look like rough-cut semiprecious stones, served in a silver bowl along with the tea and coffee. My dad drank a lot of wine. He had a new bat, one he was excited to deploy; I went with him after lunch to the car to fetch it, just before the start of play. He was already dressed in his cricket whites, with a red blazer over the top. He looked like he belonged, among these actual stars of screen and page. Pride tied a little loop around my neck.

From the boot of the car Dad pulled the new bat, which he'd already battered with a mallet and rubbed down with linseed oil the night before. My dad was always good at pretending to fit in at events like these, acting posher than he was; I asked him how many times he'd actually played cricket and he laughed, wryly, and said, 'Oh, fewer than you'd think. See if there's film in the camera, why don't you?'

Fiddling with the back of my mother's old Nikon, I was standing too close to the boot of the car. It was my fault really. But Dad – perhaps more nervous than he cared to admit, perhaps loose-armed from too much to drink at lunchtime (and Mum would never forget this; she would never let him forget this) – didn't see me behind him as he began warming up with the bat. Two or three times he swung it up into the air and round in generous, wide-wheeling circles. The third time, or else the fourth, he hit me – a good hard bone-cracking knock at the edge of my right eye. I remember an eclipse: a round red moon that bloomed across the circle of my vision; I remember my mother screaming, and how the wives of the famous people seemed to draw away a little before they came rushing towards me.

There was nothing Dad could ever do that would prove how sorry he was. In the hospital he cried beside me, and that seemed to make Mum angrier, because she didn't cry herself.

I lost the sight in my right eye for nearly two months. I spent dark hours at Moorfields Eye Hospital, robbed of the ability to read. I missed school. When – in tiny, flickery darts of light and fractured shape – my vision began to come back, my parents hired a tutor named Jason to help me catch up with my schoolwork.

Unlike a lot of the kids I knew, I'd never had a tutor before, but it seemed to me straight away that Jason was everything you'd want in one: calm, focused, knowledgeable. He made the prospect of catching up on everything I'd missed seem less daunting. He would often put music on while we studied: something rich with organs and woodwind, or moody, beautiful piano pieces. If Mum and Dad were arguing downstairs, he'd turn the music up. Sometimes we'd make mind maps and stick them to the wall. Sometimes we'd record history or geography notes onto the computer, so that I could keep them in iTunes. For each session, he'd make a target sheet, written out in his delicate, calligraphic hand with his special pen, a Rotring. Knowing how much I loved to see the colour change, he kept a supply of different ink cartridges – red, turquoise, brown – and would make sure to change from one colour to the next during our sessions, so that the line of his writing would modulate smoothly from, say, green to blue, via every magical shade in between. And each time we hit a target (memorising the different plate boundaries, reciting the key aspects of the Norman invasion), he'd let me shade in the box.

'Target met,' he'd say. 'Onwards, Ben.'

He also had an extraordinary store of hidden facts and trivia and folklore. He would tell me why it would be possible to build habitable colonies on Mars but not on Venus; he knew the name of every bird we saw in the garden. And it was Jason who introduced me to the Norse Gods.

He'd say, 'Ah, Ben, you mustn't worry about only one eye. You know who only had one eye? Odin!'

And then he'd tell me the story of how Odin sacrificed the sight of one of his eyes in exchange for wisdom.

'You're wise, too, Ben. Plus you'll get your sight back perfectly,' Jason would say. 'Hold tight. No rush.'

I loved the parallel he'd drawn, so quickly and so easily, between me and the world of the Gods. I remember thanking him for it, in a clumsy kind of way. He told me that it came sort of naturally to him, because he also had something in common with one of the Gods, a kind of physical quirk. I forget the story, if he ever told me. It was related to something that had happened early in his childhood, he said.

He bought the Old Norse grammar for me, one of the few birthday presents I received that year, and even helped me to learn some of the verbs, though he didn't know the language himself. Sometimes we'd sit in the park and drink coffee and read together. Jason's favourite of the Gods was Heimdallr, the watchman, who sat on the rainbow bridge, Bifrost, and watched everything that went on in the world. Jason was, I suppose, quite like Heimdallr. He was a good observer, and he didn't judge.

When I started seeing little halos, trails of coloured light that formed into the faint edges of what appeared to be faces, figures, I imagined it was some by-product of the recovering muscles in my eye. But they persisted, growing brighter and more intense. I began to associate each colour with one of the Gods. Sky blue for Odin. Blue-green for Tyr – brave Tyr, whose hand was bitten off by Fenrir. Burnt orange for Heimdallr, honey-gold for Baldr, fire-red for Loki – not really a God, but often counted as one. Lemony-green Frigg. Greenish-bronze Hermódr. Sea-blue Freyr and purple-pink Freyja. And two uncoloured trails of light, one pearlescent and one midnight dark, that I knew were Hati and Skǫll.

I christened it the Otherlife.

I wasn't afraid; I was curious. I could see the Gods; I was quite sure of it. For some reason *I* could see them. And I was glad that I could, because I was lonely. I became an expert seer, constantly on the lookout for signs of the Otherlife. Odin's hand extending from behind a fallen tree, pale blue and blinding. Jǫrmungandr billowing beneath the undertow in the murky waters of the canal. Best of all were glimpses of Skǫll, who sometimes showed up as the shadow of some smaller dog: a sharp-jawed, magnificent flicker against the hot dirty pavement. Faint: outlines only. Suggestions. But enough. It was like a channel that was always on, if you tuned into it right. Their stories played out, forwards, backwards, over and over, in my secret cinema; their world was the underlay of mine, and it made sense when mine did not.

I feel a hotness behind me: heavy breath condensing in the May morning air. I become sure that someone – something – is following me. I quicken my pace. Near the cemetery gates I hear twigs breaking, gravel scuffled by sharp-clawed feet.

A whispered growl, camouflaged by the howls of cars and motorcycles.

I stop, listen again.

Silence.

The house reproaches me for leaving it unattended. I chuck my keys onto the table. They make a hard noise, like money in a slot machine. I make coffee. There's no point in going to bed for half an hour. Better to get changed, head into school and hope I stay conscious. Out of no more than habit (my headache, for the moment, is gone) I open the drawers in the kitchen, sifting through bulldog clips and clothes pegs, candle stubs and string, in search of triangular pills. Mum's driving licence. Booklets of stamps: first class, second class, cartoon Santa. A rectangle of warped cartridge paper. I lift it out of the drawer and take a look.

On one side, a wolf, masterfully drawn with a calligraphy pen. A hundred thousand times more accurate, more powerfully captured than my tattoo. On the other side, a handwritten certificate that says, *I, Benjamin Holloway, have survived a week of intensive study*. It's dated 8th November 2008, and it's signed by the person who drew it.

Jason.

For most of Years 4 and 5, he was more than a tutor really. He was a friend too, a protector. Once, just before he arrived for our session, Mum had taken Dad's favourite wineglasses and smashed them, two by two, on the paving stones in the garden. It was the precision of it, the way she took them out in pairs, a glass in each hand, that really affected me as I watched from my bedroom window. It made me think of the Ark, in some kind of weird, backward fashion. There were three sets of expensive-sounding crashes: delicate high-pitched screams that broke the silence. I retreated from the window and listened as Dad yelled at her for breaking his *favourite glasses* which were a *wedding gift* and she yelled back that it was *symbolic of her deep frustrations* and then, as they always did, their voices became nothing but angry music, sounds I couldn't decode.

Mum had already gone out by the time Jason arrived on his bicycle; Dad was upstairs, barricaded into his study. As Jason boiled the kettle to make coffee I crept into the garden to survey the damage. Suddenly it struck me that my parents shouldn't have just left it all there like that, for the neighbours to see. The stones were strewn with minuscule shards of glass. I told myself that it was a glorious trove of diamonds, one I was lucky to have discovered. Then I knelt down and swept up the pieces.

Jason came out and found me sitting in a sea of broken glass, hands bleeding. Without saying anything, he took me inside and mended me, washing the cuts, bandaging me properly with crepe and safety pins. He went back outside with a dustpan and brush and disposed of the remains of my parents' argument. Instead of tutoring, we read about the time when Thor dressed up as a woman, and by the end of the hour and a half I was laughing inside and out.

I carry the wolf certificate upstairs – carefully, by the corners, like a museum specimen – and after a little thought I take my clump of Blu-Tack and stick it, wolf-side out, just above the Otherlife mural. Then, slowly, I stick the photograph of Hobie next to it. There's a song my dad really likes – I don't know who it's by, a duo from the sixties or seventies – which he likes to sing, in his vague way, when he's doing the washing-up. I don't remember it perfectly. It's about a time of innocence, and having a photograph, and preserving your memories. And it's this song that I think of now, as I look at the photograph. It's like looking at a relic from another era.

Strange. Forget the Otherlife, with its definite article. I had, once, an*other* life: one where I didn't know Solomon, didn't take pills every day and loiter by night in cemeteries and parks and fire escapes. My daily uniform, instead of black and grey, was green and burgundy, with a pale pink tie and the school initials on my peaked *Just William* cap. And I was friends with Hobie. Best friends almost, you could say. I was innocent; he was confident – magnificently so, with his rugby swagger and his ability to get away with anything. There was a famous story about a penis – or perhaps it was a swastika – drawn in chalk on the back of Frodo's blazer before a Summer Concert. Hobie's first line of defence: deny it ever happened, and then blame someone else. (The chalk was later discovered in Archie's violin case.) Some people harboured a strong suspicion that Hobie, in order to be put into 8 Upper, had cheated in his end-of-year exams, though there was no proof of this and he was too savvy to own up to it, even to me.

How did we become friends? When did he stop alarming me and start trying to be nice, and – more – why? I remember playdates, heavy with snack food, where we ran away from his little sister and hid on the roof, smoking. I remember his house. It was built like a luxury battleship, all sturdy cream walls and impenetrable bars on the windows. There was a certain novelty in being there. If you left a towel on the floor it would be replaced, silently, with a fresh-minted one from some unseen laundry cavern. Everything smelt of hundred-pound candles: lofty, unnameable scents with anagrammed French labels. But the real novelty was Hobie. At the start of Year 8 he ignored me, like everyone else did. Suddenly he changed. He wanted to sit with me. He copied my work – that infuriated me at first, before I started really wanting him to do well and feeling sorry for him, because he couldn't keep up with the rest of the group. I changed too, I suppose. But Hobie . . . why did he suddenly want to be friends with me?

I feel, as I so often do, that I cannot remember. But suddenly I realise that I do.

The *tattoo*.

That was why.

During the long, sad summer of 2008, my parents' arguments were nightly and the panel of glass in the front door shattered, not once but twice, from the force of being slammed. I didn't have school. I didn't have friends. I didn't even have a tutor, for there was no more money for luxuries such as Jason by the time I reached Year 6, and besides, I didn't need him any more, they said. I had the Otherlife, and I had Old Norse, and I had metal. I started a collection of heroes, preferring, for some reason, (perhaps because they'd been killed or died for their art, which added a certain nobility), the dead ones. And their tattoos were fantastic – literally, inked fantasies that took up whole arms, backs, shoulders. I decided that I wanted one. I liked drawing. I didn't mind pain, if I could control it. A tattoo would require both, and it would give me something to look forward to over the holidays.

It didn't feel right to attempt to emboss myself with one of the Gods. I considered some Norse, but felt anxious about getting it wrong. I loved wolves. When Ragnarok, the day of judgement, came, Skǫll raced across the sky and devoured the sun, plunging the world into darkness. Similarly, when my parents argued in the kitchen, I used to long for the lights to go out. In our house, in all the houses on our street, in the whole of London.

So: Skǫll it was.

I made my plans carefully, borrowing a needle from the sewing box and taking some plastic gloves from the nurse's station when Dad took me to the GP to have my ears syringed. I toured the house in search of clingfilm, Sudocrem, kitchen roll. I drew my design, keeping it outline-only, not worrying about shading. I waited for a full moon, for the stroke of midnight. With the wardrobe mirror to guide me, I traced Skǫll onto my ribs and poked Winsor and Newton Indian ink into the lines with a sterilised needle. Over, and over, and over. I listened to 'Orion', by Metallica as I did it, as loud as my headphones would allow.

One by one, the Gods came out to watch me. They hung in the air like fireflies while I worked, drifting in and out of sight. When I was done, and the tattoo was a bloodied mess under a neat patch of clingfilm and healing cream, they'd gone.

It felt as if they approved.

It's funny. I've become so used to Skǫll being on my ribs that I've forgotten what I needed him for. Not just, as I remember fiercely intoning to Hobie – standing, furious, on his roof, struggling to explain – for *meaning*. But because the Otherlife appears *on the edges of things*. And when I blurred my own edges, forcing ink beneath the layers of my living skin, I was looking in exactly the right way. The way you need to look if you want to really see the Otherlife.

My tattoo was the one thing I had that Hobie didn't have, couldn't buy, couldn't ask for as a present. It must have made me strangely cooler in his eyes – which makes me smile now, because I was definitely *not* cool. I was not cool then, and I am not cool now.

Before I leave for school, I send Mum a text. *Have changed mind re tutor. Cld you pls get hold of Jason? Think he cld help with chem and phys.*

The more I think about it, the better I like the idea. Seeing Jason again. Letting him help me. He made me feel calm, when everything around me was anything but. When my head was hurting, when my vision was wobbling, when I felt like I couldn't write anything more. Jason always knew the answer.

She doesn't reply until about eight fifteen, just as I'm walking from the tube station to school, entrenched in the sublime riffage of Metallica's *And Justice For All* album, which I decided to listen to from start to finish on the way in.

*Sorry, darling. Jason's not available.*

Shame. He must've become fed up with tutoring spoilt rich kids. Even not-so-rich, not-so-spoilt ones like me. As I pound up the stone stairwell to the last strains of 'Dyers Eve', kick-starting my brain to cope with another day of revision notes and shouting teachers, I wonder what Jason's doing now.

# HOBIE'S DIARY

Monday 29th September 2008

Yesterday afternoon we went to Whole Foods Market on Kensington High Street. It is what we do as a family, when Dad isn't away. Mum likes to buy weird wilting leaves and sprouting seeds and unbleached toilet paper. Dad likes to peruse organic Californian wines. Whole Foods is huge, like an airport. Once I shut Zara in the cheese room because they sometimes leave it unattended and she screamed and screamed until someone let her out.

When you walk into Whole Foods the first thing you see is these enormous mounds of bread loaves and meringues and scones, like leaves waiting to be set on fire. For a shop that's so obsessed with being healthy, they have a lot of sugar-loaded stuff in the entrance hall. But maybe it's like a trailer for a tacky action movie before some turgid foreign subtitled arthouse bollocks. It draws you in. I wondered if Ben had ever been to Whole Foods and what he'd make of it.

Zara and I made straight for one of their artistically positioned tasting trays, full of bits of chocolate brownies and things. I picked up three or four and shoved them into my mouth. Just as Za was doing the same, I said:

'Mum thinks you're going to be too fat to pass the 11+. Did you know that?'

She shot a look at me, quite a wavery one because you could tell she just hadn't been expecting that.

I looked her up and down. She was wearing pink leggings and ballet shoes and a grey cashmere hoodie with diamanté crystals stuck onto it in the shape of a unicorn. I smiled sort of knowingly.

'I'm not fat,' she said. She made it sound a bit too much like a question.

I shrugged. 'Sure, sure.'

Now she was tearing up. Easy. Too easy.

'What do you *mean*, Hobie? What do you—'

I put my head on one side. 'You need to be *hungry*, Za.'

Mum and Dad were wafting over with their big blank trolleys.

'Hey, hey,' said Dad, reaching his arms around Zara. 'It's all right, little monkey.' She turned around and hid her face in his jacket, letting the mini brownie squares tumble from her fingers.

Then they both looked at me.

'*I* didn't say anything,' I said.

Mum glanced at the sacrificial heap of baked goods. 'I don't think we should get any of these this week. You children are having far too much sugar.'

When Mum and Dad had set off again I caught Zara's eye and winked. *I told you so*.

## Wednesday 1st October

I messaged Ben again, asking about the tattoo. One thing I've realised about asking for things is, if you just keep on and on at it, and the other person is significantly more weak-willed than you are, eventually you'll get your way.

He replied, 'You have to understand what the Otherlife is about. Otherwise there's no point.'

I said that was fine, and he said he'd try and explain it a bit, although he probably wouldn't be much good at it. He'd also give me some books and things to read.

I forgot to discuss it properly with him earlier this week because there was so much going on. We had this massive Science test on acids and bases which I think I failed and I'm worried I'm going to have to have extra sessions with Mr Keynes who I don't like because he is weird. Then there were auditions for *Lord of the Flies*, which we're going to be putting on in early December. I love plays. Miss Atkins and Mrs McRae held auditions on Monday after school in the hall for Years 6 to 8.

*Lord of the Flies* was on our reading list last year. It was quite good but had too much description. I wanted to be Ralph because that's the biggest part and because I have fair hair, but Miss Atkins thinks I should be Roger.

'But Roger hardly says anything!' I said to her. 'I have a

really loud voice. You said that last time, when we did *The Pirates of Penzance.*'

'We'll see, Hobie,' she said.

'We'll see' is almost as ridiculous and see-through as *pas devant l'enfant.*

In the end she said she'd cast me as Jack, who is almost as big a part as Ralph, so that was all right, and the Nicholson Twins as Sam and Eric (of course) and Norville as Piggy although he'll have to put on about four stone in order to play him. Are the teachers really stupid or something? Frodo would be perfect for Piggy. He even has moobs. And they cast Matteo as Roger and Archie as Ralph and they asked Ben to play Simon but he said he'd prefer to paint scenery and build props out of bits of wood, so they've cast Simon as Simon which at least makes some kind of sense. I hope they film it all and put it on YouTube.

Miss Atkins said they'd need a few days to finalise their decisions. She asked Ben to compose some special music on the harp to play offstage and he went dark red and said that he didn't have his harp any more.

'His mother sold it,' said Frodo importantly. 'It was worth, like, ten grand.'

I think that was what it cost per day to charter the yacht we went on over the summer. Or maybe that was euros.

As Miss Atkins was gathering up all the scripts I noticed that her stomach was poking out a bit more than usual under her wrap-type dress. I mean, all women's stomachs do, and Miss Atkins doesn't always wear the most flattering outfits, but as I was on my way out I asked her anyway.

'Miss Atkins, are you . . . pregnant?'

She reacted like I'd hit her in the face and then stood up a lot straighter, furiously shaking her head. Most of the scripts slithered out of her arms and fell to the floor.

'Hobie, you can't ask those kinds of questions. I mean – *honestly*—'

She and Mrs McRae scrabbled around, picking up the scripts, while Norville and Ben and Simon helped.

'I told you,' I could hear Miss Atkins muttering to Mrs McRae as I departed. 'I told you he should play Roger. God knows where that child will end up. Juvenile detention, I'm telling you.'

## Thursday 2nd October

I failed the Science test. I told Mum it was Mr Keynes's fault for forgetting to give me some extra sheets like he said he would, and she was all fired up to have a massive go at the school, but then Mr White emailed her with some 'concerns' because apparently I'm behind in French and Geog and Greek and also my last two English homeworks have 'fallen short of the standard expected from Scholarship candidates' or something stupid like that. So, faced with this pile-up of evidence, Mum did the only thing she could do under the circumstances, which was to blame Jason.

Today he arrived five minutes early as always, on his falling-apart bicycle that would've looked dated 100 years ago, and Mum was waiting to collar him in the hall. I could already tell from the shade of her lipstick that she was getting ready to fire him and shop around for a better tutor. One with royal connections maybe, or a double-barrelled surname.

Crouching on the other side of the sitting-room door, I knew that it wouldn't really be fair to hold Jason responsible. And he probably wasn't going to be much good at standing up for himself. He's so weedy and gay-looking, with his silly Adam's apple and his awful stripy shirts.

I was wrong.

Jason made it totally clear that he's kept a meticulous note of every single piece of work he's ever done with me

AND date-stamped it on his crappy laptop. I reckon he knows my syllabuses better than the teachers do. He even tailors all our work to my Learning Style (kinaesthetic, which means that I like to throw things while I learn).

Even Mum couldn't really argue with that.

I could hear their voices bobbing up and down behind the sitting-room door. It was like some awful play on Radio 4.

'Really need to make sure Hobes is properly focusing . . .'

'Mrs Duvalle, these Scholarship exams are very demanding. There's bound to be a steep learning curve at this point.'

'But even so, surely he should be performing . . .'

'Have you considered redoing his Ed Psych?'

'Why, do you think he . . .'

'Perhaps it might be . . .'

Then the key turned in the front door and Dad came in, depositing his briefcase and coat with military exactness and rubbing his hands together from the cold of the evening.

'Hey, Hobie, what's up?' Dad always looks so pleased to see us when he comes home from the office. 'What's going on in there?'

'Mum and Jason are talking.'

Dad decided that the best thing to do would be for me and him to go and join them, so we sat around together for another *FIFTEEN MINUTES* while I poked all Mum's coffee-table books (called things like *La Terre Vue du Ciel* and full of pictures of lagoons) so that the edges didn't line up with each other any more. And it was agreed that Jason and I should continue working together on Mondays and Wednesdays and Thursdays, but for an extra half an hour so we can go over more basics. And Mum asked Jason if he would come to our country house for the second week of half term and his eyes lit up and he said he would have to miss a tutorial but, yes, he'd like that very much, and I fervently hoped he'd consider buying some new jumpers or something with what Mum was proposing to pay him. He looks like he shops at Oxfam.

And then Rebecca arrived, in her little green jacket and purple hat, to work with Zara, and Mum decided on the spot that Rebecca should come to the country too so that Zara could have some intensive sessions and I could get a bit of help with Latin and Greek. I quite like Rebecca. Sometimes I think I make Jason nervous, though I don't know why. Rebecca always just smiles and looks sort of amused by everything.

This evening I ate the whole of Zara's veal escalope. She didn't seem to want it, even without breadcrumbs.

## Friday 3rd October

'You could have just copied me,' Ben said. I was in the squash court, slicing my racket with precisely the same amount of vigour each time, sending the ball ricocheting crazily back and forth like a rabbit trying to dodge a pack of hounds.

Ben doesn't understand that I only enjoyed copying his work before, when I didn't really like him. It isn't any fun copying off someone you think is actually OK.

'Nah,' I said, hoping that the racket would snap from the force of my strokes. Willing it to. 'What would be the point? I've got to take the same stupid exams as everyone else.'

'So maybe you need to study a bit harder.'

I disagreed. What I needed to do was find a way of getting a Scholarship anyway. I needed to give it some more thought. Maybe I could bribe some kid at Eton to get hold of the papers and fax them over? Could I blackmail Miss Atkins into giving me a heads-up on the content of the Latin and Greek papers? Of all the teachers, she's probably the easiest to manipulate. I thwacked the ball in an alternating forehand, backhand pattern, thinking furiously. Then I noticed what Ben was doing. He was standing completely still and staring at the back wall, just above the line.

I caught the ball in my hand and said, 'What? What is it?'

He shook his head abruptly. 'Nothing.'

'Bollocks. You're looking at the Otherlife, aren't you? What can you see?'

Without shifting his gaze he said, 'It's Mjǫllnir. Thor's hammer. Just the edge of it.'

*'Where?'*

'Sort of emerging from the paint. Like it's coming up from underneath. Look for the way the colour changes. Thor's always a dark blue, a kind of indigo.'

I stared at the wall so hard I could've burst a blood vessel. But I just couldn't see it.

Then Ben asked if I would spend the first week of half term revising at his house, and I said yes immediately, not because I wanted to do any more sodding work, but because (a) Ben doesn't have a nanny or anything, so we could do whatever we wanted, and (b) I liked the idea of getting out of my own house. Even though I hear Ben's is really small.

'So, were you pissed off about your mum selling your harp like that?'

'No.' He looked surprised. 'I mean, it was never properly mine, was it? It was hers to sell. My parents bought it.'

Ridiculous. As soon as anyone buys anything for me it becomes 100% my property.

'But you liked it.'

He sighed. 'Yeah.'

'What's happened to your dad?'

'I dunno. He's gone off to finish his book.'

Ben's dad never made as much money as Ben's mum did. I really can't imagine what that would be like. My mum worked in an art gallery for about three days once and then she met my dad in a club called Annabel's. I did, however, once tell the whole of my class that she used to be an air hostess because I knew it would really infuriate her when she found out.

'I never really see my mum either,' said Ben.

'Who makes your breakfast and packed lunch and stuff?'

'I do.'

'Jesus, Ben, that's like slave labour. You should ring Childline.'

'Don't be stupid, Hobie.'

He walked out of the squash court, slamming the door. An unusually forceful gesture, for Ben.

Today we were studying Purpose Clauses in Latin. Such as, *ad forum ivi ut panem emerem* – I went to the forum to buy bread. To express intent, or purpose, use *ut* + subjunctive. Follow the rule for sequence of tenses. It came to me, as I subtly rocked my desk back and forth so that a series of tectonic vibrations undermined the studious note-taking of the Nicholson Twins, Hobbitboy and Jean-Jacques, that the lesson summed up quite a lot of stuff really. We study Purpose Clauses so that we can do well in Latin. We do well in Latin so that we can get Scholarships. We get Scholarships to bring Prestige and Fortune upon ourselves and our families and our schools, and do well at our next schools. We do well at our next schools so we can go to the best Universities. We go to the best

Universities to get the best jobs. It's all one big, ludicrous Purpose Clause.

But where does it end? We're all going to die eventually, aren't we?

'Hobie!' said Miss Atkins. 'What are you *doing*?'

I looked down. With the nib of my Pelikan I had dug a massive rip in the pristine cover of my new *Latin for Scholars, Part Three* by R. J. Thoroughgood.

I don't think Miss Atkins has forgiven me for the pregnancy comment. She swept my textbook off my desk and replaced it with her tatty old copy, which is covered in Post-it notes. 'If you do anything like that again, I'll have to bill your parents.'

It sounded a bit like 'kill your parents'. For a moment I had a hilarious vision of Miss Atkins in a safari park, aiming at Mum and Dad with a rifle.

'And you can stop smirking,' she snapped.

She gave out another ream of past papers to start going over for homework, and added, as she was on her way out:

'The cast list is up, by the way, boys. Outside the gym.'

We already knew who was playing all the big roles, but most of us ran over there anyway to see which of the Year 6s and 7s would be littluns and the minor characters like Robert and Bill and I forget who all the other ones are. Those officers that rescue them at the end, maybe. And someone should be the pig's head on the stick, because that would be quite fun to do, with flies buzzing around and blood leaking from the neck and stuff.

I got there a bit after the others, and when I arrived Frodo was doing this obscene dance and yelling, 'EPIC FAIL!' and I knew I was playing Jack so it didn't occur to me that he was doing it for my benefit, but then I went a bit closer and sort of scanned the cast list all the way down and up and down again and I realised.

Jack was being played by *Frodo*, who was still gyrating around and trying to knock me over with his huge hips.

My name wasn't there.

Not even as the pig's head.

Nothing.

So I went to the Staff Room and banged on the door and then asked really politely if I could please speak to Miss Atkins, please, thank you, sorry to disturb you on your tedious lunch hour where you all just sit around eating ginger nuts.

And Miss Atkins came to the door and I said, 'I'm really sorry about defacing the cover of my book, miss.'

And she said, 'That's all right, Hobie. I accept your apology.'

I said, 'I should have been more respectful of school property.'

And she smiled and said, 'I'm sure you won't do it again. It's a shame you won't be playing Jack, by the way. But your mother rang and said that you were working so hard at the moment that you wouldn't be available for rehearsals.'

The door of the Staff Room shut and I just stood there, staring into it, thinking that I'd never really noticed what wood grain looks like before.

## Monday 6th October

My mother is a cow.

When I came home on Friday she was on her cross-trainer in the small room by the playroom that my parents use as a gym. She was wearing a tracksuit from Sweaty Betty and Masai Barefoot Technology trainers and had no make-up on so you could see how much older she is than she looks most of the time. Her hair was tied up in a ponytail and her roots were showing up the outrageous fakery of her blondeness.

'Why don't you just have brown hair, Mum?' I said, dumping my bag on the floor and picking up a kettlebell.

She took one hand off the wheeling arms of the cross-trainer and muted the flatscreen TV.

'What did you say?'

'I said, how was your day today?'

'Oh, it was all right,' she said. 'I had lunch with the Gala Committee and we had a lot of things to decide about the flowers and so on. I'm just working off a few calories because we're going out for dinner this evening.'

'When is your gala? Can I come?'

'It's during half term, and no, Hobes, I don't think so.'

My mum is patron of some massive children's charity. Sometimes they organise parties. Sometimes there are leftover goodie bags with sweets in them.

I sat down on the kettlebell like it was a miniature

spacehopper, considering how to get Mum to change her mind about the play. If I'd just yelled at her straight out she would've got all defensive and might have taken away my Xbox privileges for a couple of days. I decided to do that deep-breathingy weirdly calm voice that I imagine they use in her stupid Pilates classes or reiki healing or feng shui or some other ritual that my mum's a sucker for.

'Mum, can we talk?'

At once she dismounted from the cross-trainer and passed a completely unnecessary towel over her forehead. She sat down on the treadmill so our eyes were level.

'Of course we can. What's wrong?'

'Well, Mum, I'm a bit—' I searched for some kind of magic word – 'I feel a bit *belittled* about . . . that I can't be in the play any more . . . because you know I was going to play Jack and that's one of the lead roles and—' inspiration dawning – 'I've been told that senior schools are, like, really impressed with acting achievements and things and I don't want to . . . to jeopardise my chances of . . .'

It was time for the Hug. She zoomed in, both arms in their baby-blue velour reaching tight around my back while a cloud of figgy perfume engulfed me. There was no choice but to give in to it so I allowed myself to bend a bit, like chocolate left out in the sun or something.

'Oh, Hobie,' she said into my hair. 'It's so sweet that you're worried, but you needn't be. They'll award the Scholarships to the most academic students. It doesn't matter about drama. I promise. Besides, I do think that with all the extra hours we need with Jason, you just wouldn't have time for that kind of commitment.'

'I could have made time!'

'Well, you did fail that test last week. And Mr White said—'

'I'll work harder. I really will. I just really, *really* want to be in the play.'

She sighed, checked her watch, and got up. 'All right,' she said. 'I'll email Miss Atkins. Maybe you can have a small non-speaking part. But you'll have to promise to—'

She just. Doesn't. Get it.

'No, Mum!' In my distress I had forgotten about the Zenlike monotone. But it was an emergency. 'No, Mum! I want to play *Jack*. That was my part.'

'Hobie, they can't possibly *take it away* from whoever they've given it to now. And anyway, it's far too large a role. I really feel quite sure about this.'

'But they've given it to Frodo!' I howled at her departing tracksuit. 'And he's too fat to play Jack!'

At the doorway she turned. 'That isn't a nice thing to say about your friend. And he was simply amazing in *Oklahoma*. A really beautiful singing voice.'

Yes, because Jack is totally going to burst into song every time he spears a wild pig, now, isn't he? *Jesus*.


I was too furious to go on my computer or PSP or Xbox, which is what I usually do each night. I ended up staying in the gym with most of the lights off, reading a book Ben lent me called *Gods of Northern Europe*. I can't begin to explain how frustrating it is that I can't have a wolf tattoo until I know what it's for and that means I have to read this book first. Or something.

I don't believe in God. I mean, I understand about Our Father Who Art in Heaven and so on, but that's just something they make you say in Assembly in order to usefully bridge the gap between lost-property announcements and 8.58 a.m. I think Zara believes in God because she used to actually say her prayers each night, asking for people to be happy, even people she didn't know, which is ridiculous, and sometimes if she loses something she asks God to find it and promises to be really good in return and not tell lies or eat too many cookies. As if God cares. I teased her about the prayers so much she stopped, but I suspect her of continuing in secret. When her hamster died she thought it was because God was angry because she'd done something wrong. That's how stupid Zara is. If she passes even one of those exams she's taking next year, I'll be amazed.

Anyway, this book is quite different re. Gods. For a start, in Norse mythology there are loads and loads of them, a bit like the Classical ones like Zeus and Athena and so on, but I was completely bored stiff of studying them, interfering in wars and running around disguised as old women and bickering like a bunch of morons on *Big Brother*. I mean, how many times do I have to draw a picture of Pandora opening the stupid box and then feeling really guilty about it? Those evils were just about the coolest thing that ever happened. She should have felt glad.

These Gods were much, much more interesting. The main one was Odin, also called the Father of Battle, but I liked Thor best. He was Odin's eldest son. I can't believe that Ben can actually *see* them. Why can't I? I bet my eyesight's better. Then there was a bunch of others and some Goddesses who aren't as important. Loki was the son of a giant and he was the mischief-maker, sort of unpredictable. I liked him too. And Loki was the father of Fenrir the wolf and also the World Serpent and the woman who ruled over the Land of Death whose name was Hel. (Awesome.) As you can see it's all quite complicated. Ben must have studied this for ages. The Gods lived in a place called Asgard and feasted on an endless supply of pork and drank mead (like ale or beer or something) which they got from a goat. And right in the middle of Asgard was this massive sacred tree called Yggdrasil, or the World Tree. Yggdrasil was the tree of life.

Normally I dislike reading, but I read for quite a long time.

## Wednesday 8th October

Today we had a fixture against St Martin's and I was really, *really* up for a match. I felt different as I stepped off the coach, swinging my kit bag against Archie's back. One of the good things about fixtures is that it's normally just me and Archie from 8 Upper. Everyone else comes from the other classes or from Year 7. It's quite refreshing after hours and hours with the Nicholson Twins and Hobbitboy all talking about the conditional-perfect tense in French or finding the volume of a cone.

Ben didn't sit with me on the coach, although he'd come as a spectator.

'Good luck,' he said, and shuffled off to sit on his own under a tree.

Before matches I have this feeling in me, like an itch or a glow. Like I just need to get out there onto the pitch and go flying. I breathe in and I feel this unbelievable rush of oxygen, the red blood cells charging around in my veins. I raise myself up onto the toes of my trainers, wait for my muscles to come alive. Stretch my hamstrings against the ground. And I want to go out there . . . and *nail* it. And today I felt just like that, but like alcohol when you boil off lots of liquid and you're left with this kind of distilled essence. I felt, honestly, like I might crush the skull of anyone that came near me.

My position is outside centre. Sometimes I wish it wasn't

Rugby we were playing though. I wish it was fighting. I wish we had swords. We won the toss and as we shook hands with the opposition I saw three or four kids who were definitely not St Martin's pupils on their team. They looked, like, a foot taller at least and seriously muscular, with jaws that jutted out aggressively over their mouth-guards.

'Who are *they*?' said Archie, pulling up his socks.

Mr Voss said they were some French exchange students who were visiting from Toulouse.

'Mr Voss, that's so unfair!' we all chorused.

He said that as far as he knew there was no reason why they couldn't participate, since they were temporarily pupils at St Martin's.

'What the hell,' I said. 'Let's beat them anyway.'

And we did.

Towards the end of the second half it was 21–21 and we needed to score. So I just kind of went for it. I mean, what was there to lose?

At one point I dived between both of their centres to get the ball and I felt invincible, even when they came running after me and one of them grabbed the back of my shirt and I felt it rip with this amazing scratchy sound that sounded like freedom and I set off up the pitch hugging the ball against my chest and I *swear* I have never run that fast in my life. And then someone tackled me from the side and I lost balance and fell and barrelled over and over in this frenzied somersault and the blood in my ears was going mental and the grass of the pitch had this really high earthy smell and I felt something give a bit in my arm and I didn't give a shit and I rolled back onto my feet and kept on running. I realised my nose was bleeding because my mouth felt hot and wet and these overdressed mothers on the side were screaming for the ref to stop the match, but I was so close, so close to the try line. And I dived for it, just as two of the French kids landed on me from either side like the velociraptors in *Jurassic Park* when they try to take down the T. rex. I'd been travelling at such speed that even with the bulky foreign students weighing me down I managed to hurl the whole of my body over the line and the ball was all smeared with blood and my arm was tingling and when I stood up I couldn't feel it any more.

'Dude,' said Archie, 'that was *epic*.'

And the whistle went.

It turned out that I had sprained my wrist and dislocated my elbow and possibly broken my nose and I was covered from head to foot in the most spectacular bruises that looked like someone had done them with purple spray paint. The first-aid person from St Martin's said I needed to go to hospital to check that nothing was broken, so they called my mother and she arrived in an Addison Lee almost immediately, smelling of white wine.

'Oh, *Hobie*,' she said, covering me with kisses.

'He was definitely Man of the Match, Mrs Duvalle,' said

Mr Voss respectfully. He turned to me. 'Good work, champ. Don't go too crazy on a regular basis though. We're going to need you for the inter-schools tournament at the end of term.'

He patted my hair, which was a big mess of blood and turf.

I eyed my mother. What if she was planning to add Rugby to the list of things I wasn't allowed to do any more? But it turned out that she was actually thinking about whether I could get a Sports Scholarship to go with the academic one I was definitely in the running for. She made an *I'll call you* gesture at Mr Voss, who was busy filling in about eighteen different Incident Report forms.

The cab was waiting to take us to A&E. We got it to go via Marks & Spencer because I had missed tea.

'I don't think my arm is broken, you know,' I said to Mum as she opened the box of Bakewell tarts, which I intended to finish before we arrived.

'I should hope not,' she said. 'But at least it's not your writing arm.'

## Friday 10th October

Ben agreed to come round to my house again after school and I was really pleased. Jason was there for a short while to make up for the session we'd missed on Wednesday because I was in the hospital. Mum put us all in the playroom to whizz through our homework.

'You don't mind if Hobie's friend joins in with the session?' she said to Jason, as Clothilde carried in a tray of hot chocolate and Duchy Originals lemon biscuits.

But Ben had already flung himself at Jason and was giving him a massive hug, and Jason was laughing and saying, 'All right, little man?' Which I thought was an absurd thing to say to a twelve-year-old. But I suppose Ben must have been pretty small when they first met. I was beginning to feel a bit left out, and when Zara sneaked in to see what all the fuss was about I shoved her back out the door and slammed it shut just short of her ponytail.

We all sat around the playroom table and I got that weird feeling you get when you're out at dinner and a really famous person walks past your table, and you realise there's someone more important than you in the room. Sometimes Jason would murmur these little asides to Ben in a funny language, quite slowly, and Ben would nod and reply super-fast like he was completely fluent, and then at one point Jason said to Ben, 'I see you're still reading the Edders then,' and Ben was all solemn and serious and pleased. It was like watching a totally different Ben.

'What're the Edders?' I said, and Ben and Jason both corrected me simultaneously, saying they're spelt *E-D-D-A-S* and represent these two massive old texts that tell the stories of the Norse Gods. Whatever. How was I meant to know?

After Jason left and Mum and Dad had gone out for dinner we climbed up onto the roof. Ben accepted a cigarette and we sat and smoked in our coats, which we'd smuggled upstairs because it's getting a bit colder now, and darker. It was harder to get up there with my arm in a sling, but I managed it.

'What I thought was so magnificent about Wednesday,' said Ben, 'was how you just didn't seem to feel any pain. When they all fell on you.'

'I didn't.'

'Why not?'

I thought about it.

'I felt kind of charged up. You know. Like when you give your dog loads of sugar and it goes mental and starts running around the house peeing on the curtains like Matteo's did that time when we fed it Haribos and Lucozade. I felt like I didn't have any nerves in my body for feeling pain. I mean, I sort of knew something had happened to my arm, but I swear, I really couldn't feel it. I just wanted to get the ball over the line.'

'Berserk,' he said.

'What?'

'That's what you were. A Berserk.'

We sat and smoked and the sun bled out into the sky and the aeroplanes cut across the clouds making their steady downwards glide into Heathrow and Ben told me about these warriors, called Berserks, that were sacred to Odin and were supposed to get special powers from him. They were phenomenal in battle, totally fearless, consumed with this mad rage that meant they feared no pain. They painted their bodies black and fought in the dead of night. They had no weapons and wore bearskins. Sometimes they believed they were wolves or bears. And that's where the word *berserk* comes from. Awesome.

'I think I'm starting to get it,' I told Ben.

The Otherlife. It's a place that you think doesn't exist, this far-off place with its icy mountain ranges and lawless warriors and wolves and savage Gods. And then you find it inside you. When I touched down and the blood from my face danced onto the rugby ball and the screams of the mothers and the other kids felt like they were actually inside my body, like it was my blood itself that was screaming, I knew. It was in me.

That's why the tattoo. It's not because Ben wants to be a wolf. Or even a warrior. He just wants to know that the Otherlife is there.

'So am I ready?' I asked him.

'Tell me the name of Odin's father.'

I thought frantically. 'Baldr.'

He snorted. *'No.'*

'Buri!'

'Wrong again. I thought you were reading the books.'

'I am! But the names are so bloody complicated.' If it'd been anyone else, I'd have kicked them, but I didn't because it was Ben.

'One more guess.'

'Dammit, I know it begins with a *B*. Wait. BOR.'

And Ben got out a square bottle of black ink with a round lid and gave it to me, and said I could find my own needle.

# BEN

I don't have many friends. Not at school, not anywhere. I hang out with Jake and Ally Stonehill, because they're metalheads, and metalheads stick together. But my best friend – by miles – is Solomon. Ever since we were paired together in chemistry in Year 9 and he put my hair out with Evian when I stood too close to the Bunsen burner. I can tell Solomon almost anything. I can ask him almost anything too, and if he doesn't know the answer then he'll try and find out later and ring me up at midnight to tell me he's spent an hour on his father's LexisNexis but he's *finally* worked it out.

We are loitering in the lunch queue. No one is ever in a hurry to get through the dining-hall doors, into the steam-puffed air and the starch-and-chemical smell of the Pasta King machine.

'Do you know a tutor called Jason?' I ask him.

Solomon has a different tutor every day. Like day-of-the-week underpants, he once commented. He doesn't need them any more, but his parents can't let go.

'Nope. Never had a Jason,' he says, polishing his watch with his shirt cuff. 'Any good?'

'Yeah. Pretty good.'

'I must wash my hands,' he says.

Solomon shoots off in the direction of the toilets. He's a hygiene enthusiast. My headache is back: a stubborn squatter in my burnt-out head. Reflexively I shake a pill out of my sleeve, ready to take with my drink when we sit down.

'Holloway. What've you got there?'

Chadwick bears down on me, enormous in his three-piece suit and preposterous 'comedy' waistcoat, emblazoned with picnicking teddy bears. Like a six-year-old caught with something disgusting in the sandpit, I stare blushingly at his shoes. Open my fingers. Hold out my palm. Neatly he removes the pill.

''Fraid I'll have to hand this in at the office.'

'It's just for migraines, sir.'

Chadwick looks at me closely.

'The only people authorised to dispense medication are the school nurse and the secretary. Personal supplies are strictly forbidden; you know that.'

His voice bounces off the marble floor. Amid the crush of bodies I sense eyes on me. Watching. Quietly condemning. Solly slips back into the queue, making a point of looking fixedly at the vast mixed-media collage of the Last Supper that a group of Year 9s did about twenty years ago.

'Ah, Green. Just the person I was looking for. You and Holloway are both due in after-school detention from four till five.'

'What for?' says Solomon weakly.

'Plagiarism is the most atrocious of crimes, Green. Even auto-plagiarism. Your attempt to disguise your distinctive writing style with cheap spelling mistakes and misplaced semicolons was easy to see through. Especially since you happened to use the same watermarked paper for both your essay and Holloway's. Holloway, if your migraines are impeding your ability to put pen to paper, you have only to show me a note from your mother. I'll see you both later.'

And off he goes, wobbling from side to side like a carnival float.

'*Busted!*' hisses a voice from behind Solomon's back. It's a kid called Lawson in Year 10, indulging in a moment of Schadenfreude.

Solomon hates being late, ill or rebuked. These things disturb his core philosophy, which he claims is a Japanese mode of thought called kaizen. According to Solly, everything must exist in a state of perpetual, gradual improvement. Or else it falls apart. Once he asked me what my philosophy was. I thought about it. And I realised that I just . . . didn't know. Yet, once upon a time, I remember standing on Hobie's roof, hair turning in the wind, and telling him that *everything has to have a meaning*. Truly, surely, I believed in something once.

I believed in the Otherlife.

'I'll miss Scrabble Club. Dammit,' says Sol. 'God, Ben, cheer up.'

He shoves me in the ribs as the space ahead of me in

the queue opens up. I drag myself forward. I fix my gaze on the Last Supper, a mosaic of weathered glass, torn fabric and ripped-up newspaper, surprisingly effective because of its size. It's easy to make out the long table studded with wine glasses and plates, the central figure of Jesus among the bent heads of his apostles. Solomon is chatting to me, some anecdote involving his French exchange partner, a Westfield gift card and a lost iPhone. I've heard it before. I keep staring at the collage.

As I'm about to go in, something draws my attention back to the Last Supper. I catch a final glimpse of Judas Iscariot, and see, indistinct, shimmering beneath it, the flame-red hair and secretive sneer of Loki. Judas Iscariot catches my eye, and winks.

'I'm *starving*,' he mouths conspiratorially. 'My nanny was supposed to drop off my snack. But she didn't.'

Shaking my head, I push through the doors of the dining hall.

Lunch today is some kind of curry with rice and green beans. Baked potatoes. A salad bar with sad folds of lettuce, hard-boiled eggs and wedges of beetroot, leaking an artificial fuchsia juice. My head vibrates. They report you if you don't take any food, so I ask for a piece of bread and throw a couple of foil-wrapped cheeses onto my tray.

'Is the pill that important?' asks Solly as he holds out his plate for grated carrot.

'What pill?' I say. I take an apple from a bowl.

'The one you were clinging onto like some kind of panic button. What are those things?'

'Nothing. I just get these headaches during exam time.'

'You shouldn't take painkillers.' Solly is pious about healthcare; his mum's a homeopath or something. 'Try vitamin B3.'

We make our way over to our usual corner table. As we edge past a particularly rowdy group of Year 12s, Solomon stops and says, 'Oh, *I* know who you should ask about your tutor.'

'Who?'

'Friedman, of course.'

Friedman. He's right. Solomon always figures out the answer to things. When he warns me that my blood-sugar levels will crash if I skip lunch, I tell him I'll get hold of some vitamin B3.


Friedman is our age, but so smart they moved him up a year. The sixth-formers have small studies all along the top corridor in the south wing of the main building, and I imagine I'll find him there, proofing the next edition of the school magazine, or revising for one of his five AS levels. It's hard to say how he found the time, but alongside these activities and others – the model United Nations he organised among the other London day schools, the *Pearl Fishers* aria he performed so touchingly in assembly last week – Friedman has also designed an app which he is reportedly about to sell to a software company for a fantastical sum. Called TutoReal, it uses something like a combination of GPS software and a vast and intricate database to match clients with a suitably qualified tutor who lives or works within close proximity. Solomon's right: if anyone can tell me where Jason is, Friedman can.

I knock on the door. '*En*-ter,' says Friedman, in his famous baritone.

He doesn't swivel round immediately, so that – even though we ought to be in the same year, and have known each other since we were nine – I'm forced to stand in the doorway like Oliver Twist until he's ready. I watch his broad back, hulking over his laptop, the bulk of his curly head. Finally he turns around.

'Oh,' he says, 'it's you.'

'Hi, Frodo,' I say.

'It's Alexis now, if you don't mind.'

To the horror and fury of his mother, Friedman decided a while ago that his first name didn't have enough gravitas for someone of his intellectual standing and plumped for his more appealing middle one.

'What can I do for you?' he says, turning back to his computer, where I see among the tabbed pages a property search engine, the FTSE 100 index and a couple of sites that he must have broken through the school firewall to access.

'I was wondering if you could look up a tutor for me.'

'I'm incredibly busy at the moment, Ben. Try Google,' says Frodo, taking a swig of bottled Frappuccino.

'I've done that already. His name's too common to search for, and he didn't have a website. Not one that I can find anyway.'

Without looking, Frodo throws the empty Frappuccino bottle in the general direction of the bin; I remember that he was never much of a sportsman. Not like Archie, say. Or Hobie.

'Well, come back tomorrow, why don't you?' says Frodo.

I take a step further into his hallowed sanctum.

'I've never really seen your app, you know,' I say. 'Solomon says it's perfectly optimised for OS X.'

I'm actually not sure Solly ever said that, but it sounds plausible.

'Of course it is,' says Frodo loftily. 'I built it.'

'Please,' I say. 'Just one search and then I'll leave.'

A shrill staccato bell rings out from the courtyard: five minutes until lessons.

Frodo sighs huffily and then says, 'Fine. Actually I'm quite excited by some new features. I want to incorporate a secret search parameter for the female tutors, like *Hot or Not*, you know? So you can get a really fit tutor instead of some hideous dog, but in order to access the function you need to pay for an upgrade.'

'Wow,' I say. 'That sounds like an amazing idea.'

He clicks on an icon in the dock of his laptop; a royal-blue screen pops up.

'Tutor's name?'

'Jason.'

'Jason what? I have over five thousand tutors; I expect a good many Jasons.'

'Young.'

'Age?'

'I . . . I don't know.'

'Specialisms? Qualifications?'

'Maths. Science. Some other stuff. He was doing a PhD.'

The royal-blue screen shuffles and reshuffles its results. Frodo scrolls through the square photographs – it's a little like a dating site, the ones I've seen Mum use sometimes – of pink-cheeked girls and serious-browed boys, sorting and resorting with his many intelligent filters, but we come to the second-last page of Jasons, and Youngs, and then the last, but there is no Jason Young.

Jason is not there.

'Sure you've got his name right?'

'Pretty sure,' I say. 'I used to know him quite well.'

Frodo stares at me with what looks like a flicker of interest. 'Wait, wait. Not the guy who tutored you at Cottesmore House? That Jason?'

'Yes, that Jason,' I say, my arms twitching. 'Why?'

There's a pause, and then Frodo says, 'Nothing. Don't

worry about it. But he's certainly not on my database. He must have got a real job.'

By the way he swivels back round to face his desk, I know that I have been dismissed.


I find Solly in the library, where he is writing a long, alliterative letter of apology to Chadwick. It is very like Solly not to blame me for the detention, even though it is sort of my fault.

'Any luck?' he asks.

'No. Jason wasn't on the app.'

'Questionable piece of design work, that app,' says Solly, who is possibly jealous. 'Frodo probably misspelt the name on the database.'

'Doubt it. I guess he doesn't tutor any more.'

Solly folds his letter into perfect thirds and slides it into an off-white Conqueror envelope.

'Well, do you have any mutual acquaintances?' he asks.

My thoughts flicker at once to Hobie. But I can't ask Hobie. I think briefly of his sister, Zara. But she was only little when we were in Year 8. I can't imagine she'd have a contact number for Jason. And I wouldn't know how to get in touch with her anyway. I suppose my mum must have a number for Hobie's parents, but I don't want to go down that particular avenue.

'Not really,' I say.

'What about his alma mater?'

'Sorry?'

'His *university*,' says Solly, with dwindling patience. 'Didn't you say he was doing a PhD?'

When I call Imperial College from the payphone outside the dining hall (my phone, as usual, has no credit), I find myself in a maze of a switchboard. I don't know which extension I require, and the operator is possibly having lunch or something, because I keep getting put through to some kind of answering machine. With the last of my fifty-pence pieces, I try once more, and this time instead of holding for the operator I press a sequence of random digits and somehow end up talking to a human being – a kind-voiced woman, whose gentle vowels remind me a little of Frigg.

'Can I help you?' she says, and it seems almost as if she'd like to. There's so much warmth in the way she says it.

'My name's Ben,' I say. 'I'm trying to find a contact number for someone who was doing a PhD at Imperial about four years ago.'

'Well, he may still be studying here,' she replies. 'Let me check.'

I give her Jason's full name. I'm sure he was doing something scientific, so I tell her that as well, and then I listen to the woman breathing, and typing, and then typing some more.

'Bear with me,' she says. 'I'm just getting into the system. It takes a while to load.'

Then there is a pause.

'From our records it seems that Jason Young did not complete his studies,' she says, her voice growing fainter, and heavier. 'Computational Biology, it says here.'

'That's right,' I say, remembering.

'I . . . wait a minute, I . . . there's a note in his file. Oh. It seems that, oh dear, I am sorry to be telling you this over the phone. Are you a friend?'

'Yes,' I say.

'I'm afraid that Jason Young is dead,' says the woman, in her slow, kind voice.

My insides have been scooped out. Liquid cement has been poured in. It has solidified, filling my cavities, blocking my tear ducts. My blood has stopped. How can Jason be dead? He read the Norse tales to me, taught me about fractions, held my hand when we crossed the road. It is not possible that Jason is dead.

At the nurse's station I am offered a single paracetamol and a glass of water. I am sick on her apron, and she offers to call my mother.

'Don't,' I say. She knew. My mother knew, and didn't tell me. It's Reg of Putney all over again. It's the *what you don't know won't harm you* school of thought she keeps on subscribing me to, even though I didn't ask to be a member. I hate her.

*Jason's not available*, she texted this morning. Right. Of course he's not available, *because he's dead*. Just as Hermódr said. *He is dead*, he said, when I saw him and his horse in the garden. I just didn't know who he meant. When did Jason die? How? Chadwick lets me off the detention and I take the tube home, listening to the whole of *And Justice For All* for the second time today. It's the album James, Lars and Kirk wrote after the death of Cliff Burton. Some people say you can't hear the bass on it at all, because they couldn't bear for it to be there, played by the newly recruited Jason 'Newkid' Newsted instead of their beloved Cliff. I turn it up so loud that my pulse reawakens and pounds brutally in time to the down-tuned moan of 'Harvester of Sorrow'. Several Italian tourists glance at me in horror and change carriage. Wedged into a corner seat like a hunted-down animal, vibrating messily, my headache spelt out in pain marks on my forehead and bleeding Metallica from my earphones, I must look terrible.

Mum's already home when I get back. The kitchen clatters with the sounds of tidying and food preparation and never-silent Radio 4. She's laying the table, setting the cutlery exactly perpendicular to the edge.

'Ben,' she says. 'How was your day?'

And then: 'What's the matter? What's wrong?'

'Mum,' I say, measuring each word out carefully, like I'm doing an experiment with them, 'you didn't tell me that Jason was dead.'

She looks at me, surprised. I watch her, suspended, a fork

hovering in the air. I watch her trying to decide which lie to tell next. I watch her wrestle with them, sifting the quick and easy lies from the dark and heavy ones.

'I'm sorry,' she says. 'I can see you're upset. Try and stay calm.'

'How long have you known?'

Now she crosses over to the sink, where she decorates the stacked plates from breakfast with economical bursts of Fairy Liquid.

'I rang the tutoring agency at the start of the Easter holidays,' she says, her words flat, like hockey pucks. 'I was thinking of getting him to come and do some revision with you. They told me then. Pass me those mugs, will you?'

I don't move. She fetches them herself and holds them under the tap. A coil of steam rises.

'But when did he die? How?'

'He . . . I don't know. Why don't we talk about this after your exams are finished? I don't think it's the right time to be—'

'What's the name of the agency?'

'I don't remember, Ben.'

I almost feel sorry for her, which is weird. She's lying; she's lying again. She can't stop. Jason never had an agency. He worked for himself. He always had.

Head on fire, nerves chattering, I go back upstairs and sweep the contents of my desk into a rucksack. My revision notes, my set texts. I swallow another pill. Mum appears at the doorway, her face dark.

'Ben, where are you going? You've got maths tomorrow; you need to rest!'

'Dad's house.'

She doesn't try to stop me.

# HOBIE'S DIARY

Monday 13th October 2008

Mum made the most of my inability to go to Saturday Football Club by getting Jason round for an extra couple of hours of tutoring.

'Been in the wars?' he asked me. I had a staggering black eye as well as the sling.

I explained about beating the French exchange students and he did his little laugh that sounds more like an embarrassed sneeze and asked me if I had any homework.

Now, quite surprisingly, because I could easily have got Jason to basically do it for me, I had already done my creative writing homework. The instruction was to 'write about a powerful moment in your life'. Inspiring stuff. We were of course meant to write some kind of weepy bollocks full of similes and things about the death of a beloved grandparent, but I couldn't think of any more powerful moment recently than last week's Rugby match. A moment when I literally felt so full of power that it took an entire evening of lying flat on the sofa, watching television and getting Clothilde to microwave me popcorn, to calm down again. I think I like writing more than I used to because of this journal thing, which seemed so irritating at first and is now just a way of putting things down and is sort of automatic, like breathing or blowing your nose. Anyway, it was the first creative assignment I've ever wanted to complete, voluntarily, without two or three gentle reminders and a parent or tutor breathing down my neck.

So I gave it to Jason to read, and instead of fiddling with toys and surreptitiously checking Facebook or whatever I normally do to kill time during tutoring, I sat there and watched him read it.

It took him forever.

Eventually he laid it down on my desk and said, 'This is terrific. Really, really good.'

And I felt pleased.

'I like the bit –' he pointed to it with his pencil – 'where you suddenly shift into this almost mythological landscape, and the rugby players metamorphose into warriors in war paint and you become a wolf. You really build the tension. And communicate this feeling of power that you had. I can see Ben's influence too.'

I could tell that Jason had never had a similar experience on a playing field. I mean, I doubt table tennis gives you the same sense of exhilaration, and I can't imagine he plays anything else.

'I don't know about this bit though.' He read aloud: *I felt like I could crush the skull of anyone that crossed my path.*

'How come?'

'Isn't that a bit strong? I mean, you didn't actually feel like that, did you?'

'OK,' I said. 'Let's change it.'

But I did feel like that. I did.

I asked Jason where he lived because I realised I didn't know, and he said Bethnal Green, but I don't know where that is.

And then Mum, who thinks a colon is something you get irrigated at the spa, put her head round the door and asked Jason if he'd checked my sentence structure and punctuation, and Jason said he would.

## Wednesday 15th October

I searched on Google Images until I found what I wanted, which was basically pretty close to Ben's wolf but more sprawled-looking, more poised for attack. I didn't want any of the ones with curly lines or silly clothes or wings. Some people have really idiotic ideas for tattoos. And I printed it out and hid it under the bed, and I felt really excited about it, which made me realise that I don't often feel really excited about things. Even when we were on the yacht, which was quite cool with the butler bringing whatever you wanted and the jet-ski bike on the deck, I never woke up in the morning feeling like I couldn't wait for the day to get going. This tattoo is definitely going to help me to see all this stuff that Ben can see. I know it is. All these Gods showing up like glow stars, or the hidden shapes in Zara's NVR papers. It's driving me literally crazy that I can't see them.

Ben had told me to wait for a full moon because full moons are more special and potent, and it turned out that last night, Tuesday the fourteenth, was one, and that was perfect because Mum and Dad were going to the opera. They went out at about half past six, looking like they were going to a première or something.

Clothilde made pasta pesto with vile, slimy rice linguine, which is apparently better for you than normal pasta, and served it to me and Zara while we watched a box set of *Friends*. It was a Thanksgiving episode where Monica is shown in a flashback to have once been really fat and Joey gets a turkey stuck on his head.

'They're all so thin, aren't they?' said Zara, looking at Rachel and Phoebe and present-day-Monica on the screen.

'Thinner than you, you mean?' I said, yanking the cashmere throw over to my side of the sofa. 'Though that's not difficult. I mean, you could make a twelve-ton walrus look svelte.'

'You children, you are not eating your dinner!' said Clothilde. '*Vous êtes malades, ou quoi?*'

So Zara ate a bit more of her pasta although she hid quite a lot of it under her napkin. And I (for once) just didn't feel hungry. I wanted night to fall.

'Hobie, can I play Xbox with you?'

'*May* I.'

'May I, please?'

'No, you may not. I have stuff to do. Play with your horrible dolls instead. Or . . . I know. Go and find me 28 things beginning with *c*.'

That got rid of her.

I had a shower and put on my pyjamas and got into bed at about 9.30 p.m., and when Clothilde came in to try to kiss me goodnight I made a big show of being sleepy, and let her switch off my light. I listened to her clumping about, flushing the toilet, answering her phone a couple of times. And then the house went quiet and I knew it was time.

I traced the wolf onto my ribcage on my right-hand side,

pretty much where Ben's got his. And yes, I knew that it was only a matter of time before Mum found out about it, but our next tropical beach holiday hadn't even been booked yet, and I was sure I could argue my way out of laser removal or surgery or whatever if it came down to it. Anyway, it wasn't really my problem.

I got out the fat white candles that I'd found in one of the kitchen cupboards and lit them with my lighter. I dragged open my curtains. Everything took a bit longer because of my sling, but that didn't matter. The moon was a bit obscured at first but gradually it came out and lit the room with this opally, milky-blue light that I thought would have been exactly the right kind of moonlight for the Berserks to fight beneath.

I hunted around for the needle that I'd hidden in my sock drawer and unearthed Ben's bottle of ink. I looked on Facebook for the instructions he'd sent me, but for some reason I couldn't find his message in my inbox. And it made me really cross because I was totally geared up to tattoo myself *at once* so I thought, what the hell, and Skyped Ben. It was about elevenish by this time but I was sure he'd be up, reading his Norse books or playing one of those weird multiplayer online quest games he likes so much.

The call blipped and beeped and eventually he answered it. I saw his fringe bobbing about in front of the camera.

'Hobie. What are you . . . ? It's kind of *late*, you know.'

'Yeah, sorry. I can't find that message you sent about bandages and stuff.'

There was a scuffle and the sound of his laptop being rearranged, and a loud sigh.

'I've got my design and the ink and the needle and some kitchen roll, and I've lit some candles,' I said.

'Have you sterilised the needle in boiling water with a bit of salt?'

'Um, no. Hold on. Don't go anywhere, OK?'

His face loomed and receded and I could see him crossing his legs as he sat over his computer.

'Fine,' he said.

I raced off to the guest bedroom where there's a kettle and all these different teabags laid out on a tray for when Grandma comes to visit, like our house is actually a hotel. As I boiled the kettle I hopped feverishly on one leg. There wasn't any salt and I briefly wondered if sugar would do, then decided it really didn't matter either way.

'I'm back,' I hissed, plonking myself in the middle of my carpet.

'Did you sterilise the needle?'

'Sort of.'

'If you haven't, just hold it in the candle,' said Ben.

So I did.

'You also need some healing cream and some clingfilm to tape over it when—'

'I'll get it later.'

'Can I go back to my game now?' he said.

'Can't you stay online? I need moral support. Why don't you do a sort of chant or something?'

He sighed again. I swear, Ben should go on daytime TV as a really disapproving chat-show host.

'I suppose,' he said, 'it would be a fitting part of the ritual.'

'Great!' I said, opening the bottle of ink with my teeth. 'But you'd better keep it down, OK?'

So he began this really low chant that sounded like his mouth was full of toffee. It had a slightly *Lord of the Rings*-y feel to it if you know what I mean. I like all that stuff, but there isn't enough blood. And the elves and princes and whoever are all quite gay and always looking meaningfully into the middle distance for about twenty minutes before they speak, which is why those films are so bloody long.

This (I found out after) is what Ben was saying:

> *Skeggǫld, skálmǫld,*
> *skildir ro klofnir,*
> *vindǫld, vargǫld,*
> *áðr verǫld steypiz*

Which apparently means:

> *An axe-age, a sword-age,*
> *shields will be cloven,*

134

*a wind-age, a wolf-age,*
*before the world's ruin.*

I put the mirror on the floor between the candles, unbuttoned my pyjama shirt again and began.

As the point of the needle touched my skin I felt a rush of cold all along my side like just before you jump into a massive freezing lake and you shiver because you know how it's going to feel. Ben kept chanting and I joined in a bit (making up gibberish) in an undertone.

*Skeggǫld, skálmǫld,*
*skildir ro klofnir . . .*

The candles warped like they were doing their own strange dance in time to the words. I poked the ink into my skin, over and over, at the point of the wolf's tail, blotting the blood with kitchen roll. It didn't even hurt that much. When you've had a whole bunch of kids fall on you in a scrum and practically rip your arm out of its socket, a tattoo is honestly just child's play, really.

'This is easy!' I said to Ben. 'I could actually—'

But I didn't finish what I was going to say (which was that maybe I could do the moon as well as Hati and go for a much larger, more impressive tattoo), because just at that moment my door flew open and Mum and Dad came in.

\*　　\*　　\*

Now I know what people mean by the expression All Hell Broke Loose.

I have to say, at first my parents couldn't quite figure out what on earth I was doing. From the look of the candles and the mirror it must've seemed like I was trying to summon spirits or something. But then there was the biro on my ribcage and the needle and the ink and, well, a fair bit of blood and stained kitchen roll and the fact that I was half dressed. And Mum might not be the sharpest, but she worked it out and was screaming as loudly as she could in a whisper so as not to wake up Za, while Dad kept shaking his head and saying 'Jesus Christ, Hobie!' and ranting about septicaemia, which is blood poisoning. Luckily Ben had immediately signed out of Skype and my laptop was a bit to the side so they didn't pick up that I'd been talking to someone online.

They took away everything and mopped up the blood and put a dressing on the 1mm area that I'd managed to ink in, and Mum cried and said we would have to go and see the GP for a tetanus jab first thing in the morning, and why would I consider doing such a self-destructive thing and was I not happy and then she cried some more, sitting on my bed in her opera clothes.

'Mum,' I said eventually, 'why did you guys come into my room?'

She reached for the kitchen roll to absorb some of the mascara gunge from her face.

'What do you mean?'

'You couldn't have seen a light. And I don't think you heard me. So why did you come in?'

She sighed and then pointed upwards to the shelf above my bed.

'The NannyCam.'

I followed her gaze, to where Jimmy my old yellow dinosaur reigned over a court of kangaroos, polar bears and Buzz Lightyears. And a rectangular digital clock, sort of boring-looking, that I'd always thought was just a clock. But apparently not.

'Mum, you've got to be *joking*.'

'We don't use them much. It's just nice to check on you and Zara sometimes. To make sure you're safe. The cameras are linked to a monitor in the study.'

The idea that my parents have been spying on me for the last however many years with a NannyCam, no doubt relayed to their laptops so they can make sure I'm not trying to look at porn and am spending an appropriate amount of time on my homework and sleeping soundly each night, *revolted* me.

'I thought only celebrities did that kind of thing!' I said to her.

'Hobes, I'm not going to apologise to you after what you've just done. Don't you know how dangerous it is? And how *tacky* tattoos are?'

'I can't *believe* there's a NannyCam in my bedroom!'

She got up. 'We'll talk more about it tomorrow.'

On her way out she staggered a bit, wobbling onto the landing in her shiny, pointy shoes. Maybe it was because she was drunk, or maybe it was because she was upset. I didn't especially care which.

## Thursday 16th October

I ended up missing an entire day of school. We couldn't get an appointment at the local GP so Mum rang the Harley Street people and then she decided that while we were in the area we should see this Educational Psychologist man as well who had an office nearby. Under other circumstances I would have really liked that sort of day, maybe with some shopping thrown in before lunch and a bacon cheeseburger at Black and Blue, but I could tell that Mum was Exceptionally Pissed Off and treats were unlikely to feature in the schedule. She was obsessed with the idea that I had somehow *grazed my ribs* with the needle and it was all Dad could do to stop her from calling an ambulance. Honestly, if Mum had taken air hostess exams, she wouldn't have been clever enough to get in – not even to, like, Ryanair. No wonder Zara has so much trouble. I have one-sixteenth of a wolf's tail on my skin and it looks like a stupid *mole*. I wish they'd just let me finish it.

She kept looking over at me and trying to hold my hand and then abruptly withdrawing it, as if she couldn't decide how she should be behaving. I got on with eating my stack of pancakes with maple syrup. I noticed she was wearing her Harley Street Outfit, a camel-coloured suit with a knee-length skirt and a silly collar. She wears it when we go to the dentist too. I wonder if she knows she has a uniform. It got me thinking anyway, and I endured the tetanus jab with the patronising private doctor ('Oh dear, haven't *we* been a silly little boy!') and a forced amble around Regent's Park to admire the last of the summer roses by keeping this pinned in my mind. Because I had to do *something*.

Then we went to see a man called Dr Tibbert. I seem to remember I'd seen him before, years ago. He had sweets in a clay bowl on his desk. The whole thing took *hours*. It was just like Zara's ghastly Assessment Papers: find the odd one out, which shape on the right does not belong with the group on the left, underline the two words closest in meaning, and then about twelve pages of codes with 'the alphabet written out to help you'. It was all piss-easy, and although I was tempted to sabotage my scores by filling in the multiple-choice answer sheets at random, I just sat there drawing neat little pencil lozenges in the blanks and feeling pretty confident that, whatever happened, Dr Tibbert wasn't going to say I was an idiot.

We also had to talk about my feelings and things.

'Do you feel that you are under any particular pressure at the moment?' he asked me. He had very small hands. They unnerved me. Why were they so small? Were his feet also undersized? I kept trying to get a look at them, but they were hidden by his immensely imposing mahogany desk.

I didn't know how to answer him, so I said I didn't know. It was sort of true. I don't know what pressure is. It comes from Latin *premo, premere, pressi, pressum*. There is atmospheric pressure. Pressure = Force over Area. I feel pressure to knock people's teeth out when I play Rugby. But I didn't want to tell him that. And I didn't want to tell him about Ben's Otherlife, or Skøll, or the wolf Hati that I really wanted a tattoo of so that I could be reminded of it every day.

Dr Tibbert seemed to want to discuss it, though, probably at Mum's insistence. He asked me if I'd wanted to feel pain when I did it. I thought of the Berserks flying into battle, smeared in dark paint, gone mad with the desire to win, fearless. I looked at Dr Tibbert's neat round face with his neat round glasses, like Harry Potter's, fixed with geometric precision above his nose. I imagined picking up the clay bowl and smashing it on the floor. Just by looking at it I felt like I knew exactly the sound it would make, exactly how many pieces it would break into.

'I don't know,' I said.

'Do you feel frustrated that your arm is in a sling at the moment?'

'I don't know.'

And I answered *I don't know* to every single thing he asked me after that.

When I came out Mum was reading a brochure from a clinic called The Body Beautiful that specialises in non-surgical liposuction. What she needs is a brainlift.

I enjoyed the silence in the taxi on the way home.

## Friday 17th October

'What happened?' Ben asked. We were at lunch. Clothilde had made me a focaccia sandwich with Parma ham and goat's cheese. There were also carrot sticks and a mini pot of hummus and a yogurt called Forbidden Fruits. I stared at it all, arranged on the red-and-white checked mat that my lunchbox artfully unrolls into. And I felt completely *defeated* by it. The small plastic spoon for my yogurt, the dark blue paper napkin folded into triangles, the perfection of Clothilde's artistry. All for what was basically just a tray of fuel for my body to turn into glucose and thenceforth into energy.

Maybe that's why Zara doesn't eat much any more. Because she just can't be bothered.

'Fail,' I told him briefly.

'Sorry.'

'Why are *you* sorry?'

'I'm not,' he said. 'I mean, I'm sorry you didn't manage to do it. But you will eventually.'

Then he told me my mother had rung his mother and invited him to stay with us at our country house for the second week of half term. She's just so transparent. She knows Ben is likely to get a Scholarship, so she figures if she lures him down to our country house, bribing his mother with the prospect of free tuition, some of his precocious intelligence will rub off on me and my chances

142

of getting one myself will magically treble. Well done, Mum.

But actually it was a wicked idea.

'So will you come?'

'Will Jason be there?'

'Yeah, and another tutor. A girl. She can do Latin and Greek and History and stuff. She's quite pretty actually.'

He half smiled. I don't think I've ever really seen him smile. He doesn't do it often.

'Yes,' he said. 'I'll come.'

I attacked my focaccia sandwich, in a much better mood all of a sudden.

'Although,' he went on, 'it is my birthday that week. I suppose Mum forgot.'

Bloody hell, that's awful, I thought. But I said, 'Don't worry. My mother's amazing at birthdays. And Zara and Cloth-head will probably bake you something.'

I decided I'd tell him about the NannyCam another time. Didn't want to put him off coming.


After lunch they told us we'd be having Mock Exams after half term and we had to spend forty-five minutes making a revision schedule. The Nicholson Twins had already done theirs on matching pieces of card with fineliner gel pens and kicked up a massive fuss about doing them again, so they were allowed to go to the library instead. Norville spent so long inserting a table into his Word document and then changing all the fonts for each section and colouring in the background that he still had an empty timetable at the end of the lesson and started hyperventilating.

Ben and I worked on a joint schedule since we were going to be revising together. He opened a new Word document while I wrote ideas down on paper. We came up with some-thing we thought looked quite workable. Five hours a day, and for the second week Jason and Rebecca would be there so we scheduled most of the Latin and Greek and Science for then. Jason can kind of do everything, but I think his PhD is in . . . now what is it again? Conversational Biology? Is that even a thing? I forget.

## Saturday 18th October

Mum and Dad are making a big effort to act like nothing ever happened, regarding my brief flirtation with self-mutilation (as they see it) or symbolic tribal body art (as I do). Yesterday after school I saw the repulsive physio woman and she said I could take my sling off, which was a massive relief. When your arm's in a sling *everything*'s a hassle. You have to move slower. Doors swing in your face and you have to catch them with your shoulder because your other arm is carrying all your stuff. You can't push people so easily. Most frustrating of all is missing Sport. There's something indescribably painful about standing by the sidelines watching the Nicholson Twins fall over each other and cry because they have migraines when I should be there, chasing them down the pitch. It's like being outside a bakery that hasn't opened yet and really, *really* wanting one of those apple-turnover things. I'm still not allowed to do anything like Rugby, but I'm sure they'll let me play again after half term.

So, anyway, my parents have decided that I've been punished enough by their disappointment or whatever and now are behaving as normal. Supper tonight was fillets of sea bass with steamed green vegetables and buckwheat noodles. Disgusting. I poured so much soy sauce over every-thing that it all just tasted like salt and then I needed sugar as if my life depended on it. It felt like I'd swallowed a tidal wave. I went to the larder, which has colour-coded baskets stacked with treats, and I had three snack packs of Oreo cookies and five strawberry shoelaces and some yogurt-coated cranberries as well, because once you start eating those things you can't stop.

'Zara, you must finish all your fish. It's good for your brain,' Mum was saying.

'Yes, baby, you're looking a little bit peaky,' said Dad.

'Well, she's lost some weight which is really a good thing, but you absolutely must get all your nutrients, Za,' said Mum, switching awkwardly from the third person singular to the second person singular and indicating the untouched noodles on Zara's plate.

Zara was smiling at them blandly. Under the table, though, I could see her ripping her paper napkin to shreds. I recognised the look on her face. It's a look that I do some-times too, when I don't want my parents to know what I'm thinking. The thing about Zara is that mostly she'll do what she's told. On Wednesday morning I found 28 things begin-ning with *c* neatly stacked in the White Company laundry basket outside my room. Four pairs of Christian Lacroix earrings, one bottle of Cristal champagne, ten Crayola crayons, a family of moth-eaten toy chipmunks, some Colgate toothpaste and an assortment of chocolate and crisps which I devoured before breakfast. What's vaguely interesting is that she's not doing exactly what my parents are telling her to any more. They can say this stuff about vitamins and nutrients and five-a-day, and she'll just hide her food under her fork and knife. Maybe she's growing some sort of spine.

After supper I showed Mum and Dad the revision time-table that Ben and I had made and they were both ecstatic. Mum photocopied it four times so there was one for the kitchen corkboard and one each for Jason and Rebecca and one to take down to the country house.

'Ben's such a good influence,' I heard Mum saying. 'It's a shame they're not applying to the same school, but I gather the Scholarship provision is very similar.'

Good influence. Ha! She should see his tattoo.

And then they made one with Zara. Comprehension, Composition, Vocab-building, VR, NVR, Fractions, Decimals, Times Tables.

Of course they did.

# BEN

Dad comes to the door on the third ring of the bell, rubbing his eyes, his hair sticking up like unmown grass. I used to have a key, but Dad locked himself out a few months ago and cabbed up to Kensal Rise to borrow mine and I haven't got it back yet.

'Fell asleep in the garden,' he says ruefully. 'Had lunch in Soho. Came back and went out like a light. Christ Almighty. I thought it was Thursday today.'

'It is Thursday.'

He gives me a proper Dad-hug. He's much better at hugs than Mum. Every time he hugs me, I feel the waves of *sorry, sorry* coming off him. He will never stop being sorry about the cricket bat. But I'm sorry too, because sometimes I think if it hadn't happened my parents would still be together.

'Is it OK, me being here?' I say. 'I'm not due until tomorrow.'

'Of course. You're always welcome.' Dad smells of damp grass, salt, something sweet and pungent. His hand rests against the side of my head, a protective gesture he's done for years.

The landline rings and I know it's Mum.

'Let the machine pick up,' I say curtly. 'I'll text her, let her know I'm here.'

So he does. I spread my revision out on the beaten-up oak table. It's Maths tomorrow. English next week. Dad tells me he can help with poetry and short stories.

'Ted Hughes,' he says. '"The Rain Horse". I remember reading this when it first came out. I was a little older than you are now. It made me pathologically afraid of country walks.' He laughs, peering at where I've highlighted words, underlined things.

I tell him it's too obvious the horse is a figment of the man's imagination. I'd prefer it to be more ambiguous. The strange black horse that roams around, tormenting the man for forgetting about this isolated farmland – it seems so . . . surreal. Not horse-like.

'Don't you think it's real *because* he believes in it though?' says Dad.

I shrug. 'Maybe.'

When it's getting on for 9 p.m. Dad begins assembling dinner. He's a random, haphazard cook. When I was little he'd make sculptures for me out of toast, ice-cream puddings with faces splodged onto them in almonds and chocolate sauce. The faces used to scare me a bit, but I ate them out of politeness. Today's ingredients, unearthed from the back of the fridge: feta cheese, green olives, red peppers, black-edged mint and half a pomegranate. Dad decides to make a rice salad. He puts the radio on, gives me a knife and a couple of peppers; for a while the kitchen is filled with vintage rock and roll and chopping and slicing, and Dad opening and shutting the fridge. And I feel something slip a bit inside me, like I've been holding on to something, clenched in my chest, and I'm finally allowing it to give. I almost feel . . . calm.

Then I remember that Jason is dead.

The rice, when we open the jar, is seething with weevils. Tiny insects that writhe, rice-like, causing the surface to shift so subtly that for a moment I think it's the Otherlife, wriggling its way into the dry goods. Dad roars with laughter and rings for pizza.

We eat in the sitting room at the tiny fold-out table, while the TV flickers on mute in the background. The room is crammed with falling-apart books, woven rugs hanging on the walls, wooden carvings of things Dad's found on his travels or in antiques markets.

'So, they're going well then, are they?' says Dad, a bit awkwardly. 'The exams, I mean. *Aeneid* book twelve and $E=mc^2$ and all that.'

I dropped Latin as soon as I could, but he never seems to remember that.

'Fine, I guess,' I say. 'I need to get A stars though.'

Dad pours himself a tumbler of water. I'm drinking apple and raspberry juice, which he buys if he remembers, because he knows I like it.

'I suppose you've been through it all before. When was it, three years ago? When you did Scholarship?'

I nod. 'It felt more intense then.'

It may have been more intense when I was thirteen, but I'm just not as clever now. I've addled my brain. It's tired, like a machine that needs servicing. I'm tired. What's the same is the expectation. The desire for me to do well. It's a desire that's so strong you can properly see and taste it: a thick, amber, oily desire that leaks from the bricks at school. Infusing the membranes. Bewitching the parents.

'Ben. What's the matter?'

'What d'you mean?'

'Well, you show up here out of the blue. You're white and shaking. You've been on autopilot since you got here, and I may be a terrible father but I'm perfectly aware that something's up. So why don't you tell me? Is it something to do with your mother?'

I start to cry. It feels awful and quite good at the same time, and then awful again because I don't want to feel good. I don't want to feel anything. My head aches, and there's an exam tomorrow, and Mum's a liar, and the Otherlife keeps coming and going and it's been gone for so long that it doesn't make any sense that it's here now, and Jason is . . . Jason is dead.

*Jason is dead.*

Dad just lets me cry, his hand with its funny signet ring

that he never takes off resting lightly on my arm. He doesn't speak.

Eventually I do.

'I didn't know,' I say carefully, 'that Jason died. You remember Jason, right? My tutor.'

His phone squirms on the table.

'Dad? Did you know?'

'Who told you he was dead, Ben?'

'I wanted to get in touch with him. I didn't know how. I ended up calling Imperial College. They told me.'

Dad pours himself another glass of water. 'I suppose you would have found out eventually.'

A mosaic of small memories of Jason begins to form in my head, like goldfish rising to the surface of a pond. His beard: always midway between patchy stubble and a triangular goatee. *I don't like my chin*, he'd once told me, when I asked him about his obsession with facial hair. His Rotring pen poised like a surgical tool in one hand, while the other played a scale on the desk, thumb to little finger and back again. His voice, ash-grey from smoking and coffee and long hours of study, telling me always, *Take your time, Ben. No rush.*

'How long have you known, Dad?'

His hand twitches reflexively, just touches the edge of his phone. I reach out and move it away.

'A while, I suppose. A few . . . a few months.'

'But Mum says she found out a couple of *weeks* ago.'

This is a lie, but I've learned from professionals. It's the right thing to do. It catches him out, and I watch his face collapse, as if the structural supports, spillikin-thin, have given way, taking his skin down with them. He couldn't possibly know anything related to my life, school, the world of revision and tutors and certificates, before Mum. It's as impossible as dinosaurs on Mars.

'Ben,' he snaps, 'sometimes you're not told things for your own good. Have you never considered that possibility?'

'She lied to me. And you're lying too.'

'We just emphatically couldn't tell you at the time. Maud was worried about your exams. She was so desperate for you to pass them—'

'Which exams? My GCSEs?'

'No,' he says. 'Your Scholarship exams.'

The room has too many details in it suddenly. Too many books, haphazardly stuffed onto slanting shelves. Too much red, too much blue. The carpet swirls and heaves and buckles.

'You're saying Jason died before I took Scholarship? That was in May 2009! That's *three years ago!*'

His phone beeps again, urgently. Dad is starting to get that helpless look, the one he used to get in airport queues, busy galleries.

'I don't know how to do this,' he mutters to himself, emptying his glass in one quick swallow. 'She won't want me to say anything.'

'When did he die? When exactly?' I say, the skin around my nose and mouth blistering, seizing up.

'He died at Duvalle Hall, Ben. Hobie's house. That November. The night of the fireworks.'

The room finally stops its evil merry-go-round spinning complete with headless horses and flashing strobes, and I say, 'OK. Just tell me whatever you know. Tell me everything.'

It's funny. I know that I was there for a week, during half term, revising with Hobie. I remember, vaguely, parts of Duvalle Hall – the airing cupboard on the landing, for some reason. A patchwork quilt pinned to a wall. A bridge over a lake. I know my parents were there. My mother was a house guest, and my father turned up unexpectedly. But so much of that week I just don't remember at all. People say, sometimes, when they cannot remember, that things are a *complete blank*, but that is not the way I'd describe it. A *complete dark* would be more appropriate.

Dad leans back in his chair, bringing his glass to rest softly against his chest in contemplation.

'I came to Duvalle Hall, Ben, because I wanted to see you. I'd missed your birthday, and I knew where you were.'

'So . . . you were only pretending you turned up by mistake.'

'Your mother wouldn't let me see you! You may have forgotten, Ben, but as soon as she found out about Marti she wouldn't let me within a hundred metres of you.'

I frown.

'Is that true?' I say.

'I swear to Almighty God. Ask Maud.'

'She never told me that. I thought you just vanished.'

'She was incredibly angry with me, Ben. For leaving and being generally useless, the good-for-nothing waste of space that I indisputably am. It's only been in the last year or so that she's let you come to stay with me. The timing was bad. The divorce, her losing her job . . .'

'Because of the financial crisis, right? The firm downsized.'

'Actually, no. She was in a hearing and lost her temper with another solicitor. She slapped him. They had to restrain her.'

I never knew that. Thinking about Mum though, it kind of makes sense.

'You were in bed,' he goes on. 'Maud was spitting with rage . . . there was no reason for me to stay. But the Duvalles insisted, and I was starving hungry, I remember. I avoided Maud's eye and talked mostly to the girl tutor; what was her name?'

'Rebecca.'

'Ah yes. Rebecca. The little girl was there too. Hobie was holding court, telling some outrageous anecdote about a chap called Bilbo—'

'Frodo,' I say, my eyelids hot.

'Frodo – yes. Dinner was spectacular. Some kind of casseroled beef, creamy potatoes. A cheeseboard. Pudding of some kind. I had quite a lot to drink, out of nerves more than anything else, and I'm fairly sure the room was spinning a little by the end of dinner. The walls of the dining room were a dark plum colour and hung with tapestries, and all along the table were silver bowls of pine cones and guttering candles.'

He's doing his writer thing, adding unnecessary amounts of description, but I don't want to interrupt him.

'It all became rather Gothic and haunted after a while, and I remember starting to feel a strange sense of dread, as if something terrible was going to happen. After dinner we all put our coats and boots on and went out onto the lawn and watched the fireworks. It seemed horribly lavish for just a few people, but I suppose that's what they were used to. There were more drinks: some mulled wine or cider, even champagne. Ike kept opening bottles, doing a kind of Lord of the Manor act. And then your mother dug me in the ribs and said wasn't it time I went home before I embarrassed myself. So I took the hint and wandered back to the Braithwaites' cottage.

'I actually phoned Maud the following evening, to apologise for turning up the way I did. And to see how you were. That's when she told me that Jason had been found, dead, in the rhododendrons or the roses or somewhere, early that morning. I wasn't to tell you.'

'But I was still there in the morning!'

'She drove you home straight away, before anyone could tell you. Remember, you really weren't well at all. What did you have? Pneumonia, or bronchitis, no?'

'Pneumonia,' I say. I'd forgotten about it entirely too. Now I remember. I was in bed for four weeks; there was even a suggestion of hospital at one point. I missed the November mocks, not that I cared. For various reasons, exams were the last thing I wanted to think about. I was barely capable of thinking in any case. Being so ill was almost a relief in some ways. For months I felt a jagged scrap of scar tissue in one of my lungs. I remember the lengths I went to – the fixed obsession I developed with staying in my pyjamas, with bathing on my own, even when I was coughing so hard I could hardly breathe – so that my mother didn't see my tattoo. By Christmas I was almost better, but I remained, I guess, for the rest of my time at Cottesmore House, in that curious, cotton-wool, invalid state, where words hover unheard in the air and nothing seems particularly real. Even the Otherlife took on a faded, patchy quality. In fact – and I can't believe I'm only remembering this now, but then, how easy is it to remember the point of forgetting? – I think perhaps that by the New Year the Otherlife had pretty much vanished completely. I papered my room with Late Greats, and I began to worship them instead. From one set of Gods to another.

'I believe the police were quite annoyed about Maud taking you away like that,' says Dad. 'She had to go back later in the week to talk to them.'

At his mention of police, I remember something else that I'd forgotten, somehow, until this moment.

'They came to see me in London,' I say slowly. 'When I was better. But they didn't say that Jason was dead. Mum must have asked them not to. They just wanted to know . . . they wanted to know what he was like as a tutor, if I'd got on well with him, if I thought Hobie liked him. That kind of thing. I didn't understand why they were asking me questions about Jason. I thought . . . I suppose I thought they were asking me more about Hobie, considering . . .'

But I can't quite finish what I'm trying to say.

Dad begins to clear our plates, with hands that are not quite steady.

'How did Jason die?' I ask. 'Didn't they do an autopsy?'

'I imagine they must have done, but I never heard what they found.'

'Isn't that . . . isn't that a bit strange?'

Dad pauses, a plate in each hand.

'I've always thought,' he says slowly, 'that it was something we weren't meant to find out. Something – I don't know – something that the Duvalles would have considered a scandal of sorts. They both sit on the boards of various organisations, some political, some cultural. You know.'

'I don't have a clue what you're talking about, Dad.'

'I mean that they're a prominent family. They couldn't have afforded to have a suspicious death on their doorstep, could they?'

'Suspicious *how?*'

'Well, Ben, come on. Jason was a young man, a student.

He looked . . . vaguely alternative, with that goatee and so forth. He was rather emaciated. I've always been absolutely sure that Jason took an overdose of something or other.'

'That is not possible,' I say, fighting to articulate the words. My breath comes quick and uneven; my hand aches to retrieve my painkiller from my pocket. Dad is wrong. He is completely wrong. He's doing what he always does, which is to take some small scrap of truth and embroider it, make up something many-coloured and brash and shouty. Something fictitious.

He pats me clumsily on the shoulder. 'Look, Ben,' he says, 'it's a sad reality that more people are grappling with addictions than we know about.'

Then he walks into the kitchen, where the radio is still blaring away. While he's out of the room I quickly tip a pill into my palm and swallow it. In my haste, I drink from his glass, not mine. I nearly spit it out in surprise.

It's not water in Dad's glass.

It's neat vodka.

I freeze as he comes back with a plate of truffles. As though he's caught me, when actually it's the other way round.

'Someone gave me these. They're wheat-free, or dairy-free, or something. Try one,' he says. 'It'll cheer you up; chocolate always does.'

'Dad,' I say, and it comes out sounding more accusatory than I meant it to, 'I thought you'd stopped drinking.'

His eyes dart sideways, a swift flicker that I only notice because I'm expecting it. It means he's about to tell a lie.

'I have. More or less.'

'You've got vodka in the water jug.'

'Look, Ben,' he says, 'I know you've got a lot of revision and exam stress and the like, and this must all have come as a terrible shock to you, but I wish you wouldn't waltz over here and give *me* a hard time. I told you what you wanted to know, didn't I?'

He gets up and hunts for the remote, un-mutes the TV and makes a show of going through every channel. A jarring sequence of sound-snippets crowd the room: newsreaders, weather girls, detectives. He sits in the armchair, the twin of the one we've still got in Kensal Rise. They looked better as a pair.

I make up the bed in the spare room, digging around in the airing cupboard for clean sheets. There's no bulb in the bedside lamp, so I leave the overhead one on. I sit on the bed, next to the radiator, which is turned up far too high for May. Dad's socks are drying on it, tragic-looking grey-white things, unravelling at the ends. I'm not unwelcome here, but I never feel totally at home.

A knock.

'Come in,' I mutter.

Dad is bringing me a replacement light bulb.

'Forgot. Sorry. I know you need the light on,' he says.

He sits down on the bed, like I'm in hospital and he's been allowed into the ward for a visit. He has a tongue-tied, tactful look about him.

'Ben,' he says, 'I'm sorry we didn't tell you the truth. To say there was never a good time feels like a poor excuse.'

'There is no excuse.'

'But you have to admit that, given the circumstances . . . I'm sure your mother meant to tell you. But, well, after everything else that was going on at the time, don't you think it's understandable that she tried to keep you from becoming too distressed? You were very ill, besides.'

There's nothing to say to that.

'Is there anything you would like to talk about, Ben? Because I'm here for you, you know that. We both are. Or if you ever want to go and see Hobie. You know I'd come with you. If you wanted.'

There's nothing to say to that either. I do not want to see Hobie. I used to, at first, but . . . it was just too difficult. I did go, but only once, or perhaps twice. I remember I went on my own, shunning my mother's attempts to drive me. I stayed no more than a quarter of an hour or so each time, hating each minute.

For a while my father and I sit in silence.

'You're wrong about Jason,' I say. 'He wasn't a drug addict. He worked with children. He was . . . *responsible*.'

But Dad doesn't reply to this. Perhaps he is thinking about something else.

'Dad,' I say, 'what happened to Marti? Why did she leave?'

He looks taken aback.

'My nanny,' I say deliberately. 'The one you disappeared with. The one you were going to marry.'

'Yes, yes,' says Dad. He gets up and ruffles my hair. 'You'd best get some sleep. Your mother's left three messages about your exam in the morning.'

'But why did Marti leave, Dad?'

He turns off the overhead light, becomes a black silhouette against the doorframe.

'She left,' he says quietly, 'because she knew I still loved Maud.'

And this, oddly, doesn't sound like fiction. It sounds like truth.

Before I go to sleep I stand at the window, just as I would at Mum's house. The forget-me-not curtains Dad bought on eBay do not fit the frame, because he didn't know how to measure up properly. The wood of the sill is rotten: if I clawed at it, I'd be able to rip it away with my hands. I've taken more painkillers today than I have all week: very bad news, especially with maths tomorrow. The narrow Battersea street is lamplit and silent; a cat crosses the road, its tail waving lazily, as if to acknowledge ownership of the night.

I close my eyes. I listen for hidden sounds: an owl, a lone car.

When I open them, he is there.

Haloed by the streetlamp, he stands in a long dark coat. His hair is golden, white-gold on yellow-gold. The threads of light are honey-coloured and slow-moving. I lean out of the window and call to him.

'Baldr!'

He raises a hand in a half-wave. He smiles: a kind of soft rearrangement of the currents of light in his face. I know that wry, almost-embarrassed smile. I'd know it anywhere. He doesn't speak, but I can hear him: *Everything in your own time, Ben. No rush.*

'*Jason* . . .'

And I'm out of the room and down the stairs before I've had time to think, pelting down Dad's boot-cluttered hallway, to throw myself into his arms and tell him it'll be OK. *I will find out what happened, Jason, I promise.* The cat is washing its face on a jasmine-draped fence over the road, pausing only momentarily to look at me in surprise as I hurl myself at the gate.

'Jason!' I yell, holding my hands out as if there are threads of gold still floating in the aura of the streetlamp. 'Jason!'

But he's gone, he's gone, he's gone.

### Hermódr Visits Hel
### By Ben Holloway
### 22/10/2008

The grief of the Gods was terrible, and Odin was saddest of all, for he knew Baldr's death foretold their doom. It was the first of the dark prophecies to be fulfilled. Now the Gods had no choice but to realise that, after Loki's cruel trick with the mistletoe, their world must inevitably come to an end. Ragnarok, the day of reckoning, would be upon them soon.

Frigg longed for someone to ride to the kingdom of death to bring Baldr back, and Hermódr, another of Odin's sons, offered to make the journey. He rode Sleipnir, Odin's eight-legged horse. As he approached the bridge, he saw Heimdallr, the crooked-backed watchman. There he sat, with the rain trickling down his face, gazing into the distance. Hermódr crossed the bridge of glowing colours and went down, down, down to the gates of Hel.

He cantered through the iron gates and plunged into the bleak mists of Hel's kingdom. There he found Baldr, sitting on a high chair, with Hel, Loki's daughter, at his side. Baldr's face was white and his eyes were dull.

'Release my brother,' said Hermódr.

'I am willing,' said Hel, 'on condition that every living thing weeps for him.'

Hermódr rode back to Asgard, bearing this news.

'Cry, sob, weep for Baldr! Weep, weep, weep for him!'

His call echoed around the woods and mountains, towns and valleys. And every living thing did indeed shed tears for their dear Baldr: the birds and beasts, the men and women, even the silver and gold that lived in the earth.

All wept, except one.

There was a giantess who dwelt in a cave. She refused to weep for Baldr. 'Alive or dead,' she said, 'I've no use for Odin's son. He's nothing to me. Let Hel keep him.'

The Gods, knowing that the giantess was none other than Loki in disguise, were furious. Loki fled and built himself a hut with four lookouts, where he thought he would be safe.

# HOBIE'S DIARY

Sunday 19th October 2008

I wasn't allowed to do Saturday Football Club. I ranted at Clothilde but she was completely inflexible: Mum had said under no circumstances could I go until the physio woman said it was OK. I couldn't confront Mum because she'd gone to a wedding at Chelsea Town Hall. Za and I both needed to study, she said. I think she wanted to get drunk. I hate weddings anyway. You have to sing hymns and then sit at the children's table at dinner which they call breakfast (how stupid can you get?) and drink sparkling fruit juice and Mum makes me put gel in my hair. Zara loves it all, of course. Flowers and bridesmaids and people crying into Kleenex and then throwing confetti.

Since there wasn't anything else for me to do yesterday apart from more tedious work (English *in*comprehensions and an essay about China's economic future), I thought I might as well put my plan into action. Clothilde was doing some ironing and the cleaner was faffing about somewhere and I could hear Zara watching a repeat of *X Factor* in the sitting room, warbling a tuneless rendition of some American pop song that she'd presumably choose as her Fantasy Audition Piece.

The time was nigh.

I went into Mum and Dad's room, which is on the floor below ours. Everything in it is cream or beige or a really wet-looking bluey-greeny colour. There are window seats with lots of cushions that never get sat on and an antique carpet called an Isfahan. I know what it's called because I once left a red felt-tip pen on it with no lid, and was in big trouble. They used to have a wall-mounted flatscreen television, but then this feng shui man came and said it would disturb the *precious* Qi of the bedroom so they took it down. I asked if I could have it but they said no. The bed is always made. There is a chaise longue, which is French for long chair.

Mum's dressing room is in a little room off the bedroom. It is all wood, even the ceiling, really polished reddish brown wood, a bit like in the cabins on the yacht. The shoes are arranged by colour on long shelves at one end. Some I have never seen Mum wear. The hats are in hatboxes. She was wearing one today that looked like somebody ate some feathers and then sicked them up onto a ball of wire netting. The jumpers and scarves and tops are in drawers that slide out completely noiselessly. There are lavender sachets hanging everywhere, like Christmas-tree decorations. And when you open the sliding doors, that's where the dresses are. Some of them are in bags.

The problem was, what to take.

In the end I picked four dresses off the rails and two handbags, which were in an organised *testudo* like a Roman battle formation. One was black and one was cream.

The dresses looked like summer ones, which I thought Mum wouldn't miss immediately – although part of me sort of wanted her to realise they were gone and wonder why. I chose a frothy orange one by Alice Somebody and a hideous flowery one by Matthew Something and a black leather one (ugh, imagine Mum wearing it!) and another black one with no sleeves. I put everything in a bin bag which I'd had some difficulty locating because I'd never had to look under the sink before.

I picked up the spare key from the suede thing in the hall where Dad leaves business cards and foreign coins and loose change (which I pillage for cigarette money), waited till the roar of the hoover was hovering just overhead and left the house.

I always get away with it when I try stuff like this. Partly I think it comes down to sort of *assuming* that I'm going to. It's like those silly confidence-building exercises Mr White and Miss Atkins get us to do sometimes. I've got loads of confidence. Zara's the reverse: she assumes she can't do things, so she messes them up. Loki got away with *everything*. Well, almost everything. Recently I've been reading about how the Gods caught him after Baldr died.

Loki knew that in order to hide from the Gods he would have to disguise himself again, so he experimented with lots of different shapes and eventually decided to change himself into a salmon. Then he wove himself a net out of some stiff grasses, but seeing that it would be able to catch fish (so why did he do it in the first place? What a *retard*!) he hastily threw it into the fire. He looked out of the window and saw the Gods were approaching, so he turned into a salmon and leaped into the river.

The Gods came to the hut and found no sign of Loki. But Kvasir, who was very wise, looked into the ashes of the fire and saw the remains of the net that Loki had burnt there.

'Let us use this as our model and construct another net for ourselves,' he said to the other Gods.

So they made a net, using Loki's as a pattern, and they threw it into the river. Loki saw it, and managed to leap over it, but Thor caught him by the tail in midair.

The Gods took Loki to a dark cave where they set three slabs of stone in the ground. To bind him they used the intestines of one of Loki's sons, which turned to iron. When Loki was safely bound they placed a serpent at his head, and the poisonous venom dripped onto his face. Loki's faithful wife, Sigyn, held a bowl beneath the serpent to catch the drips, but each time she went to empty the bowl the poison would fall again on Loki's face. The whole earth shook with his struggles. And Loki stayed there, until Ragnarok.

Pretty harsh.


There's a whole bunch of shops near Notting Hill Gate and some of them are Exchange places where you can take in CDs, books, clothes etc and swap them for cash. Or so it's advertised. They smell of old sweat, like Jason's vile holey jumpers, and I've never been in. But I've walked past enough times because they're on the way to and from school. There was a man selling the *Big Issue* outside a newsagent's and I wondered what the *Big Issue* actually was. I didn't buy one though.

I went into the shop that said 'WOMAN' in big white letters. Inside there were rails and rails and rails of fur coats and pouffy ballerina dresses on hangers and glittery belts descending from the ceiling like snakes and glass cases full of shoes and jewellery. Everything had big labels on with prices that had been crossed out and rewritten to make it look like the shop was full of bargains. I said I wanted to exchange some clothes, and they made me go downstairs to a basement with a really low ceiling stuffed with even more rails of clothes, including vests and faded jeans and things I couldn't imagine wanting to buy if you knew someone else had worn them first.

There was a counter at one end with two women sitting behind it. They had loads of bags full of clothes, and they were sorting through them and holding them up and checking the seams and putting those white plastic things on them so they couldn't be stolen. As if anyone would want to!

'Can I help you?' said one of them. She had a lot of piercings in one ear.

The other one was staring at me strangely.

'Yes, please. My mother asked me to bring all these dresses and bags in.'

'Let's have a look,' said the first one, only it sounded more like *lessavvalook*, all one word.

She tipped everything out onto the counter and they both pawed at the dresses, turning the necks out so they could see the labels.

'Are you sure your mother doesn't want these?' said the second one.

'She's got loads of others,' I said confidently. 'And these ones are –' what was that expression? – 'last season.'

'Nah, mate,' said the first one, but she was more talking to the second one than to me. 'This one here's new season. And this one.'

'Oh, well, if you don't want them . . .' I said.

But I knew they would. They went into a little huddle and then did lots of adding and subtracting incredibly slowly, but I suppose if they were good at Maths they wouldn't be working in this rubbish-looking shop and then the first one said:

'We can do you £160 cash or £200 exchange for the lot.'

I asked for the cash of course, but just as I was leaving I noticed this enormous clown suit, all white with balloon sleeves and big black pompoms down the front, and I thought I might get it for Zara as a joke. So in the end I left with £135.

I never actually have any money. I have lots of things like computer games and a MacBook Pro and designer clothes, and of course stuff like my grandfather's model ship collection and a cricket bat signed by Kevin Pietersen. And if I ask for something I usually get it, and if it's really big then maybe I have to wait until my birthday or Christmas which are conveniently nearly six months apart so I never have to wait longer than that. But I never have any cash on me and I don't have a bank card. This annoys me. It's one rule of Mum and Dad's I've never managed to get around. Until now. I crossed the road and went into Pret and bought a Super Club sandwich and a packet of crisps and then crossed back again, thinking I needed to hurry up because Clothilde would absolutely call the police if she realised I was out of the house.

I walked down Pembridge Crescent, thinking it was where Archie lives and maybe I could put a dog turd through his letterbox as I was passing, to make his day a little more interesting. And just as I was thinking this, I saw a dog, not on a lead, sort of pottering around on the pavement in front of me. It was small and white and annoying-looking with a brown patch over one eye and another near its tail. I wondered whether I could steal it and take it into one of those grotty pubs where the same old men sit outside drinking Guinness and smoking, day in, day out, and sell it. I'd read in the *Daily Mail* about people selling dogs in pubs. I could say my mother didn't want it. I could start a whole business, selling things my mother didn't want. But I probably had enough money now, and anyway I couldn't think who'd want such a weaselly, unattractive dog. Just then a gate opened and a woman came rushing out, and she scooped up the dog and practically snogged it, saying things like, 'Oh darling Percy, naughty Daddy left the door open,' and this show of affection was putting me off my sandwich. And she put it down and it pissed on her shoe.

I turned left down Chepstow Villas and then walked nearly the whole length of Portobello Road, which was seething with people buying street signs that said *Portobello Road W11* and bits of lace and silver candlestick holders. The houses are quite pretty and it looks like a film, but you have to walk at a snail's pace, like when everyone's leaving Assembly and the hall is massively congested with Year 4s and 5s. I passed the Hummingbird cupcake shop, and was debating popping in for a Red Velvet when I saw this old grey-haired man standing behind a table of flasks and lighters, and I got a *feeling* like he'd have something I wanted to buy. Sure enough, after a spell of rummaging I unearthed a dull silver lighter with a wolf emblazoned on it in relief. It was only a fiver so I bought it immediately. It was a Sign.

As I walked I tried to do what Ben does, and look on the edges of things. I stared at the side of the Falafel King van, tried to force the air to move, the particles to start glinting or whatever he says they do. I waited for the Gods to show up. It made me a bit dizzy. Then I crashed into a Japanese tourist.

I couldn't quite remember where the tattoo place was,

but I knew I'd seen one somewhere, among all the shops selling identical-looking flowery dresses and the fruit stalls and that place with loads of bars of soap that you can smell from across the street. When I eventually found it I marched in with my envelope of cash and went straight up to the man at the counter, shoved my picture of Hati the wolf under his nose and said, 'One tattoo, like this picture, please.'

This man was literally a map of ink. His arms were covered in vines and there was a headstone on his shoulder with some crosses and dates on it and RIP which is from the Latin *requiescat in pace* (and in Latin you're supposed to put the verb at the end, so how come it's at the beginning there?) and even his hands had tattoos on them. He was bald and there were three little stars under his right eye.

He smiled at me. His teeth were very white and square.

'I'm, uh, going to need to see some ID.'

'I don't have any ID and I'm in a hurry,' I said. 'Can't we just get on with it? I don't mind paying extra.'

He laughed.

'Sorry, kid, but you don't look a day over eleven.'

'I'm *twelve*,' I said angrily.

'Yes, well, according to UK law, you need to be 18 to get a tattoo, or 16 with parental consent. Come back in a few years.'

Why does everyone have to follow the rules the whole bloody time? But I could see there was no point arguing with him.

## HOBIE'S DIARY

My iPhone informed me that I had thirteen missed calls. By the time I rang Clothilde back she was completely hysterical. That word comes from the Latin for *womb* so it's appropriate that women are always being it. I managed to get her to believe that I'd been called by school to go in and help them with an Open Day at the last minute and had got a lift with Simon, and even though it was unlikely that Mum would buy this story, it got me temporarily off the hook. I walked home because buses are really dirty, and I bought another Super Club sandwich on the way and ate it, even though I wasn't really hungry.

# BEN

Mum calls seven times over the weekend, trying to get me to go home. We assure her that I am fine, I am fed and watered, I am revising, that I went to my exam on Friday and that it went OK. We are unreliable in this regard. I am watered and fed – according to the best of Dad's intentions – but I am barely revising, and I am not fine.

I really am not fine.

I sit in Dad's garden, with *The Five Stages of Grief* on my lap. One good thing about my father: he always has a book for every occasion, and if he doesn't, he'll go out and borrow one. I feel like an invalid. Solomon calls, with his unerring instinct for distress, and then arrives on Saturday afternoon with St John's wort and spirulina and vitamin C, all in fancy dark-glass bottles, and a bunch of tulips from M&S.

I haven't slept properly for days, and my nights have been peppered with nightwalking – including an uncomfortable moment when I woke up at a petrol station, propped up against a diesel pump, and another when I found myself in the middle of Brompton Cemetery, having somehow climbed over the wall – and the filaments of horrifying dreams. Omitting, for now, the story of the Otherlife, which will be too long and too strange in the telling, I sit with my eyes closed and explain to Solomon everything I've found out about Jason. He listens with exceptional patience, never interrupting. At the end he breathes out in a single, solid sigh.

'Ben, you poor old suffering thing,' he says, patting down Dad's IKEA garden chairs with antibacterial wipes. 'That's quite a conspiracy, not to tell you.'

'They wanted me to get my Scholarship,' I say darkly, thinking about that phone call from school (*We are delighted to offer your son a Major Scholarship – he's done exceptionally well across the board, Mrs Holloway*), and how, after I'd called Dad, the first person I'd wanted to get in touch with was Jason. I hadn't seen him for many months, but the frenzy of Scholarship preparation had been so all-consuming that I bought without particularly questioning it the statement that Jason had too much work with his PhD to come and tutor me, and besides, all the hard work – that mad week of revision at Duvalle Hall – had now been done. But when my result came through – I'd done the best in the class, apart from Frodo and one of the Nicholson Twins who had made a late bid for his own identity by massively outscoring his brother – I demanded to talk to Jason, no matter how busy he was. But Mum's BlackBerry had deleted half of her contacts in some mysterious malfunction, so in the end I wrote a postcard instead, and posted it myself. *Dear Jason, I got a Scholarship!! Thank you so much for all your hard work.*

*You are awesome. Ben.* My mother wrote a postscript herself, in her lawyerly scribble. My mother is a woman who can bring herself in cold conscience to write a note to a dead person. That she managed to do this still astonishes me.

'*You* didn't know, did you?' I ask, suddenly.

'Me? Of course not! Why would you think that?'

'I think that Frodo knew,' I say.

There was something about the way he turned his back to me, his tone of voice when he said, *That Jason.*

'Not a thing,' Solomon replies. 'But there are all kinds of stories that go round about tutors. You hear them from time to time. That marriage that broke up, you know – and the mother ran off with the tutor. People talking about getting off with their tutors, and you never know quite if they're telling the truth. *I* certainly never have. There *was* a story – and it was a very long time ago, now, that I heard it – about a tutor being found dead, outside a house somewhere. Only I got the impression that it was abroad.'

'Oh,' I say. 'OK.'

I'm glad he didn't know. I couldn't bear it if he too was somehow part of this web of collusion. Then again: if he did know, he'd almost certainly have found out the truth. *All* of it. And that's something I need to do, more than ever. If my father thinks Jason took an overdose, there are probably other people who do as well. I know he didn't. He was too sensible, too measured in his approach to things. He was too serious about life, and all the things he wanted to achieve in it. One day, I remember him telling me, he was going to be a professor.

'How are you feeling?' says Solomon.

According to *The Five Stages of Grief*, I'm supposed to feel: fear, anger, bargaining, depression, acceptance. I'm not entirely sure what stage I'm at: drug-fuelled emptiness and mind-fogged paranoia? GCSE-revision-induced traumatic nothingness? There's probably a label; I just don't know what it is.

'I don't know,' I say.

Dad is drinking colourless liquid out of a Tom and Jerry mug in the kitchen. Solomon raised an eyebrow when he arrived: *Is this what I think it is?* I smiled a flat non-smile: *Perhaps.* I'm not sure what stage Dad is at either.

A beetle crawls like a tiny tank across the arm of my chair. I watch it, willing myself to concentrate on the deliberate placing of each foot, on its slow, sure, uninterruptible progress.

'What are you going to do now?' Solomon asks, gently.

It's a good question. What am I going to do?

Hermódr came first, to tell me that someone had died.

Then Frigg appeared, to ask for my help. I can still hear the anguish in her voice, and how the syllables seemed to stretch out into longer notes, discordant and heartbreaking. *Hjálpaðú . . .*

And then, on Thursday night I saw Baldr in the street – faintly, but definitely. He *was* Baldr, but he was also Jason.

The Gods themselves have asked me to find out what happened to Jason. And I have to know, for myself.

'Ben?' says Solomon.

'Find out how Jason died,' I say, tracing my fingers over the ancient wine stains on the old wooden boxes that Dad uses as outdoor tables. 'No one knows, or else no one wants to tell me.'

Finally, on Sunday evening, I run out of boxer shorts and T-shirts and Dad runs out of washing powder, and – not wanting to look at another Domino's delivery box for a while – I take the bus back to Kensal Rise. Mum opens the door; our eyes meet. This is the moment for us to talk, for her to say she's sorry.

She doesn't.

'It was for your own good, Ben,' she says, her hands spread. When are my parents going to understand that cheap clichés about *my own good* and *circumstances* and *finding the right time* are an insult to the intelligence that they claim I possess? I push past her, go up to my room and lie on the bed. My mural watches me. Letting my vision go soft, I stare, and stare, waiting.

Sure enough, slowly, the mural begins to move.

Millimetre by millimetre, the clouds roll in a leisurely way towards the sea. The leaves on the tree float, like feathers, onto the shore, where they disappear into the stones. And now the corpse of Baldr appears, honey-gold, darkening, against the base of the tree. Over in the corner, at the mouth of a rocky cave, fire-red Loki is tied down, furious, squirming beneath incessant drips of poison. Some of the other Gods stand around him, watchful, jittery. They know it is too late. There is nothing they can do, after the death of Baldr, to prevent their world from ending.

I swallow another painkiller, close my eyes and sleep.


Big Days come and go. Sometimes I nightwalk, and sometimes – too exhausted, maybe, to venture outside – I don't. I'm living to the rhythms of my alarm, the announcements on the tube, the giant clock in the exam hall. I have no other biological functions; I feel like an automated puppet, a thing made out of cardboard and basic electronics. I take two more exams, English and physics. English is OK: I bend my head close to the page, coax a thought-flow from my brain down my arm to my pen and just keep writing, writing. Physics is a minefield. I can't remember any of the formulae. I look at the blank spaces, as unfilled in as my stages of grief, and know that my head-state just isn't right for exams.

Mostly I make a point of ignoring my mother. At mealtimes our conversation goes like this:

Her: Have you revised for (fill in blank according to timetable)?

Me: Yep.

Her: Do you want some more (fill in blank according to menu)?

Me: Nope.

And I know I'm being horrible to her, when she's trying to help me do well, like she always does. But I'm just so angry. (This, maybe, is a good sign: I've reached an identifiable stage.) Partly I feel like she doesn't even care that Jason is dead. That he died in this weird, unexplained way. To her, I suspect it was an inconvenience, in more ways than one. It was an event that would have deeply upset me, had she seen fit to let me know about it, and might have affected my exam scores. I wonder sometimes whether Mum has proper feelings at all.

She's like the giantess who wouldn't weep for Baldr.

A sleepy, cloud-covered Saturday. London simmers in a do-nothing haze. I'm lying on the floor, reading my old Free Creative Writing book, hoping I might find some clues: the Gods grieved for Baldr as I am grieving now, but what should I do next?

On my wall I have stuck a picture of Jason, next to the wolf certificate and the picture of me and Hobie. It's beginning to look like a serial killer's shrine, or the desk space of a criminal psychologist. Not for the first time, I wish that I could ask Hobie. He was there, after all, on the night that Jason died. He stayed up for dinner; I didn't. He'd have seen more than me. But I can't ask Hobie. I wish I knew how to reach Jason's family. But if I couldn't find Jason online – and I spent days trawling through Google searches and old Myspace pages, trying everything I could think of – I can't imagine how I'd reach his relations. I don't even know what family he had. I tried calling Imperial College again, but I couldn't get through to the woman I'd spoken to before, and they said it was against their policy to give out any details about their students, living or dead.

So there's no other resource but my brain. What's left of it.

The sides of my vision go soft. I stare at the middle of the page, looking at my twelve-year-old writing. A line stares out at me, somehow bolder and darker than the rest:

Hermódr crossed the bridge of glowing colours and went down, down, down to the gates of Hel.

Hel.

*The Underworld.*

If I didn't take so many painkillers I'm sure I'd have made this connection sooner, but it strikes me, suddenly, that if I'm meant to go to the Underworld, I can actually get there with relative ease. I drop the book and reach for my shoebox of gig flyers, where I rummage around until I find a leaflet for Infernal Damnation 2012. Tonight. At the Underworld in Camden Town.

'I need a break from revision,' I say to Mum as I thunder down the stairs. 'I'm going to this gig in Camden.'

'Taking a break is not a good idea . . .' she begins.

'I'll be back before midnight.'

'You haven't always been back before midnight.'

'Are you saying I'm a liar? You lied to me about Jason for three and a half years, remember?'

Ignoring this, she gives me fifteen quid from the drawer of loose change and tells me to remember my key.

The 31 bus takes forever. I arrive in time to catch the last part of Ctulu and all of Funeral Throne. The Underworld is salty and sour with sweat and spilt beer. People of all ages and sizes jostle and mosh and sway in time to the symphonic, down-tuned soundscapes. One thing I love about metal (good metal) is that so little has changed since its early days, the late 1970s and early 1980s, when the New Wave of British Heavy Metal started sending its dark vibrations into the post-punk community. It makes me feel like I could almost be there, at an early Iron Maiden or Motörhead gig.

I buy a beer, thread my way to the back and lean against the wall, letting the noise consume me. A strobe begins to pulse and I close my eyes: strobes used to do funny things when my eye was bad, and I'm seeing enough unwanted stuff as it is.

When I open my eyes again, Fever Sea are onstage doing their line check, tapping the microphones, plugging in their leads. People are milling about, going to the bar, drifting outside to smoke. I transfer my gaze from the stage to the crowd of black-clad metalheads.

There's a girl directly in front of the stage. Unusually for girls at metal gigs, she's on her own. It makes her stand out exquisitely, like a pine tree on an ice shelf. I squint at her. Her hair hangs down on either side of her face. Her arms sway gently at her sides, but oddly out of time to the music. She looks as if she's waiting for someone. I study the knots of bone at her elbows and wrists. The lights change from murky green to a clearer blue as the band begins to play, and I stare, and stare, and am sure.

That's *Zara*.

Slowly, because you can't really move fast when this kind of music is playing, where the chords are lordly and wallowing and wide-spaced, I nudge and apologise my way through the crowd.

But when I reach the front, she's nowhere to be seen.

I find her outside, leaning against the heavy bar of the fire-escape door. She looks anxious, fiddling with a jewelled iPhone and a pink-strapped watch. She's tall, much taller than I remember, like a plant starved of light. That makes sense: she must be fourteen now. Her hair, which used to hang in crimped, blondish-brown twists, now lies flat against her head, as though it lacks the will to move. Her skin is shadowy and pale. I can almost see through her, she's so thin. She is very beautiful. Or she would be, if she didn't look so ill.

'Excuse me,' I say, and she looks up, her eyes cross-referencing me with memory, with Facebook, with mental snapshots of everyone she knows. 'Are you Zara Duvalle?'

'Yes.'

The sounds of Camden on a Saturday night are turned up too high, like Dad's radiators. The screams of drunken women and police sirens intrude on the silence of her face, the sweetness and seriousness of her expression, as she tries to work out who I am.

'I'm Ben. Ben Holloway.'

She jumps slightly, like she's heard something unexpected. Her eyes take on a pale, frozen glaze. She puts out her hand, a reflex born of years of cocktail parties and social interaction. I shake it, feeling the dryness of her skin, the bolts of her knuckles. As I look into her eyes, the same open-sky blue as Hobie's, it occurs to me that I don't often look properly *at* people. And just at that moment, I feel like she's really looking *at* me too, because her expression changes again, and I see the old Zara. The Zara who would follow me and Hobie wherever we went, begging to be allowed to join in.

She says, 'Oh my God. Ben.'

And smiles.

'Do you often go to metal gigs?' I say. My mouth feels drained of saliva. I don't really know how to make conversation with beautiful girls.

'Sometimes. Once, twice a year, maybe.'

A gaggle of under-dressed women clatters past; they're decked out in devil's horns and five-inch heels, their arms flailing at the air, as if to keep them from falling. The night buzzes with noise. Broken beer bottles and Chinese takeaway boxes gather in the gutter below us, like washed-up sewage.

Zara checks a doorstep for obvious debris and then sits down, carefully. After a little hesitation, I join her.

'I don't much like metal gigs,' she says.

'So why do you go?'

'For Hobie. He can't, so I do, sometimes. It makes me feel . . . I don't know how it makes me feel. I just think he'd like it if I went on his behalf. That sounds stupid.'

'No, it doesn't,' I tell her.

'Do you really listen to this music?'

I nod. 'It's a lot more complex than it sounds.'

'I remember – you once told us about it over breakfast. When Hobie gave you the poster of that Metallica guitarist who died.'

'Bassist,' I say automatically, then wish I wasn't quite so pedantic when it comes to metal.

'My parents think I'm at the theatre,' Zara says, 'but I'm going to have to get back. I have to work.'

We both make a study of the side of a bus, something to do with the Olympics. A sprinter in sunflower yellow, a slogan: *Flow faster with VISA*.

'It's nice to see you,' I say.

'It's strange to see you,' she replies at once, and I remember as well how Zara always had to say what she felt, all the time. She had no emotional filter. The bus pulls away; lurid chip-shop signs glitter in the space it reveals. A motorcyclist pulls up at the traffic light; on his helmet there are wings of red and gold. He turns his head to spit, and I see that he is not human; his face is covered in dense fur as he bares his teeth in a grin. Around him the air hums and quivers.

Blink: he's gone.

I shake my head, gently. I never saw anything quite like this when I was younger and saw the Otherlife. There's something alien about it now. Something I can't put my finger on.

'You know,' I say, 'nobody told me about Jason.'

Immediately she puts her hand out to touch my sleeve.

'Oh, *Ben*,' she says. 'And you really loved him, didn't you? He was your tutor when you were small. He wasn't just Hobie's tutor. He was so great with you both. And he was so kind to me. I was in such a state about the eleven-plus and he just . . . he made it OK if I didn't understand how to convert top-heavy fractions into mixed numbers, and he always drew those little target squares on the wall, with that pen he had . . .'

'A Rotring. It was a Rotring.'

'He was an amazing tutor,' says Zara.

'But . . . how did he die?' I say. 'You must know.'

'I don't . . . I think . . . It was just one of those really sad things. Like Sudden Death Syndrome or something. I was too young at the time for anyone to tell me. I don't know if I asked. That sounds really awful, Ben, I'm sorry. But honestly – I really don't know.'

Although she falters as she says it, tripping delicately over each phrase, it still sounds a little rehearsed to me. Like she's been told to say it, if anyone ever asks her about Jason. Maybe I'm paranoid; maybe I'm mad. But that's how she sounds.

I try again.

'But you don't think . . . I mean, he definitely didn't take an overdose, right? Nobody said that? The police, the medical people . . . ?'

She pauses.

'I never heard anything like that,' she says at last, and I can't be sure if she means it. 'But that weekend . . . it just isn't something we talk about.'

Delicately she picks at the edge of a shell-pink fingernail. Somehow the mood has changed. Zara looks up. A solid, glossy CompuCab hovers beside the kerb.

'I must go,' she says.

She hesitates, as though she can't make up her mind about something. I find myself longing to know whether her hair smells the same as it always used to. (Buttery and sweet, like popcorn.) Then she looks in her bag and takes out a business card, a tiny one with a cartoonish strawberry print on one side and *Zara Elspeth Duvalle* on the other, with an email address and phone number. She holds it out to me.

'You can call me,' she says, 'if you like.'

She climbs into the car, her legs origami-folding beneath

her, and the car drives away, as smooth and silent as a predatory fish.

I stand there watching until it's out of sight. Then I head back inside.

Metal is metal, after all.

# HOBIE'S DIARY

Monday 27th October 2008

It doesn't feel like bloody half term, even though we have two weeks. Ordinarily we'd have gone abroad, somewhere warm where they bring you drinks by an infinity pool. The Maldives maybe, or the Bahamas. It feels monumentally unfair that we're staying in England for the entire time.

Anyway this week I am going to Ben's house every day from ten till four. His mother has a copy of our revision timetable. I suspect there may not be enough food, so I am equipped with the following:

1. 5 sherbet Dip Dabs
2. Three loaves of sliced Malt Loaf
3. 2 bags of Babybels
4. A large tangle of strawberry shoelaces
5. An enormous tin of Melt flakes for hot chocolates

'D'you think they'll have milk or should I bring that too?' I fretted this morning as Clothilde cleaned my shoes. Dad has this thing, which he apparently inherited from his dad (Hobart Duvalle II), about clean shoes on Monday mornings. Whatever.

'I'm sure they will, darling,' said Mum, who had taken a croissant from the basket of pastries and was delicately picking flakes off it in much the same way as gorillas check each other for fleas. She doesn't eat bread products usually, so I assume she was entering into the festival spirit of the school holidays.

Dad put down the bunch of papers he'd been studying, fixed me with an earnest eye and said, 'Hobie, it's great that you're sensitive about your friend not having, ah, access to the same kind of resources that he once did—'

'No, I'm just worried they won't have any milk for my hot chocolates, because apparently his mum goes shopping kind of sporadically. That's all.'

'Listen,' he said sternly, 'from where I'm sitting it's coming across as a little bit sarcastic. Ben's parents have had a difficult time, he and his mother are living in a much smaller house and they can't pay full school fees. It's good that you're aware of that, and that you don't flaunt things that you have in his face. But, Hobie, I'm sure there'll be milk for hot chocolate, OK? You mustn't get carried away. There's a thin line between understanding and mocking.'

I had *no* idea what he was talking about. It could have been in Ancient Peruvian for all the sense I could make of it. As for flaunting things in people's faces, it's one of my favourite occupations. Only Ben and I have far too much to talk about for that to be the case with him.

Just as Clothilde and I were leaving for Ben's house the post arrived and my half-termly report was among the letters.

There was also a thick posh-looking envelope marked *Tibbert and Taylor Consultants*, which must've been my Ed Psych report. Mum put it in the pocket of her robe. Then she opened my school report. Dad and I watched, soundlessly, like someone had paused a DVD.

My grades were a mixture of Bs and Cs for achievement (and a D in Greek – damn you, Miss Atkins!) and 2s and 3s for effort. So, sort of average. Absolutely fine, really, except for one thing. They weren't good enough for Scholarship.

'If we don't see a marked improvement across the spectrum of academic subjects,' Mr White had put at the end, 'we will, unfortunately, have to consider moving Hobie into 8 Middle, where he may feel more at home.'

'Well, Hobes,' said Dad, putting on his overcoat and gloves, 'the ball's in your court now, isn't it?'

I felt sure he'd chosen a sporting image on purpose. Mum smothered me in a hug and said she knew I was going to be trying my hardest over the next two weeks, and then she left to go and visit the venue for her Gala Dinner for the massive children's charity which is on Friday night, same as Halloween. God knows how Mum's any use at these things. I suppose she just puts ribbons around the chairs and fixes bits of paper to clipboards and shouts at the caterers. She's got Zara and a couple of ghostly work-experience girls making up goodie bags today with organic hand cream in them and salted caramels and Manuka honey lip gloss. Two hundred of them. I know because I demanded to be allowed to eat the surplus caramels and Mum, meanly, said no.

Clothilde can't drive because she's pathetically afraid of it, so she took me to Ben's house in a taxi. We went along Ladbroke Grove and round a roundabout and past this massive Sainsbury's and then we were driving along the Harrow Road and turning into a maze of little streets with teeny tiny little houses, almost cottages, mostly covered with creepers and roses and the whole place had a really eerie, empty feel to it, though if Zara'd been there she'd have probably thought the houses were adorable.

Ben's house was about halfway down one of these little labyrinthine streets, with a blue door that needed painting. I got out with my rucksack and my food bag and my laptop and charger and phone charger and a couple of DVDs in case we finished ahead of schedule. At that moment Ben's mother opened the door. I recognised her from plays and concerts and things and of course she looked the same, not noticeably poorer after all. Ben's mother has got dark hair that sort of sits exactly in these long curves like a house plant that drapes its leaves on the floor. She was wearing a black suit and flat shoes and a silky scarf with all these orange and peach triangles printed on it. Pretty hideous. Her skin is too pale for such bright colours. And she was waving and smiling and then Ben appeared behind her looking completely different, smaller somehow in his non-school clothes.

Ben's mother said, 'I hope you don't mind, Hobie, but I'm not going to be able to stay with you boys today. There's a crisis in the office and they're really short-staffed. Ben's got my number and Jovita will be here for most of the morning. If you have any problems, just ring me.'

And then she showed us what was in the fridge and reminded Ben not to leave the lights on in rooms that we weren't using and how to use the gas cooker if we wanted to heat up the New Covent Garden soup.

'Who's Jovita?' I asked Ben.

'The cleaner,' he said.

I don't know my cleaner's name. I've never asked. I guess they could still afford one of those. Maybe not every day though. And it definitely looked like there was milk in the fridge. Which was good because I hadn't had my mid-morning hot chocolate yet. Or my mid-morning snack.

While I embraced the novelty of heating milk up for myself in the microwave and mixing my own paste of sugar and Melt flakes in the bottom of a Mr Men mug, Ben made himself a cup of tea and we discussed the day's activities. Now, like I said, ordinarily I'd have been the first person to dispense with the revision schedule, which looked about as enjoyable as another day with Dr Tibbert, a wasps' nest and a power cut. But I was beginning to concede that I needed to do some actual work.

So we sat like adults at Ben's super-small kitchen table and instead of routinely taking the piss out of the teachers and their monotonous and demanding expectations, we checked our timetable, set the timer on the oven, plugged in our laptops and got started.

By eleven thirty I was ready to kill myself. I'd already made myself two and a half hot chocolates (the milk had indeed run out by the time I got round to my third), made substantial headway with my bag of assorted snack food, broken the arm of the chair I was sitting on by assuming it would support my whole weight (well, I didn't know it was cracked already, did I?) and been told off by Ben for scuffing the walls with my trainers.

'I'm so bored,' I told him. 'I can't go on.'

'Hobie, you agreed that we don't have a choice about this. Isn't it better to just get it done? Haven't your parents promised you, like, a treat or a holiday or something if you get a Scholarship?'

Now *that* was an idea that hadn't yet crossed my mind. I haven't really focused on the actual Scholarship exams themselves. Firstly because next May seems quite a distance away. Secondly because, well, all right, I'll admit it, I've been feeling constantly like I shouldn't even be in 8 Upper. I shouldn't be doing Scholarship, but I am, and I hate, hate, *hate* to fail at stuff. I pretend I don't care and that everything is other people's fault, but, honestly, I really don't want to fail. The worst thing is, if you do really badly they can make you take Common Entrance, whereas ordinarily even if you don't do well enough to get a Scholarship they'll usually let you in anyway. I don't know if I could bear the humiliation. It's hideous to even think about it, which is probably why I haven't.

As if he could read my mind, Ben took a pint of milk out of the freezer and put it on the counter to thaw. Two goldfish globbed tragically around a spherical bowl next to the fridge, as though they were looking for something but couldn't remember what. The kitchen was dark and gloomy.

'Look,' said Ben, 'do you think you can do it or not? Are you just afraid to try?'

I threw a pencil at his head. It missed and tinkled against the side of the bin.

'I am a Berserk. I am *fearless*,' I said, digging around in my food bag for a strawberry shoelace, which I proceeded to cram, whole, into my mouth, letting the overspill hang out like intestines.

Ben sat back down and opened his Geography textbook, a monumentally humourless tome entitled *The World and Man's Place In It*, which is full of detailed maps of microclimates. 'Right then,' he said. A smile twitched at the corners of his lips.

That's the thing about Ben. He's nice.

## Wednesday 29th October

So the days seem to be falling into a pretty regular pattern, like *amo*. I wake up, have a shower, eat breakfast, take a taxi to Ben's house, study from ten till one and two till four, come home, get changed, run on the treadmill, piss about watching TV, eat dinner, mess around on the Internet, go to sleep. Every night Mum and Dad check up on what we've been doing and mark their copy of our revision plan with careful ticks and bracketed notes. Zara annoys me in small doses but I'm largely spared the burden of her company.

The thrill of being unsupervised (good thing my parents assume that's not the case) is dampened by the fact that Ben's mother rings up every hour, on the hour, to see how we're doing and to check we haven't been electrocuted or abducted by the people that come to the door with leaflets about Christianity. She's obsessed with Ben doing well. Often she comes back in her lunch hour (she works somewhere pretty nearby in some office) and sits at the table with us, maniacally checking through all of Ben's notes and revision cards and patting her hair over and over.

'We've *got* to show your father,' she said to Ben when I was in the bathroom and she thought I couldn't hear. 'We've got to show him. Just because he's run off to sit on his behind writing self-pitying claptrap that no one's going to read, doesn't mean we can't get on with our lives. And when you get your Scholarship he'll know that we don't need him to be happy, do we?'

Wow. I've never heard anyone sound so angry without shouting. I wonder what Ben thinks.

In keeping with his suggestion, I have demanded a reward if I get a Scholarship. Dad laughed and said that he, personally, was sure that I'd feel so proud of my achievements that it'd be a reward in itself, but I could tell Mum would jump at the chance to dangle another carrot in front of my nose. And even though I greeted with derision her idea of taking me to Paris, just the two of us, to look at boring sculptures and buy Fendi handbags *for her*, I liked the idea of Tunisia and some of the other places she came up with. In Tunisia there's this awesome hotel where the breakfast buffet has, like, everything you can think of and you can just keep filling up your plate.

It occurred to me that Ben's mum and dad blatantly weren't going to reward Ben if/when he gets his Scholarship except, like, by buying him a pencil case or taking him to the zoo or whatever. It's his birthday next week and they probably aren't going to bother much about that either. So I went on Amazon and found the biggest Metallica poster they had, because Metallica is his favourite band and the poster was of this guy with really long hair called Cliff Burton. Ben loves Cliff. And I got Mum to put in her credit card details and the Duvalle Hall address and she said I was very nice to be thinking about my friend.

Of course, Mum and Dad had to think of something for Zara too, in the unlikely event she passes the 11+. I thought she'd be well up for the Paris idea in a girlie, *Sex and the City* sort of way. Wearing frilly accessories and skipping about on the banks of the Seine, buying little trinkets, etc. But Zarie was totally apathetic about it and just blinked at them. Eventually she said she didn't want to think about it in case she failed everything. She keeps getting ill at the moment and has a kind of permanent sniffle, which is an additional reason to stay away from her. Mum is going to take her to the doctor.

Last night I found the unmarked carrier bag from the exchange place where I sold Mum's clothes and inside was the oversized clown suit. I'd totally forgotten about it. I went into Zara's room, which as you can imagine looks like a flamingo threw up in it and has so many fluffy rabbits and weasels and squirrels peering down from the tops of cup-boards that the air is thick with glitter and artificial fur. She was sitting on the floor arranging her Sylvanian families into cutesy little groups and I suppressed a flickering impulse to snatch one and bite its head off, like Ozzy Osbourne once did with a live bat, so Ben says.

'Here, Zarie,' I said, flinging the suit at her. It flopped against her head and slithered over a family of fieldmice and their rainbow-painted furniture.

'What is it?' she said. Like all girls, she likes things made out of shiny fabric.

'It's a clown suit. I got the biggest one they had, of course, so you can fit into it.'

Her shoulders twitched, but she didn't reply. Didn't call for Mum and Dad, didn't shout at me. Zara just doesn't know how to defend herself. She'd be useless on the rugby pitch.

'What, don't you like it? Look, it'll last you forever. Unless you manage to outgrow it of course.'

Her lack of response slightly spoilt my enjoyment, so I left her sitting there with the clown suit in her hands and went back to my room to read some more about the Gods.

At the moment I'm rereading one of my favourite bits: the Binding of the Wolf – the wolf, of course, being Fenrir, Loki's son, and father of Hati and Skǫll. Fenrir grew up in Asgard but gradually became so huge and ferocious that nobody could feed him because they were so afraid. And Odin knew that Fenrir was fated to kill him one day, but even so he wouldn't allow the Gods to destroy the wolf. Only Tyr, the God of swords, was brave enough to try to feed him. Thor forged a chain, which Fenrir smashed to pieces as easily as if it was made of cobwebs or something, and the whole earth shook. They tried again and the same thing happened. So in the end they got the dwarves to make a new chain out of mountain roots and the footsteps of a cat (weird!) and the breath of a fish and bear sinews and it looked like silk. And the Gods basically tricked Fenrir into letting them bind him with it, but he asked for one of them to put their hand in his mouth as a way of promising that it wasn't a trick. And of course Tyr was the only one daring enough to do this.

So the Gods bound Fenrir with the chain the dwarves had made, and even though he leaped about and flamed with rage, he couldn't get out of it, because the chain was enchanted. And foam dripped from his jaws and his eyes blazed black with anger and he bit off Tyr's hand. The Gods pulled the silken chain through the middle of a rock which they had sunk deep into the earth, and when Fenrir sprang upon them they propped his massive jaws wide open with a sword. And that's where Fenrir stayed, right up until Ragnarok and everything ended.

When I think about it, about the moment Fenrir bit off Tyr's hand, I feel all weird and headrushy like when you go on Thunder Mountain at Disneyland. I love how brave Tyr was. I want to know if I'd be that brave. Or would I be more like Thor, who of course was really courageous but couldn't sacrifice his hand because of always throwing his hammer? It was pretty hard having my left arm in a sling for two weeks, so I understand that.

I also love Fenrir. When he realised he'd been tricked, it must have been so satisfying to take that final downwards bite.

# BEN

Reg of Putney arrives to take Mum out for a pub lunch on the river. They will read the Sunday supplements and eat traditional roasts, and talk about traditional Sunday things. They will watch people rowing with easy precision; they will watch boats go by. Reg of Putney appears to be quite a nice guy. He's older than Dad. He's wearing cords and a russet-coloured jumper, drinks half a glass of cider and asks me if I've read *The Decline and Fall of the Roman Empire*.

Contrary to Mum's fears, I am not rude to him. I don't have the energy.

'Ben,' says R of P, 'why don't you come with? Be nice to get to know you.'

'Ben has a lot of work to do,' says Mum quickly. 'He's got exams every day next week, and he was out late last night.'

'Yeah, but thanks,' I say.

As they leave, Reg of Putney offers me his hand. He smells of cinnamon and cloves and half a glass of cider. I wonder if this is the attraction for Mum: she has found a man who can stop at half a glass. Dad would have finished a whole bottle of something by now.

I sit on the carpet, my English set texts laid out in front of me. The sign in my head flickers. An amber glow: *warning*. It's weird – in addition to the usual growl of my headache, I have the jangly overlay of a hangover. I can actually *feel* the different types of pain competing for space in my head. In sharp contrast, the view out of the window is almost blissful. The trees along our street are riotous explosions of leaves. The sky is blue; it makes me think of the light that comes from Odin.

I compose a text to Zara, asking if she'd like to go for a walk. I have no doubt at all that she'll be busy, possibly too busy even to reply; surely she too is doing Sunday things – revision, ballet practice, reading the papers – but she texts back almost immediately, suggesting I wait for her near the top of Ladbroke Grove where it meets Holland Park. I text back: *Great. See you then*. I think about getting changed, but all my non-school clothes are variations on the same theme: black or blue jeans, long-sleeved tops with Metal logos, hoodies. In deference to the occasion though, I put on something clean that doesn't have a skull on it, or Iron Maiden's Eddie, and try to do something with my hair to make it look less like a purposeless thicket.

It's a direct bus from near my house, but it'll do me good to walk. The fresh air, the tug of my hamstrings working after weeks of solid revision and exams, the dribble of sun onto my face make me feel more alive than I've felt in a long time. As I walk past the boarded-up shops and the boxing gym my phone vibrates in my pocket, and I wonder if it's Zara, cancelling. I wouldn't be surprised. I'm not sure, really, what we're going to talk about. She doesn't seem to know anything about Jason, or, if she does she isn't telling me, and as for other things . . . they're like scabs you really can't prise away in case there's unstoppable blood underneath them.

Oh well. It's such a nice day that we can definitely talk about the weather for a while.

But the text isn't from Zara. It's from Solly. A picture message.

I enlarge the image.

No. No *way*.

It's a pair of tickets to Download in June, a couple of weeks from now. The festival I've always wanted to go to, but never been able to afford. And Metallica are headlining! Not to mention all the other bands I'm desperate to see: Opeth, Soundgarden, Lamb of God. The message beneath says: *early birthday present*. My birthday's not for six months.

I call Solomon immediately. 'You're awesome. You're ACE. How did you get them?'

'My aunt works for the promoter.'

'But it's right in the middle of exams,' I say, excitement temporarily stilled.

'Well, is it a Mum weekend or a Dad weekend?'

I calculate, tapping out the weeks against my leg.

'Uh . . . Dad, I reckon.'

'You should be able to get out of that, then. Tell him you've got a study session at someone's house. Listen, though. I want to make a deal with you.'

'What's that?'

'You'll give up those orange painkiller things. If we go.'

'Sol, I don't . . .'

'Yes, you do. You've got an actual problem, Ben. So my proposition is: we go to this dreadful place, with its undisinfected toilets and disorganised camping and lager louts, and you *take your last pill*.'

After what feels like a long time, I say, 'OK.'

'Well done. Acceptance, Awareness, Action, as they say.'

'But I don't really get what's in this for you, Solly. You prefer jazz and stuff.'

He laughs. 'Kaizen, my friend,' he says. 'Kaizen.'


As I head to the top of Ladbroke Grove, the church bell strikes the hour. It makes me think, as church bells always do, of Metallica's 'For Whom The Bell Tolls'. It's a song that just drags you into another place altogether. Right from the opening, where, somewhere not too far away, a giant bell begins to toll.

*Doooonnggggggg* . . .

*Doooonnggggggg* . . .

A horrible, hollow sound, almost de-tuned, like food that's gone off.

The bell keeps tolling, every two bars, even after the

guitars come in. Two sets: a low, staccato riff that dances around a minor-second interval, and a high, wailing one reminiscent of ambulance sirens. And relentless and savage drums, like pounding footfalls.

When the riff changes, becomes more frenzied, I see men, marching. Men raising guns to their shoulders. Cannonfire. And then . . . then Kirk Hammett's breathtaking riff comes in, the one that cycles round a set of just four notes. There's something in the sheer repetitiveness of this bit that makes me think it's about the mindlessness of war, the rhythms of battles fought and lives lost between daybreak and dusk. It's got a certain beauty to it. If it were a colour, it'd be blue – a shot of clear, almost electric blue against the murky dark of the landscape. It's not until two minutes and seven seconds in that James Hetfield starts to sing. Despite Hetfield's ear for powerful but not overblown imagery, I think that in the case of 'For Whom The Bell Tolls', the music tells the whole story by itself. No need for words at all.

The song ends just as I'm reaching the top of Ladbroke Grove. The houses here are so stately, so perfectly painted in soft greys and creams and blues, that they look as if they've been cut out of quality cardboard and pinned against the sky. As I reach the church, the congregation comes milling out in dresses and suits. I slow down, letting them walk in front of me.

'Ben.'

Zara is standing on the paved path that leads from the

church door to the road. She's wearing a grey skirt, a pale mauve blouse and a white jacket and looks exactly like all the other people who came out of the great wooden doors. Her clothes are too subdued, like a teacher's. In the daylight, she somehow looks even thinner than she did last night. A small halo of sunlight plays around her head.

'I didn't realise you went to church,' I say.

I feel stupid immediately. Why shouldn't she go to church? Mum does ballroom dancing and runs ten kilometres before breakfast; Solomon takes vitamins and reads books on self-improvement. I listen to metal. Everyone has a church. In fact, I might not go into the church itself, but there's nothing I like more than a quiet cemetery, full of tumbledown graves and straggling creepers.

'I go with Mum and Dad, sometimes,' she replies. 'When they're in England.'

She gestures to the other side of the road, where Ike and Elsie are coming out of the newsagent's with bundles of papers. Ike's bald patch is more pronounced; Elsie looks the same. A little more gaunt, but she was always gaunt. I remember the newsagent's; I think I went there once with Hobie. It was the only place, at the time, that stocked Reese's Peanut Butter Cups.

'Do you want to go and say hello?'

I hesitate. Part of me wants to jump at the opportunity to ask Ike and Elsie about Jason. But I can't imagine they'd take kindly to that. They'd be horrified by my rudeness, my insensitivity. Zara said outside the Underworld that they don't talk about that weekend; I can't expect them to start talking about it now, to me.

'Um. No. Thanks,' I say.

'OK,' she says quickly. 'That's fine. I didn't think you'd want to. Which way do you want to walk, by the way? Shall we go to Kensington Gardens?'

We fall into step, turning up Ladbroke Road towards Notting Hill Gate. We talk blandly about neutral things: the gardens we pass, the weather. We compare the respective atmospheres of our schools and decide that they are very alike, though hers is a girls' school and mine is for boys.

It's only as we cross the road past the tube station and begin heading towards Bayswater that Zara, tapping the railings as she walks, says, 'It's funny.'

'What's funny?'

'Going to church. We never used to, you know. Not regularly. We used to go to Whole Foods on Sundays. Mum and Dad are really into prayer now. Sometimes they even hold these extra prayer meetings at home.'

'What do you think they're praying for?'

She blinks at me, as though the answer is obvious.

'For Hobie,' she says. 'For his soul.'

'Do you pray too?'

'Sort of. Not really. I don't go that often. I used to, to keep them company. Then I gave up. I found myself wondering what the point was, of praying to something I didn't believe in.'

'So you don't believe in God,' I say.

'Again, I used to,' she says shortly.

I wait, sensing that there's more to come.

'But recently, a couple of weeks ago, I started . . . seeing things.'

'What things?'

'Strange lights. Flickers – like when you have a Christmas tree in a dark room and the fairy lights reflect off the tinsel and the mirrors. That kind of light, but changing shape, changing colour.'

I slow down, staring at her in disbelief.

'What kind of colours? Blue?'

'Blue, mostly, yes, and green. Pink, sometimes. And voices. Whispers. I think they're *angels*. Does that make me crazy?'

'Of course not,' I say, thinking, I've got to tell her.

'So one day a couple of weeks ago my parents had the vicar round at our house for tea, and they went to take a conference call from one of their financial advisors and I was just sitting there, you know, passing the biscuits to Reverend Lewis, and then suddenly I felt this tremendous desire to, you know, ask him about the angels.'

'And what did he say?'

'He said if it got worse to tell the doctor. But I haven't. I'm sick of doctors. Anyway, I got quite interested then about dreams and visions in the Bible. People seeing things.

It seemed to happen all the time in the Bible. And so lately I've been coming to church with Mum and Dad, just to listen to what he's saying. To find out more. I'm wondering if there's a story in the Bible, some parable or whatever, that I need to read. Reverend Lewis said angels bring messages. I think he's right. I think it is a message, though I don't know what.'

'What sort of message?' I say.

An ice-cream van sits at the entrance to the park. We watch as a little boy in a Spider-Man T-shirt elbows a group of children out of the way, insinuating himself into the front of the queue.

'Billy, don't *push* people,' says his mother from the bench nearby, but she lets him stay where he is. The other children protest and whine, but fall back to let him through, giving way to his vitality.

'Sometimes it's a woman's voice and sometimes a man's. It's a language that I don't understand. But, somehow, I know that something is *wrong*.'

Watching the little boy make his purchases, thrusting a crumpled fiver through the window of the van and grabbing his ice creams – a Twister and a Feast (and I just know they're both for him; he's that kind of kid) – I make a decision.

'They aren't angels, Zara,' I say. 'They're Gods.'

Sitting on a bench while the world goes about its Sunday business around us, doing its best to recreate that pointillist painting of people in a park I remember once copying at Cottesmore House, I tell Zara everything I know about the Otherlife. As I would expect, she is a wonderful listener and stays pin-drop silent while I talk. It's the longest I think I've ever spoken uninterrupted. As I speak, I find myself getting used to my voice, acclimatising myself to forming proper sentences. I am revealing myself, removing piece by piece an armadillo suit of armour.

I begin by telling her how it began. I tell her about the cricket match, and Dad's new bat, and how for a while I was completely blind in my right eye. How Jason comforted me with tales of Odin, who also lost an eye, and how by the time my vision returned the Norse tales were as real to me as anecdotes from my own life. How the coloured lights started, and how I recognised in their wispy formations the shapes of the Gods. How I painted a mural; how I tattooed myself with a wolf (at this I slide up my T-shirt, briefly, to prove it), and how the Otherlife, by the time I was in Year 8 and became friends with Hobie, had become more real to me than my own existence.

Zara tucks her feet underneath her and says, 'I see.'

Her tone of voice suggests that she thinks I'm borderline certifiable. But then she goes on: 'The older I get, the more I find I look for rational explanations. I'm not the kind of person who can accept things without proof. I don't believe in imaginary things any more. When I first saw the coloured lights, I wanted so much for them to be some kind of neurological disturbance – even though that in itself was quite frightening. I needed there to be a reason, a scientific reason, for them. But at the same time, I knew there wasn't one. I had a feeling that they were coming to me from somewhere outside of my brain. That's why I asked Reverend Lewis.'

'So you do believe me?'

'I believe you,' she replies.

A ripple of relief runs through me. I couldn't bear to confide the truth about the Otherlife – something I've only ever told, I suppose, to Hobie – and for her to not believe me.

'But I don't understand about the relationship between the stories of the Otherlife and the Otherlife itself,' says Zara, frowning. 'Did you see the stories playing out in the correct order, or did you not see the stories, so much as just the Gods themselves?'

It's a really good question.

'I did see little pieces of the stories,' I say, after a bit. 'On my mural, especially. The paint would sort of move about sometimes. But mostly I would *read* the stories but *see* the Gods, and the landscape that they lived in. It felt like the stories could almost be told in any imaginable sequence, and therefore that I could see bits and pieces from any part at any time. It didn't really matter. It was all just one big cycle.'

'What do you mean?'

'I mean that from creation to destruction it wasn't a straight line, so much as an endless circle, or a spiral. Ragnarok was the end, but also the beginning. The world began anew each time.'

She's silent for a while. It all takes some getting used to, I suppose.

'But why now?' says Zara. 'Why is this happening now, to me?'

'I'm seeing it again too,' I say. 'And I haven't seen it for years.'

'Do you think it's something to do with Hobie?' she says suddenly.

'Is there any reason why you'd think that?'

'I just wondered,' she says. 'I think . . . I think I might have seen one of those lights before. Just once.'

I wait for more, but she doesn't say anything else.

'Is he . . . I mean, how is he?' I say.

'Oh, Hobie. He's the same.'

Her voice is flat and quiet.

'I think it has to do with Jason. I think we need to find out how he died,' I say.

'But his death was unexplained. I'm sure it was.'

I don't say anything, but I'm thinking, If she cares so much about finding out the explanations of things, it doesn't make much sense that she should accept something like the death of a young and healthy person as *unexplained*. But there's a weird tranquillity seeping into me, in spite of it all. It's the kind of afternoon you'd think of as golden, like the beginning of *Alice in Wonderland*. It's something about the people sprawled under trees with dogs and picnic baskets, the children scootering by, the smell of summer flowers. I can't quite bring myself to ask any more questions.

So we get up and go for a long walk, past the Diana Memorial Fountain and all the way to Marble Arch. We don't talk much; I give her one of my earbuds and we listen to *The Black Album*, which she claims to enjoy. Then we take different buses home. Before she leaves (her bus, the 94, comes first), she gives me an awkward hug goodbye, and says, if I like, I can meet her again next Sunday, same time, same place.

As I get on my own bus, a 23, I think: I still might not know what's going on, but I don't feel alone any more.


Reg of Putney is reinstalled in the sitting room when I return, eating Tesco Finest biscuits and watching the racing. He's certainly making himself at home. Mum is nowhere to be seen, but from the laughter reverberating from the kitchen I deduce that she's on the phone to Aunt Jane in Canada. Aunt Jane is one of the few people Mum lightens up around.

'Join me, Ben, why don't you?' says Reg, seeing me pass the sitting-room door.

At first I pause; then, thinking that Zara wouldn't hesitate to behave with due propriety under the same circumstances, I do.

215

'Tell me about yourself,' says Reg.

'There isn't much to tell. I'm doing GCSEs at the moment.'

'Favourite subject?'

'Nothing really.'

A tenseness begins at the tops of my arms. I hope that Mum hasn't said anything to him about Jason. I am not ready to share my grief with a stranger.

'What sort of music do you like?' asks Reg.

This is a preferable question: metal is one of the few things I will genuinely go on at length about to anyone, even strangers. And – even better – it turns out that Reg has fond memories of Black Sabbath, from back in the day. One of his best mates was a roadie at an Ozzfest. He even saw Jethro Tull play one of their first-ever gigs! I have a real envy of people who were around for the early days of British Metal. I grill him in earnest, pressing him for sensory details. I find myself eating a biscuit, and offering to make him another cup of tea.

'Of course, I didn't have much time for concerts and the like when I was in full-time work,' says Reg.

'What kind of work do you do?' I ask him, thinking how rude I am, that I haven't already found this out.

'I'm a coroner. Semi-retired now.'

The uneaten half of my biscuit quivers in my hand.

'A coroner . . . really?'

'That's right. Know what a coroner is?'

A sprinkle of shrieking – oh-no-you-never, oh-yes-I-swear-to-you – tells me that Mum is still on the phone. I don't want her to hear me quizzing Reg of Putney. But this is too good a chance to miss.

'How would you establish cause of death, usually?' I ask him casually.

He settles himself more comfortably on the sofa; I realise I'm relieved that he's not sitting in Dad's old armchair.

'Depends on the circumstances. If the person had been ill, we'd want to know if they'd seen their usual doctor in the fortnight before. The doctor would then issue a certificate. If that was not the case, and there was no obvious cause of death, a postmortem would be carried out. After that, if there was still no explanation, you could hold an inquest. Planning a murder, are you?'

'Is it normal for a death to be . . . to be registered as "unexplained"?' I say, still trying to sound as casual as I can.

'Not usual, no. We always want to try to find the cause, if at all possible. People don't die for no reason.'

'What are you two taking about?' says Mum, arriving with coffee cake and giving the question word her usual legal emphasis.

I make my excuses and go upstairs. I was right; I knew I was right. Whatever Zara thinks – whatever she says – it is very, very unlikely that Jason's death was 'unexplained'. Someone must know. And I will find out. With an automated hand-to-mouth action, I reach for another painkiller, but, reflecting that it's not that long until I have to give them up completely, I put it back in the bottle. On the wall there's now a proper collection of trivia. There's my wolf certificate. There's Zara's business card. I have pinned it exactly straight, because I know it would not please her to be even slightly askew. There's a photocopied magazine cutting I found in my *Gods of Northern Europe* book entitled 'Cannibal Ate My Mum with Ketchup and Peas'. I can't remember the significance of it exactly, but it looks like something from one of Hobie's magazines.

And then there's the picture of me and Hobie, arms around each other, smiling our feral, free-and-easy wolf smiles as though we haven't a care in our hearts.

# HOBIE'S DIARY

Thursday 30th October 2008

Ben has the most amazing mural in his bedroom. He painted it himself. On the first day he gave me a guided tour, and I tried and failed to imagine what it would be like to live in a house that small. I mean, no gym, no home cinema or dedicated TV room, and just a bedroom each for him and his mum and then a minuscule one she uses as a study. I don't know if I could cope with that. How would I get away from Zara? Ben's room was at the back of the house over-looking the garden and about 19 other gardens as well, and from his window I could see loads of falling-down sheds and laundry lines with pegs dangling half-heartedly in the wind and cats slinking up and down the walls.

But when he opened the door to his room I was fairly knocked out by the painting that stretched all the way along the end wall. In the foreground are all these flat rocks and marshland and then there's a big stretch of sea the colour of slate with white tips on the waves and in the background massive mountains with snowy peaks, but the whole thing looks kind of grainy like it's covered in mist. And somehow, even on, like, three or four metres of wall, Ben's created this incredible sense of space like it goes on for miles and miles. And, best of all, there was a Viking longship just visible through the puffy white cloud. Ben knew enough to just suggest that it was there. He told me he painted it mostly with bits of sponge dipped in acrylic and a palette knife. His mum went ballistic at first, but in the end she said they'll paint over it when they move to a bigger house.

Ben says he likes to just sit in front of it, watching. Sometimes, he says, it moves. The longship changes position. Berserks appear and disappear. And the sky changes colour, meaning that the Gods are there. I've tried a few times, but all I can see is paint.

Frodo's Halloween party has been a major source of comfort all through the first week of half term. Now, I don't like the guy, and I can't imagine he likes me all that much given what I've done to him over the years – drawing a penis on the back of his blazer in chalk before the school concert (at which several minor members of the Royal Family were present), putting rocks and live snails in his sleeping bag on the Geography Fieldwork Trip, making that Facebook group called Stupid Fat Hobbit with his face as the profile picture . . . I forget what else, but a fair amount. But the rule at school is on pain of torture you always invite your *entire class* to your parties. And everyone was going apart from Matteo who was in Florence and they'd taken one of those Super Tutors with them, whose catchphrase was *'Motivation, kid, you get me?'* I know because one time I saw them in the park, sauntering up and down with a pile of History notes. The guy was smoking roll-ups. I've asked Matteo whether he's actually learning anything from this dude, but Matteo seems to be completely blown away by the Super status and is unable to recall what they do in their tuition time.

I've been trying to persuade Ben to go with me to the party, which will involve trick-or-treating around all the streets nearby followed by supervised games and a frenzied consumption of collected loot. After five days of work, side by side in his dismal kitchen with only an endless supply of cheese pitta breads and microwavable M&S pasta meals to sustain us (or rather me – the quantity of food I brought with me increased daily), I think even he saw the benefit of an outing.

Both our mothers had spent all week using the party as a bargaining chip. Any insubordination was instantly greeted with a 'Listen, Hobie, if you do that to your sister again you will *not* be going to Frodo's on Friday night,' etc etc. But I don't think we gave anyone a reason to deny us the right to go. Jesus, I got into the minicab every morning at precisely 9.35 a.m. like a veritable *angel*.

Over the course of the week, we've done the following:

1. Essay plans for English, History and General Paper
   – three of each in bullet point or mind-map format
2. *All* our global locations (incl. rivers and seas and mountain ranges) and map symbols
3. Complete revision of the periodic table, properties of metals and non-metals and the reactivity series

4. A French reading and writing paper plus revision of all irregular verbs

5. Two Maths papers, on which we marked what we didn't understand so that Jason could explain it to us the following week

6. Revision of tenses, third, fourth and fifth declension nouns and reported speech in Latin (but there's so much that really we need Rebecca's help with that)

7. The first six chapters of our Greek textbook, doing questions at random.

Eventually I made the decision to treat what we were doing as a kind of drawn-out version of super-intensive physical training, like I'd do in Tennis Camp, or before a really important match. Remembering that I'm a kinaesthetic learner, I started charging into Ben's garden (which is the size of a five-pound note and mostly paved over, but at least it's outside) and doing press-ups and star jumps every half-hour. The blood rushed around my body and jarred my brain into gear, and it felt really good. Ben would come and sit on the rickety picnic table and call out verbs so that I could complete the principal parts.

'*Cado . . .*'

'*. . . cadere, cecidi, casum.*'

'Meaning?'

'I fall.'

'*Caedo . . .*'

'. . . *caedere, cecidi, caesum.*'

'Meaning?'

'I cut, beat, slaughter.'

As we ran in and out, kicking the kitchen door shut and slamming our textbooks down, I caught myself, to my horror, *enjoying* the charge of adrenaline that I was experiencing from getting things right.

I was becoming a swot. Jesus.

But I couldn't really piss about all day and distract Ben. He genuinely needs to get a Scholarship for financial reasons, so it wouldn't be fair. That's my excuse. As soon as these bloody exams are over, I'll go back to normal. Jason can do my homework and I'll coast by on the bare minimum and they won't be able to do anything about it. Anyway, they say Scholarship is harder than A level, don't they, so it's possible that I'll never really have to do any proper work ever again.

By Wednesday I felt confident enough at predicting the unannounced visits of Ben's mother to risk smoking on their doorstep. (They do have a teeny-tiny loft but Ben wouldn't let me go up there because there was definitely no way of getting on to the roof plus he was worried I'd put my foot through the ceiling. Since I'd already broken not only the arm of the kitchen chair but also a table lamp and two mugs, perhaps it was a fair point.) I'd bought a packet of Lucky Strikes at the very dodgy but quite cool corner shop next to lots of similarly random shops: one that sold chainsaws and big bags of compost, one that sold really hideous furniture and second-hand ovens, a couple of really cheap-looking hairdressers. I had no idea you could get a haircut for less than forty quid. I'd also bought an awesome magazine called *It's My Life*; on the front cover it said 'Cannibal Ate My Mum with Ketchup and Peas' in orange italics. And I was sitting reading and smoking and thinking that for some reason I didn't resent not being in the Bahamas as much as I'd thought I would, when I realised I could hear Ben on the phone to his mum.

I listened.

'I dunno,' he was saying. 'Yeah . . . no. Not too bad . . . Hobie's helping loads. We've made a list of things to do with the tutors . . . Jason and Rebecca . . . I dunno. Oxford or Cambridge, I think . . . OK.'

Was his mum questioning Rebecca's qualifications? Ridiculous. Shouldn't *look a gift horse in the mouth*, as they say. Is that to do with the Trojan horse? I wonder.

'Mum, I really can't tell you whether I'm going to get a Scholarship or not . . . I don't know what the other candidates are like, do I? I just don't . . . OK, yeah. Yes, I will. See you later.'

Then silence.

I made a point of shutting the front door quite loudly to let him know I was coming back inside. It was nearly time for lunch and I was thinking about what to put in the microwave.

Ben was slumped down, his head resting on his arms. I prayed he wasn't going to cry. I don't know what to do when people cry, except make fun of them. Then he raised his head and looked straight across the kitchen, through the glass door and over the garden wall, past the line of houses backing onto it and towards a little chink of pale sky between the chimneys.

'Dude, are you OK?' I asked.

He didn't speak for a while, and then said, 'Ragnarok.'

I sat down beside him.

'The mountains are shattered. The World Tree shakes,' murmured Ben.

'The stars disappear from the sky,' I joined in.

'The monsters break loose,' he said.

'Tell me about it,' I said. Ben likes nothing more than telling stories. And I quite wanted to hear this one. I'd read about Ragnarok, but even so. Eventually I managed to persuade him. He fetched his Free Creative Writing book from his bag and fumbled around for a while. Then he cleared his throat a couple of times, and began.

'It was the end of everything. Fire and frost giant joined forces on the plain of Vigrid, where the final battle would be fought. Heimdallr sounded his horn. Odin and the Gods rode out from Valhalla. Here God met monster on the massive plain, and all met their death. Thor slew the serpent, and then fell to the ground, overwhelmed by its deadly venom. Heimdallr did battle with Loki, and each killed the other. Tyr met the great dog Garm, who had broken loose from its fetters in the Underworld. Freyr met the giant Surtr. Mighty Odin stood among his fallen warriors as the wolf Fenrir came near, and though Odin fought to the last, he was swallowed up by the furious beast. His death did not go unavenged, however, for Odin's son Vídarr set one foot on each of Fenrir's jaws and ripped them apart. Finally, Surtr hurled a wave of fire over the world, so that the race of men perished alongside the Gods. The world sank beneath the sea.'

He finished speaking. The kitchen was quiet. I thought about it: the Gods, waiting for the world to end. The wicked way that each God was paired with an enemy combatant – perfectly matched, like wrestlers or fencing champions. I was just sorry that Loki had to die too. Though, as Ben has tried to explain to me, the way the Otherlife works is that it's constantly beginning and ending, and that sort of cheers me up because in one way Loki will live on forever.

'Awesome,' I said. 'Dude, you read that really well.'

His eyes were almost back to a normal colour, I was glad to note. Sometimes that frozen look of his sort of chills me.

Then I had an incredible idea.

'Hey!' I said. 'Hobbitboy's Halloween party on Friday! We should go as *wolves*. Hati and Skǫll. Why the hell not?'

Ben managed a smile.

'OK,' he said.

\* \* \*

I still had my envelope of cash from the sale of Mum's gear and I hadn't spent much of it. Normally I spend everything I have on me sort of automatically. For example, if we're abroad and I have some euros I'll just go into the nearest cafe or newsagent and buy a random selection of sweets or pastries or whatever. Or if Mandy, my godmother, comes to stay, sometimes she'll give me a Hamleys gift card and we'll go together and I'll make sure I've used it up completely. But somehow I still had about £120 and I had it with me in my rucksack, just in case.

It took some real skills on my part to get Ben to leave the house, but since his mum had just rung up it wasn't very likely that she'd come back any time soon. And she doesn't mind if Ben goes out on his own, not the way my mother does. My mother thinks the world is one big nest of murderous kiddy-snatchers.

'Come *on*, Ben,' I said. 'We need some air anyway. Let's just leave a note saying we've gone for a walk.'

Ben was looking really stressed out. He's really good at all this academic stuff so I don't know why he's so wound up at the moment, but maybe it's because his mum keeps pestering him about his progress. I basically dragged him out the door and down the road, past all the dodgy shops full of girls with prams and Ugg boots and people muttering to themselves and pushing tartan shopping trolleys. We walked over the canal and through an estate and eventually we got to the Golborne Road, which I know about because

Clothilde and I drive past on the way to Ben's. And there were a few shops along that road that I knew would be *perfect*.

The first one we tried had exactly what we needed: loads and loads of fur coats of all shapes and sizes hanging up outside or lumped together on rails. I started rifling through them and pretty soon Ben began to see the point and helped me look. And finally we found two coats small enough to fit us. One was grey with white flecks and the other was quite dark, almost black, with a big fat collar, and when we tried them on they came down to about mid-thigh. The shop lady obviously thought we were delightful, and when we explained to her that we wanted to be wolves for Halloween she pointed us in the direction of this massive bin full of hats and gloves and scarves, and we pulled out big hats with flaps that could cover our ears and were nearly the same colour as our coats. I wanted the black one, of course, because it was cooler, and Ben said he didn't mind which one he had. And we got black gloves for me and white gloves for Ben that were made of really thin material like suede or something. And the woman told us that if we went into a couple of other shops we might be able to find some wolf masks if we looked hard enough. So I paid her £90 for everything and she threw in some moth-eaten old fur wrap things she said we could cut up for tails. Then we trailed about poking around in all these different shops until we found a proper fancy-dress place that had loads and loads of masks; I mean you could get a rubber head of Prince Charles if you wanted, or about fifteen different clown ones that made me think of Zara. Perhaps I could make her wear that enormous clown suit when she goes trick-or-treating with her pathetic little friends. That would amuse me loads.

'Here,' said Ben, chucking what appeared to be a piece of black leather at me. I looked down and saw that it was half a wolf's head with holes for eyes and all over it this amazing spidery design in patches of shiny silver. *Awesome!* He'd found one for himself too, in red and gold. Last but not least, we bought a couple of packets of fangs. We were sorted.

Like I said, once I start spending I honestly feel like I can't stop. I made Ben go via the newsagent's with me on the way back to his house (I'm starting to like the man behind the counter who blatantly doesn't care that I'm under 18) because I wanted a can of Coke, something I'm routinely forbidden from drinking at home. Just as we were going inside Ben sort of froze and I asked him impatiently what the matter was, thinking he'd had a sudden vision of Odin descending from the dusky clouds or whatever. But he stood totally still and I followed his gaze, which led across the road to this cafe place, and there, sitting in the window, was Ben's mum.

And sitting opposite her was Ben's dad.

I stared from them to him and back again, trying to figure

out what might be going on in his head. I know Ben hasn't seen his dad (who is a novelist, apparently quite a crap one according to the reviews on Amazon, but then they're probably all written by Ben's mum or something) for like weeks and weeks. I think he misses him, although he never says so. If I was Ben, I'd definitely miss living in a bigger house and going out for dinner and stuff. But Ben's weird. Who knows what he thinks about anything?

A solitary tear, like one of those glass beads Zara puts in her dolls' hair, trailed down his cheek. I thought of Freyja, twin sister of Freyr, who wept tears of red gold when her husband disappeared.

I didn't know what to say.

Then Ben took off across the street, sending two cyclists and a 228 bus skidding to a standstill as he went. I looked on as he tugged open the cafe door and waited for his parents' heads to turn. I felt like it just wasn't right to watch what happened next, a bit like when you walk in on someone changing and you know you shouldn't stare at their naked body. Normally I don't care or I think it's funny. But I went into the newsagent's, like I'd meant to, and bought my can of Coke.

I hung about in there for a while, figuring that Ben'd be embarrassed if I loomed into view while he was talking to his dad who he hasn't seen for so long, and who appears to be meeting his mum without bothering to come and see Ben as well. I cast around for something else to buy, something else to do. And my eye lit upon the super-cheap photocopier in the corner of the shop.

Now *that* was an idea.

Although the corner-shop guy seemed bemused by my desire to photocopy the same page 200 times, he was perfectly happy to let me get on with it.

# BEN

Solomon and I are in the ICT Room, looking at hotels within a two-mile radius of the Download site, and running a couple of Bitesize Revision pages on separate tabs in case teachers are about. We have a history paper after lunch. Source questions on the Cold War. School vibrates with that strange, stifling quietness that always creeps up around exam time. It seems at odds with the blue skies and lush trees, the carefree games of cricket and tennis that go on in cinematic Technicolor on the outside.

'So,' says Solomon, 'who is this Zara person?'

'Who?'

'The one you keep texting under the table.'

'Just . . . someone that I used to know,' I say, inadvertently quoting a song that's always on the radio.

'But who *is* she? Is she one of the Carlisles? It's the family that owns all those racehorses, isn't it? Or is it the toilet-seat manufacturers? I think their youngest is called Zara.'

Solomon is a kind of walking database of social trivia. His parents instilled this in him at birth: an innate need to 'place' people on a social scale that takes into account money, property and titles.

'She's no one,' I say. 'Nobody.'

'Oh, just a face then. Or do you like her for her brain?'

He unwraps a sandwich. We're allowed to bring in our own food during exams.

'What's her last name?'

'Duvalle,' I say, with reluctance, thinking how right he is: I do like her for her brain. 'Look, Sol, why don't we just camp at Download? It's so much cheaper.'

'This hotel's only a hundred and twenty-eight pounds!' he protests.

'Per night.'

'Per night, that's nothing. That's – what, oh, you do the maths, Bennikin. It's only three stars though. That might be a challenge.'

I look out of the window at the low brick walls of the science block, its tinted windows strangely sinister in the late May sun. The ICT suite is empty apart from us: everyone else is in the library, stocking up on dates and quotes for the last two-hour paper of the week. Or they're outside, free from worry, free from duty, on their backs on the lawn, absorbing the sunlight.

'It's about the music though,' I say.

Solly pats my arm. 'Yeah, I know. Course we can camp. I'll borrow some gear off my sister. She's always racing off to the Isle of Wight and whatnot. Peeing into a funnel and wearing face paint. Aren't you eating?'

'Maybe in a bit. Got a headache.'

'The thing about you, Ben,' says Solly, 'is that you're continually deeply uncomfortable in your own skin. You want to be somewhere else all the time. You are not actually in pain; you've manifested a constant sense of being in pain in order to necessitate the taking of medication. This gives you a feeling of control.'

'Spare me your therapy-speak,' I say.

'Don't forget our deal,' he replies.

Suddenly the room erupts into a burst of body odour and unwashed hair and I feel fat hot hands clamping my shoulders. Jake and Ally Stonehill: hockey champions known for their brutal stickwork and ferocious tackling. Feared by the entire lower school, and most of the teachers. Jake is one year above us; Ally is two. Committed metalheads. I don't hang out with them a lot at school. Sometimes we go to gigs together. I think maybe they've been abroad somewhere; I haven't seen them since their house party.

I half get out of my chair as Ally grabs me in a headlock. Up close, the sweat on his face threatens to diffuse onto mine. The threads of his corn-coloured fringe are greasy and stale from late nights and beer-clouded gigs. Jake and Ally see every band that plays. Even school nights, whatever. Their parents fear them too.

He pulls at the back of my head.

'Looking gooooood, Benny! Looking good!'

'Yeah, not too bad,' I say. I've been trying to grow my hair for a long time. Sooner or later someone'll make me cut it.

Jake makes the sign of the *mano cornuto* at me. Also known as the *maloik*. Index and little fingers pointing forward, out of a balled fist. I make it back.

Solly coughs. He's edged himself all the way over to the other side of the bank of desks.

'What ho,' he says.

Jake blinks at the screen in front of me. He looks at the train times, the hotel dates, the location. Puts two and two together and, eventually, makes four.

'You're going to Download!' he exclaims.

Exams don't figure prominently in the Stonehills' Life Priorities. They're so rich that you can see their house on Google Earth. School would have evicted them long ago had it not been for the newly refurbished (and rechristened) Stonehill Sports Hall and the fact that they're unbeatable at games.

'Awesome,' yells Ally. 'Gods . . . of . . . RAWK!'

'We got tickets already,' says Jake. 'Early bird.' He smirks.

'Are you taking the 5.36 on the Thursday night?' Solomon asks politely, no doubt planning an alternative. 'Or are you driving?'

'Yar,' roars Ally. 'Want a lift?'

Solly is the kind of person they'd beat up for fun, except that I like Solomon. And Jake and Ally like me. Die-hard metalheads stick together.

When they've gone, overturning box files, swearing, kicking the door, Solly turns to me and frowns.

'I know, I know,' I tell him. 'We don't have to hang out with them when we get there.'

'It's not that,' he says. 'I've just realised who Zara is. Hobie's sister!'

It's my turn to frown. 'How do you know that?'

'Our mothers were friends,' he says. 'Hobie and I used to have playdates in Year 3. He once tried to make me eat a spider.'

A pause.

'Let's not think about him,' says Solomon, turning back to the computer. 'Not now anyway. Sorry, Ben.'

Solly's wrong. I haven't been thinking about Zara. I haven't been texting her constantly. Just a couple of times. I may have written her name once or twice on the back of a past paper, but that was just to see how it looked written down in my handwriting. Hobie often called her Za or Zarie, I remember. In my spidery scrawl, the Z looks too harsh, too forbidding, with its jagged angles and straight lines. I try to make it more calligraphic, curving the lines slightly, as Jason would have done. I wish I had a Rotring.

Hobie was always pretty horrible to Zara. I didn't really know her at all. I only saw her at playdates, and then that half term at Duvalle Hall. I remember her as a gentle – almost too gentle – person, who loved animals and soft fabrics and pretty colours. Her room in Duvalle Hall was beautiful. There was a patchwork quilt pinned above the bed, something she'd inherited from her great-grandmother.

Rosy hexagons, a riot of flowers and polka dots, a dark purple border. On the shelves between the windows that looked down across the lawn were six or seven large, real-looking dolls, with long eyelashes and placid faces. Each one, Zara once told me, was an American Girl, from a different period in history. There was a Settler one with blonde plaits, a 1920s tomboyish one, a princessy Victorian orphan in a sumptuous velvet dress. It was the Victorian one that I most often saw her wandering about the house with, whispering in its ear. Samantha, I think it was called.

Hobie found me in Zara's room, listening to her explaining the histories of her dolls, and extracted me with typical urgency. 'What are you doing in there?' he demanded. 'You'll become infected with gayness. Let's go outside. Come on.' And he manhandled me out of the room, fingers digging into my arm. The only game he really liked playing with Zara was Lose Zara in the Maze.

I want to say that I told him he shouldn't be so cruel to Zara. But I'm not sure I did. It makes me feel a bit sick, the thought of that. He used to tell her she was fat; I remember that quite clearly. She wasn't fat, not ever. Even if she had been, I don't see why it should have mattered to anyone, not unless she was life-threateningly overweight. She wasn't even plump. By the time I went to stay at Duvalle Hall she was skin and bone. And he still laughed at her for being chubby. It amused him, I think, to see how much power he had over her. Also, he liked to eat her food.

OK, maybe I have been thinking about Zara a bit. And, since it isn't really possible to think about Zara without thinking about Hobie, I've been thinking about him too.

'Ready?' says Solly, pouring a sachet of powdered vitamin C into his water bottle.

'Ready,' I say, logging off.

Side by side, we make our way down to the exam hall.

I wake up on Sunday with a foul, bone-splitting pain between my ears. It feels as if my mouth is stuffed full of cloth. My eyes, when I open them, jam themselves shut in horror. *Emergency*. The glass by my bed is empty, so I go downstairs in my tracksuit bottoms and *Sad But True* T-shirt to fetch a drink. I will take a *third* of a pill, and no more. Solomon is right: I ought to cut down.

Mum is sitting at the kitchen table. The blinds are shut; the garden door is closed. She's on the phone. Her mobile is palmed against her cheek, and she's whispering into it.

'Can't tell him now,' she says.

Then something I can't hear, as I stand in the doorway.

'Just . . . hold tight. I'll be . . . but try not to . . .'

She looks up and our eyes lock. Her tone shifts, becomes bright. Fake, like plastic flowers.

'But we'll speak later, all right, Jane?'

Unlikely that it would Aunt Jane on the phone, at 9 a.m. Greenwich Mean Time.

'Bye for now, then. Bye.' She puts the phone down, like

it's perfectly normal to be sitting and whispering in the gloom of an unlit kitchen.

'Ben, you're up early!' she says warmly. She twiddles the blinds, floods the kitchen with light. Soon she'll be in full-on breakfast mode.

'Coffee? A boiled egg?'

'Who was that on the phone?' I blurt out. 'Was it Dad?'

I don't know why I've just said that. But I can see in the sudden flash of panic in her eyes, the way her nostrils flare slightly, that I'm right.

'What's wrong? What's wrong with Dad?'

She takes a box of eggs out of the fridge. Lifts one up to the light, checking for cracks.

'I should have got some smoked salmon,' she murmurs. 'They have offcuts at Co-op.'

'I don't want any smoked salmon! What's the matter with Dad? Is he ill?'

'Ben, calm down, please. Your dad's fine.'

'Why do you keep lying about everything?' I shout at her, my voice catching, as if I've surprised it with my own daring.

She stops rifling through the fridge and looks at me – actually *at* me, rather than through me. Like Zara did, for a moment, outside the Underworld. Then she sits down at the table, her forehead in her hands. When she speaks, she speaks quietly.

'I'm sorry. I'm sorry I didn't tell you about Jason. You probably think I didn't care about him, that I only cared about your Scholarship exams. He was a deeply brilliant tutor and a very nice person who didn't deserve to die, suddenly, like that. I'm sorry your father and I couldn't make it work. I'm sorry I lost my job. I'm sorry I sold your harp. I'm sorry about the goldfish. I'm sorry about everything.'

I don't know what to say. I stand there, looking out from under my fringe.

'You told the police not to tell me,' I say accusingly. 'When they came to talk to me. You are such a liar that you actually got the police to lie to me too.'

'Not lie. Just . . . not tell you the . . . the whole truth.'

'Big difference.'

'It was for . . .'

'*Don't* keep saying it.'

She closes her eyes for a second.

'As for your dad,' she says, 'he's had one of his episodes. You know how he gets.'

'Are you going to go and see him?'

'I think I should. He sounded in quite a bad way.'

'When I went round the other day he was drinking again,' I tell her.

'Poor Robin,' she says.

'He thinks Jason took an overdose,' I say. 'Did you know that? Is that what you think too?'

She tilts her head a little, as though it's a new thought.

'No,' she says at last. 'That's just the sort of thing Robin would think.'

'What do you think?'

'I thought perhaps he was diabetic, asthmatic . . . I don't know. There are so many possible reasons why he could have died. But an overdose: no. I wouldn't allow a drug addict to tutor my son.'

'Did you not ask the Duvalles?'

'Believe it or not, Ben, I haven't seen either of them since. I haven't particularly wanted to. Hobie was *not* a good influence on you. I should never have let you play with him.'

I watch the knot of her dark hair rise and fall as she busies herself at the worktop, her back turned. I don't see how she can be right, any more than Dad can be right. I don't believe there are so many possible reasons why Jason could have died.

I down a pint of water and accept her offering of a boiled egg. We eat in silence, with the radio tinkling in the background.

After breakfast, Mum loads up the car with books and mineral water and cake and drives to Battersea. I don't know how I feel about this. She used to hate Dad. Now she's going on a rescue mission.

'What about Reg of Putney?' I want to ask. But I don't really care. At least, for once, she's told me the truth about something.

I make sure that I am not late to meet Zara. I don't think lateness is a quality she'd admire. I take a different route today, crossing the canal, just as I once did with Hobie, when we went shopping for our wolf suits.

Early, I stand outside the church at the top of Ladbroke Grove, and I realise I haven't just been thinking about Zara a bit. I've been thinking about her a lot.

It's a greyer day than last Sunday. Swollen clouds drift solemnly overhead. I listen to the soft rise and fall of embarrassed British singing. The alleluia choruses peak and drop, peak and drop. Hymns always seem so sad. This one sounds like 'Onward, Christian Soldiers'. Whenever we sing it at school it makes me think of 'For Whom the Bell Tolls'.

Then the doors swing open and people trail out. A young couple carries a newly baptised infant, wrapped in a pink-and-white blanket. Well-wishing godparents step smartly in shiny shoes. Ike and Elsie climb into a dark Mercedes. I look for Zara.

When she appears, my heart surges a little, like it's been charged with an extra amp. And then it surges again, with recognition.

Next to Zara, in a long purple skirt and matching cropped jacket, is Rebecca.

# HOBIE'S DIARY

Sunday 2nd November 2008

Early on Friday Ben's mum texted and asked if I could go round after lunch instead of arriving at 10 a.m., and although she didn't say why I presumed it was something to do with Ben's dad. I went through a number of possibilities aloud while Clothilde boiled me a second egg because the first one was too runny. Maybe Ben's parents were getting back together and they were all sitting round in pyjamas watching television or something. Or maybe Ben's father had tried to kidnap Ben and take him to France and half the Greater London police force had been after them in a massive car chase and they'd caught up with them just as Ben's dad was getting on the Eurostar with his unconscious son stuffed into a sports bag.

'Or maybe you watch too much television and read too many stupid magazines, Hobie,' said Zara, staring down at a piece of white toast that she was bizarrely eating with her knife and fork.

I thought fondly of 'Cannibal Ate My Mum with Ketchup and Peas'.

Dad had left for a breakfast meeting and Mum was panicking about her Gala Dinner, racing round the house as fast as her high heels would permit, simultaneously putting on face cream, yelling down the phone at someone called Kirsty about whether the caterers had the vegetarians marked on the table plans and necking vitamins straight from the bottle.

'What are you doing for Halloween?' I asked Zara.

She recoiled as if I'd suggested a merry jaunt to Wormwood Scrubs to feed the convicts.

'Nothing. I need to work.'

Recently Za has started asking if she can go to boarding school. I think Mum and Dad were a bit taken by surprise because she is hardly an independent spirit. I mean, she's still frightened of the dark, isn't she? But they went along to some Open Day and predictably Zara was enchanted by the flowery cushions in the boarding house and the fact that you could keep your own rabbit in some dedicated pet area. And Mum and Dad, you could tell, were not unexcited by the prospect of having us both out of the house next year so they could go on more holidays and things. So Zara is studying all the time, writing new bits of vocabulary in a pink book with a fluffy cover, reading *Little Women* and *Pride and Prejudice* and working with Rebecca twice a week like clockwork. The doctor apparently said that Zara was a bit underweight so now she has to keep a food diary and Clothilde and Mum have to make sure she's eating at mealtimes. If anything, I think Zara's eating less as a result.

I didn't mind not going to Ben's after breakfast. We'd done enough bloody revision, even by Hobbitboy's standards. I had one of my favourite sorts of morning instead, roaming around the house half-dressed and playing computer games. I ran 4 kilometres in the gym (at least I'm allowed to do that, if no other exercise) and watched *Cribs* on MTV and had a very splashy bath where I read the Gods book (Ben won't mind if it's a bit waterlogged). Then, when Mum's masseuse came round, I spent a good twenty minutes in the second sitting room, which no one uses much and is just full of sculptures and poncey art books, and where the goodie bags for the Gala Dinner were sitting in solemn white rows, like those war graves in Flanders Fields.

'What were you *doing* in there?' Zara asked suspiciously as we collided on the stairs. 'You'd better not have taken the salted caramels out of the bags.'

When I got to Ben's house the kitchen felt different. Sort of cleaner and lighter, like someone had mopped it very thoroughly. Funny, I felt almost sad about the week coming to an end. I'd actually sort of enjoyed working at Ben's house, which, apart from his mother barging in every lunchtime and ringing up and harassing Ben all the time, had been really peaceful and constructive. We got a lot done, and I am prepared to care about it as long as the teachers don't move me down and say I can't take Scholarship. I wish Ben and I were applying to the same school.

'What was going on with your mum and dad last night?' I asked Ben as we sat at the table on Friday trying to get through everything at top speed, scribbling the last of our

Geography notes by hand rather than waste time formatting them in Word.

He put his pen down and started building a house out of the colour-coded index cards we'd been writing on. Clothilde has been dutifully trotting back and forth from Ryman's all week, satisfying our every demand for stationery supplies. His face was all tight, like he didn't have enough skin. I waited.

'My dad's getting married again.'

'Whoa, no way! That's kind of *fast*, isn't it? Who to?'

The top of the card house wobbled and gave way, and the index cards collapsed into a messy mix of pink and blue.

'My old nanny, Marti,' he said shortly.

That's when I saw what was different about the kitchen. Following my gaze, Ben said, 'We came home and mum went mental and smashed some things. Plates, bowls . . .'

The empty space on the counter next to the fridge looked like a massive yawn.

'Shit! What happened to the goldfish?'

'They died pretty much straight away.'

I tried to imagine Ben's sleek-haired, boringly dressed mother breaking the goldfish bowl. Had she just dropped it straight downwards to the floor or hurled it across the room? A watery stain, low down on the white wall opposite, confirmed my suspicions.

'Wow,' I said. 'Maybe she's a Berserk too.'

He put his finger to his lips. 'She's upstairs.'

\* \* \*

I thought perhaps Ben wouldn't want to go to the party, but he seemed really up for it in his quiet way. Maybe he didn't want to spend the evening with his mother, who when she came downstairs at teatime looked as if she could definitely give Morticia Addams a run for her money. Her eyes were red and bloodshot and for once her hair was all nasty and scruffy like a mass of wires. Like my mother when she has no make-up on, she looked loads older. She made herself a cup of tea and looked blankly about the kitchen, and asked me if I would remember to take all my chargers and pencils and mini Post-it notes and Tupperware containers with me as it would be very nice to regain the use of her kitchen table. That sounded rather sarcastic, I thought, but I was in the middle of a buttered raisin muffin with strawberry jam so I didn't wind her up about the dead goldfish or anything.

So I packed up my stuff and Ben and I got into our wolf suits, which took a hell of a long time. I wore black jeans from DKNY Kids and Ben put on some old faded grey ones. We cut up the tatty old fur stoles and safety-pinned them to our trainers so they could be wolf paws. We actually sewed strips into long sausages for tails, sitting on the floor with our backs against the bed and listening to this awesome music called Heavy Metal that is really quite old but still incredible. It sounds like how I often feel before rugby and football matches, furious and frenetic, with huge drums that beat really fast and whole armies of guitars on top of it and mad high-pitched screaming. And a lot of the songs are about war and madness and death. Like I said, awesome.

'How come your mum lets you listen to this stuff?' I asked as I attached my tail to the back of my fur coat.

'She used to make a fuss about it,' he said, 'but then she read an article about how children that listen to heavy metal have higher IQs.'

With our fur hats and leather masks and fangs, with just the bedside lamp on and Ben's mural as our background and the chug-chug-chug and drone of the music, we stopped being Ben and Hobie and became Hati and Skǫll. One song by a band called Metallica was actually called 'Of Wolf and Man'. Like it was written specially for us! I was jumping up and down on the bed and trying to bat the ceiling with my tail and Ben was leaping about the room in that slightly shifty way that he has, shaking his hair about. He was chanting, '*Bǫðvar úlfr brandi tekr!*' over and over and I asked him what it meant and he said it meant 'Wolf of combat takes up blade' which was about as far as he had got at teaching himself Old Norse and I thought it was one of the coolest things I'd ever heard. He wrote it down for me on one of our revision cards and I told him it was really quite impressive the way he'd managed to learn all the spellings and things. And Ben explained that it was sort of out of respect to the Otherlife, which was why he preferred to use the proper Norse names for most of the Gods, even if it takes a bit of time to get it right. Then he taught me a Heavy Metal sign called the *mano cornuto*, which you make by holding up your hand with all the fingers clenched into a fist except your index and little fingers, so it looks like a pair of devil's horns.

Awesome.

Ben's mother opened the door and said she was ready when we were and could we please turn down the music and stop ruining the furniture. 'Good Lord!' she said, presumably taken aback by our wolf suits. Then we drove to Frodo's in absolute silence.

Frodo's house, which I hate to say is bigger than mine, was lit up neon green by these massive floodlights on either side of the door. Life-size cutouts of Frankenstein and Dracula were parked between the bonsai trees. His housekeeper and cleaner were stationed inside the hall, each holding a gigantic wicker bowl full of organic sweets. I lunged at them, and was immediately pulled away by the scruff of my wolf suit by Frodo's mother, who appeared out of nowhere. Now, if I find Frodo irritating, fat, pretentious and boring, then it's highly probable that his mother is responsible for all of the above except the fatness, which he gets from his father. She has a dried-up face and scraped-back hair and wears all black all the time. I have never seen her smile, even when she is talking about Frodo and his amazing gifts and talents. According to her, he was playing the violin at eighteen months and composed the music for his grandmother's funeral when he was only seven, never watches television because he would prefer to have private classes with a member of the Olympic fencing team and knows how to make crème brûlée with a mini blowtorch. Oh well, I suppose that's the pudding that matches his personality most accurately. His mother is called Vonda and she hates me as much as I hate her because of the chalk penis episode. Quite often she sends Frodes into school with vomit-inducing cookies like pumpkin seed and molasses, which none of us will eat, so we take them home and then the other mothers see what a stupendous Baking Talent she is.

We were the last people to arrive, and apart from Matteo everyone was there. Norville was in a bespoke £300 chicken suit. The Nicholson Twins had come as Jekyll and Hyde. Archie was Little Bo Peep but spattered with blood and with a lightsaber instead of a shepherd's crook. Only Archie, who is strong enough to hit you back, could get away with something as tempting-to-violence as dressing as a girl. And everyone was rushing around shrieking and jumping on balloons and the whole of the downstairs floor was decked out with cobwebs and huge toadstools that lit up and changed colour and scary ghost noises were playing through the speakers.

There was a photographer there, sidling around all the groups of kids with his camera. He had one of those old

Polaroid cameras that are supposed to be really cool because they're from like the 1950s or something.

'A pair of wolves!' he said.

'I don't want to be in a photograph,' said Ben.

But the photographer was hustling us into an empty space in front of a cobwebbed wall.

'Smile!' he said.

I put my arm around Ben and whispered, *Wolf of combat takes up blade!*'

He chuckled. The camera popped and flashed and I felt Ben cringe and tense up a bit but when the photograph came out it was really cool because we were both doing proper wolf grins and I decided that I liked it more than the signed picture of me and Tom Cruise. Ben didn't seem to want it so I put it in my jeans pocket, folded in half.

Somebody coughed loudly from the landing and we all looked up at the massive curvy marble staircase because Frodo was coming down the stairs. And I have to say it was pretty cool of him to dress as an actual Hobbit, complete with pointy ears, hairy toes and a flagon of ale in each hand. Almost as though Frodes has a sense of humour after all. Knowing him and his mother, it was probably an actual costume from *The Lord of the Rings* and I was half expecting her to say she'd put in a call to the director and he'd had it shipped over specially, just for Frodo.

And then she did say just that.

Frodo's nanny took us trick-or-treating and we traipsed

up and down the sloping tree-lined roads ringing on all the same doorbells as the other convoys of kids. We must have passed fifty or sixty other groups of ghosts and goblins and devils and witches and so on, marching with the sugar-crazed intensity of army recruits and yelling insults at each other across the street. Our Happy Halloween bags groaned under the weight of chocolate coins and packets of Haribo and Oreo cookies. I had the idea after a while to start howling instead of shouting 'trick or treat' and then Ben and I both began howling non-stop and capering from side to side, dangerously close to the edge of the pavement.

We fell behind the others and then met a phalanx of Teletubbies coming the other way, which caused a bit of congestion.

Ben caught hold of my sleeve with his paw.

'Let's run away,' he said.

So we did.

We tore off down the road, jumping high in the air and howling bloodcurdling howls and *'Boðvar úlfr brandi tekr!'* which I'd pretty much got the gist of by that point, cannoning into the other trick-or-treaters. Just as we were coming up behind a group of really little kids, no more than seven or eight I'd say, it was like we both had the same idea, because Ben leaped around one side of them and I leaped around the other and roared really loudly, which made several of them start screaming. As an afterthought I snatched one of their bags of treats and then we sprinted away on our wolf feet, fast as torna-does. The father who was with the little kids started yelling at us to come back and apologise and what did we think we were doing etc, so I reached for a handful of Quality Street and flung them behind me as I ran and yelled, '*Bǫðvar úlfr brandi tekr!*' although I guess I should've replaced the object noun with the word for sweets, but they probably didn't have those a thousand years ago.

We rounded the corner and pelted down the street and crossed the road and crept along it in exaggerated steps, like burglars do in cartoons. We pressed our masks to the windows of shops and soon came to an incredibly posh restaurant that my parents go to sometimes on dates. It was low-lit inside with candles on the tables and was full of expensively dressed people with wine in silver buckets and waiters with white tea towels over their arms. We crouched down behind the door, under the dark green awning.

I looked at Ben. He looked back at me. No one needed to say the words *I dare you*.

We were Hati and Skǫll.

We opened the door, and although it jangled loudly I could see the maître d' lady with her massive appointment book on a little plinth and her back was turned because she was saying goodbye to someone. We sprang into the room and ran around the tables, doing a sort of Wild Rumpus dance from *Where the Wild Things Are*. This caused a wave of diners to break abruptly from their boring conversations about house prices etc etc and give little, polite screams (some were louder than others) and the maître d' started marching in pursuit, but of course she couldn't properly shout at us because the restaurant is what my mum calls *hushed tones*. And we met a waiter coming the other way and he was holding a wooden board with a huge, perfectly cooked steak for two people to share which I think is called a *côte de boeuf*, and there was a glittery serrated knife artfully poised among some rocket leaves and I pounced at the waiter. But Ben pounced first.

Randomly, I started thinking about last week's creative writing homework, which had been to write a story called 'Crossing the Line'. When Ben seized the *côte de boeuf* and made off with it, and I followed him, I think we probably crossed it.

We ran for what seemed like an hour but actually just took us around the block. And finally we collapsed on someone's doorstep and howled with wolf-howl laughter.

'Wolves of combat take up steak!' I said.

Ben looked down at the frankly enormous steak, charred on the outside and oozing juices.

'It should be raw really,' he muttered.

'We should have got hold of some chips,' I said.

We tore it in half and devoured it.

It felt like being free.

\*    \*    \*

The rest of the evening was, of course, dull by comparison. Hobbitboy's nanny is so moronic that she had actually failed to notice that we were missing, and we managed to catch them up just as they were approaching the house. Frodo had slowed to a waddle, encumbered by his excessive bulk and the acquisition of about four tonnes of treats. Archie had broken his lightsaber and was trying not to cry.

Then there were games and feasting supervised by Frodo's unsmiling, witchlike-in-all-seasons mother. Ben and I didn't join in as much as we could have done because we felt full. Full, and sort of smug. To be honest, I hadn't thought Ben had it in him to be that naughty.

I really slept in yesterday morning. It had already been agreed that I could take the whole weekend off from revision. Despite being mightily pissed off that I *still* wasn't allowed to go to Football Club, I was looking forward to some proper lounging about.

My father is half-American so really goes in for brunch on Saturdays – when he's not on a business trip, that is. Brunch involves smoked salmon, freshly baked bagels, orange juice squeezed by Clothilde using our Kenwood Multipro machine, fruit salad and eggs cooked by Dad any way you like. Awesome.

I could hear Zara in her room, so I put my head round the door. I resisted the temptation to boast about the Great Steak Heist, perpetrated by ferocious mystery wolves.

'Coming down, Za?'

She was sitting at her desk, halfway through a Non-Verbal Reasoning paper.

'Not hungry,' she said, not looking up. 'Got to finish this so Rebecca can mark it.'

I peered over her shoulder. 'That's wrong, *that's* wrong and *that's* wrong,' I said, pointing at Find the Missing Shape and Which of the Shapes on the Right Contains the Hidden Shape on the Left. She flung her head down over the paper and wrapped her arms around it.

'Go away, Hobie!'

'OK, okaay!'

I pottered downstairs.

Mum and Dad were at the second-cup-of-coffee stage. The radio was burbling in the background. Newspapers were littering the table, providing a comprehensive spread of Sports, Travel and Money news. I poured myself a big glass of orange juice and picked out the strawberries from the fruit salad while I pondered what mode of eggs to choose. Fried are the most greasily satisfying. If you go for scrambled it always feels like it's not quite enough. Poached? They look like boobs, I always think, which is diverting.

'I just can't imagine who would have done something like that,' Mum was saying mournfully. She was swaddled in a white robe.

'Oh, how did your gala go, Mum?' I asked with my mouth full.

Dad sliced a bagel in two and began smothering it with Philadelphia.

'Someone at the venue with a sick sense of humour?' he said. 'One of the waiters perhaps?'

I froze with my hand still out to grab a handful of papaya chunks from the bowl. Were they talking about the Great Steak Heist? Had it somehow reached the national papers? Wicked!

But they weren't talking about that.

The Gala Dinner had been a huge success, apparently, with a silent auction thing that had raised a hundred thousand pounds. Mum had come home elated and triumphant and had already started planning next year's event.

Then, at 9 this morning, the phone had started ringing.

It turned out that all those Gala Dinner goodie bags had contained, along with the salted caramels and hand cream and spa vouchers etc, a photocopy of a tasteless magazine article entitled 'Cannibal Ate My Mum with Ketchup and Peas'.

No one could think how it had happened.

# BEN

It's Rebecca who plunges towards me, a rush of familiar, heathery perfume reaching me first.

'Darling, dearest, lovely *Ben*,' she says into my earlobe, squeezing me tight. 'How are you, my friend? Zara said she'd been seeing you.'

We stand on the stone path that leads from the church to the street. Breezes ruffle the tops of the trees. Zara's hands are blue.

Rebecca slips an arm around Zara's shoulders and says to me, 'Come for tea? We'll go to my flat. It's a nice walk from here. Quickly though – it's going to pour with rain. My geraniums will be thrilled!'

As we hurry down Ladbroke Grove, I try to figure out what Rebecca's relationship is to Zara now. Is she still a tutor, or more of a friend? A big sister? The way she holds Zara's arm, just above the elbow, as we cross the road, makes me think that she's still in a position of authority. Or perhaps she just cares about Zara, who seems so fragile. Another person from the past has crept back into my life. It's hard to accept that Jason never will.

Rebecca keeps up a carol of conversation the whole way.

'And what about your heavy metal, Ben? Are you still a fan, or have you moved on to postmodern jazz?'

'Still into it,' I say, thinking of Solomon.

'I remember you and Hobie going absolutely nuts over it at Duvalle Hall. There was a song about wolves, wasn't there? And then one by Hemingway.'

'Well, it was by Metallica, but—'

'Oh yes. "For Whom The Bell Tolls"!' Rebecca laughs.

I tell her about Download in a couple of weeks' time. Less. In one week and four days, I'll be there. I don't think I've ever looked forward to an event so much.

'Download?' says Zara. 'That's held in the grounds of Donington Park, I think. We see signs for it, on the motorway. It's quite near Duvalle Hall, isn't it?'

'I don't know,' I say. I only ever went to Duvalle Hall once, by car. I don't remember its location. I do, however, remember Hobie telling me that Duvalle Hall was the second-largest estate in the whole county.

'Well,' says Rebecca, 'Zara and I will be there that weekend, so if you get sick of the noise and the smell, you'll know where to find us.'

A group of tourists headed to Portobello straggles past us, spilling onto the road. To our left is a funeral parlour, dressed solemnly in black. Zara goes into BestOne to buy a Diet Coke; Rebecca and I wait outside. If Rebecca ran a funeral parlour, I find myself thinking, she'd dispense with the tedium of tradition. No more shiny black. No more urns and lilies. The outside would be cobalt blue with baked-in sparkles. Inside there'd be a fountain, where mysterious fish with bright, feathery tails would swim, and a string quartet would sit at the back making gentle music.

'What's the deal with you and Zara?' I blurt out, hoping I'm not sounding rude.

'I suppose what you'd call me is a mentor,' Rebecca says thoughtfully. 'I do offer some homework support, but that's not really the kind of help that Zarie needs. I keep an eye on her, especially if Ike and Elsie are away. She's been very ill for quite a while. I try to phone or text every day, and then I go and stay there sometimes. Or at Duvalle Hall. You really should come and visit us there some time. She'd like that.'

I look at her. 'Don't you think . . . ? Don't you think it will bring back bad memories?'

'For Zara, you mean?'

'For everyone.'

We watch Zara in the queue. I'm not quite sure, but from the way she is holding her purse, I think she's counting out, in pennies and five-pence pieces, the exact price of her drink. To save the cashier from having to give her change.

'I wonder if sometimes we are all pushing those memories away,' says Rebecca, 'when actually we need to face up to the past. Then again, I think to myself, sometimes, that I will try to talk to Zara about Hobie, but . . . I don't.'

\* \* \*

Rebecca's flat is on the third floor of a narrow terraced house in a tree-lined street. There are no cobalt-blue surfaces or floating fish, and you could fit the whole of it in any of the rooms in either of Hobie's houses. But the floorboards are glossy and white and the walls are covered with pictures and sketches and photographs. There is a tiny roof terrace crammed with herbs and flowers. The air smells of warm milk and baking spices. There are toys everywhere and a big wooden abacus sits in the fireplace. Rebecca must do quite a lot of child-minding, as well as looking after Zara. I wonder if she ever did any more acting. I remember she was an actress once.

As though she's reading my mind, Rebecca points out a long row of silver discs in wooden frames, like they have in recording studios. Above, the CD sleeves in separate frames: dragons, trains, a full moon. Children's books. Some of them famous.

'Those are mine,' she says. 'Audiobooks. I did the voices.'

Zara is making tea. She spoons loose leaves into a wire holder and pours boiling water into the pot.

Rebecca takes a cake out of a tin and cuts big, healthy slices.

'You aren't allergic to nuts, are you, Ben?'

I shake my head.

'This is my grandmother's recipe. The secret is soaking the fruit overnight.'

We don't sit on the terrace, because the rain is now

pattering down, in that gradual way that suggests a full-blown storm is on its way. The roof is alive with drums. You can hear the whoosh of trains hurtling across the flyover, the clink of Zara's spoon in her teacup.

I watch Zara pull her cake apart, raisin by crumb. Her hands aren't blue any more. They're white, the skin almost translucent. The lines of her bones are clearly visible. Rebecca and I talk about books, about my GCSEs, about my plans. All the time I'm answering, I'm trying to use more than monosyllables, because Rebecca's one of those people who makes you want to speak properly, with good adverbs and interesting synonyms. I'm looking at Zara's fingers undoing her cake, the too-slenderness of her wrist. And despite the hollowing out of my stomach, the acid wave of sickness that always kicks in when my head hurts, I force myself to eat all my cake. To show Zara that it's possible. In all fairness, it's delicious.

The doorbell rings and Rebecca jumps up.

'That'll be my neighbour,' she says.

When she returns, she is carrying a little boy of maybe two or three. His hair is the colour of weak sunshine and his arms are wrapped chubbily about Rebecca's neck.

'Ben, you must meet Ashley. Ashley, shake hands,' she commands.

The little boy extends a pudgy arm, with a pudgy hand at the end of it. His fingers fan out, like seaweed fronds, or a tiny starfish. I shake hands with just my index finger. I've never done that before.

'He's grown,' says Zara.

'He'll be as tall as an oak tree one day. Won't you, my little acorn?' says Rebecca, as she kisses him. I stare at his face, his little round nose and olive-green eyes. Watch as he kisses her back.

'Zaza is here,' the child pronounces, reaching messily for a fragment of cake.

Rebecca passes him over to Zara and he reaches out for a strand of her hair, his face smeared with icing sugar and spittle.

'How old is your son?' I ask.

'He'll be three in July. It goes so fast.'

'I like the name.' In Norse mythology, Askr was the first man. Ash and Elm, the two original trees. I wonder if Rebecca knows that.

'He doesn't look an awful lot like me,' she muses, 'but I'm holding out for his acting abilities.'

I wonder if I look like Mum. I think I have her features: her beaky nose and serious brow. I have Dad's eyes though.

'Then again,' Rebecca goes on, 'he's the spitting image of his father. You can probably tell, can't you, Ben?'

I blink at her. Wonder what she means.

And then I see.

I see whose son he is.

'He's . . . *Jason's*?'

Rebecca sighs. 'I thought Zara would've told you. Jason and I weren't exactly going out. But we did get – close, at

Duvalle Hall. That lovely converted stables. You can sort of imagine. Of all the strange things to happen to me, it must have been the strangest. An accident. A death. A life. The events of that weekend . . . they changed me. I cared too much about how things looked, before, about the surface of things. It's only when something like that happens to you that you realise there are stronger undercurrents in this world, that there are things more powerful than beauty. Sorry. That probably doesn't make sense. I tend to ramble.'

'It's fine,' I say.

'I'd like to say that I loved Jason,' says Rebecca, 'but I didn't know him well enough. I love him in retrospect though. I love his memory.'

She smiles. Her eyes look moist.

'He talked about death quite often, oddly. He had all these deep-seated beliefs about honouring the dead, proper burials for people in case they came back and haunted you . . .'

'Did you go to his funeral?'

She shakes her head. 'It was very small, I think. Up in Yorkshire. You have to remember, I wasn't really a friend of Jason's. We knew each other as fellow-tutors; that was all. It wasn't until a couple of weeks after he was buried that I even realised I was pregnant.'

I say, more harshly than I mean to: 'I would have wanted to be there. Nobody even told me he was dead.'

'Oh, Ben. That's . . . I suppose your parents wanted to protect you. It was such a difficult time.'

'They wanted him to get his Scholarship,' adds Zara, refilling our cups.

'How did he die, Rebecca? Do you know?' I ask.

She winces.

'I'll never forget it, Ben. Finding him. We weren't even meant to stay that night, but my car wouldn't start. It had been a long week. You were adorable and really motivated, but trying to get Hobie to work properly was like pulling teeth. The meal went on for ages. Then the fireworks . . . I couldn't see Jason, and I thought he must have gone to bed early. In the morning I knocked on his door, and when there was no answer I thought that perhaps he had gone for a walk. But I got a feeling, Ben, a kind of eerie feeling that something bad had happened. I went into his room, and saw that his bed hadn't been slept in. I ran outside and found him, curled up on his side, just near the rhododendrons. His face was all swollen and puffy. His eyes were closed.'

'Sorry, Rebecca,' I say. 'I'm so sorry.'

Ashley clambers over her, his fingers closing over a small gold *R* around her neck. She kisses his hair, inhaling him.

'Wasn't there an investigation? A coroner's report?' I say.

'Of course there was. Yes.'

Zara gets up and crosses over to the window. She places her hands on the pane in five-point stars. Rebecca glances at her, and then at me.

I begin to feel another presence in the room. The air curves inwards, bending into a different shape; hot and cold currents cross and recross, jostling for space, as the floral-print cushions, the children's books and house plants take on the unreal gloss that tells me that something else is here, something other. Subtly, a golden light hangs for a moment near Zara's head. A red light. A light of lemony-green. They tense and pulse, briefly, and are gone.

Zara turns around suddenly and says, 'It's OK. You can tell us.'

Rebecca pauses briefly. 'It was an allergy of some kind. People do have terribly bad reactions to things sometimes. They go into anaphylactic shock. That's how Jason died.'

'But an allergy to *what*?' I say.

'I really, truly don't know,' says Rebecca, taking a sip of tea. 'I was never told. I don't think anyone ever established it. Maybe he was stung by a bee.'

In November? That hardly seems likely. Does she really believe that he might have been stung by a bee? I realise it's quite hard to tell what Rebecca is really thinking.

'What about his parents?' I say. 'You must see them sometimes. Surely they must have told you what he was allergic to. Have you never asked them?'

'Both his parents had died, long before he did. The only relative of Jason's I ever met was Great-Aunt Ivy. I took Ashley to meet her in Fortnum & Mason's. We had tea. It was all very polite. We didn't talk about his death. It didn't really seem like the place for it.'

\* \* \*

266

When we come out onto the doorstep it's raining hard. The street is deserted. Water paints it a dirty, tarnished silver. I walk right out into the middle of the road, taking off my hoodie, allowing the water to drum into the fibres of my T-shirt, the pockets of my jeans. If I stand here long enough, the rain will erode me like a limestone stump, dissolving me into the gutter. Either that, or a car will run me over. I tip my head back so that a shelf of water cascades onto the plane of my forehead. In my head, Slayer's 'Reign in Blood' begins. Distilled into my senses, arms out in a scarecrow's pose, I wait to be washed away.

'Ben. What on earth are you doing? Are you OK?'

The uninvited roof of a small umbrella interrupts my silence. Now a hand on my shoulder. She guides me back to the kerb.

'Put your hoodie back on,' says Zara, eyes blue and unavoidable. 'And tell me what's wrong.'

'I'm sick to death,' I say, relishing the unpleasantness of the word, 'of being lied to.'

'What do you mean?'

'She's lying. She knows. She knows what really killed Jason and she's lying.'

Zara's voice is measured and composed. 'Rebecca never lies. She isn't like that, Ben. It's just the way she is. She doesn't think about things that are painful and ugly, like death. And she doesn't . . . She wouldn't want to upset me, by talking about it all.'

'An allergy?! It sounds completely made up. If Jason had been allergic to anything, I'd have known about it. *She'd* have known about it. She'd have remembered what they found, instead of being all vague and mysterious and . . .'

'Calm down. Breathe.'

Her hand rests on my arm; her fingers are white-and-blue from the cold. There's a damp heat around my nose. Tears at the corners of my eyes. I imagine Jason's PhD papers stacked, unfinished and waiting for him on a desk he'd never return to. I imagine Rebecca, carrying a child he'd never meet, her earrings glittering in gentle sorrow.

*I will find out what happened, Jason.*

'Cry if you want to,' says Zara, reaching her arms up around my back. Her teeth are chattering. So are mine. The top of her head comes to just beneath my chin. Her hair is darkened by water to a burnt-toast brown. The roof of the umbrella roars with syncopated rain. I cannot cry in front of her.

'You're a very kind person,' I say.

I place my hands on her shoulders and move her away from me slightly so we're staring at each other. I notice that she has tiny freckles across the bridge of her nose. Her teeth are white and even and small. She was probably wearing lip gloss earlier today; there's a tiny smudge of coral above her lip line. Her eyes are vivid and clear-seeing. I wonder at the roundabout of my emotions; that the tangled rage of five minutes ago could have been so completely replaced with something so completely different.

And just as I am about to kiss her, she kisses me first.

This is the closest I have ever stood to another person. I can feel her hands on my shoulder blades, where my wings would be; for the sake of symmetry, I find myself putting my hands in exactly the same place on her. Although she looks so cold, her skin is warm.

Now we break apart and look at each other in a new way. She smiles. I smile back.

Then, like an idiot, I say, 'Zara, don't you think there's more to Jason's death than everyone is saying?'

She moves slightly away.

'What do you mean?'

'You know what I mean. Who in the house liked tricks and practical jokes? Who was constantly in trouble for—'

'Ben!'

'I'm sorry,' I say. 'But we need to look at all the evidence.'

'There is no evidence to suggest that *anyone* had anything to do with Jason's death. The police—'

'But the police didn't question everyone, did they?'

They barely asked me anything myself, I think, recalling the brief visit, the sequence of seemingly random questions, the omission of the fact that my tutor was dead.

'I can't believe you'd accuse the one person who can't defend himself,' Zara says, slowly and sorrowfully, like an adult.

'But I—'

'I don't like where you're going with this. There are some questions people really shouldn't ask.'

*But I promised*, I say in my head. I promised the Gods. I promised Jason. I can't stop now. Even if Zara wants me to.

I escort her to the corner, where she hails a cab. She climbs into it without saying goodbye.

# HOBIE'S DIARY

Monday 3rd November 2008

So here we are at our country house. We drove down late last night and this morning Rebecca and Jason arrived, Jason taking the train to Loughborough and Rebecca in her green Mini, which is a silly car but somehow suits Rebecca who likes small, neat, brightly coloured accessories. And Rebecca said, 'Ooh what an amazing house,' and started asking Mum lots of tedious questions about paint colours and extensions, which of course Mum was only too thrilled to answer. Jason had a whole briefcase full of exam papers and old textbooks and he immediately went off to the dining room where we'll be working, me and him and Ben, and started arranging everything in a fussy old-womanish way.

Our house is called Duvalle Hall, although it used to be called something else until Grandpa bought it in, like, the 1960s or whenever, and changed it. It's properly enormous, and when I go to other people's country houses I always feel pleased that ours is the biggest. Alongside the house itself, which I think dates back to the 16th Century though I could be wrong, there's a whole bunch of converted stables and outhouses which are really plush and modern, and there's a games room out there too, with a snooker table etc. We have a croquet lawn and a swimming pool, but it's not that big, and to be honest I mostly can't be bothered to swim in it unless it's really, really hot. It's covered at the moment and there's puddles of rainwater and dead leaves on the plastic surface that look a bit like chicken pox. There's also a gigantic lake at the bottom of the south lawn which looks good in photographs, Mum always says. To the right of it there's an ornamental maze that's quite cool (one of my favourite games ever is called Lose Zara in the Maze and I'm definitely going to make sure that we play it this week) and then there's a lot of woodland up towards the top, near where our land ends and some random farmer's begins.

The house is made of grey stone with a pebbly drive and rose bushes on big lawns on all sides of the house. The hall is huge and then there's this massive wooden staircase that splits in two directions to go upstairs, with a landing halfway up and a mahogany table with flowers on it. I am sharing my room with Ben. There's about ten other bedrooms, but I want to share with him. Rebecca and Jason are staying in the converted stables. There's another, actual stable bit, but it's empty now since they got rid of Zara's pony. I want them to put an indoor climbing wall in it, or maybe a music studio. I don't play an instrument. I used to but I would always refuse to practise and then eventually each teacher (recorder, violin, etc) said there really was no point in me learning. But I'd quite like a drum kit, now I think about it. I think I would be very good at the drums.

As soon as we get down here, Mum suddenly gets into cooking in a big way. She rallies the troops (Zara, Clothilde,

Anna the housekeeper, maybe the other women who clean and stuff) and I come along if there's something I can lick from the spoon, and this huge production line of gloriousness gets going in the kitchen. I'm getting hungry just writing this and we only had supper an hour ago. Sometimes Dad and his friends go on shoots, and if they shoot things like pheasant or partridge or whatever then we eat them too. I'm not allowed to shoot yet, but sometimes I'm a beater, which means I get to rampage into the undergrowth and startle the birds out of their cover so that they fly up and get shot.

The first thing I did when we got here was check my room very, very carefully for hidden cameras. I'd done a bit of research on the 'digital clock' in my bedroom in London and I reckon it was on a timer and had a motion-sensor function so it just captured footage when there was someone in the room. I'm not sure, but I don't think it picked up sound as well. Luckily I never tried to smoke out of the window, but I'm trying to figure out what else they've seen.

Anyway, I'm looking forward to sharing a room with Ben. It's an awesome room, even bigger than my London one, and packed full of board games and my Grandpa's antique model ship collection which he left me when he died, although I'd have preferred cash. They're still rather magnificent though. I'm hoping I can talk Ben into tattooing me on the sly, and we have loads to talk about, with all the Gods and Monsters and Otherlife things.

We did a hell of a lot of work last week. And it wasn't all just Ben, you know. I feel like I made quite a big effort. Last night, me on the lower bunk bed and him on the upper one, we even went over the subjunctive.

'You do the imperfect and I'll do the present,' I said.

'*Amarem, amares, amaret, amaremus, amaretis, amarent.* Your turn.'

'*Amor, amaris—*'

'That's the passive, not the subjunctive.'

'They're the same thing, you idiot. Aren't they?'

He sighed and said I should get Rebecca to explain in the morning. We abandoned the subjunctive and went through the indicative instead, person by person, until the silence fought its way into the gaps between the words and we both fell into that really deep sleep that you sleep in the countryside.

It's Ben's birthday on Wednesday. He was born on the 5th of November. Quite cool, sharing your birthday with the anniversary of a failed assassination attempt on the King, when people ritualistically burn an effigy and set off shit-loads of fireworks. The cardboard tube from Amazon was waiting on the marble table in the hall when we arrived which was awesome, as with our stupendously exacting tutoring schedule there's no way I'd have been able to get to the nearest town to go shopping. We are working with the same timings each day because Jason and Rebecca say that students like routine or something. Zara has less to do, but she's smaller and there aren't so many subjects at 11+. Also she and Rebecca are doing reading aloud every morning and evening and trying to incorporate all the useless new words Zara's collected into her creative writing (examples: *desiccated, esoteric, coop*. I mean who's going to use the word *coop* in a sentence unless they keep chickens?). Zara is so bad at creative writing it makes me almost sick. She always, always, puts in something about a boy who has 'eyes like melting chocolate' or a girl running through the wintry forest trying to find her mother who abandoned her when she was born or something. It's not like I read what Zara writes, but sometimes she leaves her books lying around.

Rebecca is also charged with making sure Zarie is eating at mealtimes. Zara adores and clearly wants to be just like Rebecca, so she is actually copying what Rebecca does. Rebecca is vegetarian. Anna has been making quiches and risottos with goat's cheese and semi-dried tomatoes, home-made ravioli stuffed with spinach and mascarpone, and more cheese straws than Zara has active brain cells. And Zara's all chuffed that she and Rebecca are getting special meals and she's eating everything on her plate. I wonder if they'll be paying Rebecca extra for this. Now Za wants to be vegetarian too, and Mum and Dad aren't arguing with her about it just now because they're so grateful that she is eating. She was beginning to look a bit weird, I guess.

Anyway this afternoon Rebecca patiently re-explained the subjunctive and then got us to spot it in translation passages. Purpose clauses and result clauses contain the subjunctive. So do indirect questions and indirect commands. My question is, did the Romans actually write in this awful constipated way or have the examiners/textbook creators/teachers just pretended that they did in order to make us work harder? And the phone rang and – surprise, surprise – it was Ben's mother ringing up for another Progress Report. Jesus. Who gave her the landline number? I want to know. It never bloody stops ringing. I suppose Ben doesn't have a mobile so she has no choice but to keep ringing up the house phone. If Ben tells her he got something wrong she really starts freaking out. Even from the next room I could hear this ghastly, high-pitched interrogative squeaking, like a grumpy mosquito.

'So, is Ben your best friend, d'you think?' asked Rebecca as she leafed through my grammar book.

I considered this. 'I suppose he is, yeah.'

I told her about Ben's birthday, and she got all excited and said why didn't I make something for him?

'Like what?'

'What about a cake in the shape of something Ben likes? And perhaps Zara could help?' Another of Rebecca's policies is to do lots of creative cookery with Zara so she stops thinking food is something evil that will hurt her and is more like one of her Barbie houses.

'He likes wolves,' I said carefully.

'*Done.*' Rebecca laughed her little laugh that sounds like baubles clattering together as you fix them to your Christmas tree. She wears these dainty pear-shaped earrings made out of semiprecious stones like onyx and labradorite. I know because I asked.

As Ben shambled back into the room she patted my arm and gave me a conspiratorial wink. If Rebecca was my nanny I think I would quite like that.


I go for a lot of walks in the country. I like to get away from the house to smoke and stuff. It's nice having Ben here because we can go out together. We went out just after five today, taking big pieces of apple pie with us, still hot from the oven. It balanced the late afternoon chill very well.

Ben notices everything. He knows the names of the birds that call out (wood pigeon, raven) and of the little flowers that grow in the hedgerows. He sees foxes and deer. I don't because I'm not quick enough and they flash by me while I'm still trying to figure out what direction he's pointing in. He likes the woods that cover the top part of our land. He looks for owl pellets. He reads the clouds and knows what the weather is going to do. People used to think the Gods were responsible for the weather. I wonder if Ben thinks it's all Odin's doing.

Today I took him on a massive tour. We crossed the bridge that spans the ornamental lake and then we went into the maze to look at the weird wicker statue that Mum commissioned some famous artist to design. Zara was working with Rebecca, more's the pity. Otherwise we could have left her at the centre. I love hearing her crying as she tries to remember the difference between left and right. Then we climbed up into the woods.

'Do you like it here?' I asked him. A question I've never asked anyone before. Usually I don't give two shits whether they like it or not.

'It's great,' he said. 'I like being close to nature.'

Once upon a time I'd have disagreed roundly with this statement, but I understand it more now. Being close to nature is being close to the Otherlife. Thor didn't pop into the village shop to buy a scratchcard. Frigg didn't have a Knightsbridge hairdresser. Trees and fields and rivers and sky: these are the things of the Otherlife.

'Will you tattoo me while you're here?'

'Maybe. I still think you should do it yourself.'

'Plee-*ease*.'

'We'll see.'

I swiped at him. We walked on. I lit a cigarette, making a mental note to sit close to the wood fire when I got back to disguise the smell. The trees stood around, their leaves hanging limply, like guests about to leave a party. I kicked the ground, sending stones skimming away in low arcs.

When we got to this really massive tree we both stopped at the same time and we were both thinking the same thing.

'Yggdrasil!' I said.

We both stared up at it. I don't know what kind of tree it was. It towered over us, its branches knobbly and evil-looking, twisting up and away. I chucked up a couple of rocks and we could hear them tumbling down inside the trunk, knocking against its walls with satisfying clunks as they fell.

'Hollow!' I said. 'Awesome.'

Odin's Day, 5th November

This morning I got up at 6am, which was completely unprecedented, but I really needed to find a time when I could make Ben's present without Ben finding out, didn't I? I squashed my alarm really aggressively, rolled out of bed and went into the bathroom to get dressed so that I didn't wake him up. Briefly I wondered what he was dreaming about. I'm jealous of Ben's dreams. He tells me about big landscapes full of frost giants, the great bridge in the sky, hearing Odin's voice over the sound of storms and trumpets. I only ever dream about being in restaurants and not getting served quickly enough.

It was still eerily dark and cold as I crossed over the courtyard, trying not to crunch too loudly on the pebbles, and opened the door to the converted stables. Rebecca had suggested going over there because the guest annexe has a fully equipped kitchen and it would be more of a secret like that. I was rather hoping she wouldn't be dressed yet but maybe wearing one of those silky nightgown things that look gross on Mum but (I could imagine) would look exactly right on Rebecca. Sadly, though, she was already dressed and wearing an orange-and-brown striped dress and little red shoes, and was sitting in the tiny kitchen drinking coffee. Jason was also up and reading an immense book called *Algorithms and Sequences* and underlining things in pencil. He was also drinking coffee. I've never seen Jason without some kind of caffeinated beverage at his elbow.

'What are you doing up so early?' I asked him. I sort of wanted to be alone with Rebecca.

'Studying,' he said in his Northern accent. 'You lot aren't the only ones, you know.' He chuckled.

Rebecca had already, in consultation with Mum, assembled all the ingredients for Ben's cake on the work surface and was pre-heating the oven.

'We'll start by measuring everything out,' she said. She didn't look like she minded being up insanely early to bake a cake. 'Oh, Hobie, I forgot. You need to pick a design.'

She pushed her laptop towards me and began showing me all these different wolf cakes that she'd found on the Internet, telling me that of course I could do my own if I wanted. I thought of my drawing of Hati for my as-yet-unfinished tattoo, and decided it wasn't as good as the ones she'd found.

Rebecca had decided on a Black Forest cake because she said it would be totally appropriate for wolves, with a painted design of a wolf howling at a full moon on it, and some wolf cupcakes with ears and snouts and eyes and teeth that Jason said looked pretty complicated and disgusting (you had to use cut-up marshmallows and about 4 different kinds of icing) but that Rebecca and I were convinced would be a piece of piss. The thought of cherries and chocolate made me realise I hadn't had breakfast and I ran back to the main house to see if Clothilde was up yet, and if so how many bacon sandwiches she'd allow me to consume. But she wasn't.

I stood in front of the open fridge spooning Greek yogurt out of a carton while I debated whether I could be arsed to fry myself some eggs. There wasn't a lot of time and it was possible that Ben would emerge from the bedroom, although he's given to sleepwalking and/or wandering about at night (as I've discovered) and thus is normally pretty hard to rouse in the mornings. By now it was about a quarter to seven. In the end I shook half a packet of Special K into a bowl and added whole milk, sliced banana and some Melt flakes as an experiment. I put a pain au chocolat in the microwave but left it for slightly too long so it went all spongy and gooey. I was just nudging the door open to carry my break-fast back to the stables when Zara came in with her hair all sticking up like a haystack.

She was wearing the clown suit.

Momentarily lost for words, I eventually said, 'Blimey, Za, I'm glad to see my present's such a success.'

She shrugged. 'I forgot my pyjamas.'

Then she looked at the open door.

'You're baking Ben's present!' she squealed. 'Rebecca said I could help. She *did*.'

Her upper lip was giving way as it always does when she's about to cry. I sighed dramatically. Actually I was pleased at the thought that someone else could do all the boring weighing and measuring.

'All right,' I said. 'Keep your voice down, OK? Come over when you're dressed.'

There was something about the sight of her, all bones and sticky-outy hair under the drapey, shiny folds of the clown suit with its massive sleeves and droopy pompoms, that made me picture a starving orphan or something.

Two hours later we were finished. A dozen wolf heads sprouted from vanilla cupcake bases, marshmallow snouts wide open and packed full of icing spikes for teeth. They were awesome, those wolf heads, with wicked red-and-yellow eyes made from halved M&Ms and covered all over with tufty grey-brown icing. Jason had done the icing bit as he seemed to have the steadiest hand. My contribution was to order everyone around and dispose of the unwanted marshmallows. The Black Forest cake looked so good that I really didn't know how to restrain myself until teatime. It was a shame that Ben, who's so good at painting and whatnot, couldn't have done the wolf design himself, but Jason didn't do a bad job, and Zara helped with the pine trees. Rebecca took lots of photographs and put them on Facebook.

'Lucky old Ben!' Rebecca said, decanting the cakes into large Tupperware boxes. 'You're a really thoughtful friend, Hobie.'

I licked a stray smear of icing from my wrist. I couldn't imagine being away from home on my birthday. The festivities begin in the morning with celebratory Skype chats with my aunts and uncles and cousins and grandparents. I get to eat and wear and do whatever I want all day if it's the weekend, and if I have school then I bring in loads of Hummingbird cupcakes or something made by Clothilde and make sure that I do no work at all. And I can choose where we go for dinner and maybe we'll go to a play or a musical if it isn't something really tedious. And I get loads and loads of presents. The only crap part is writing thank-you notes on headed paper, which need to be sent off within, like, five minutes of me opening all my loot.

'Do you think Ben's parents don't love him?' asked Zara, her eyes all big like an owl's. She was thinking, like I was, that the phone hadn't rung yet. And no cards arrived in the post yesterday or anything like that.

'Of course they do!' said Rebecca cheerfully. 'Now, my love,' she said to Zara, 'I'd like you to have a bowl of porridge for breakfast. Why don't I come and sit with you and we can read *Anne of Green Gables* at the same time?'

Jason and I both looked after them rather mournfully as they crossed the courtyard and went back into the house.

When Ben came downstairs Mum and Dad made a huge fuss of him and gave him a dark grey cashmere jumper from Paul Smith and a *Collected Works of Shakespeare*. The tag said *From Ike and Elsie and Zara and Hobie xxx* but actually I hadn't chosen any of it, although I suppose some Shakespeare is all right.

'Happy birthday,' I said. He ate half a muffin, looking like his birthday meant absolutely nothing to him. Maybe they don't celebrate them in the Otherlife. Then I gave him the Amazon tube (I hadn't wrapped it or anything gay like that) and when he pulled out the poster and unrolled it he must've been pleased, because he went purple and muttered that it was a really good choice.

'Why is that man wearing such weird clothes?' asked Zara suspiciously. 'And why does it say RIP at the bottom?'

'Because he died in 1986,' Ben explained. 'Cliff Burton was the original bassist in Metallica. He was a classically trained musician. You can really hear his influence, especially on the second and third Metallica albums.'

It was the longest speech anyone (apart from me) had heard from Ben. We all sat in respectful silence, eating our breakfasts.

Later on, we were sitting through the first segment of the day's planned timetable (a rather monotonous review of Shape, Space and Area) when we heard the familiar sound of car wheels grinding on the gravel. I thought it was probably a delivery van with a sculpture from some Italian workshop or yet another Ocado order. We turned our heads as footsteps crunch-crunched over towards us, and just before she knocked on the dining room window we saw who it was.

Ben's mother.

'Did you know she was coming, *brúðr*?' I hissed as Ben slid out of his chair. He slipped out of the room, not even bothering to put his shoes back on.

Jason drew a neat line through the session on his time-table and said he hoped we'd be able to stay on task for the rest of the day, as there was still a lot to get through.

*NB I was quite pleased that I managed to remember the Norse for *brother*. Unfortunately, when I looked it up later on, I realised that I'd confused the correct word – *bróðir* – with the word for *bride*. But at least I tried.

# BEN

I only have three pills left. Nine corners in all. I will splinter them into cut-glass shards, roll them under my tongue. And it won't be enough. It will never, never be enough. I know I promised Solly – that I'm going to stop, that I won't start again, that I won't take them, if I find them lying around the house – but I can't believe I've only brought three.

But at least I'm at Download.

This morning I woke up in the White Campsite, unzipped the flap of our tent and peered outside. The festival was sleeping. Low snores carried on the chill wind. A few stragglers were staggering back from the giant toilet huts. Beer cans rolled on trampled grass.

Freedom.

We got a lift with Jake and Ally on Thursday night after all, because we realised we needed them. Ally, specifically, because he's eighteen. Solly and I wouldn't have been able to get in on our own. Jake drove wildly fast up the M1 to a soundtrack of Pantera, Rollins Band, Deftones. *Deaf*, said Solly, was very much the operative word. Every hour or so he drip-dropped a trickle of Rescue Remedy onto his tongue. He doled out water bottles and M&S sandwiches from the 'food bag', transferring wadded-up wrappers and spent cigarette boxes to the 'rubbish bag'. Wiped the condensation off the windows. I wondered, all the way, why he was coming. He paid for everything for me, too: cereal bars, apples. Kept nudging me to eat.

It was easier than I thought to lie to Mum: I told her I was staying with Solly, whose parents have a house in Gloucestershire. I used the magic word (*revision*) and gave her a landline number with a missing digit. I rang up Dad and said I was sorry for missing one of his weekends, and he said, a little too quickly perhaps, that it didn't matter. I texted Zara, to say I was sorry that I upset her. But I didn't hear anything back.

It took an hour to park the car and a further hour to crawl along in the queue towards the entrance gates. It made me think of soldiers with standard-issue gas masks, waiting for something big: a boat, a war. Thousands and thousands of us, sorted into lines, awaiting entry. I'd never seen so many people all dressed in black. Only the tattoos were different, and the hair, spangly and backcombed and many-coloured. At festivals, people communicate by the slogans on their T-shirts: Crowbar, Sepultura, Fear Factory. Apart from Solly, who is top to toe in Abercrombie & Fitch, down to his three-ply welly socks. He's in a tribe all of his own.

It's not freezing, but it's cold. The sky is a wet-looking off-white. Metal and rain: they go well together.

'That's the law of festivals,' said Ally when we arrived.

'It's always shit weather.' He had two bottles of rum in his rucksack, for adding to hot chocolate: a good way to ward off the cold, he said. Solly looked doubtfully at the mud, already building to a slow wave on the footpaths, and said it wasn't too late to check into a hotel. But I could tell that he was kind of intrigued. Camping would be a novelty. Like owning a caravan, doing your own washing or visiting a car-boot sale. He wants to know what all the fuss is about.

'Good morning, good yawning,' he says groggily from the humid interior of the tent. 'I must brush my teeth.'

'Sol, can I have a bit of your Rescue Remedy?' I say.

He eyes me as he hands it over. All his toiletries are arranged in pouches along the side of the tent. He's brought four bottles of hand sanitizer, some cashmere fingerless gloves, an eye mask, earplugs, a memory-foam neck pillow and twelve spirulina protein bars on which to subsist until Sunday.

The drops of Rescue Remedy go straight to my head. The whole of Download stretches out for miles, as far as I can see. Fields of tents, as bright as Zara's patchwork quilt. The big blocks of the stage, the funfair rides, the rows of food vans parked in semi-organised lines. Jake and Ally have been eating huge burgers that drip with grease and shredded lettuce. Baguettes stuffed with roast pork. Crisps and chocolate bars, washed down with booze. I take an apple from the food bag.

'Ben, you need to wash that,' admonishes Solly.

'You're such an old woman, Sol.'

'Least I'll live to *be* old.'

The ground in front of our tent is crystallised with dew. I unfold one of Solly's picnic blankets and stretch out, staring up at the sky, imagining watching myself from a great height. Again and again, I try to remember more about that week at Duvalle Hall. Zara's dolls. A bonfire. A maze . . . and Zara at the centre of it, screaming . . . Cupcakes with *wolves* on them . . . yes: for my birthday, Hobie made me cupcakes.

Could Jason have been allergic to something in the wolf cakes? Or was that on a different day?

'Oh, look, the mutants are crawling out of their cave,' says Solly, picking his way over the guy ropes and plastic bags, puffy with assorted trash. The thing about camping is it's hard to stay asleep in the morning: the tent roofs let the heat and the light in and you're warmed up like a microwavable meal. Sure enough, a furry blondish head is emerging from Jake and Ally's tent. Ray-Bans. Stubble and unwashed skin.

Jake and Ally don't really stand out here. There's so much wild behaviour: people vomiting behind trees, girls walking around in nothing but bikinis and body paint, wild capering to rival me and Hobie on the night we stole a steak from a restaurant. Besides, Jake and Ally haven't come to kick people in the head, vandalise the school chapel or pick on the Year 9s. They're here for the same reason I'm here: to listen to metal. More or less.

'What time is it?' slurs the blond head.

'Nine thirty.'

He moans in horror. 'I don't know what that means.'

'It means,' says Ally, emerging also, 'that we're at DOWNLOAD.'

We spend the day hanging out in the campsite, drinking beer and playing cards. Solomon amuses himself by trying to persuade the Stonehills that they'll be seeing themselves into an early grave if they maintain their current intake of sugar, salt and saturated fats. He's such a clever orator that I can actually see Jake's resolve begin to falter. He nearly tries one of the spirulina bars before his robust manliness gets the better of him.

'Seriously,' says Solly. 'You ought to have a pre-diabetes test, at the very least. And *don't* get me started on cigarettes and drugs.'

'Sol,' I say, 'I don't really think this is a great moment to be lecturing people on excess. It's a festival. People are by nature excessive at festivals.'

He raises an eyebrow. I know what he's thinking: I've become more talkative, more able to speak in sentences. It's Zara's influence. Her mind is so unfettered, so razor-bright, it makes me want my own to operate with such clarity and focus. Every hour or so, wherever I am – in a queue for beer, at the water fountains, in some tent or other waiting for a band to begin – I find myself wondering if I will ever see her again.

'There's many a tragic accident that's taken place because people *haven't known better*,' Solomon says. 'Like mixing beer and fondue. You can die from that.'

'That is an *urban legend*,' says Ally, full of scorn, copying Solly's italics in his thick-vowelled voice. He lights a cigarette. He's smoking Lucky Strikes: Hobie's brand, I think, with another jolt of memory.

'Or, consider psychedelics. Not only could you do yourself immeasurable damage while on a trip – it makes me feel faint just thinking about it – there have been plenty of well-documented cases in which people have mistaken a poisonous mushroom for one containing psilocybin.'

'That is not how you pronounce it,' says Jake. 'It's got, like, six syllables.'

'I think Solomon would know how to pronounce it,' I say, lying back, mind elsewhere. I know where this little chat is coming from. It's not actually for the Stonehills' benefit; it's directed at me.

Later on today, Solly's going to make me throw my painkillers away.

At festivals people move in tides. In the big areas – the tents, the open spaces – you get a more random milling about, like gas particles in a box. Near the stages, of course, the crowds congeal, silt up. But in the in-between places, you see these slipstreams making their steady way from one place to the next. If you look from far enough away, it's like watching cross-currents. We are in one now, threading our way towards the main stage. We need to be in good time for Metallica.

As Jake and Ally forge ahead, barging lesser beings out of the way with their gigantic sportsman shoulders, Solly pulls me back.

'Ben. I think it's time.'

'For what?'

'You know what.'

And he's off, cutting across the stageward flow to the row of blue toilet huts that squat along one edge of the central arena. Reluctantly, I follow.

'You've got them, right?' he calls over his shoulder.

I pretend I don't know what he means, but eventually I grunt in the affirmative, my hand closing protectively around my last three pills in their clingfilm wrapper.

We are standing in the doorway of the toilet. The stench of chemicals and stomach acid travels to meet us.

'Horrendous,' mutters Solly. 'Makes one want to avoid solid food entirely.'

It's an actual toilet, with a seat, if not a lid, rather than the hole in a bench I've seen at other locations on the site. Still, not exactly the epitome of luxury.

Solomon is wiping his hands with a Sanex tissue.

'Now, Ben, what you have to do is utterly straightforward. You need to take those last three pills, and throw them in there. God knows you won't be trying to get them out again.'

I draw the wrapper from my pocket. The pills sit in my palm, their familiar corners almost purple in the reflected blue of the toilet walls.

'Why are you doing this again?' I say.

Solomon turns away to take an inbreath of festival air.

'My sister, and I don't tell people this often, had an addiction to painkillers in her teens. They had to put her in a clinic in Arizona. I don't ever want that to happen to you. It's all been a bit rubbish for you lately, what with you finding out about Jason and everything. And I care about you. I'm sorry if that sounds weird. But I do. Even if your . . .'

He trails off before he can finish this. *Even if your parents don't.* That's what he meant to say.

'I'm not . . .' I start to say. But I stop myself.

Am I?

Am I addicted to painkillers?

They're just the things I take to stop my head from hurting; they don't mean anything. I could stop today, tomorrow, any time.

But if that's true, why am I still holding onto them?

'I do understand,' Solomon says, 'really. You're in pain. I would be too, if I were you. But it's time to say goodbye.'

'I suppose I'm scared,' I say, before I can stop myself. I take one of the pills and chuck it into the murk of the toilet.

'That's good. Keep going. What are you scared of?'

The second pill joins the first. It flies so lightly, so carelessly into the undertow. I long for it to have more weight, more gravity.

'I'm scared . . . about what will happen if I don't take them.'

'You're afraid of the pain, yes? You think you won't be able to control it. But, Ben, just *think* about what they're doing to your brain. You're stronger than you think you are. You're one of the strongest people I know.'

I've never felt like a strong person. I feel oddly light-headed as I take the last pill between my finger and thumb, resisting the overpowering urge to press it into my mouth.

'So, farewell then,' says Solomon. 'Let this be end of the painkillers.'

With a heavy arm, I cast the last of my pills away from me. It lands without sound, swallowed up.

Gone.

'*Now* let's go and watch this Metallica of yours,' says Solomon.


The sounds are too loud, the black too black, the colours too bright. The sky is too wide, the air is too cold. The world has become curved, like a fisheye lens. I am curved too. My spine wobbles. I tell myself: Metallica. The syllables clatter like corrugated tin.

We push and shove and wrestle into the dark heart of the mob. The air is thick with perspiration, a hundred thousand gusts of exhaled $CO_2$. Beer fumes. A man in a wheelchair with a deferential circle of space around him. Two tiny children with bright pink ear defenders. If Zara was here, she'd choose pink too. Giant screens on either side of the stage pulse with moving images.

I watch Ally piss into an Evian bottle and hurl it high, high up over the massed crowds. He roars with amusement, raw-throated from drinking and smoking. Solly's pale, freckled face is creased up in a reluctant grin.

'*Now* you're getting into the spirit of it all,' Jake tells him.

It feels as if I've waited my whole life to see Metallica play live. The crowd is seething with anticipation, like a swarm of millipedes. As the opening bars of the intro music kick in, a howl rises up. Scenes from an old Western movie flicker on the screens.

'D'you know, I'm rather enjoying this,' shouts Solly. 'Cinematic.' He darts me a look. 'How are you holding up?'

I grunt.

'Do you want to go to the medical tent?'

I glance behind us at the thickening mass of people. It's like another hundred, another thousand people are joining every second, like ants to honey. I try to make a judgement. Not easy. The pain in my head, the bolt of nausea in my middle – they're bad enough, almost, to make the trip worthwhile. Maybe a couple of Nurofen will ward off the worst of it.

Maybe.

But as I'm thinking about it, James Hetfield, Lars Ulrich,

Rob Trujillo and Kirk Hammett walk onstage and start playing 'Hit the Lights', and I know I'm going to stay.

'Good man,' says Solly, and hands me a pint of water.

I let the pain come for me. I offer it up to the giant altar of the stage. To Metallica, as they motor into a version of 'Master of Puppets' that they must've played millions of times in hundreds of countries and *still* sounds as fresh and savage as the recording from 1985. I let the crowd buffet me. Jake and Ally disappear into twin blurs of frenzied headbanging and air guitar. Elbows elbow me. Feet fight for space on the torn-up ground. All the time, Solly stays close by, his Paul Smith hoodie firmly up to ward off projectiles.

James Hetfield addresses the congregation:

'METALLICA IS WITH YOU!'

The cry of the crowd is almost singular.

'ARE YOU WITH US?' he yells. 'ARE YOU WITH US?'

I give myself up to the gig.

I am going to be sick. It's an unstoppable wave, coming from deep down. I palm my forehead; it's sticky with sweat. I don't feel the headache yet, the headache that I'm sure will inevitably come. Just *sick*. In my bones as well as my stomach. The smell of rubbish rises up from the festival floor, creeps into my nostrils. Cigarette smoke from the couple on my left. The kids in front are jabbering like rabid monsters, arms in the air, camera phones aloft. And now – suddenly – the metalheads are gone, and a rabble of Berserks surrounds me. Iron-limbed and savage-toothed, hurling themselves about in front of the stage. The air is rich with battle cries. A line of food stalls stretches away to the left of the stage, each containing a skewered hog turning on riotous flames, and I can see Berserks throwing themselves at the roasting meat, tearing off limb-sized chunks that glimmer with grease in the fluorescent light.

As fast as I can, I begin to edge my way backwards and out of the crowd. The Otherlife – this strange and almost-unrecognisable Otherlife – is all around me: a looming, menacing circumference. I cannot escape it. If the painkillers were the only thing keeping it at bay, I cannot escape it now. A Berserk seizes my arm, his eyes pale yellow and rolling about in his head.

'Watch it, mate,' he says, the saliva gathering at the corners of his mouth.

I jump as a rattle of gunfire explodes from the stage. Fireworks are starting. I turn my head, catch a glimpse of pink and green starbursts dissipating into the inky sky; the green starbursts wriggle and twist like tiny flies, taking on a yellower hue. They form the face of a weeping woman. There she is: huge, etched in the sky above the stage. Firework tears flow, lemony-green, as Frigg cries for her dead son Baldr.

Finally I reach the fraying edge of the crowd, where the

bars and kebab vans begin, where the less hardcore are watching from the relative comfort of rugs and chairs.

The queue for the toilets is immense. I won't make it. I pull away and veer behind the backs of the stalls, towards the high wire fence that separates the parkland from the festival site. Rubbish is strewn over the ground. The screwed-up paper and discarded cartons look like angry flowers. I stumble this way and that, looking irrationally for an unlittered spot. Then I give up. I sink to my knees and litres of wet vomit pour out of me: water and part-digested apple, and Ben-ness. I am throwing up my own identity. In this landscape of roasting meat and metalhead Berserks, I may as well disappear entirely.

'Ben!'

It's Solly, kneeling at my side.

'God, Ben, I totally blame myself. We need to get you to the medical tent. I didn't think you'd go into withdrawal so quickly.'

He helps me to my feet, and we start back towards the complex of shops and fairground rides. Strains of Metallica float in the air behind us. I'm walking away, I think, from the only thing I've ever really wanted to immerse myself in fully. From the music I love best. It feels hollow, somehow: unsatisfying. I too am hollow. There is nothing inside of me.

Three girls overtake us, each waving a glowstick above her head, like a sword. Long trails of blue light, green light, purple light spread out from the tips of the glowsticks, and now the girls are girls no longer, but Valkyries mounted on horses, flame-haired and victorious. Shrieking, translucent, they take to the skies, wheeling in cawing circles like birds of prey.

'What are you looking at?' says Solly. 'What's happening?'

I stumble on a tuft of earth and he holds me up.

'Something I can't do anything about,' I whisper, my throat sticky with phlegm. 'Can't tell what's real any more . . .'

'Shush. You're just quoting from Metallica.'

'No, it's . . .'

'Right now you are a *poster boy* for addiction,' says Solomon. 'I hope you've learned your lesson. I know that sounds heartless, and trust me I have no wish to sound heartless, but there's many a tragic accident that's taken place because people—'

It's his speech from earlier; he must have planned it before we left London.

'I know,' I say. 'Because people haven't known better. I'm an idiot.'

'You didn't even know what was in those painkiller things.'

'I know,' I say again.

Another huddle of Berserks surges past us, bear-coated and beer-laden. A heavy, orange-brown light plays about their heads. Is it the Otherlife? Or is it the painkillers leaving my system? I wonder if maybe it's some hideous combination of both.

I feel it now: the glittering. The sides of my world curving. The soft, sad hum of Frigg's voice, asking me for help.

And all at once a memory pushes itself up to the surface: me and Hobie, roaming through the woods on the edge of the Duvalles' land – wolves ourselves, chanting in Norse, throwing ourselves onto the damp-leaf ground, rolling around . . . his white trousers darkening with soil . . . sun setting overhead . . .

*'Wouldn't it be amazing if the Berserks were here?'*

*'Imagine a line of them coming out into that clearing . . .'*

*'Painted . . .'*

*'With Odin watching . . .'*

I stagger again, and then – suddenly – I stop, and grab his arm.

I remember.

*I remember.*

'Solly. What was the thing you were saying earlier?'

'About drugs?'

'About mushrooms. You said it's easy . . . it's easy to . . .'

'I said it's easy to mistake a poisonous mushroom for one containing psilocybin. That what you mean? But what—'

I bend down and throw up again. With damp hands I wipe my hair away from my face. I can feel the little dent in the side of my head where Dad hit me with the cricket bat. I can feel the broken beat of my pulse in the middle of my forehead. Solly hands me a bottle of water and I drink from it, feeling the liquid trickle down my throat, cooling my heart.

'Ben. Are you OK?'

I look at him and say, 'I don't know how, or why, but I think I do know what killed Jason.'

# HOBIE'S DIARY

Thor's Day, 6th November 2008

It turned out that Ben's mother's arrival had been planned by Mum as a kind of birthday surprise. I don't think Ben much likes surprises, and you'd have thought his mum would have known that, frankly. Anyway. Getting Ben's mother to come and visit (and not just for the day – she's bloody staying until the end of the week, which is awful) is just the kind of thing that my mother would think of. Mum is the Year 8 Parent Rep and likes doing showy-offy things like ordering cupcakes personalised with initials and edible glitter and getting celebrities to come in and do workshops. I can just imagine her doing her Bountiful Lady of the Manor thing down the phone, all 'Oh but you absolutely must come for a few days . . . No, we don't dress for dinner, don't be silly . . . Ben will be so thrilled' etc etc.

I'm not too sure Ben is that thrilled. In his house, all last week, you could really feel it when his mother was around. She was kind of suffocating, like a really hot sleeping bag. The way she stared at him sometimes when he was bending over his laptop, murmuring to himself. Like she wanted to eat him. The more I think about it, the less strange I find it that she smashed the goldfish bowl. No wonder he's always thinking about the Otherlife. No wonder he has it on the wall. He must want to really live there, I reckon, to get away from the way she looks at him.

Of course she wanted a detailed update from Jason and Rebecca and insisted on being shown all the work we'd done so far. I mean, obviously first she hugged Ben and gave him a present of a new laptop case and begrudgingly showed him an email from his father that she'd received earlier this morning saying happy birthday, and *then* she practically frogmarched both tutors into the dining room for a full-on Progress Report.

She was suspicious of Rebecca.

'Really? You're an actress? Did you study drama?' she was asking in the manner of a courtroom judge, oblivious to the fact that she's not the one paying £200 per tutor, per day, so she could just shut up and be grateful Rebecca wasn't a lunatic/paedophile/Communist.

'No, Classics,' smiled Rebecca, her earrings dancing.

'Where?'

'Oxford.'

Ben's mother seemed appeased. Then she cross-examined Jason about whether he had access to the mark schemes for the Maths and Science papers.

'Well,' he explained, 'the schools don't tend to release their marking criteria. With Scholarship it's often about looking for a kind of brilliance, displayed in a certain way.'

'I don't understand. Are you saying Ben isn't brilliant?'

Like Rebecca, Jason was very patient. He must be used to it, I guess.

Ben and I looked at each other and crept out of the room.

We raced out of the house, crossing the courtyard, climbing over the gate behind the guesthouses and then running through the old paddock where Zara used to ride. Then we charged up the hill and into the woods. It was a really crisp afternoon, already almost getting dark, the trees loaded with red and gold. The edge of the forest is where I normally turn back if I've just left the house to stretch my legs and have a smoke or whatever, but Ben dived into the woods and I could tell that he was being Sköll again, without the wolf suit this time, and I thought, What the hell, and ran after him.

Twigs and dying leaves crunched under our feet as we careered in and out of the trees, baying crazily in the setting sun. The air was thick with the smells of wet earth and decay and pine bark. Ben threw himself to the ground and started rolling around in the leaves and I thought it was amazing how he can just *become* Sköll like that. I still feel like I'm pretending to be a wolf. Pretending to be Hati. I wish I believed everything the way Ben does. I didn't want to roll around on the ground because I was wearing these new really expensive trousers.

'Ben,' I said, 'teach me some more Norse.'

He unrolled to his feet and shook his fringe.

'Like what?'

'I don't know,' I said, aiming a kick at a low-hanging branch to see if I could break it. 'Like a verb or something. Like *être* or whatever.'

'*Ek em, þú ert, hann er, vér erum, þér eruð, þeir eru.*'

'Jesus! Slow down. Again.'

He recited the verb once more and I did my best to repeat it back to him while we walked on into the middle of the forest. (Later I checked, so I could copy it down properly, with all the accents and everything.) How does Ben have time to learn this stuff? You'd think we had our hands full enough with Scholarship work. I breathed in cold air and closed my eyes as I walked and tried to imagine that we weren't in the middle of England at all, and that it wasn't 2008 any longer. It was hard. Normally when I close my eyes I see random shapes and holographic lights, imprints from computer games. I see menus, rows of sandwiches in Pret a Manger, set out like library books. I hear gunfire. I think about what I want people to give me. I think about Rugby. But I tried, I really tried. I realised I'd never heard the proper sounds of the forest before, but now that I was listening I could hear the swoosh swoosh of the wind in the branches and the chatter of birds, the noise of twigs breaking. Everything was alive. I squinted at Ben and he had his eyes sort of closed too. I knew that he could see the Otherlife. I knew that it was inside him and he was inside it.

I opened my eyes and said, 'Wouldn't it be amazing if the Berserks were here?'

'Yeah.'

'Imagine a line of them coming out into that clearing—'

'And another one on that side—'

'Dressed as wolves—'

'Painted—'

'With Odin watching—'

We looked at each other. I could almost feel it in my bones. Why couldn't it be real? Why couldn't I see what Ben could see? After Halloween, he told me that when we robbed the little kids and were racing away down the road, before the Great Steak Heist, he actually *saw* part of *Naglfar*, the awesome ship made of dead men's nails. Just sort of sailing down Westbourne Grove.

Yggdrasil was waiting for us. At its base was this crop of mushrooms, a perfect cloud of them with white helmets. Quite big too – bigger than puffballs. I fell on them immediately.

'Awesome! We can pick them and eat them.'

One of my favourite starters is smoked mozzarella with mushrooms and Parma ham, which I always order if we go to our local Italian restaurant. I was already fumbling in my pocket for a Kleenex or something to wrap them up in.

Ben said dreamily, 'Some people think the Berserks ate hallucinogenic mushrooms before they went into battle. They think that's why they were so frenzied and fearless.'

307

'What do you mean, hallucinogenic?'

'The mushrooms sent them into a trance. They had visions.'

I breathed out. *Even more awesome.*

I reached out my hand to break off a mushroom at the base of the stem. Ben opened his eyes.

'Wait, Hobie. No.'

'Why not?'

'They could be poisonous.'

'Don't be ridiculous, Ben. Either they're food or they'll send us into a psycho Berserk state. Which'd be amazing.'

'They could be poisonous,' he repeated obstinately. 'You need to check.'

Then, to my surprise, Ben took a running leap and began to climb. I hesitated, then followed. I'm much better at gym and sports so I should have been leading the way really. The tree was sticky with yellowy moss, and pieces of bark peeled away as we scrabbled for hand and footholds. Ivy covered the surface like a fur wrap, and sprigs of white berries clung here and there. It was harder than a climbing wall, but much more interesting. Ben laid his head against the tree.

'What are you doing?'

'Listening to it breathing.'

We got to the top and crouched together in the nest of branches, peering down into the hollow, which was spectacularly black like a ghost-train tunnel. Anything could've been down there: a roosting owl, a monster of some kind, the skeletons of long-dead cats. I wasn't about to suggest that we should climb down into it, but I could tell that Ben wasn't going to be persuaded not to. He turned round and slithered backwards and then jumped and I heard him land with a muffled crunch.

'Are you OK?' I yelled.

'Fine. Come down!' he yelled back.

'Can you get back up?'

'Yeah.'

'Watch out then.' And I dropped into the hole.

It was weird, like being inside the stomach of a strange beast. I flicked my wolf lighter and Ben's skin leaped out like a pale flash against the black walls. His pupils were huge and he was grinning. Ben really loves secret places.

'I wish we could stay here,' he said, 'in the tree. I could live in a tree.'

Well, I bloody couldn't. Breathing was a bit difficult, for a start. I crouched down and craned my neck to catch a glimpse of purple sky, crisscrossed with branches like one of Mrs Ottoboni's woodcuts. It made me feel like there was definitely some oxygen coming from somewhere, which was a relief. I wished I'd brought a snack, even just a Fruit Roll-Up or something. It was definitely getting on for teatime. And it was cold. On the other hand, I liked being down there with Ben. Away from the grown-ups. Away from Zara. No books and no papers. Just Norse words and being wolves and the Otherlife.

'Tell me a story,' I said. For a weird, scary moment I really wanted to hold his hand. I didn't though, of course.

So he told me about the World Tree, and how it was watered by maidens called Fate and Being and Necessity, and preyed on by animals like the serpent that was curled at the root along with hundreds of other snakes. And a squirrel called Ratatoskr scurried up and down the tree carrying insults back and forth from the serpent to this huge eagle that sat at the top.

'What kind of tree was it?' I asked. I was beginning to feel sleepy, like the cold was slowing my bones.

'An ash tree.' His voice echoed slightly.

'Like this one?'

'Nah. This is an oak.'

Shit! Suddenly I remembered about the wolf cakes. It was a special tea and we were going to be late. We climbed back out of the tree, which was seriously quite frightening at certain points, but luckily there were a few knobbly things to hold on to and the prospect of eating my own bodyweight in cupcakes (and maybe some hot buttered toast – I don't know why but I always want a lot of hot buttered toast when I'm in the country) propelled me to the top. I helped Ben get up too and then we fairly hurtled out of the woods and down the lanes while the sky grew darker overhead.

'What's the massive rush all of a sudden?' he panted as we scrambled over the gate.

'It's your *birthday*, you moron. You can't miss your own birthday tea, can you?'

We clattered into the house just as Clothilde was setting the teapots and cups and things in front of the fire. 'Where have you been?' she cried. 'Your mothers were *inquiètes*.'

Dad came wandering into the sitting room, looking much more comfortable in his chunky knitted sweater than he ever does in his office suits.

'Hey, boys,' he said. 'How was your hike? Did you find anything interesting?'

We shrugged and piled onto the rug in front of the hearth like the wolves we still were on the inside, huddling as close to the fire as we could.

Mum came in. She was wearing a dark green dress and a pink cardigan which I thought was a silly combination. Her face looked sort of twitchy and I found out later that she'd been weighing Zara, which had ended up with both of them screaming at each other. Zara had gained half a kilo and had gone into this massive panic despite Mum and Rebecca telling her it was a good thing, and apparently Zara shouted at Mum that it was all her fault for putting her on a diet in the first place and she hated her and she hated herself and she was going to fail the 11+ no matter what happened. It was lucky Rebecca was there because she succeeded in talking Zara out of the bathroom (Zara had locked the door) and now she'd taken Zara to the guesthouse to watch *The Princess Diaries*.

When she saw me and Ben on the (admittedly white,

probably expensive) rug, Mum let out a small scream not unlike the one she'd emitted when she found me in the act of tattooing myself.

'Boys! You are covered in mud. Go and change. Now. No, Hobie, not after tea. Right now.'

Then she turned on Dad. 'Didn't you notice the state of them?'

'Relax, Elsie,' he said, not looking up from the enormous book he was reading about the life of some dead American president. 'It's Ben's birthday and he's a guest. Ben and Hobie, why don't you just change into some other trousers?'

We went and changed. I kept really wanting Ben to see the wolf cakes *now*. Like it really couldn't come quickly enough. I'd never managed to keep a secret for an entire day before.

When we got back Ben's mother was curled up on the huge L-shaped sofa. She's all spindly like a spider and she didn't really take up a lot of space. You could tell she found the house intimidating because she'd lost all her money and stuff and was probably annoyed that she didn't have a house remotely like it any more. I've seen that jealous look loads of times on grown-ups' faces.

'Hey, Mum,' said Ben.

She reached out for him like he was a special pet that'd been trained to sit on her lap and he dutifully went and sat with her. It looked like every nerve in his body was on standby. She stroked his hair.

'How are you, my darling? Did you boys manage to get any work done this afternoon?' She cast an acid glance in the direction of the corner, where Jason was nursing a pile of textbooks and marking. He looked up and did an embarrassed cough.

'I think they went on an adventure,' said Dad mildly.

'Sure, but since you have tutors here—'

'Once in a while can't hurt.' Dad stretched his legs out and I suddenly felt really strongly that it was crazy that we didn't have a dog, something wild and messy and waggy-tailed, to roll around at his feet. Why the hell didn't we have a dog? And also, why couldn't Dad be here more often? He's in America and Europe and Japan so much that I sometimes forget he's a real person.

And then the lights went out and the fizz of miniature sparklers could be heard advancing into the room.

Rebecca and Zara and Clothilde brought in the cakes on big silver trays and we all sang 'Happy Birthday to You' and even though you could tell Zara had been crying she was smiling at Ben as if she was genuinely excited that it was his birthday. I suppose Zara is quite wet and emotional and can be relied upon for that kind of thing. I couldn't take my eyes off Ben. Would he like the wolf cakes? I didn't think they would count as a bad surprise. I was really hoping that he'd be pleased.

He didn't say much, but he really looked chuffed with all of them, the wolf cupcakes with their marshmallow snouts and the Black Forest one which I have to say really did look awesome. He was incredulous that I'd got up to bake them, with a bit of help from others, while he was still asleep. And Mum took loads of pictures and Dad led a round of 'For He's a Jolly Good Fellow' and Jason was looking almost as hungry as I was and surreptitiously edging a bit closer to the smoked salmon sandwiches with wedges of cucumber that someone – maybe Anna or Clothilde – had made with bread baked in our bread machine, and Rebecca hugged Ben and I wished it was my birthday too.

Ben blew out the candles on the Black Forest cake and Zara said, 'Make a wish.'

He looked really old suddenly, with that dark look in his eyes. His Otherlife look. I wanted to know what he was wishing for. Maybe for his parents to get back together. Maybe to get a Scholarship. Maybe that he could live in the Otherlife instead of London. That would be just like Ben.

I really, really wanted to know.

And then I realised I had a wish too.

I wished that Ben could come and live with me. Not just for this week. All the time.

If it had been my birthday, I would have wished for that.

I'm starting to really hate that Ben's mum is here. She has this really annoying way of coming into the kitchen while people are cooking and talking and generally milling about and she leans backwards against the rail of the Aga like she's on a cruise ship and posing for a snapshot. Plus, she has taken to 'sitting in' on our sessions with Jason and Rebecca, and although they're really good-natured about it I can tell that they feel like she's checking up on them to make sure they're as good as my parents think they are.

Or she comes bursting through the dining-room doors and pounces.

'What was that word you just said?'

'Um, heterochromatic.'

'Which is what exactly?'

'Well, it means that two things might be different coloured, such as irises.'

'You mean people's eyes?'

And Ben will be twitching silently and staring out of the window and I'll be looking at Mrs Holloway like she's an absolute retard and Rebecca will be like, 'Yes, exactly, and I thought Ben and Hobie might be able to use it somewhere in their creative writing.' And Ben's mother will scrabble through our notebooks with her skinny white fingers, ablaze with the desire to find mistakes. All this time I thought I didn't have any allergies (Zara has loads, such as sesame oil and oysters and penicillin, and even Jason's allergic to something bizarre, he told me once, like grass seed or dandelions or something) but I think I was wrong. I think I might actually be allergic to Ben's mother.

And now *my* mother, inspired by Ben's, has also taken to barging in on our sessions. I think she feels like she's losing Mummy Points by not taking a frenzied interest like Ben's mother. It's not enough to produce a fat cheque at the end of the week. No, now she has to be there too. It's getting more and more like a police interview or something. Except neither of them wants to be the Good Cop.

Today, just as we were tidying up (well, I say *we*, but I mean Ben and Jason were tidying up while I fashioned darts out of scrap paper and chucked them at their heads), both mothers came in like Valkyries on the hunt for dying warriors. They opened our completed Maths papers and scanned them for the red biro marks that signalled Jason's assistance or correction. They whispered. They traded looks of excitement/consternation. They were unbelievably annoying about the whole thing.

'84% – is that good? That's good, isn't it?' said Ben's mother, pretending not to notice it was 13 more per cent than I'd got.

'Oh, is 71% all right?' my mother was saying. That's one thing she hadn't reckoned on with the joint tutoring: seeing someone do better than me.

Ben and I and Jason made for the door, leaving them to feast like vultures on the carcasses of our work. We were all three of us looking forward to supper, which was pheasant with red cabbage and parmesan mash and an autumn trifle for pudding.

Ben's mother hovered, arms outstretched.

'Well done, darling,' she said, making an awkward grab at his neck for some kind of cuddle. He flinched. 'You're making such fantastic progress.'

We were halfway down the stone passage that leads from the dining room to the hall when I heard a voice that can only be described as wrought from steel and sheer ice summoning me back again.

*'HOBIE! HOBART DUVALLE!'*

What? I thought irritably, trotting back again like a gundog. What was it this time? I couldn't think of anything that I'd done recently. I let Zara help with the stupid cake. I hadn't played Lose Zara in the Maze even once, and we'd been here nearly a whole week. The clown suit, although a bit tactless maybe, could totally be explained as a cross between a joke and a spontaneous gift. There were no cigarettes knocking about as far as I knew, and if there were I'd blame them on Jason. Oh. The clothes. Had she found out about the clothes that I sold? Did she have ELSIE DUVALLE nametapes on the things? I thought I'd checked, but . . .

My mother was standing like some sort of accusatory statue in the middle of the dining room. One hand rested on the back of a mahogany chair for support. The other held a piece of paper. Uncrumpled, smoothed out. Jagged-edged.

Shit. *Shit.*

Why the hell did I hang on to it? Perhaps it was just

forgetfulness. I don't know. I hadn't been expecting her to go through my rucksack. But then, this is the woman that keeps tabs on her children with state-of-the-art hidden cameras, so it was doubly stupid of me not to throw the thing away. Frantically I tried to string together a lie, a lie good enough to explain what it was doing in my bag.

But it wasn't any use.

There, in her manicured hand, was the original 'Cannibal Ate My Mum with Ketchup and Peas', in all its lurid glory. The chocolate smears on the edges were further (unnecessary) proof that it was mine.

# BEN

I'm an uncomfortable person, and I've felt uncomfortable many, many times in my life. But nothing – not dark days in Moorfields Eye Hospital, not Zara walking away from me in the street, not even the worst of my nightmares or headaches – comes close to how uncomfortable I feel at this moment. If I'm right, and Jason died for the reason that occurred to me, suddenly, just now . . . but I can't be right. I don't know. I don't know what to think. I need to go somewhere; I just don't know where.

Giving Solly a shallow hug, and telling him I'll see him later, I wander away through the festival. I pass the medical tent, with bored gap-year students sitting outside with clipboards and pamphlets; I pass the emergency supplies stall with its overpriced batteries and shaving kits. The tattoo tent blares in neon: *Argon Ark*. Pairs of animals are lit up in gaudy silhouettes: lions, kangaroos, ducks. I slip my hand under my T-shirt, press against my ribs.

As I watch, the letters of the pink-lit sign swim and jumble and swap places.

*Ragnarok*

Slowly, I back away from it. I walk and walk, limbs

uncoordinated, until I reach the outskirts of the Download site. Then I dive under a barrier, weave through skips and caravans, jump over a dry ditch. I turn and tramp up a narrow lane paved with corrugated iron and lined with blackberry bushes, lit with emergency lighting. I come to a car park, one of an interlocking system of car parks, spreading out like great lakes. Giant fluorescent lights smoulder on strings. There's no one about. The cars look like slabs of stone.

A car alarm goes off, and then another and another and another. A chorus line of beeps and wails gets louder, and louder.

'*Ben Ben Ben Ben Ben!*'

I start to run, heading to the top of the car park. I must get to some place *higher*, I think, higher up. Some place with a view. I climb over barbed wire, clamping my hands freely over the spikes, uncaring.

'*Ben Ben Ben Ben Ben!*'

Now a hedge meets me and I slither through it, desperate to get away from the noise. I find myself alone in a giant field. It is curved, like the top of a huge dome. The only light now comes from a sullen three-quarter moon that lurks behind swollen clouds. Distant behind me, the angry cries of the cars. I make my way to the top of the field, my legs automated.

A bonfire at the far edge of the field. Dark shapes around it. Four – five. *Berserks*, I think. But there's nowhere to run to. I know they've seen me; I hear whoops and high-rising catcalls. One of them stands up, waving. I look for my phone, but there's nothing in my pockets. In any case, there's nobody to call.

'Ben! Get over here!'

Perhaps they are going to kill me, I think. I remember going to the headmaster's office – it must have been six weeks ago, already feels like a different year, a different me – and standing outside, knowing that when I got in there'd be a long, sorrowing conversation about my lack of ambition, the poorness of my predicted grades. And I remember thinking, Just get rid of me now, if I've failed so badly. Just let me go.

Feet slow, I approach the group around the bonfire.

White-faced, black-clothed, they squat around the flames. Some of them hold guitars. Their hair is long and matted. As I get nearer they all look up, their smiles wide and welcoming.

'It's Ben! He finally made it!'

'Take a seat, dude.'

Space is cleared for me on the ground. A warm beer is pressed into my hand. I look around the group. Berserks they cannot be, nor Gods. But . . . now I'm looking at them up close, I can see – just faintly – a flickerwork of changing light about their heads. Slowly I study their faces, all turned towards me with expectant expressions. The bonfire rustles and sizzles; sparks pop and chatter, springing away like shooting stars.

There's Dimebag Darrell.

Layne Staley.

Randy Rhoads.

Gar Samuelson.

And Cliff. My beloved Cliff Burton.

My Late Greats of Metal, assembled here like old friends.

'What are you doing here?' I mumble.

'Oh, we don't like to miss Download,' says Gar Samuelson, his curled hair rippling.

'We don't like to miss anything,' adds Randy Rhoads. 'But tonight there's another show about to start. Just across those fields, there. Look.'

I follow his outstretched arm. He is pointing down, down across the valley. It's so dark that there's nothing to see at first; then the image sharpens, lightens, so that I can almost make out the individual shapes of the Monopoly houses, the tiny sheep and cows. I gaze over the knitted fields with their treeline hems, past outhouses and barns, past the snaky glint of river to a small village. It's about a kilometre or two away, I'd say, though Ordnance Survey map work was never one of my strong points. For a moment I think I recognise the church spire, the curve of the footbridge as the river meets the edge of the village.

'What is it?' I say. The village is sleeping, so silent it could be uninhabited. 'Nothing's happening.'

'Just wait. It will,' says Cliff, in his Californian accent.

'What is that place?'

'I think,' says Cliff, his thin, intelligent face lit up by the flames, 'you could call it Valhalla.'

Together around the bonfire, the Late Greats and I watch as the lightshow begins on the horizon.

Over the sleeping village the colours bloom: pink, bruise purple, silver and bronze. Otherlife colours. Silent lightning: tinsel spears the sky. Shadowy figures are stirring. I watch the roil and swell of the clouds: flamenco dancers gathering up their skirts. It begins to rain. Fat, angry drops burst on my skin like grenades. The lightshow seems to fade and brighten, brighten and fade, bursts of brilliant intensity alternating with dim flickers. It's like watching an enormous underwater creature breathing in and out, its gills edged in iridescence.

I climb to my feet, walk to the edge of the field.

The church spire, that line of willow trees, those thick dark woods tucked away behind the lofty grey house . . . Something in my brain is still tick-tocking away, like Solomon's does when he's trying to figure out what school someone goes to, which university their siblings are at, which side of the square someone's house is on. Even through my drug-heavy haze, I'm thinking, I know this place. I know this.

As the lightshow pulses and grows, the air swirling with purpose and menace over the village, I keep thinking, tracing the outlines of the buildings and mapping them against my memories. I swing back to the Late Greats, but – of course

– they're gone; not even a circle of stamped-down fire remains to suggest they were ever there. I turn again to look at the lightshow.

I have been here before.

I have been to that lofty grey house over whose turrets and shingles the lightshow is gathering.

*Valhalla.*

The steps appear in front of me, rainbow-edged and translucent, and then, gradually, the whole of the bridge assembles, unfolds, reaches over and across the valley towards the lofty grey house at the edge of the village.

It's Duvalle Hall.


'Ben!'

I look back. It's Cliff, whiter and thinner than ever, barely there.

'Good luck,' he says.

It's raining harder now; it's difficult to hear him.

'Are you . . . in the Otherlife?'

'Who knows where we are . . . or where we're going, Ben . . . We just . . .'

'What?'

'We just came to show you the way.'


I never thought – never – that I'd be watching my grimy trainers take their first faltering steps upon Bifrost. I never thought anything like this would ever happen to me. The

Otherlife was born out of books; it came to me in shadows and glow-worm gleams. It hummed quietly in corners. It told me stories. It was never this bright, or this loud, or this . . . present. At this moment, for some reason, it is the realest thing that I've ever felt in all my life.

I'm up above the valley now, still climbing. The rainbow bridge shimmers under my feet. It feels tremulous, like thick slime. The air sings with rain. I take off my sodden hoodie and throw it off the bridge, and watch it flap-flapping down into some fields far below, like a broken kite. I am alive, I think, but I might also be dead, because I don't know how this can be happening.

I look for Heimdallr, the watchman, and find him at the apex of the bridge. In one hand he holds a heavy-looking horn. A blazing, burnt-orange glow outlines him as he raises the horn to his lips and tips his head back, and blows. A single note rises into the air, like a siren call.

Silhouetted against the rainclouds he stands, neck taut, waiting. He does not notice me as I pass.

The bridge begins to curve downwards now, towards the village. I see the green with its cricket pavilion, the handful of shops and cottages, the bigger houses on the fringes, rising up to meet me as I descend.

I get off by the footbridge over the river. There's no need to look behind me: I know Bifrost will have already dispersed into the night. There's no sign of the Otherlife now, as I walk through the sleeping village, past the putting green and the small playground, past the post office and the bed and breakfast. But I'm wrong: in the sky, two wolves hover in clouds of luminescence; one is white, the other dark. High up, they twist and writhe, straining to be unleashed.

*Hati will eat the moon. Skǫll will devour the sun. All will fight, and all will fall*, I think uneasily.

Ragnarok is the end.

But the end of what?

Now I turn down a gravelled lane and walk past the church and the graveyard and all the way to the end of the road. Here, finally, I come to towering iron gates, built tall and impenetrable, but the wall is loaded with creepers, which make it easy for me to clamber over. A slither and a jump and I'm on the other side. It's silent: the only sounds are the rain on the trees and my breathing. Still, I'm wary as I approach the house, keeping to the trees and avoiding the winding pebbled driveway. I don't know who's out there.

Duvalle Hall rises out of the shadows. It's larger than I remember, and more imposing. Ike and Elsie must have extended it. I don't remember the extra wing on the left; I don't remember the two towers that point like a *mano cornuto* from the roof. Surely it never had so many windows, so many rooms? But it's definitely Duvalle Hall. I recognise the yew hedges, the outhouses. The converted stables appear as I get nearer, tucked away behind the house. There's the croquet lawn, and over to my right I make out the glint of the lake and the ornamental bridge, and the maze beyond.

No lights burn in the windows. Shivers eddy along my arms as I come to the front door. I put out my hand to push it, and it opens at once, swinging back with oiled grace. My heart is a kick drum.

I step across the threshold.

'Zara?' I call out. 'Rebecca? It's Ben.'

They did say, didn't they, that they'd be here this weekend? Perhaps I've got that wrong. The marble floor is cold under my feet as I wander into the centre of the hall, my steps tentative. There's nothing here, I think. There's no one. Hati and Skǫll in the sky, the Late Greats – all just the chemical glitches in my brain. But if that's so, then how did I get here? Because I sure as hell didn't trek across the fields; I *felt* Bifrost quiver under my trainers. I *saw* Heimdallr raise the horn to his lips, so close I could have reached out to touch it – and I know it would have been smooth and slightly warm under my fingers.

'Christ, it's dark in here,' comes a voice. 'Why don't you have the light on? Ah yes, the power's out. Hold on.'

Muscles drawn tight, I wait.

Someone is shouldering the sitting-room door. Footsteps on stone. A match is struck, then another. A candle illuminates the hall.

'Ben! Great to see you! How was your hike?'

It's Ike Duvalle, coming towards me, beaming with lordly confidence.

'What do you think of our new bridge? Pretty handy, huh?'

He claps me on the back; something feels odd about his arm.

'You'd better head on upstairs. Careful on your way up. There's a lot of work going on in this house. Ah, but that's the way Elsie likes it. Now, I should see about brunch. You will be staying for brunch, right?'

As he speaks he walks me towards the stairs, as though he's in a hurry for me to go.

'What kind of eggs do you like? Fried are the most greasily satisfying. Poached eggs look like boobs, or so I've always thought.'

He doesn't seem to notice that I haven't said anything. I don't know what to say; I'm too disorientated. He's not how I remember him at all. He leans down to a row of bulbous glass-jar candles on the mantelpiece and there's something strange about the way he strikes the matches – holding the box awkwardly, his left hand at an odd angle – that bothers me. He catches me looking, and holds his hand up.

'Prosthetic. You like? Pretty cool.'

Now that I'm looking at it properly, I can see that it's artificial: jointed, flesh-coloured, the fingers opening and closing with mechanical stiffness.

'Ike, what happened to your hand?' I say.

'Had an encounter with one of our resident beasts. Unpleasant-looking animal. One of our gamekeepers took a shot at him, but I'm not sure we nailed him.'

He holds open the door to the stairs.

'Thank you,' I say. There seems to be no choice but to go through.

Just as I pass him, Ike clutches my arm with his artificial hand and whispers, 'I just wish I knew, Ben. I wish I knew where I went wrong.'

This is a staircase I don't remember from my time at Duvalle Hall. The stairs I remember were wide and mahogany; they split into two like the ones on the *Titanic* and had a river of rich dark carpeting running down the middle. The stairs I'm currently climbing are both shallow and steep at the same time; sometimes I take a step and am surprised by how high I have to lift my leg, and other times I stumble, misplacing my foot. It must be a hidden passage. It smells of mould, and something tangy and metallic, and expensive room freshener. The walls are rough-hewn stone, porous, the colour of the inside of a mouth. The stairs twist like DNA strands, so many times that I find I can't figure out my orientation, or how far I've climbed.

A small round window appears, like a porthole. I crouch down and peer through it, and then draw back in alarm.

Through the porthole, Elsie Duvalle is standing in a bra and knickers, going through her wardrobe with quick, cross hands. Her clothes – silver and gold robes, jewel-coloured shawls – are flowing past her on some kind of invisible carousel. Boxes with expensive-looking logos and labels are piled up around her; ropes of fish-scale gems are slung over the free-standing mirror. Elsie pulls a kimono onto her shoulders. She calls to someone out of sight.

'Clothilde! It is unbelievable. He has *stolen* some of my dresses. He is *literally unbelievable*. What are we going to do with him? Can you go and fetch him at once, please? And get the decorator to call me.'

She looks up sharply; I pull back from the edge of the porthole. She has the same waxy appearance as Ike does, as though if I were to peel her skin away there'd be nothing underneath but air.

'Who's there?'

She comes towards the porthole. Her hair billows out from her head in a cloud of woven gold. A lemony-green light flickers about her ears as she begins to cry.

The stairs are steeper now. I notice that the walls are inlaid with a web-like substance, like electrical wire, that seems to connect one porthole to another. Some of them are blocked or bricked up, others have curtains or panes of glass. These I peer through, each time with a pulse of hesitation, a buckling in my gut.

Through one porthole, a wolf sits in Pret a Manger with a Super Club sandwich.

Through another, two wolves tear down Westbourne Grove with a chargrilled steak.

Through a third, the boys from 8 Upper are auditioning for *Lord of the Flies*. Frodo stands on the stage, his fine voice echoing proudly as he delivers one of Jack's speeches. He ducks as a pair of highlighter pens, bound with rubber bands, freewheels through the air towards his face.

Some of these images are faint, others clear and sharp-edged. I pass a branch of Hamleys, overstuffed with toys. In the centre of a shelf sits a blonde doll dressed in a clown suit. Her hair has been jaggedly cut, and she is crying.

I pass a factory floor where wolves in white aprons are icing hundreds of tiny cupcakes that are dancing quietly by on conveyor belts. Each cupcake has a pale-faced, dark-haired boy delicately painted on its surface.

It's me.

Higher, higher I climb. I'm nearly beyond thinking; it's as much as I can do to keep going. One thing I'm sure of: something is wrong here. Ike's bitten-off hand, the lemony-green light in Elsie's face . . . none of this is right. I don't know what's happening, but it is something very strange. It's as though Ike and Tyr have become oddly melded into a single entity; meanwhile, Elsie is Frigg. But why?

This is not my Otherlife. Parts of it are familiar, but parts of it are not. And this is not Duvalle Hall either. It's somewhere, or something, else. Every few minutes the house shakes, as if a giant hand is clenching in its foundations. The smells are stronger the higher I climb: the copper of blood, fresh-baked chocolate croissants, new-mown grass. The web-like substance on the walls glistens with quick-travelling sparks. Somewhere below, I can still hear Elsie screaming.

And now the stairs are coming to an end. The door at the top of them is heavy and oak-solid and lined with red felt, and it takes all my strength to push it open. With the whole of my weight I lean against it, feeling the threat of cold air on the other side. Suddenly, without warning, the door gives way and I half fall out onto an immense stretch of rooftop covered entirely with grass.

It's a rugby pitch.

I take a couple of steps out onto the pitch. The rain has died down. The twin fireballs of Hati and Skǫll – one over to the east, one over to the west – leer down from above, like giant floodlights. I squint upwards. Now, above me, a constellation of ice-blue points appears in the sky, and each point gets larger, larger, growing limbs and weapons until they stand, side by side, and ready.

An army of frost giants.

Unannounced, the wolf pounces, knocking me down. Iron-hard body, flailing legs, hot breath. Diamond eyes. Its jaws close on my upper arm. The scream, when it comes, doesn't sound like mine. It's the disembodied scream of computer games, heavy metal, air-raid sirens. My arm howls with pain.

I lock eyes with the wolf, wishing I had more violence in me, and prepare to knee it in the throat. Its head comes closer, till its nose is nearly touching mine.

And then, instead of ripping out my jugular with one swift-clawed slash, it licks my face, with a rough tongue that feels like it's studded with salt crystals. It whines, softly, nudging my nose.

'Skoll?' I whisper.

'Wrong!' it says triumphantly, rolling off me and doing a blurry, furred somersault. It scrambles to its feet, shaking its coat. Its four legs become two and it climbs to stand, dressed in white trousers and a red shirt. His curls gleam like butter. He gives me a rugby tackle of a hug.

'It's so good to see you,' says my old friend Hobie Duvalle. 'Sorry I bit you, dude.'

# HOBIE'S DIARY

Freyr's Day, 7th November 2008

I am obviously in disgrace.

I've never seen my parents so angry. The Tattoo Incident pales into insignificance. I mean, my mother isn't Ben's mother so she didn't break anything, but she actually seized me by the wrist, sat me down in a chair like I was about to be tortured by the Secret Police and shouted in my face. The problem is, I guess, that apart from exercise and lunches my mother doesn't do much stuff, so apparently the children's charity thing is of, like, Huge Importance and therefore it was about the worst thing I could have done, ever. Much worse than if I'd just eaten all the salted caramels, which is what I'd planned to do initially.

First of all it was the fact that people had paid £250 for tickets to this thing which had several celebrities and football players among the guests and some BBC man doing the auction, not to mention a famous old jazz singer performing after dinner. So, in Mum's mind, sabotaging the goodie bags was a bit like scratching the bonnet of a Maserati. An act of great devaluation. Second of all it was the content of the magazine article. (Dad said: 'It was so disgusting that it actually made me sick – not only that someone would do such a thing, but that people would publish and read it. I'm utterly ashamed of you, Hobie.')

Thirdly, everyone in the article, from the cannibal to the victim's family, was a complete chav. And that of course made it worse. Not that Mum would have seen the joke if they'd been posh, but she might not have freaked out quite as badly as she did.

I am now not allowed the following:

Puddings
Salty snacks
Sugary snacks
Xbox
Heavy Metal
Any TV apart from shitty documentaries about whales
   and plankton
My iPhone.

I demanded to be told the timeframe of this punishment and apparently it's till the end of half term and that's only three days away. So actually it's nearly over. Normally I'd be desperate to get back to London, but I'll be sad when Ben isn't staying with us any more. Even if we've had to put up with his dreadful mother.

I don't care much about my phone because there's not much signal here anyway, and I'd only have used it to text Frodes or Archie something belittling or designed to derail their day in some small way. The lack of Xbox hurts more, but we don't really have time for it anyway, and I'd rather go to Yggdrasil with Ben. Same goes for TV. Plus the one down here isn't nearly as large as all the London TVs. Once you're used to a 42-inch screen, you can't really adjust to anything smaller, I find.

However, the sunflower and pumpkin seeds that Clothilde doles out to me in a little glass ramekin like I'm a pet budgerigar or something are *really humiliating* and totally inedible. Even though Rebecca says they're really good for you and full of essential fats. I think I will die if I have to keep eating them. They taste like bits of cardboard.

'Think about the Berserks,' said Ben today when we took a break from Geography. 'They fought on empty stomachs.'

'Bull*shit*. Weren't they stuffed full of hallucinogenic mushrooms or alcohol or something?'

'Yeah, but no food. Probably.'

'I'm sure they had a few carcasses to barbecue at the end of it.'

'Maybe.'

'Definitely not bloody *goji berries*.' Morosely I helped myself to another handful.

We were all in the kitchen. The tutors were making coffee and looking at each other's notes, murmuring things about 'timing' and 'showing your working' etc. Me and Ben and Za were at the kitchen table, staring down at our ration bowls like prisoners who've been let into the courtyard for an hour's forced exercise before going off to build railroads or whatever. Ben has nobly refused to eat any of the things

I'm being denied. A bit like a protest hunger strike. Not that he ever really seems to care about food.

I spat a pumpkin seed across the table, aiming for Zara's Longines wristwatch that she got for her tenth birthday. She jerked her arm out of the way and I noticed how narrow her wrist looked, with the pink crocodile bracelet of the watch slithering over it. Her fingers were a bit like Twiglets (another snack I'm permitted to consume). Sort of snappable, with sticking-out knuckles.

'Stop it, Hobes,' she muttered.

'*Stop it, Hobes,*' I mimicked, with my mouth full of what felt like hamster bedding. 'How's the old verbal reasoning going? Learned how to spell your own name yet?'

'Ho-bee,' sang Rebecca above the roar of the Nespresso machine, 'be *kind*.'

Jason was looking out across the kitchen garden to where our head gardener was overseeing the building of the most ginormous bonfire you could ever dream of. Tomorrow is our Bonfire Night celebration. After dinner we'll watch fireworks by the side of the lake and bedtime will be a whole two hours later than usual. I love bonfires. Ordinarily I'd be out there chucking deadwood onto it and then scrambling up the climbing frame and leaping off to land *snap crunch* on the top of the heap, but as you can imagine that wasn't on the agenda for today. Too much like fun.

'Whoa,' said Jason. 'That'll be some bonfire.'

He strode outside, knotting his scarf over his Adam's

apple. Rebecca went with him, closing the kitchen door carefully behind her. She kept pulling at her sleeves so that the cuffs of her sweater (which was the exact pink of summer pudding) covered her hands and she was leaning close to Jason for warmth. Their heads bobbed together. He lit one of his roll-ups, and they seemed deep in conversation. Sometimes Rebecca threw a kind of half-glance back through the window in our direction, and I wondered why. Sometimes she shook her head, as if something was quite sad.

Zara slipped out of the room like a little ghost.

'You shouldn't be so mean to her,' said Ben.

'I'm not *mean* to her,' I said. 'She's used to it anyway.'

'What you did . . . I felt so sorry for her.'

He was referring to the game of Lose Zara in the Maze that we played yesterday. Zara is just so amazingly trusting each time. That's what makes it so funny. You lead her into the maze, getting her to bring a couple of those awful dolls and say maybe they can do a fashion show or a concert or something, and then you blindfold her and run away. Then she has to find her way out – ideally while it gets dark – and you crouch outside making ghost noises. Anyway it was all going brilliantly yesterday and Zara was crying and screaming and then Ben, totally unbelievably, went back in to get her.

'It was extremely lame of you to go in and fetch her,' I said. 'She'd have gotten out eventually.'

Suddenly I saw that Zara had left her halloumi and red pepper wrap completely untouched. I seized it and crammed it, whole, into my mouth, feeling the glorious ooze of Hellmann's mayo onto my palms, only chewing as much as I needed to facilitate swallowing it as fast as was humanly possible.

I couldn't resist a victory cry.

'Soooo good!' I snarfed. 'Want some?'

Ben shook his head. 'Won't you be in trouble?'

'S'not sugary, s'not salty,' I said, or words to that effect. I needed to be economical with speech in order to eat faster. 'Jesus, I was getting *so hungry* I almost—'

And then Clothilde came in with a massive basket of ironing and saw me and went into a torrent of stressed-out French, and then, *surprise!* Mum came tap-tap-tapping in wearing her suede knee-high boots and, lo and behold, I was in trouble again. This time for eating a snack that was a) contraband and b) Zara's. FOR GOD'S SAKE. DOESN'T MY MOTHER HAVE ANYTHING BETTER TO DO?

'Mum, I *need* snacks in order to do the amount of work we've got to get through,' I whined.

'Yes, and you can have dried fruit, nuts and seeds.'

'But they're rank. They're foul. I hate them.'

'The point is not for you to like them,' she said, wetting a piece of kitchen roll and dabbing my mayonnaise-anointed face in a way that I found ludicrously over the top and like she was just *trying* to embarrass me. 'You have too much of what you like.'

339

'It was only a halloumi wrap. It would've gone to waste otherwise. I was just trying to—'

'*Enough!*'

I hate it when she gets properly cross. It must be because we're not in London. She must be bored or something.

She chucked the remains of the wrap – the frayed bits of tortilla I hadn't had time to hoover up – into the bin. Then she went over to the sink and started flinging potatoes into a colander. (Peeling potatoes = she *definitely* didn't have enough to do with her sodding time.)

'I emailed Mr Voss this morning, Hobie . . .'

My heart did a little *du-dumm* of surprise.

'To say you won't be doing Rugby for the rest of the term.'

I felt like my stomach was going to involuntarily erupt like Vesuvius and engulf the kitchen table and the whole sorry household in an ash-cloud of chewed-up halloumi.

'What the f— What the . . . ? *Why*, Mum, why?'

Very slowly, she turned round. She was drawing on these floral oven gloves that looked like massive gauntlets, smoothing down her matching pink apron.

'I spoke to the physio. She said it wouldn't be wise after your arm injury.'

'But my arm is fine!' I said, flailing it madly to prove it. She winced.

Tears. There were tears at the back of my nose. Traitors.

'Off you go now. Time to crack on.'

Like probation officers, Jason and Rebecca were waiting to usher me and Ben back to the dining room, where two hours of War Poetry awaited.

'But, Mum—'

'Stop showing off in front of other people, Hobie.'

And she turned back to the sink.


'Why's she doing it, Ben? Why?'

We were perched at the top of Yggdrasil again. It was almost raining, but not quite. Sort of misty, with water suspended in the air, a pinkish greyish sky. Tutoring was over for the day. If we'd been in London, you'd have been able to smell that firework smell that always hangs about for a few days either side of bonfire night. The mushrooms were still there, jostling at the foot of the tree like a bunch of disgruntled football fans.

Ben lowered his left leg into the hollow trunk and waved his foot from side to side.

'Your mother likes power. Mine does too.'

I reached above my head for a branch, considered letting it take the whole of my weight, thought better of it.

'Why do they have to have more power than us? They're *women*.'

'Frigg and Freyja are women.'

I thought about the Norse Goddesses. There aren't that many, obviously. Other than a lot of blonde hair, they had zero in common with Mum, as far as I was concerned.

'At least our mothers aren't immortal,' Ben went on. He shivered. He was looking really pale.

'D'you think we'll pass the exams next week?'

'Dunno.'

'I think I'll die without Rugby.'

We sat in the arms of the tree while the light faded.

Saturday 8th November

Today is the last day in the countryside. We are driving back to London tomorrow. Ben will leave with his mother in the morning. I want to go in their car but I can't apparently because it 'doesn't make sense'. On Monday we have exams. I know that if I fail them, they'll move me down. I'm trying not to think about this.

I will miss:

1. Going to Yggdrasil and talking about the Otherlife
2. Doing stuff with Ben
3. Being on holiday, no matter how crap and arduous and work-orientated it's been
4. Rebecca

I will not miss:

1. The sunflower-seed snack regimen unfairly imposed by my mother
2. The tutoring
3. Being with my family
4. Jason

OK, maybe that's a bit unfair, because Jason's all right really. He just doesn't let us run around every ten minutes like Rebecca does. And he's too bloody serious about everything.

Tonight we're having people over for drinks before dinner and they're bringing some other people who are staying with them, which is what people do in the country. Personally I hate it when someone that I don't know comes to one of my parties, say like when Matteo's cousin is visiting from Geneva, or one of Frodo's lame orchestra buddies accompanies us to Byron Burger. But for Mum and Dad it's a chance to mingle/connect/show off how nice the house is. And they sit and talk blah blah mingle crunch sip guffaw and the kids and Clothilde pass around the canapé nibbles that've been knocked up earlier, and then at exactly eight fifteen they all roll back into their cars and drive six minutes back to their houses.

Mum has relented on the boring food front as it's our last night and, let's face it, I've sat there with Jason and Rebecca for FOUR HOURS every day, working my socks off. She asked what I wanted for dinner and I said boeuf bourguignon, which is one of my favourite-ever suppers, with potato dauphinoise and then hot chocolate and raspberry soufflés and she must know she's been a real bitch to me for the last few days because she said yes to all of that.

I went into the kitchen to find Anna browning the meat. She was salting and peppering the cubes of beef, dabbing them in a bowl of flour and then sliding them into this massive casserole dish where they sizzled in butter. When they were brown on all sides she lifted them out with a slotted spoon, leaking juices, and put them aside. My hand shot out immediately and she smacked it lightly away.

'Hobie, absolutely not.'

'Why not?'

'Because it's not cooked yet, only browned.'

'Raw beef can't kill me!'

'Perhaps, but I'd still prefer not to take the chance. Would you like to chop up those onions?'

'That's not *my* job,' I told her and ran out again, seizing a couple of Frusli bars from the counter on my way.


Ben and I finished the last of the French papers, the last of the Maths papers, the last of the History Source questions. It was all done. I didn't know about Ben, but I felt drained. Some bloody holiday. One by one the textbooks went back into our rucksacks, the revision notes and index cards were filed and put away, our files stacked in the hall with labels on.

Jason, quite lamely, but I suppose with some inner core of decency, high-fived us both and gave us these handmade certificates that he'd drawn on cartridge paper.

'I, Hobart Duvalle, have survived a week of intensive study,' said mine. He'd done it quite well, to his credit, with a frame of vines and roses and thorns. Ben's was the same but with his name, obviously. Benjamin Holloway. Both of the certificates had a wolf on the back, so beautifully done with a calligraphy pen that I stared at old Jase briefly with new respect.

'*That's* going to be my tattoo,' I whispered to Ben in an undertone. 'And it's much better than yours!'

'Hobart,' Rebecca was saying. 'What a name! Where's it from?'

'It's an old version of Hubert, isn't it?' said Jason.

I explained that it was my grandfather's name and his grandfather before that, making me the Third.

'Hobart Duvalle the Third,' Rebecca said dramatically, giving me a salute. 'That's a name to do serious mischief behind. And I suppose your grandson, Hobie, will be the Fourth. Imagine that!'

And she hugged me.

'You boys have been so focused, and you've worked so well together.'

She wrapped her arms around Ben and kissed him on the cheek and I was inwardly furious because she only hugged me and what was all that about? Especially since it's my house. Then she frowned, and reached out to touch his forehead with the back of her hand.

'Ben, you're awfully hot. I think you're coming down with something, my love.'

The guests crunch-crunched onto the gravel through the massive gates that have stone pineapples on either side.

From the kitchen we heard the muffled slam of car doors, wellies scuffling towards the door. Drinks were being served in the drawing room, which is a bit like the sitting room but fancier and with more oil paintings in it and no TV. Dad was opening champagne.

Outside, the gardeners were lighting the bonfire while some men from the village strode to and fro on the big lawn, setting up fireworks. Ben and I watched from the window on the landing.

'It's a funeral pyre,' Ben murmured. 'Remember Baldr.'

'Tell me,' I said.

Ben drew a deep breath and closed his eyes.

'Everyone came to Baldr's funeral. Odin was there, with his ravens and Valkyries. Freyr came in a chariot drawn by a boar; Heimdallr on his horse. Freyja's chariot was drawn by cats. The frost giants came too, for they all had loved Baldr deeply.

'Baldr's body was carried down to the sea, where his ship, *Hringhorni*, waited on the shore. The Gods found, however, that it was too heavy for them to launch. So they sent for a giantess, whose name was Hyrrokkin, who came on a wolf, with vipers for reins. She went to *Hringhorni* and pushed it into the sea with a shove so powerful that the world shook.

'The Gods placed Baldr's body on the funeral pyre that they had built onboard the ship, with Baldr's wife, Nanna, beside him.'

'Oh, did they burn her alive?'

347

'No,' he said. 'She died of grief.'

'Huh. I'd rather be burnt alive than die of feelings.'

Ben went on: 'Slowly the great ship rolled down to the sea, blazing with the flames that Thor had consecrated with his hammer, Mjǫllnir, and to which Odin had added his gold ring, Draupnir. As they watched, the Gods wept for the departed Baldr until the ship was no more than the faintest glow on the horizon.'

'Awesome!' I said. I stared out at the growing flames. Funerals in England are so dull and drab. Lame-arsed singing and silly flowers and eulogies that are so bland and unfunny they might as well have been downloaded off the Internet. I wouldn't want that, if I died. I'd want what they had in the Otherlife.

The bonfire hissed and crackled as the dry leaves and branches caught fire in the gathering dusk. We stared at it, willing the body of Baldr to appear above it, as a sign that the Otherlife really did exist.

From the drawing room came the sounds of hooting laughter, glasses clinking together and the *fwah-fwah* noise that grown-ups make when they're interacting.

Ben's mother came out from her room. She smelt of some super-strong perfume and her hair was completely straight and shiny.

'Hello, darling. Hello, Hobie. Are you boys coming down?'

It wasn't a question, so we trotted down the stairs after her, Ben first, me following.

'Ben,' she was saying, 'you must make sure you answer clearly when people speak to you, all right? Don't just mumble like you would at home. Are you feeling OK? You look terrible.'

As I watched them go in, side by side, I was assailed by this terrible wave of sickness and sadness. I shook it off immediately. Just for a moment, though, I felt, as he passed through the door, like I would never see Ben again.

# BEN

'I thought I was never going to see you again,' he says, fingers pressing into my arm, breath hot on my cheek. 'But you've arrived at totally the right time. Come with me.'

He leads me to a swing seat and throws himself onto it, gesturing for me join him. It's a white, curlicued, wrought-iron contraption that I remember from the garden outside Ike's study. But what is it doing here, on the roof? And why is the roof so large, and flat? The swing seat faces out, across the sculpted gardens; you can see the lake and the woods, and an arena of pulsating sky. I hang back for a while; then, slowly, I go to sit down beside him.

'This is it,' says Hobie. 'It's starting.'

'What is?' I say, wanting to hear him say it.

'Ragnarok!' says Hobie, and in his voice is the full-force ecstasy of someone who's waited a long, long time for this moment.

A ship appears, blue-white, its edges swarming like insects, on the edge of the clouds. *Naglfar*, made of the nails of dead men. A flicker of fire-red on the ship's prow.

'Remember when you saw the ship on Westbourne Grove?' says Hobie. He is eating a chocolate brownie, devouring it in greedy bites, as though it's the first solid food he's had in months. 'I was so jealous. I so wanted to be able to do that. And now I can. It's *awesome*.'

'What are you doing, Hobie?' I say.

'Chilling out, enjoying the spectacle. I have to say I've been mostly bored out of my mind here. They kept me tied up, you know. Dripped with poison. No rugby! No snacks! I've only just managed to get out. I mean, Ben, it was practically a *straitjacket* they put me in! Not cool.'

He shivers. Without looking directly at him, I let the sides of my vision go soft – it's easy to do; I've had plenty of practice – and study him. He looks so changed. I remember when I saw Zara outside the Underworld, and thought that she was like *a plant starved of light*. That is almost how Hobie seems, under the myriad bursts and glimmers of the Otherlife. Taller, yes. But not as tall as I am. Not nearly. And thinner. Too thin. He looks as though he hasn't taken any exercise for a long time. It's hard to tell, in the darkness, but his skin seems papery and pale.

'They had me in some kind of hole, or tent or something,' he goes on. 'All dark, like a cave. A prison cell. Couldn't move a muscle. I'd have tried all my usual sweet-talking routines – you know, the kind of thing that generally works on Mum and Cloth-head – but I couldn't even *speak*. I could hear them, moving about. Staring down at me. Talking in Norse. Lucky you taught me a bit, though mostly I couldn't make out what they were saying. Machines making noises.

Bloody irritating. I don't know how long it went on for. It felt like months. *Years.*'

'The punishment of Loki,' I murmur.

'What?'

'What you're describing,' I say. 'It's like . . . It's the punishment of Loki, for killing Baldr.'

'Oh, come on, Ben. I didn't kill anyone.'

'What about Jason?'

'Jason?! You can't pretend that was my fault!'

'Why not? It was your fault. I know it was.'

He turns to me, smiling widely. Smears of chocolate give him the appearance of missing teeth.

'You've got no proof. Admit it.'

Another ship glides across the sky, huge and luminous with rising flames. *Hringhorni*, bearing Baldr away.

'I think I know what you did,' I say. 'I just don't know why you did it.'

We watch as *Hringhorni* disappears into the clouds. It's eerily silent. Bifrost, the rainbow bridge, suddenly dawns across the sky. *I walked over that*, I think. I was there.

'You never came to see me,' says Hobie.

'I did. I came twice.'

'Twice!'

There's a lot of pain in his voice. It's disguised as anger, but I can hear it.

'Sorry,' I mutter. 'I didn't think you'd have noticed.'

'Whatever,' he replies.

'Hobie. What did you do to Jason?'

'Like I said. *N-O-T-H-I-N-G*. Jesus, Ben. You can't show up and act like my *mother*.'

Bifrost begins to shake under the weight of the fire giants who come marching, marching, marching. Then it shatters and splinters, and breaks up into shards of multicoloured phosphorescence. Over the roll of thunder, I hear Heimdallr's horn again. It tingles in my blood.

A supernova bursts as Garm, the hellhound, comes for Tyr. In the empty space of the sky they fight, soundless, almost formless.

The horn sounds again. Now Jǫrmungandr, the World Serpent, many-coiled, hissing poison, rises up, a mass of scales over the woods. I watch as the dark blue Thor-shape dives for it, hesitantly at first, then gathering force. It's deadening. Hypnotic. It feels as if I'm locked in a circular cinema, unable to look away from the screen.

Hobie climbs off the swing seat and saunters over to the edge of the roof. I find myself following him, coming to stand not far away from him, right on the edge. Suddenly, *Naglfar* appears again before us, a shimmering mass of white and blue.

'Beautiful, isn't it?' says Hobie.

His face glows in the reflected light of the unfolding end of the world. His arms hang loosely against his sides. Loki steers the ship so that it glides alongside the rooftop. I've never seen that fire-red light so close. I can almost feel the heat of him, the demonic blaze. Now I see Loki's face, just for a moment – a wide grin of sharp teeth that reminds me a good deal of Hobie's – as he raises an arm to salute us.

'He's waited so long for this,' says Hobie exultantly, saluting back. 'So have I. It's all I've been able to think about. Like looking forward to the world's most magnificent party. Like every heavy metal song in existence rolled into one. You know, Ben, I'd never have got here if it hadn't been for you. I'd never have seen the Otherlife. It's all down to you really.'

I don't know what to say. Is he thanking me, or blaming me?

'You could stay here, you know, if you wanted to. With me,' says Hobie.

It must be the heat, or the explosions of light in the sky. The fibres of my thoughts are unravelling.

'What do you mean?' I say at last.

'It would be quite easy, Ben. You could be here all the time, like I am.'

'In the Otherlife, you mean?'

'In the Otherlife. You'd see it all the time, all around you, not just sometimes, in some places. Just think: isn't that what you always wanted? To live here?'

'I . . . I suppose so.'

Inside me a hole has opened up, a solid vault of wanting. It's the feeling I felt as a child. The longing to be taken away. The longing for the Otherlife. Loki murmurs something harsh and rapid and begins to turn the ship. Heimdallr makes for him, burnt-orange, battle cry jagged in the air.

'If you took maybe one or two tiny steps . . .' Hobie whispers.

Suddenly I am twelve again, and standing on a different roof, in another place. Hobie and I are watching the streets of west London, while the smoke from his cigarette rolls upwards into the clouds, and I tell him about the Otherlife. Our growing friendship is a suit of armour we both wear against the world. I have missed that friendship. I remember our wolf suits, and the night we stole the steak from the restaurant. I remember the taste of that steak: lemon and garlic and abandonment and delight. I've never tasted anything like it, before or since. I remember the night I helped him tattoo himself while I chanted in Norse. I remember the way we would sneak out to the squash courts at lunchtime, so Hobie could practise hitting the ball and we could talk more about the Otherlife while he played. Always, always, he wanted to hear about the Otherlife.

Perhaps . . . Perhaps Hobie is right. What is there for me in my own life? Just parents I seem to constantly disappoint, and exams I barely know how to revise for, and a future that I can't seem to look forward to, no matter how hard I try.

'We've missed you, Ben,' says Hobie.

Glancing down, I see that my trainers are barely ten centimetres away from the edge of the roof. It's a hard, straight fall. There are no terraces or ledges to catch me. I'd drop, like a deadweight, fifty or sixty metres.

It would be over very fast.

Maybe I would end up in the Otherlife, like Hobie seems to believe. Maybe I wouldn't. But maybe it wouldn't matter.

I sense him next to me, waiting.

Then I remember something Solomon used to say to me, an annoying-sounding truism that I used to ignore: *When in doubt, pause. Take three proper breaths. Think about the things that matter to you.* And despite the belt of heat that seems to grow stronger every second, and the bewildering brightness as God meets monster above our heads, and the grumbling and shaking of the house beneath us, I try to do as Solomon says. I close my eyes. Immediately my head is suffused with echoes and fragments of the things I've seen: the tangle of electrical wire on the Duvalle Hall stairs, Ike's artificial hand, Elsie's golden tears. I see Hati and Skǫll, one dark, one light, bristling and blurred in the sky. *Pause. Breathe.* My mind slips backwards: Metallica. The fireworks. The chains of lights in the Download car park. Solomon's solemn smile. *Pause. Breathe.* Zara in the park. Zara outside the church. Zara in the rain. *Again.* Portobello Road, on a bustling Friday morning. Jason buying the first of my Norse books for me as a birthday present. Jason's voice. *Take your time, Ben. No rush.*

I open my eyes. Hobie is right next to me, his hand almost touching my arm. My arm still aches from where

356

he bit me. Moving backwards, away from the edge of the roof, I say, 'No. Hobie, I can't. I came here for a reason. I need you to tell me what happened that night.'

'What night?'

'The night Jason died.'

'How could *I* possibly know what happened?' he says, eyes widening.

'Look,' I say. 'You're not going to get into trouble. You've been punished enough already. So just . . . tell me. If I mean as much to you as all that, then I have a right to know.'

A dazzle of blue as Odin and Fenrir clash above our heads. The winds are rising again, whipping the heat into strange shapes around us. Somewhere above us, I can hear the cries of strange birds.

'I know it was you,' I say. 'No matter what anyone says; no matter how much everyone pretends it was all some unexplained mystery, some strange allergic reaction that makes no possible sense, I know you killed him, Hobie.'

Hobie looks at me, then looks away.

'OK,' he says at last. 'I guess maybe I did.'

'Tell me,' I say steadily, 'why you killed Jason. Tell me you're sorry.'

'But I did it for you. I did it for *you*!'

My hands close around his neck.

'You killed Jason and you're telling me you did it for me—'

'Ben, I—'

His hands close around mine.

We lock ourselves in battle. So much heat comes off him, but his skin is cold to the touch. He knees me in the stomach and I sink for a moment, then twist into him, throwing him down onto the rugby pitch. A blur: skin darkening, nails extending into heavy claws, and he's a wolf again. And so am I. Under the bursts and explosions of Ragnarok, our jaws scissoring, our claws catching, we fight.

'You . . . killed . . . I loved him. I loved him more than anyone—' I gasp.

He swipes at my head, misses.

'You loved him more than me . . . You never loved me!'

I stop in mid-wrestle. Stop wanting to hurt him. For a moment.

'I did love you, Hobie. I did.'

He stares at me, mute and furious.

'I loved you too.'

'So just say it. Say you're sorry.'

His wolf-eyes are filling with tears. Slowly, he gets up, shakes himself. How we wanted this, I think, when we were young. We wished we could be wolves.

Surtr summons a wave of fire and sends it hurtling over the battlefield. Gigantic, all-destroying, it rises, rises, begins to crest.

'All right,' he says. 'You win. I'm sorry. I'm fucking sorry.'

The foundations of the house are shaking again beneath us. And I realise that the fire, the Otherlife fire, that comes blanketing across the sky in a single, gigantic sweep of such magnificence that it paralyses me down to my shoes, is *catching*. The roof at the far end of the rugby pitch goes up in flames, as though it's made of nothing more than cardboard. A foul smell trickles on the winds. The heat is growing.

'Hobie, we have to get out of here,' I tell him.

'You don't understand. This is it.'

Now the swing seat explodes in a glittery patter of white stars.

'Come on!' I yell. 'What are you waiting for?'

'I have to stay here. Like you always said. It's the end. I can't go with you. I have to stay here, Ben.'

I can see boy again, glowing palely through his wolfskin. He grows more elongated, two-legged, clothed again in his trousers and red shirt. I am boy too, unwolfed. I will never be a wolf again. The cries of the strange birds grow louder; I realise they are not birds, but the crescendoing sounds of battle – the clashes of swords, the screeches of Valkyries, the wordless curdled yells that accompany bloodshed and destruction.

'I wanted you to stay here,' says Hobie. 'But it was wrong of me. You should go. You still have time.'

He pushes me away from him; I can feel the strength of him, even though he's lost so much of his musculature. Then, suddenly, just as he's drawing back, he reaches forward again, towards me, and touches my hand. His expression shifts into something vulnerable, almost unrecognisable.

'Ben,' he says, 'am I going to be OK?'

He looks very young and very old at the same time.

'Yes,' I say quietly. 'Yes. I promise. You're going to be fine.'

I realise that I am crying.

Hobie draws away from me. Smiling now, he holds out his hand in farewell. Beneath my feet comes a vast and hollow creaking sound, like the bellowing yawn of a giant. I feel the turf wobble and split; I look down and see a jagged crack opening up like a mouth before my trainers. I step back, and the crack widens. I see the sedimented layers of the roof: film of rugby pitch, tiles, concrete, steel girders . . . and something bubbling up from the depths of the house, too: something like blood, or magma.

On the other side of the divide, Hobie looks smaller still.

'So long, dude!' he calls. He is still smiling.

'No, Hobie!'

I'm crying so hard I can barely get the words out. Behind me, I can hear the frame of the door I came through giving way. The roof is slanting now, like a sinking platform.

The last thing I see is Hobie's white hand, forming, for a second or two, a *mano cornuto*.

A blast of fire drowns him in a white-hot wall. I just hear him, faint but articulate: 'The *ship*, Ben. Look for the ship . . .'

I make it through the collapsing frame of the doorway just in time.

\* \* \*

I wake up, as I've woken so many times before, outside. This time though, I am screaming.

'Ben! *Ben!*'

A small hand slaps me, once, around the face. I stop screaming and open my eyes.

I am lying in a square of close-cut grass, damp beneath me. Around me are tall green people, watching. Surgeons, I think. This is an outdoor operating theatre. They are bringing me round.

'He's awake. Oh, Rebecca, he's awake.'

My arm hurts. My back hurts. My head . . . My head *doesn't* hurt.

What new world is this?

The light blue eyes of Zara are staring into mine. Her hair – buttery and sweet, like popcorn – brushes against my face in a feathery curtain as she leans over me to check I'm alive. She is binding my arm with a roll of crêpe bandage, her hands deft, professional. The tall green people are not people, I realise, but trimmed yew hedges.

'Where am I?' I mutter.

'You're at Duvalle Hall,' says Rebecca. She is carrying a sleeping Ashley in her arms. 'Funny time you picked to drop in.'

She sounds a little irritated, but she's smiling too.

I struggle to sit up. The sky glows with early morning promise above me.

I'm in the *maze*.

'How you got yourself right into the centre of the maze, Ben, I really don't know. We followed the blood,' says Rebecca. 'Something has bitten you on the arm.'

'Hobie,' I whisper. 'He's here. I saw him.'

But they don't seem to hear me. Rebecca and Zara help me to my feet and bring me back to the house. My legs are sore, as though I've walked on them for miles – which, I suppose, I have. I sense that I need to account for my appearance, somehow. But I'm not sure what to say. What would Solomon do, I wonder? Probably, he'd just tell them the truth. So that is what I do. I tell them the truth. Part of it.

As we walk across the dew-washed lawn, I tell them that I am addicted to painkillers – small, triangular things that have ruled my existence for many years. Last night, at Download, I gave them up, which opened a floodgate in my head. I had hallucinations I couldn't control. Out-of-body experiences. I stumbled over fields; I saw lights in the sky. I made it to Duvalle Hall, recognising it in some way. I climbed the wall. What bit me I really don't know – a large dog, a fox perhaps. Not wanting to wake them as they slept, to frighten them, I looked for shelter in the maze. My words jumble, tumble over themselves, but they seem to believe me, which is a relief.

'Breakfast is in order,' says Rebecca. 'Eggs. What kind of eggs do you like, Ben?'

'Doesn't . . . Isn't Ike in charge of cooking eggs?' I say foggily.

'Mum and Dad aren't here,' says Zara. 'They've gone to Barbados.'

Duvalle Hall, in daylight, is the Duvalle Hall it always was. The extra gables, the turrets and towers, the windows that glittered like fly's wings are gone now. I look up, and – as I expected – there is no long, flat roof on which rugby could be played, on which you could stand while the world began to end.

'Boiled eggs for Ben, I think. With Marmite soldiers,' says Rebecca, swinging Ashley in her arms.

I protest that I am not hungry, but – in fact – I am. And so is Zara. It's nice to see her like this. As we eat she keeps looking over at me. When Rebecca gets up to pull a tray of tomatoes out of the Aga, Zara reaches across the table and holds both of my hands.

'Something was different this morning,' she says, 'when I woke up. Like the air had cleared.'

'Well, there was the most enormous storm in the night,' says Rebecca, hearing us. 'The power went out for a couple of hours. I was quite afraid.'

'And they're gone,' Zara whispers, when Rebecca is engaged in feeding her child. 'The angels – the Gods – they're gone.'

I blink at the kitchen, at the white-and-yellow-striped blinds, the opulent, high-stacked fruit bowl and the polished worktops. I wait for the edges of things to blur. And I realise she's right.

'Why don't you take Ben on a tour?' says Rebecca. 'You can show him the new cinema room. Ike and Elsie have been doing a *lot* of work to the house,' she adds in explanation. 'Bless them.'

So Zara leads me around Duvalle Hall, and I struggle to reconcile what I remember of last night with the manicured rugs and right-angled cushions, the Old Masters in their weighty frames. It's imposing – it's huge – but not as huge as it was last night. The air smells of wood gathered for the fire, and cloves, and fresh-cut flowers.

'Zara,' I say, 'does your father have a prosthetic hand?'

'My mother has breast implants,' she replies, 'but I think Dad's fairly *au naturel*. What a weird question, Ben. Here's the dining room,' she continues. 'They've gone for dark blue. It was once red.'

This is where the final supper took place, I think. Where Jason ate his last meal. What did my dad say – a casserole, a roast? I wish I could remember.

'What did you eat, that night?' I ask Zara. 'The night Jason died.'

'I think I'd just started being vegetarian. I had what Rebecca had. Everyone else ate some kind of beef thing, I think. A stew. Why?'

'And nobody was ill, were they, afterwards? Not your parents or anyone?'

Zara looks at me. 'What are you thinking?' she says.

In my mouth, the word *poison* rolls around like a sticky

marble. I catch my breath and try to tell her what I think must have happened. But just as I'm about to, she turns, with a swish of her wavy hair, and leads me away. I follow her, thinking, I should have got Hobie to tell me what he did. He admitted it, but he didn't tell me what he did.

How is it that Jason died, if everyone ate the same thing?

Somewhere far away, I can hear the plaintive bleat of the phone.

Zara shows me the sitting room, the study. She shows me the new guest bathroom, all rippled marble and eggshell blue. She shows me the new panelling on the stairs. I look for the staircase of last night: that cramped vortex of a passageway that twisted like a periscope. But it's not here. We reach the landing and turn into the complex of rooms on the first floor.

Zara opens the door of her bedroom.

'I'm going to have new curtains,' she says. The patchwork quilt still hangs in the middle of her wall; the American dolls sit like a jury on a special shelf. She shuts the door and we walk on.

'What about Hobie's room?' I say.

'Do you really want to see it?'

'Yes. I saw him, Zara. He was here.'

'You know,' she says, leading the way along the passage, 'sometimes I see him too. I hear his voice. But he isn't here. He's where he's always been.'

Hobie's room is exactly how I remember it. Battle-lines

of toys, the elaborate painted furniture stencilled with hot-air balloons, griffins, clowns. The alphabetised bookcases look as if they haven't been touched. The bunk beds still wear their blue-and-white striped duvet covers, monogrammed with *H.J.D.* in thick cream stitching.

In the centre of the antique carpet I stand absolutely still, letting my mind go soft, allowing the shape of the window to blur, the pattern on the wallpaper to overlap with itself in an unending tessellation. I wait for the Otherlife to offer me a clue, for the lemony-green Frigg to hover at the edge of my peripheral vision, beckoning, guiding, for eight-legged Sleipnir to bring Hermódr forth with a message. But the room is quiet, still.

'I really did see him last night, Zara,' I say. 'He told me that he killed Jason. He admitted it. But he didn't say how, or why.'

Zara sits on the floor, cross-legged. She reaches for a small yellow dinosaur and cradles it in her hands, running one finger down its striped tail.

'I've always thought that perhaps he did,' she says. 'But something in me wanted to defend him. That's why I was so angry when you suggested it. Maybe I wasn't ready to hear it. Without proof, there's only the fact that of all the people in the house who might have done something bad, and purely in terms of past behaviour, that person was Hobie. That on its own isn't enough. Ben, what are you doing?'

I pull the under-bed storage boxes onto the carpet and

open them up. Board games in boxes, a beaten-up piggy bank, a stack of tacky-looking magazines. I sift through them, checking.

'What are you looking for?' says Zara.

'I've remembered something. Something that might help. At the end of Year 7 we were told to start keeping a note of things that we saw and ate and did. It was supposed to help with our writing. I didn't bother myself, because all the writing I did was in my Free Creative Writing book, but . . .'

Getting the idea, Zara goes over to the bookshelves. She takes out a wedge of Tintins, and then another, laying them in piles on the floor.

'You're right,' she's saying. 'He was so secretive about it. But Hobie did . . . sometimes. I used to see him, writing things down.'

'A blue journal, wasn't it? With a leather cover.'

'That's right.'

'Have you seen it? Do you know where it is?'

She sits back on her heels, thinking.

'Maybe it got thrown away,' she says at last.

I go back to his chest of drawers and slide open each drawer. There's something painful about the tidy way his clothes have been folded and kept, unmoved and unused, like artefacts of another time.

'It can't have been thrown away,' I say. 'It must be here. We just have to find it.'

As I'm saying this, I look upwards, towards the top of the wardrobe. I remember Hobie's last words to me.

'*The* ship, *Ben. Look for the ship.*'

I'd assumed he was talking about *Naglfar*, or *Hringhorni*. The Otherlife has many ships. But there are other ships than Otherlife ships. And there are many ships in this room.

There it is, on the top of the wardrobe. His antique model ship collection, meticulously arranged and museum-perfect. Inherited, as far as I remember, from his grandfather, Hobart Duvalle II. I seem to remember that Hobie was prouder of those ships, more genuinely fond, than he was of most of his other luxurious possessions.

Climbing onto a chair, I reach up for the biggest, the best, the most expensive-looking of the ships, and lift it down.

And I find it, scuffed and dusty, wedged against the floor of the ship.

The diary of Hobie Duvalle.

She's quick; I'm slow. But we sit on the floor, our backs against the bed, and we read it all, together.

When we've finished, she leans her head back against the starched cream valance. 'Oh, *Hobie.*'

There's nothing else to say.

'So that's what he did,' says Zara.

Rebecca is calling.

'Zara! Where are you? Zara!'

When we reach the ground floor, Rebecca is standing with the phone in her hand, and a single tear, pear-shaped, like an earring, on one of her cheeks.

'The clinic rang a while ago, when I was in the garden. I've just called them back.'

Zara gives a little gasp.

'Hobie died,' says Rebecca, holding out her arms. 'At two o'clock this morning.'

# HOBIE'S DIARY

Saturday 8th November 2008 (continued)

The total bore of a drinks party blathered on. My parents were handing out drinks while Zara passed round a plate of raw fennel and chive dip and quail's eggs and celery salt. Sir and Lady Someone were milling around near the fireplace with two enormous Labradors that Mum clearly very much wished had stayed in the car. The random couple that live on the other side of the village were deep in conversation with Rebecca about whether she'd be able to work with their daughter. Clothilde and Anna were to-ing and fro-ing from the kitchen in neat square aprons. And then there were these people called the Braithwaites, who live nearby.

Of course, when the Braithwaites asked if they could bring their house guest, and my parents said yes, of course, how marvellous, they hadn't known that the Braithwaites' house guest was, well, none other than Robin Holloway. Otherwise known as . . .

Ben's dad.

This was an Epic Fail.

'Oh my goodness,' Mum was saying. 'We didn't realise . . .'

I have to say Ben's dad was pretty glib and slick, with his hair combed carefully over the bald bit and his jeans and pea-green jacket combo. He actually looked incredibly pleased to see Ben, striding over to him and giving him an awkward hug which Ben seemed quite happy about, even though he generally loathes physical contact.

'Ben! This is such a surprise! Happy birthday for Wednesday, old boy. Have you been here all week?'

And he turned to Ben's mother, who had gone purple with the effort of not freaking out, and kissed her on the cheek in much the same way as people kiss corpses in funeral parlours on TV shows.

'Maud, you're here too. How've you been?'

There was a rather elaborate antique Korean vase on the table next to Ben's mother and I wondered if I should hurry over and rescue it before she threw it against the wall. But she didn't break anything, just looked like her shoes were suddenly far too small for her feet and like she was having difficulty standing up in them. She began showing off about how well Ben had done in all his practice papers, and how hard he had worked. She took care to make it sound like Ben was a damn sight better at hard work than his dad was.

'87%,' she was saying, swigging rapidly from her champagne glass, 'and that's with no help at all. Isn't that right, Jason?'

'Oh, absolutely,' Jason said, looking at his watch.

I couldn't believe she was adding an extra 3% to Ben's score. What a brazen liar!

My parents did a good job of getting more drinks down people as quickly as they could and everyone did a lot of very fast talking about how beautiful the garden was looking and how amazing the fireworks were going to be etc etc. I ate half a plate of smoked-salmon blinis and started on the bowl of Sevruga caviar before Anna wrestled it away from me and took it around the other guests.

'You'll spoil your dinner,' she scolded.

Sir and Lady Someone and the Random Couple and the Braithwaites had some other dinner party to go to. Ben's father stayed behind. Ben's mother and father and Ben were all sitting in the big green armchairs and I realised I'd only ever seen them all together once, in that cafe off the Harrow Road. Mum and Dad tactfully bundled me and Zara off to the TV room.

'When did Ben's parents split up?' asked Zara.

'Over the summer. Not that it's any of your concern,' I told her.

'Poor Ben. D'you think he's OK? He doesn't look great.'

Privately I agreed with Zara.

I left her in front of some ridiculous film about twins that are separated at birth and snuck back to the drawing room.

Voices were raised.

'What the hell d'you think you're doing, turning up here?' Ben's mother was saying.

'Maud, I honestly had no idea—'

'Oh, I find that very hard to believe. You knew where we were going to be.'

'I didn't make the connection, I assure you.'

'Ben and I have had enough of your *assurances*.'

Thrilled, I crept closer. Would she have a go at him with the fire irons? I couldn't hear Ben. Was he still in there? Was he OK?

'How is your *fiancée* then, Robin? Tired of her yet, are you?'

'Maud, your tone is really trying. Marti is very well.'

'Well, I'm sure you'll forgive me if I don't contribute to the honeymoon fund.'

Gradually her voice was rising. She was using some impressive swearwords too.

'You're upsetting Ben, Maud.'

'*I'm* not upsetting Ben. I'm not the one who pissed off and left us without even any way of paying for his bloody school fees—'

'We can't have this conversation now.'

'So what are you doing here?'

'I told you, I—'

'I think you'd better—'

'Ben. Ben, are you OK?'

'Oh my God, Ben!'

I was desperate to know what was happening. I was about to turn the handle when the doors opened and Ben's dad came out, supporting Ben, who looked white and faint and shaky on his feet.

'Ben's had a bit of a dizzy spell,' he said to me. 'Best get him to bed.'

Ben's mother grabbed hold of Ben and shoved his father aside, her eyes glinting like the Grand High Witch's, and said she'd take him herself.

'No,' murmured Ben.

'What did you say, darling?'

'I just want Hobie to come with me.'

So I took Ben upstairs and helped him into bed and he was really hot and I thought he probably had a temperature and I said I'd go and get Clothilde to bring the medicine box and he said he just wanted to sleep for years and years.

'Are you going to have supper with us?'

He rolled over into a ball.

'Nah. My head really hurts.'

I thought for a minute and then dashed into his mother's bathroom, which was closer than my parents', and I opened all her sponge bags, hunting around for something that looked like it'd do for headaches. Ben's mother had a *lot* of pills: green ones, white ones, packets and packets with foreign symbols on them, like Chinese or Japanese or something. Finally I seized a small brown bottle at random and raced back to Ben. The bottle was full of triangular pills the colour of satsumas and I gave Ben two with some water, getting him to sit up to swallow them.

'Thanks,' he said. 'What are they?'

'I dunno,' I said. 'They're your mum's.'

He lay back, his eyes closed. I watched him for a while.

Then I said, 'Ben?'

'Yeah.'

'On Wednesday, when you made your wish . . .'

'Yeah.'

'What did you wish for?'

He pulled the duvet up over his face and fumbled with the switch of the bedside light, plunging the room into darkness. It was totally quiet.

Finally Ben said, 'I wished my parents were dead.'

I went down to the kitchen. The trays were laden with silver forks and knives, ready to be taken into the dining room. Anna had wiped down the tabletops and it was all gleaming like in a kitchen showroom and the smell of beef and wine and herbs was all warm and delicious like a perfect sunset. Two rectangular dishes of potato dauphinoise were bubbling in the Aga. The casserole was simmering on the top, little ripples of dried juice cemented round the rim. I picked at some salad leaves and wondered what to do next.

'Where are you off to, Hobie?' asked Anna when she saw me putting on my scarf and coat. She was frying bacon and these little round mushrooms to add to the casserole.

'Going to say goodbye to this tree in the forest,' I told her truthfully.

'Well, take a torch then. It's pitch black out there.'

*   *   *

Mum and Dad were outside talking to the gardeners about the fireworks. I hoped they'd chosen properly spectacular ones, not just boring old Catherine wheels or whatever. I ducked through the door to the kitchen garden so that they wouldn't see me. As I passed by the wall, I heard them talking.

'How did he become like this?' Mum was saying. 'I feel utterly at a loss to explain it. You read the Ed Psych, didn't you, Ike?'

'*Extraordinary academic potential, severely impaired by repressed anger and a total disengagement with his studies*,' Dad said, presumably quoting from Dr Idiot Tibbert. 'It doesn't even sound like our son.'

'Is it something we've done?'

'No,' Dad was saying. 'I'm sure we couldn't have done anything differently. For Christ's sake, the kid has everything he's ever wanted . . .'

Their voices faded as I moved away. I stormed across the yard, feeling the bite of the cold, and then across the paddock and up into the woods, running the torch like a searchlight over the ground. I could feel tears burning in my mouth, and they weren't tears for me this time. They were for Ben. Because Ben is really cool and it isn't his fault that he's got no money and lives in a rubbish house and has this total freak of a crazy mother and this stupid father that isn't even around. And then I started feeling sad for me too, because at least Ben is going to pass all his exams whereas I'm going to fail miserably even with all the help I've been getting, and I'll probably never be allowed to play Rugby or be in a play ever again, and one day they'll find out about the roof and stop me going up there, just like they stop me doing everything that I really enjoy.

An owl hooted above me as I crashed through the trees, flicking the beam of my torch this way and that. I imagined Loki, God of mischief, running alongside me, chanting words of encouragement. Where the hell was Yggdrasil? I stumbled to and fro between the trees, looking for something familiar. In my head I heard Ben's muffled growl of a voice. *I wished my parents were dead.*

The mushrooms were still clustered at the foot of the tree, glowing white in the torchlight.

'*Bǫðvar úlfr brandi tekr,*' I muttered under my breath, and as I said the words it really felt like the trees were saying them with me. '*Bǫðvar úlfr brandi tekr.* Wolf of combat takes up blade.' Like the whole forest was alive with the sound of whispers. And I realised that I was crying, really properly crying.

I crouched down. I grabbed a handful of mushrooms. They came away from the ground quite easily, along with some old leaves and bits of grass and twigs. I stuffed them in my pocket and went back to the house.

As I strode away I knew that an army of Berserks was marching in the shadows behind me.

\* \* \*

The kitchen was deserted when I got back. Quickly, not bothering to look for a chopping board, I chucked the mushrooms onto the worktop and scrabbled about for a sharp knife. When I looked at them in the bright light though, I realised that they were too pale, not cooked-looking enough, to not be noticed if I dropped them into the casserole. Damn it! I seized the handful, trying not to drop clods of earth on the floor, and scanned the kitchen for something else to put them in.

And then I saw the big shiny saucepan that held the mulled wine for people to drink during the fireworks. It was chock full of orange peel and cinnamon sticks and whatnot and it'd be dark anyway, when people drank it. Perfect, perfect, perfect. I attacked the mushrooms with a breadknife, just enough for them to crumble into pieces, and even though there were still a few leaves and things I gathered up the whole lot and stirred them hastily into the mulled wine. Then I put the lid back on and slipped out of the kitchen. I even remembered to wash the knife.

It was just like the goodie bags, just like the Great Steak Heist, only better. I always get this massive rush of excitement when I've done something amusing. A bit like Fenrir when he bit off Tyr's hand. I can imagine him, lurching around in his chains, jaws poised, paws scraping at the ground. Waiting for the world to end.

I was surprised, when we went into dinner, to see that Rebecca and Jason were staying after all. Apparently her car wouldn't start, or something. For a moment I panicked. Then I remembered that Rebecca didn't drink alcohol, so that was OK. I wouldn't want anything to happen to Rebecca.

Sunday 9th November

Shit.

### After Ragnarok
### By Ben Holloway
### 29-10-2008

Only Yggdrasil remained, sheltering a handful of men and women beneath its branches.

One day the world would be born again, with a new race of men and a reborn sun.

One day Baldr would return from the dead, to rule over his new kingdom.

# BEN
## ONE MONTH LATER

We come to the churchyard in the late afternoon. Butterflies cycle lazily above the honeysuckle. The air is still: so still you can almost feel the currents, the tiny ripples as they pass. A crow alights on a headstone, its eyes bright and beckoning. Then, with a rustle of wings, it circles away into the distance.

I have measured out my life in graveyards, in shadows and dark places, I think. But my nightwalking days – or, I guess, nights – are over now. Since Hobie's memorial service a couple of weeks ago, I haven't set foot in a graveyard. I went to the London ceremony – an enormous, catered affair in a church in South Kensington – where I saw all the old teachers from Cottesmore House, and all the kids from 8 Upper too, which was sort of weird. Frodo made a speech. All I could think about was how I wished Hobie had been there, to draw something unmentionable on the back of Frodo's impeccably cut suit. Solomon came with me, and so did my parents, and we all sat together, which felt strange, but also comforting. My parents, it seems, are spending more time together now. I'm glad. She is angry, and he is weak, but – like the armchairs in Battersea and Kensal Rise – they are better as a pair.

The actual funeral was a small, family-only occasion, here in the village. Here in this church. It's a polite, pebble-grey shoebox of a church. I can't imagine Elsie's hats fitting inside it. It must have been very sad – but, perhaps, with a hint of relief as well. There was very little chance, you see, of Hobie ever waking up – or, if he had, of waking up OK.

Some of the graves are marked with wreaths and flowers. Others are sunken into the grass, untended and unknown. Our shoes, crunching on the gravel, are the loudest sounds. Zara's trainers are tied with pink laces. She hasn't worn a lot of black. I have, but then I always do.

Around the back of the church we walk, and here the graves are beautifully kept, clear of weeds and invading creepers. We come to a great, glorious slab of marble, inlaid with gold, four cherubs carved into the corners. *In Memoriam: Hobart Duvalle*, it says. *1836–1890*. A memorial for the original Hobart Duvalle, who died in America, I imagine. His wife, Mary, his son, Alfred Ebenezer, and his three daughters have adjoining stones.

Then a raised, scrubbed plinth, a solemn cross mounted at the head. *Hobart Duvalle II of this parish is buried here*, it says. *1922–2006. May he rest in peace*. Hobie's grandfather, sponsor of Latin, lover of polished shoes on Monday mornings. His wife, Henrietta, is etched politely beneath this, in a smaller, feminine font.

The grave we come to now is white and clean and untarnished by weathering. A curly-headed angel rises from its curved top. The prim bronze lettering comes into focus, and I think for a strange moment of *Star Wars* and how the writing floats up the screen at the beginning of each film, that essential paragraph you need to read in order for the rest of it to make sense.

*Hobart James Duvalle III*
*14th July 1996 – 10th June 2012*
*Taken from us too soon.*
*Rest in Peace.*

So we know, me and Zara, what Hobie did.

He took a handful of mushrooms from the base of Yggdrasil, chopped them up, considered putting them in the casserole, and then put them instead in the mulled wine. We know from the diary, and from the diary only, because all the cups and glasses, the plates and cookware and serving dishes, had been washed up and put away long before the police arrived, after Jason was found on the Sunday morning. No traces of poisonous mushrooms were found, or noted, or remarked upon, and – most important of all – no one saw him do it. But we cannot imagine that Hobie was lying. I don't think there's a single thing in his diary that he didn't mean to say. He knew the mushrooms could be poisonous, or, perhaps, that they might be hallucinogenic – that they could send the consumer into a 'psycho Berserk state'. If the latter, it would have been an excellent practical joke – or so Hobie might have thought. If the former though . . . it was no joke. He wanted someone to die.

He listened to me, when, hidden under a mound of duvet, I said the words: 'I wished my parents were dead.'

If only I hadn't said it. But I did. It took me a long time to stop blaming myself for that. In the end it was Zara who persuaded me, saying that there is a big difference between thinking something bad and deciding, in some hot-headed moment, to act on that thought. So often that was the line that Hobie couldn't see. No one knew that better than Zara. If Hobie really did want to kill someone, it wasn't because of me. Or at least, that's what I'm trying to believe. I suppose I will never know. All we know for certain is that Jason drank a cup of mulled wine, and, later, died.

So many things remained unanswered. Why was it only Jason who was affected? That was the first question. We wondered if he perhaps he was the only person to drink the mulled wine. It occurred to me to ask Dad: he is generally an expert on alcoholic beverages, and with his author's attention to specific detail he seemed to remember more than anyone else who was there. I did ask him, and he confirmed that the Duvalles had served, along with an excellent Margaux at dinner, several bottles of Louis Roederer champagne, before dinner and also later, during the fireworks. No one in their right mind, asserted Dad, would have opted for mulled wine when there was premium champagne on tap. But he called me back, an hour or two afterwards, to tell me that in actual fact he had drunk a glass or two of mulled wine, and 'it wasn't too bad'. Had he felt unwell, or sick at all, the next day? Well, yes, said Dad. But he generally did, in the mornings. Perhaps Jason drank much more of the wine than Dad did. Perhaps he just happened to swallow a mushroom, or part of one, while Dad did not.

But there were other problems too. Zara and I did plenty of research. We learned that it could take weeks, sometimes, or longer, to die after ingesting poisonous fungi. The Internet was full of horror stories, and we read as many as we could bear to. But Jason was found dead, not after days or weeks, but a few hours later. Plus: the effects of mushrooms such as *Amanita phalloides* or *Amanita virosa* are readily traceable. Why then had nobody known that this was what killed him? Why was it never reported?

As far as I was concerned, there was only one reason why there was any mystery about the cause of Jason's death. Surely Ike and Elsie somehow managed to influence the coroner's report, or suppress the real one in some way. It seemed reasonable, with their connections and their near-unlimited funds, that they could have been able to do this. And if they'd thought that Hobie might have had something to do with it – which, after what happened to Hobie after Jason's body was found, might have seemed likely – surely they'd have been all the more keen to minimise the attentions of the police, and even, maybe, the press. Zara told me that she'd been instructed not to say anything to anyone about it, no matter who asked. And this explained why nobody at Cottesmore House said anything to me – people like Frodo, who I'm sure must have found out at some point. The combination of my mother not wanting me to find out, plus the Duvalles making sure that nobody talked about it, plus my weird, wrapped-up head state, where I barely knew what day of the week it was, plus the painkillers I started taking regularly . . . all of this together was enough to keep me from figuring it out.

Until Hermódr came.

Zara and I decided that we needed to see the actual report. So, as soon as my exams were over, that – with a little guidance from the ever-helpful Reg of Putney – is what we did.

It took a while for the local coroner's office to accept that we were 'interested parties'; in the end, we took Rebecca with us. We didn't think they could deny the mother of Jason's child the right to look at his records.

Hobie had been buried for a week. It was curiously dull and grey for early July; the day had an anticlimactic feel. We waited for a while at reception, and then were shown to a small carpeted room. A woman in a blue suit told us there was a small fee, which Rebecca paid with her debit card.

And then, after so many weeks of waiting, and wondering, and speculating, Jason's report lay, at last, in front of us, in a long, official envelope. Zara, who had been content for so long not to wonder what had really happened to Jason, was the one to open it.

And it said nothing about poison at all. (Nothing about drugs either, I was glad to note.) And nothing about mushrooms.

According to the report, Jason Adrian Young, deceased, had died of 'asphyxiation resulting from severe anaphylactic shock'. In other words, Jason had had an allergic reaction. The allergen itself was not noted. Rebecca had apparently been right. Except it was not right at all.

After that, even Zara had to agree with me. It seemed that Ike and Elsie Duvalle really had managed to change the report so that it said nothing about poisonous mushrooms, which were so much more suspicious and harder to explain than a simple allergic reaction. Was that really so hard to believe? Perhaps it wasn't.

But even now, as we leave the churchyard and make our way back up the lane to the Duvalles' land, entering through the small gate that will take us into the woods, we are still not quite sure that we really know the truth.

We thread between the trees, the gnarled oaks and slender beeches, the willows with their outpoured graceful fronds. Afternoon sunlight filters through thick-layered leaves. Wood pigeons murmur from far-off places.

We come to a small grove, a clearing.

At its centre: Yggdrasil.

The sight of it, grand and ancient, fills me with sudden emotion. The history of me and Zara and Hobie and Rebecca and Jason all bundled up inside it, running deep into the memories in its roots. For a few moments we stand in its shadow, side by side but not touching, in total silence.

This is where Hobie was found.

This part is the bit that I never really knew, but I know it as well now as if I'd been there, because Zara has told me, so many times.

On the 9th of November, early in the morning, Jason was found dead. In a magazine-perfect house run with clockwork precision, anguish and confusion suddenly reigned. Amid the chaos of police taking statements, the coroner being notified, people lamenting in hushed voices, nobody noticed that Hobie had vanished. Ike and Elsie were in the drawing room with the police. Clothilde was hysterical. Rebecca was on the phone to Jason's flatmates, her voice low and choked; even her earrings had ceased to dance.

Zara padded from room to room, looking for her brother.

'Where's Hobie?' she said to the cleaner, to Anna in the kitchen, who was quietly devastated, as though she was personally responsible for the death of Jason.

She looked in Hobie's room, his bathroom, their parents' room.

Nothing.

Then, without putting on her shoes, she ran out into the cold grey morning. She thought about the maze, wondering whether he was waiting for her there. *Let's play Lose Zara in the Maze*, he'd say, tugging at her ponytail, dragging her by the hand. But the maze was silent, uninhabited. The pool was undisturbed, its tarpaulin flat and blue and ignorant.

She climbed up into the woods, following the broken stems and footprinted undergrowth that suggested that someone had passed that way. She'd trailed after me and Hobie many times besides, wanting to be part of our close-knit team of two. She knew this was the way we often came. Distantly, she heard the crackle and crash of someone ahead of her, stampeding a path towards the tree, the huge hollow tree where she knew we sometimes used to sit. The one with a funny name, a many-syllabled name.

'Hobie!' she called out. 'Where are you?'

When she came to the clearing he was already at the top of the tree. He stood, poised, one hand supporting his weight on a nearby branch. Around his head, Zara saw a fire-red light, faint, like an afterglow. (It was this light that she was reminded of, years later, when she began to see the coloured lights of the Otherlife for herself.)

Hobie looked straight at her but – she is sure of this – as if she wasn't really there. He looked through her. She wondered what it was that he could see.

He said, '*Ben* . . .'

His expression changed, from a primal baring of teeth, an elated, ecstatic snarl, to surprise, outrage, shock.

And he fell.

\*　　\*　　\*

They moved him from place to place, bringing in specialists, changing his treatments. He spent a long time in intensive care, and for a while it was hoped that he would recover. But Hobie Duvalle, the fastest, the strongest, the most vigorous and energetic of people, was trapped in a coma, as Loki was trapped in a net by the angry Gods. His brain function minimal, his body inert, his hands and feet unmoving. It was this that I couldn't bear to see, on the couple of occasions that I visited. People offered to go with me – Mum, Dad, even Frodo – but I just couldn't bear to look at his hands. In all the time that I'd known Hobie, his hands were always busy – stuffing things into his mouth, catching and throwing, scribbling, fiddling, fidgeting. I could not bear to look at hands so still.

Hobie stayed in a coma for three years, seven months, and one day. And then, on the night that I crossed the bridge to Duvalle Hall, on the night that Ragnarok suddenly appeared in the sky, he died.

When Hermódr came to me, in the Stonehills' garden, it was not *He is dead*, or *He has died*, that he said to me. It was not *hann er dauðr*, as I'd thought it was, or *hann er dáinn*.

It was *hann deyr*.

Not past, but present.

*He is dying.*

It was not Jason that he meant, but Hobie. Although I can't help but wonder if perhaps I was supposed to interpret it the way that I did, because only by finding out that Hobie killed Jason could I have ever forgiven Hobie. And I think he needed to be forgiven.

He may have pretended he didn't, but he did.

I think Ragnarok means different things for different people. As far as the story goes, it spelt the end of the Gods but the beginning of a fresh, clean world, ruled over by Baldr, under a newborn sun. It was an end, but also a beginning. Sometimes things need to be destroyed in order for changes to take place. Ragnarok is not a bad thing or a good thing. Just an eventual thing. But I also think the Ragnarok that took place on the great rugby pitch at the top of Duvalle Hall had a specific meaning, a purpose.

It was the last few hours of Hobie's life.

It really was, as he said, *the end of everything*.

And I'm glad that I got to see him, one last time.

'Do you think we've got it right?' says Zara, interrupting my thoughts.

'What?'

'About Jason, I mean.'

'Hobie said he was sorry,' I say. 'When I saw him on the roof, that night. He knew he was guilty.'

'But what you saw . . . you can't be sure that was Hobie. You can't be sure it wasn't your imagination.'

Even though she's seen the coloured lights, I don't think Zara will ever fully understand about the Otherlife. There's seeing, and there's *seeing*. Things don't always have to be physically there to be real. I *know* it was Hobie – some part of Hobie, at least. Even though his actual body was hundreds of miles away, in some secluded, bleached unit of a private clinic, I know it was him. Even though there was, of course, no enormous bridge when I looked for it the next day, I will always remember the way it glowed in the rain, the feel of it under my trainers. And even though by the time I peeled away the bandages the following evening the marks had faded to a soft, irritated pink, there was still the evidence, ever so slight, of the wolf-bite on my arm. There is more than one kind of real in the world.

I look up at the mighty tangled branches wreathed in rich dark leaves. Last time I saw this tree, it was bare. I half-close my eyes, try to remember. I can think more clearly now. My mind's my own again. I haven't taken a painkiller since Download, and I'm sure that I never will again.

'Maybe it *wasn't* the mushrooms that killed him,' says Zara, for what must be the thousandth time. Her perfectionism is so extreme that she cannot allow for errors, especially when it comes to building a story that holds water. She still hates to think that any worthy coroner would allow himself to be swayed by the promise of money, even though she can see how it might have happened that way.

'What then?' I say. 'If not the mushrooms, then what?'

'Something that wasn't poison. Something else.'

'Like what?' I say again.

'I don't know. You knew him better than me. You knew

him better than most people. What if it really was an allergy? Did he ever say anything to you about allergies?'

'If he had, I'd remember,' I say. But even as I'm thinking this, that hidden part of my brain – the part that was mired in a drugged slumber for year upon year – starts flashing, alert and awakened. There *was* something . . . something he once told me. Or was it something he told Hobie?

Opening Hobie's diary, Zara reads out a passage again, in her measured and thoughtful voice.

'*I attacked the mushrooms with a breadknife, just enough for them to crumble into pieces, and even though there were still a few leaves and things I gathered up the whole lot and stirred them hastily into the mulled wine.*'

My gaze travels upwards to the nest of branches where Hobie and I used to sit.

And I see.

I remember.

And, in my heart and stomach and bones, I *know*.

'Zara,' I say. 'Zara – look.'

Following my line of sight, she peers upwards. At the wiry clot of mistletoe that clings to Yggdrasil.

'When Hobie picked the mushrooms, he pulled up some leaves and twigs from the ground,' I say. 'We know this. You just read it out. And in among the leaves and twigs, there was some *mistletoe*. You're right: Jason didn't die of poisoning. He *did* have an allergy, a really obscure one. He was allergic to mistletoe. He didn't die of poisoning. It wasn't the mushrooms. It was the mistletoe.'

Zara breathes out, slowly.

I go on: 'He did tell me once that he loved the Norse tales because he had something in common with one of the Gods. But he never told me that the God was Baldr. Maybe he ate some mistletoe when he was small and had some kind of reaction to it; maybe that's how he knew.'

'Yes, like with wasps and penicillin and oysters. People know they're allergic and they know that it'll be worse the next time,' Zara says. 'But do you think he knew he could die from it?'

'I just don't know. He never mentioned mistletoe to me, not in so many words.'

'And isn't mistletoe poisonous anyway?'

'I don't think it's that poisonous,' I say. 'I don't think it can kill people. Also, maybe that explains why my dad said he felt a bit ill the next day. He might have had mild mistletoe poisoning. But Jason wasn't poisoned; it was definitely an allergy. And that's why it doesn't say anything specific in the report. How could they have known that he was allergic to mistletoe?'

'*Hobie* knew,' says Zara abruptly. 'He mentions it in his diary. Near the end. He says Jason's allergic to *something bizarre*. But he doesn't remember what it is.'

She knows the diary practically off by heart by now. But I think I remember the bit she's talking about. It makes me incredibly sad that the only person who knew that Jason was allergic to mistletoe was the person who caused his death.

For a while longer we stand there, not touching, not talking.

Then: 'It's just like the story,' says Zara. 'The story of Baldr and Loki.'

Later, as it grows dark, Zara and I go down to the lake. We have brought the model ship. Zara is carrying Hobie's diary. It's time for the diary to be put to rest. It's time for Hobie too. I'm sure that his funeral was very nice, in an English sort of way, and his memorial was grand and splendid, rich with organ chords and perfume. But we know what he wrote in his diary. *I'd want what they had in the Otherlife.* We owe him this much.

Today is good day for a ceremony, besides.

Today would have been his sixteenth birthday.

We stand on the narrow platform, gazing out across the flat placid surface. The Japanese bridge arches across the middle, as brittle, as artificial, as papier maché.

I do not think Hobie wanted to die, though I cannot be sure. I think he went to Yggdrasil that morning for the same reason that we always went there together: to escape. I think he didn't know what to do, or where else to go. It's possible, though, that by killing Jason in the way that he did – with mistletoe – that by acting like Loki, he somehow found his way into the Otherlife, and that when he climbed the tree on that last morning it reached out a hand for him

– a fire-red, grasping hand – and dragged him away. Either that, or he found some way of seeing it, in his unconscious state, more clearly and more vividly than I ever could. Certainly that would explain the things I kept glimpsing, all through May and June, that weren't the Otherlife I knew as mine, and the mysterious, twisted version of Duvalle Hall that I came to on the night of Metallica's show at Download. It was Hobie's Otherlife. And I wonder, sometimes, whether I started to see the Otherlife – both his and mine – again, after so long, because Hobie, in his hospital bed, wanted me to. After all, Zara saw something too. Perhaps he was reaching out to her as well.

But some things there will never be an answer for, and we will have to accept that.

We kneel down, side by side, at the water's edge. Gently Zara wedges the diary between the masthead and the curved side of the hull. On top of the diary she places a small plastic Tyrannosaurus rex. Then she takes a packet of Sun-Maid raisins from the pocket of her jeans. A Bounty bar. Adds them too.

'Snacks,' she says.

Lastly, a loose-tasselled pompom, sad and bedraggled. She puts it on the deck.

'I'm throwing the clown suit away at last, but I want him to take something of mine too,' she says.

I hesitate a moment, and then take a fold of material from my back pocket. I open it out slowly.

'What is that?' says Zara.

'A vintage Metallica T-shirt,' I say. 'Probably my favourite-ever piece of clothing.'

I imprint it on my mind one last time. The blackened scar and frayed hole from the Stonehills' party look almost right now, as though they're part of the design. I can't believe I minded as much as I did. And even though this T-shirt is incredibly rare, and I'll never be able to afford another one like it, I'm glad that I'm giving it to Hobie. Wherever he is, I think he'll appreciate the gesture.

I break a firelighter in half; it reminds me of the time I gave Hobie my sandwich. I hand a piece to Zara and we sprinkle the chalky crumbs onto the funeral mound, wiping our fingers on our clothes.

'OK. Ready?'

'Ready.'

I hand her the lighter. She flicks, neatly. A narrow tongue of fire licks the air. Slowly she holds it near the crumbled firelighter, the corner of the raisin box, the diary. Hungrily, like it's jumping at the chance, the paper snatches at the newborn flame. The edges take on a darker gilt.

'Will you say something?' she says.

I think for a while, running in my head scattered lines from the *Voluspá*. Things I read with Jason, things I read on my own, things I read to Hobie.

Then I whisper, my voice catching:

*'Sól mun sortna,*
*søkkr fold í mar,*
*hverfa af himni*
*heiðar stjǫrnor,*
*geisar eimi*
*ok aldrnari,*
*leikr hár hiti,*
*við himin sjalfan.*

*The sun grows dark,*
*Earth sinks in the sea,*
*The glittering stars*
*Glide from the sky.*
*The smoke-reek rages*
*Reddening fire,*
*The high heat licks*
*The heaven itself.'*

I think, at the same time, of that song that Dad loves so much. The one about a time of innocence, about old friends . . . about a photograph . . . and how you should preserve your memories because they're all you have left. And I make a promise, to my old friend Hobie, that I will not forget him. All these years, I haven't allowed myself to be sad about him, for fear of what I might feel. I will honour Hobie by being the alivest that I possibly can be.

And it comes to me now: the glittering. The nerves in my

palms, smouldering. The sides of the world folding in. As the diary burns on the deck of the ship, the air above it buckles and bends, and, for the last time, one by one, the Gods come out to watch. Tyr and Thor, Freyr and Freyja, Odin and Frigg. Heimdallr. Hermódr. Hǫdr and Baldr. Like a chain of luminous flowers, they hang there in the darkening light, twinkling, dancing. I know that I will never see them again.

Suddenly, beneath them, the ship erupts into amber and gold. The fabric flags shrivel up, sending up black smoke. Further and further into the centre of the lake the ship travels, as if propelled by a tailwind. The mast proud, illuminated by fire. The flames accompanied by a low rushing sound, barely distinguishable from the sound of the water. The Gods flicker, once, and then fade.

Zara is crying quietly.

'Goodbye, Hobie,' she says. 'I hated you, but I loved you too.'

'Goodbye, Hobie,' I say. 'Sleep well.'

Her hand, dry and hot, creeps into mine. Our fingers interlace.

We watch the ship as it wobbles its way across the lake. I want to see it sink, witness the crimson pool as it's suctioned under.

Eaten up by the glow of funeral fires, the ship recedes, further and further, into the distance. Until it's just a point of light.

And then gone.

# ACKNOWLEDGEMENTS

*The Otherlife* has had a long journey and many people read it along the way, sometimes more than once. They are: Sara Crystal, Rose Gardner, Calum Gray, Jennifer Johnson, Stanley Johnson, Louisa Macmillan and Laura Williams. Thank you for your wisdom and support.

Specific advice came from Dr Nalini Jasani on medical matters, Kayleigh Manson on pathology, Kat King on tattoos, Jack Maguire on heavy metal and Calum Gray on heavy metal and rugby, and I'm very grateful for all their thoughts; any errors are my own.

Very special thanks are due to Dr Richard North for his generous and invaluable help with the grammar, syntax and spelling of Old Norse; as before, any errors are mine.

*The Otherlife* was born halfway through my creative writing studies at Birkbeck, and I owe a great debt of gratitude to my tutors, and to all the students in my Writing for Young Adults module; especially to Gill Fryzer, who told me to start the book; to Julia Bell, who encouraged me to finish it; to Russell Celyn Jones and also to the Sophie Warne Fellowship.

Imogen Russell Williams: I can't thank you enough for your manifold suggestions, phenomenal patience and empathy.

Thank you to Chloe Sackur, Charlie Sheppard and all the wonderful people at Andersen Press.

And thank you to Louise Lamont, my very brilliant agent.

# BLOODTIDE
# MELVIN BURGESS

'An epic tale of treachery, deceit, sex, torture, violence, revenge and retribution' *Independent on Sunday*

*'Love. Hate. So what? This is family. This is business.'*

London is in ruins. The once-glorious city is now a gated wasteland cut off from the rest of the country and in the hands of two warring families – the Volsons and the Connors.

Val Volson offers the hand of his young daughter, Signy, to Connor as a truce. At first the marriage seems to have been blessed by the gods, but betrayal and deceit are never far away in this violent world, and the lives of both families are soon to be changed for ever ...

'Shies from nothing, making it both cruel and magnificent' *Guardian*

9781849396950 £6.99

# OUT OF SHADOWS

### Jason Wallace

**WINNER OF THE COSTA CHILDREN'S BOOK AWARD,
THE BRANFORD BOASE AWARD AND THE UKLA BOOK AWARD**

Zimbabwe, 1980s
The war is over, independence has been won and Robert
Mugabe has come to power offering hope, land and
freedom to black Africans. It is the end of the Old Way
and the start of a promising new era.

For Robert Jacklin, it's all new: new continent, new country,
new school. And very quickly he learns that for some of his
classmates, the sound of guns is still loud, and their battles
rage on . . . white boys who want their old country back,
not this new black African government.

Boys like Ivan. Clever, cunning Ivan.
For him, there is still one last battle
to fight, and he's taking it right
to the very top.

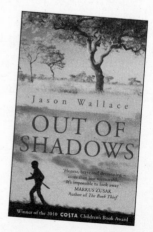

'*Honest, brave and devastating,* Out of
Shadows *is more than just memorable.
It's impossible to look away.*'
Markus Zusak, author of
*The Book Thief*

9781849390484 £7.99